THE
TRIAL
OF JOB

THE TRIAL OF JOB

CHUCK CHITWOOD

Victor is an imprint of
Cook Communications, Colorado Springs, Colorado 80918
Cook Communications, Paris, Ontario, Canada
Kingsway Communications, Eastbourne, England

Cover & Interior Design: Image Studios
Cover Illustration: Lori Bilter
Editors: Susan Reck, Greg Clouse

1 2 3 4 5 6 7 8 9 10 Printing / Year 04 03 02 01 00

Library of Congress Cataloging-in-Publication Data

Chitwood, Chuck
    The trial of Job / Chuck Chitwood.
        p. cm.
    ISBN 0-78143-308-8
    I. Title.

PS3553.H5344 T75 2000   99-047441
813'.54--dc21

To: David McGhee—The mentor I never
told "thank you."

David Terry—A brilliant life ended way too soon.

David Thompson—Serving God in spite of
great personal loss.

and

Dena—My loving wife and best friend.
Abigail—The light in my eyes.

chapter
ONE

Charlie Harrigan watched the numbers on the elevator click past in silence, as did the ten other occupants, all in pressed business suits and starched shirts. He wondered if anyone recognized him. Charlie had never really yearned for the spotlight, but he enjoyed the anticipation of what it would bring. Would there be a reception? Maybe a large banner with his name? Maybe they would enlarge the headlines of *The Charlotte Observer*, "$10 Million Malpractice Decision!" He had just been awarded the largest settlement in a medical malpractice case in North Carolina history. This was the biggest day of his career.

As the numbers continued to click, however, Charlie could not help but feel somewhat remorseful. Lawyers build their careers on the suffering of other people's accidents, losses, and heartbreaks. Someone either suffers and retains a lawyer, or someone sues to make another person suffer. Either way, many a career and fortune were built on the tears that other people shed. But if not him, then somebody else would have tried the case. Charlie tried to convince himself that another lawyer would not have been as caring and compassionate. Why should he not celebrate? Justice prevailed and the guilty was punished to the tune of ten million dollars in punitive damages, in addition to actual damages of one and a half million. Charlie was the hero who discovered the truth and enabled it all to happen. It definitely was the biggest day of his career; he decided that he should be allowed to feel elated.

Hobbes, Reimarus, and Van Schank occupied the thirty-ninth, fortieth, and forty-first floors of the newly built NationsBank Tower in Charlotte. It was the tallest and most prestigious address in Charlotte's quickly growing skyline, and Hobbes, Reimarus, and Van Schank were the most powerful occupants at that address. While NationsBank was gobbling up banks from Florida to Oklahoma, Hobbes, et al., was making a quiet fortune.

When the elevator dinged and the doors opened on the thirty-ninth floor, Charlie was disappointed. No signs. No banners. No attorneys with their hands out wanting their one third of eleven point five million dollars. Just the gold letters above the door spelling out the names: Hobbes, Reimarus, and Van Schank. His heart sank just a little, but he told himself not to get depressed. This was a prestigious firm; maybe they quietly and respectfully appreciated him. Perhaps one of the partners would treat him to a five-star dinner. Nothing was going to disappoint him today. He had just finished the five hardest months of his life in this trial. No lack of salutations was going to rob him of the satisfaction he felt upon seeing Dr. Owen Johnston's face when the jury foreman read the verdict.

Charlie turned left toward the reception desk. As soon as he reached the double oak doors, the smell of hardwood floors and money hit him. The doors opened to reveal a wall of windows that stretched from floor to ceiling on the opposite side of the foyer. The view displayed the skyline of Charlotte and Ericsson Stadium, home of the Carolina Panthers. Persian area rugs covered the hardwood floors. The foyer opened upward so one could see all three floors and take the spiral staircase to the next level of opulence. The expansive entryway and the view were designed to intimidate opponents. That is why the partners insisted that all depositions be taken in the large conference room to the right. The solid oak table that seated forty people, and the oak wainscoting with hunter green walls screamed power and prestige. The imposing view, looking down on everything else, assured opponents of the deep pockets they were facing. Charlie remembered that Dr. Leuchtenburg, his history professor, taught that medieval kings would decorate their gates and entryways with weapons and spoils of war to intimidate enemies and foreign dignitaries from ever challenging their power. The same thing happens in law firms and courtrooms today. Courtrooms are large and overwhelming by design, to make the defendant tremble under the power of the state. Law firms, however, are designed to show how much money they have at their disposal to bury their adversaries. Very few attorneys in Charlotte would feel equal to the challenge when they stepped into this firm. Charlie felt lucky to have the firm on his side. He would hate the thought of going up against these people.

Charlie greeted the beautiful but somewhat plastic receptionist, Selia, who said, "Congratulations, Mr. Harrigan! I saw your picture on the front page."

"Thank you," Charlie replied. "I was brilliant, wasn't I?" A little self-absorbed humor seemed appropriate.

Immediately after the required pleasantries, Selia picked up the phone and dialed the extension. "He's here and he's coming your way!" She spoke quickly and quietly into her headset.

Charlie turned right and headed down the hallway to his office. As he reached the conference room, the double doors swung wide open. Someone grabbed Charlie and yanked him into the room. In front of Charlie was a large congregation of dark suits and a couple of brightly colored dresses, worn by the few female attorneys. Some of these people Charlie did not recognize. In front of the crowd stood the senior partner, J. Garrison Hobbes III. Hobbes was completely bald and looked like a villain from a James Bond movie. All he needed was a monocle. He always wore black suits and a red power tie, which made his six foot stature seem even taller. He was direct and to the point. He rarely felt the need to be cordial to his employees. One could never be sure of his motives or actions. The best thing to do was to stay on his good side.

He scolded Charlie. "You're late! It's nine fifteen." Charlie's heart skipped a beat. He could not remember a firm meeting having been scheduled for today. "How dare you make us wait when the champagne has been chilling for half an hour. Congratulations, counselor!"

The crowd let out a cheer and applauded. Charlie had never known Hobbes to be this jovial, and it took a moment for him to realize that this party was in his honor.

"Ladies and gentlemen," Hobbes continued as he raised his glass to toast the hero, "allow me to formally introduce you to the latest millionaire in the firm. I have always preached to you people the benefit of a large firm doing pro bono work, because hidden under the rocks of free legal work, one will invariably find a gold mine. Our friend, Charlie, has struck it rich. Everybody drink up, but I expect you to be back to work in half an hour. You can bill this time to Charlie. He can afford it."

The lawyers laughed, the champagne started flowing, and some of the attorneys started getting a little tipsy, despite the early morning hour. Charlie mingled through the sea of people and accepted about a hundred slaps on the back. Copies of the A section from *The Charlotte Observer* were all over the conference table. Little did they know that Charlie had already purchased fifty copies for himself. In a firm with more than four hundred attorneys, it was impossible to know everyone, but it seemed that Charlie suddenly had a hundred new best friends. Most of the conversation was small talk. What would be the firm's cut? Would the doctor appeal? Would Charlie be made the next partner?

Hobbes, Reimarus, and Van Schank had five offices. The firm was established in Charlotte with branches in Washington, New York, Atlanta, and Dallas. Overall, there were more than eight hundred attorneys and two hundred partners. Making partner was the quickest way to the big time in this firm, but it was certainly not the easiest. Only one out of every ten lawyers hired had even a chance at becoming partner. The key was to bring in new clients. With the record judgment for medical malpractice in the state of North Carolina and a front-page story, Charlie could count on new clients banging down his door. He had arrived.

As the party began to die down, lawyers moved back to their offices, where they could bill other people for their time. Charlie had been on cloud nine all morning. As the conference room emptied, Charlie stared out the window, looking at the other tall buildings. He felt that remorse creep in again. A young girl had to die for him to make it big and become rich. It was a needless tragedy. Charlie's best friend at the firm, Brad Connelly, noticed the sadness on Charlie's face. Brad was slick. He looked like an attorney one would see on television. He had tan skin and perfect hair. He worked out three times a week and ran five miles every other day, the typical *GQ* lawyer with *Esquire* good looks. He had too much fun to be as serious and as driven as Charlie, which was something Charlie admired on some level.

"Hey, buddy, what's wrong? This is your party and you look like you're going to a funeral."

"You know, Brad, I was just thinking. Is it really appropriate for us to be celebrating? A teenage girl is dead. Two wonderful people have lost a child, and these people are drinking at nine o'clock in the morning." Charlie had done a little drinking in college, but his wife had rescued him from the party life.

"Listen. It's a blasted, rotten shame that Maggie Thomason died, but we are not celebrating her death. We are celebrating the fact that you brought that butcher to justice and made him pay out the wazoo. You couldn't keep it from happening, but you made it right, my friend. You're not just some rainmaker. You are a knight in shining armor."

"Thanks, Brad. I guess the whole thing has just gotten to me. All the suffering this family went through is probably the worst thing I've ever seen."

"You don't have to feel like a hero, but you sure are one in my book." Brad tried to change the subject. "So do you think they'll make you a partner for this?"

It was rare for a thirty-four-year-old man to become a partner, but it was even more rare to win such a high profile case. Unlike the movies, law is typically dull and routine. Eighty percent of the job is research and paperwork.

Charlie replied, "They should add another partner in the next few months. I don't want to get my hopes up, but man, that would be incredible."

"You got my vote. I never trusted Burchette. He always seemed a little shady."

Charlie thought briefly about the retired partner whom the firm would soon be replacing. "Thanks." He returned his gaze to the skyline.

"Well, I've got to get back to Edmund Rourke. The old guy is coming in today to finalize his will again for the twentieth time." Brad started to walk off.

"Is he leaving anything to his cat?"

"The man is the most eccentric person I've ever seen. It's like he's on another planet. He's leaving more to his cat than to his wife."

"That's what you get when you're twenty-two and marry a man in his seventies who carries his own oxygen tank around in a cart."

"Call me. We'll do lunch."

"See ya."

Charlie thought, *I guess the good guys did win this time.* He left the party and went to his office, which faced east. He could see straight up Trade Street to the police station and the Mecklenburg County Courthouse, where he had spent much of this past year. He pulled out the Yellow Pages and ordered flowers to be sent to Harold and Carlene Thomason. The card read, "I'm sorry about Maggie. I just hope in some small way this verdict will make things better. Love, Charlie." He even put the flowers on his personal credit card, instead of billing the client for miscellaneous expenses, which was the normal procedure.

Maggie Thomason was a bright sixteen year old at Providence Day High School on the southeast side. She was elected vice president of the student council and was on the homecoming court, but she was not the queen. She was a cheerleader, but did not see herself as one of the elite, which is probably why everybody liked her, especially Harley Ross. Harley was a senior and a wide receiver. He had a full scholarship to Clemson to play football. Harley and Maggie had dated a little over a year when he played his last high school football game. Providence Day slaughtered East Mecklenburg thanks to three touchdown catches by Harley. At the victory party, Maggie decided to relax her morals and have a drink or two. . . or three. Then she and Harley had their own celebration that went too far. Even though statistical probability was in her favor, she became pregnant her very first time.

Maggie and her best friend, Stacy, decided that the situation could be dealt with quickly and quietly. Maggie did not want to blow her shot at a scholarship or disappoint her family. What would the people at church say? She was a leader, an example. One Thursday, Maggie and Stacy skipped lunch and study hall to drive downtown to a women's clinic. They wanted to get far away from anyone who might recognize them. Dr. Owen Johnston, gynecologist, was less than congenial. The nurses prepped her and the doctor came in and quickly performed the procedure and left. All he told her was to "get some rest." After one hundred fifty dollars and forty-five minutes, it was all over. Problem solved.

The two returned to school in time for sixth-period English. Listening to Mrs. Brawley expound on the nobility of Hester Prynne in *The Scarlet Letter*, Maggie's whole body ached. She took some aspirin and tried to hide the pain. No one could find out. The bell rang, and Maggie grabbed Stacy and they went to the bathroom. She was bleeding. They rushed to Stacy's car and drove back to the clinic. The nurses told them the doctor was out and they would have to try the hospital.

"What about insurance?" Maggie cried. "They will want to know my parents' insurance."

"How about the free clinic on Shamrock Road?"

Being an associate of a large factory like Hobbes, Reimarus, and Van Schank had some advantages. The associates were required to do ten hours of pro bono work every month. Usually, this was very easy stuff. The elderly needed living wills and revocable trusts. Typically, there were a few lawsuits for poor people who had been evicted by greedy landlords. Charlie actually enjoyed this part of his job. Others saw it as a needless interruption on their way to wealth and fame, but to Charlie, this work was much more meaningful than being third chair on a team arbitrating a settlement between a construction company and a business owner. He enjoyed helping the people, and Charlie frequented homeless shelters, the home for runaways, and the free clinic. One Thursday at the free clinic, Charlie's life changed forever.

Charlie was talking to a mother who was having difficulty receiving her welfare check from the government, when he heard tires squealing in the parking lot. Stacy rushed Maggie into the clinic.

"Somebody help me! My friend is bleeding!" Stacy screamed.

"Can I help you?" Charlie asked.

"Are you a doctor?" Stacy asked.

"No I'm a lawyer."

"Can you sue that butcher?" Maggie pleaded desperately between sobs.

"If you hire me, I can."

That day Maggie hired the legal services of Charlie Harrigan and Hobbes, Reimarus, and Van Schank for a retainer of five dollars, which was all she had in her pocket.

A good lawyer is always prepared for action. Charlie raced to the trunk of his Chevy Blazer and grabbed his camcorder. In the back of an ambulance, Charlie recorded Maggie's statement on the way to Presbyterian Hospital. At the time it did not occur to him, but no juror could look at this horrible scene and not give Charlie everything he asked for.

The video was the last statement that Maggie Thomason ever made. She apologized for everything to her parents. She apologized to Harley for destroying their baby. She cried and repeated that this could not be happening. The last statement she made on camera was the one that sealed the doctor's fate. "Don't ever let that man practice medicine again. He's supposed to help people, but he killed me!"

In the emergency waiting room, Charlie called his wife.

"Sandy, it's me."

"What's wrong?" She could hear it in his voice.

Charlie relayed the whole story of Maggie, Harley, and Dr. Owen Johnston to his wife.

"I don't know when I'll be home," Charlie said apologetically.

"Don't worry about it. Just do whatever it takes to nail that slimy rat."

"Sandy, I think you get more upset about my problems than I do."

"That's what I'm here for."

Sandy's angelic voice momentarily lightened his otherwise depressing situation. It was not what she said; it was just the sound of her voice that made every cloud seem to dissipate. Sandy was one of the few patient women in the world who understood that being a lawyer is a twenty-four-hour job, and that being available to a client day and night is part of the territory. It was one of the things she loved about Charlie. He was loyal to his clients. He saw the legal profession as a service, not just a way to get rich. After all, money had never motivated them. Sandy had left her own lucrative career at Carolina Graphic Design when Ashley was born four years ago. Leaving a design firm that would no doubt have made her a partner in seven or eight years brought a tremendous amount of criticism from her feminist friends from college. But she was happy. Now with another little one on the way, she had all she could handle.

With Maggie's permission, Charlie had called her parents, and Stacy was waiting for them at the entrance. In the waiting room, Charlie thought about Ashley and her long brown hair and her little turned-up nose. He even began to cry thinking about what he would feel like if this were his daughter. He tried to put himself in the Thomasons' shoes and found it impossible. The hospital chaplain noticed the lone man in the corner holding his head in his hands.

"Son, are you all right?"

The question bothered Charlie for a split second. *I'm crying in a hospital, what do you think?* However, the sincerity of the chaplain's voice kept Charlie's response civil.

"It's not fair. The poor girl makes one mistake in her life and she will probably die for it."

The well-intentioned priest stroked his beard. "Well, son, many times God's will is difficult for us to ascertain. We must trust that He has everything under control."

The chaplain's words of encouragement were as ambiguous as they were noncommittal.

"Look, chaplain, first of all, thank you for your feeble attempt at comforting me. Second, if God is in control of this situation, then surely He took His hands off the wheel for a moment. And third, I am not your son!"

Charlie stormed off to the rest room to wash his face so he would be presentable for the girl's parents. He usually controlled his emotions better than that. But this whole situation was outrageous to him. He did not need fortune cookie advice from a chaplain who knew nothing about him.

Charlie was not a heretic. He believed in God and attended church several times a month. The pressure of law school and eighty-hour work weeks his first few years had made him put church on the back burner. Still, he loved God and tried to always do the right thing, which was considerably difficult for a lawyer. He was, in fact, the most moral lawyer he knew.

Harold and Carlene Thomason arrived at Presbyterian Hospital about six o'clock when the doctor came out of surgery. The doctor explained that they had tried every means possible, but there was too much internal damage and Maggie did not make it.

Charlie quickly introduced himself to the Thomasons, offered his condolences, explained why he was there, and offered to help them in any way he could. At their invitation, the following day he went to the Thomasons' colonial-style house set among the tall pines of east Charlotte. He showed them the videotape of Maggie in the ambulance. It took her parents only a few minutes to decide to keep Charlie's services and sue Dr. Owen Johnston.

Dr. Owen Johnston began medical school with aspirations to heal humanity. However, fifty thousand dollars in student loans and eventually a sailboat and a beach house in Hilton Head, South Carolina forced him to be more practical. He soon discovered that performing abortions was quick and easy money compared to routine gynecological exams. He could get through at least twenty a day at one hundred fifty dollars each. He earned three thousand dollars a day and fifteen thousand a week. In one year, that amount soared to three quarters of a million dollars. When medicine and other incidentals were added into his bill, he was a money machine.

The entire city of Charlotte watched the trial, primarily because the Thomasons and their daughter were well-respected citizens of the community. Maggie was an honor student and volunteered every Thanksgiving at a homeless shelter. The entire city wanted justice for this little girl who had not been apprised of the inherent dangers and side effects of an abortion. It had taken Charlie just one phone call to the country club to discover that the doctor had had only forty-five minutes to make it to the golf course when Maggie went in for her surgery.

Charlie brought all this information before the jury, and his last witness was the videotape. The jury watched in horror as this beautiful child related her story of being forced to pay in cash, being rushed into the doctor's office for outpatient surgery, and not being told that this procedure was more dangerous than giving birth. Everything she was told led her to believe this would be like having a tooth pulled. As the tears poured down Maggie's face and the jurors', she begged for justice.

Civil cases are usually tricky, and twelve people deciding how much money to give someone always involved long deliberations. A rash of high-dollar judgments had caused the pendulum to swing back the other way. Juries in Charlotte were hesitant to give large amounts of money to people who sometimes had questionable motivations behind their lawsuits. The jury was given the case at eleven o'clock. Charlie was in the middle of his lunch at the Uptown Café when his beeper went off. He looked at his watch. An hour and a half—and a verdict.

Back at the courthouse, the defendant was asked to rise for the reading of the verdict. One could see Dr. Johnston's knees visibly buckle when the jury foreman said, "We find the defendant guilty of wrongful death, and he should pay actual damages of one and a half million dollars. Punitive damages should be awarded in the amount of ten million dollars."

Carlene began to cry. Harold pointed his finger at the doctor and shouted that he wished someone would butcher him the way he had butchered their daughter. Journalists started running for the doors to be the first to announce the verdict. But the biggest surprise came while Charlie was hugging his clients; he looked up and saw Melinda Powell come through the back door and straight to the bar.

"Dr. Owen Johnston. I'm the Assistant District Attorney for Mecklenburg County, and you are under arrest for criminal negligence and manslaughter."

Stunned and stuttering, he tried to speak, "What . . . what . . . You can't do this! I'm a doctor. You'll hear from my attorney. We'll sue for defamation of character."

Cameras on the lawn of the courthouse got wonderful pictures of Dr. Owen Johnston being led into a patrol car in handcuffs. Charlie stood by the windows on the second floor and watched the circus proceed on the courthouse lawn. He thought about Dr. Leuchtenburg, who would say, "Ladies and gentlemen, the medieval trial by ordeal and star chamber kept crime at a low rate. Guillotines in the town square demonstrated to the lower classes the horror of their crimes and reinforced respect for the feudal lord. What would happen to crime in America if we brought back public executions on the courthouse lawn?"

Charlie laughed. His professor was a genius and highly opinionated, but he would never be elected to political office. However, Charlie thought, the guy may have a point. The only retribution civil court can offer is money. Yet ten million dollars did not seem sufficient for what his clients were suffering.

Charlie was still looking out his window and thinking about the whirlwind yesterday's verdict had caused. Who knew how many more girls had suffered under the good doctor's care? Maybe something beneficial would come out of this. Maybe he raised awareness among teenagers. Maybe another doctor would step in and take Johnston's place by tomorrow. At least he stopped one of them. About that time the phone rang. The voice was that of Samuel Reimarus.

"Hail, the conquering hero."

"I don't feel very much like a hero. Maggie is still dead," Charlie replied.

"Charlie, you are far too negative. You can't bring her back. You can't restore the love that her parents have lost. But you have the power to destroy and punish the bad guys. And you did it. And before you start feeling guilty about all that money, just remember that money is the only way this guy can be punished.

Don't look at it as getting rich; look at it as restitution."

Samuel Baskin Reimarus was the managing partner of the firm. He was tall and had a head full of white hair. He exuded a grandfatherly warmth and wisdom. He oversaw the daily operation of the firm, while Hobbes was more of a figure head and a PR person.

"I just wanted to tell you that we scheduled a press conference in the library on the fortieth floor at ten o'clock. Be yourself and call your clients if you think they would like to be there."

"You're the boss."

"Charlie, let's have lunch tomorrow. I have something very important that we need to discuss."

The partnership, Charlie thought. *They want to make me a partner.* "Sure thing, tomorrow at noon."

"I'll take you to The French Quarter, best Cajun food this side of New Orleans. Why don't you take the afternoon off? You just earned the firm over a million dollars and didn't do too bad for yourself. You deserve it."

The attorney's take was one-third of the eleven and a half million. Charlie would split three point three million with the firm. One-third went to the firm, and two-thirds belonged to Charlie.

"Whatever you say, boss. See you tomorrow."

Oliver James Burchette had just retired because of heart problems. To look at him, it would be impossible to tell that he had been one of the best litigators and trial lawyers at Hobbes, Reimarus, and Van Schank. He was a rotund man who always wore bow ties. With white hair and a beard, he could pass for Santa Claus. This jolly image made him a perfect litigator. Unlike television, the best litigator does not rant and rave. He cajoles, flatters, and acts friendly. He forces the adversary to like him and to look at things from his perspective. After thirty years as a litigator and two heart attacks, Burchette was going to St. Augustine, write his memoirs, and basically drink himself to death.

Charlie thought that since he was now a high profile lawyer, Reimarus was going to invite him to be a litigating partner. That meant that Charlie would have to be able to produce new business, but it also meant that he would get a percentage of the firm's profits instead of a salary. For a firm that generated over fifty million dollars a year in fees alone, half of one percent would earn him a quarter of a million dollars a year. Yes, it was the biggest day of Charlie's career. Nothing was going to stop him.

chapter
TWO

Charlie and Sandy watched the evening news while curled up on their overstuffed couch together. They called it couch time and it was just for each other. Ashley would have to practice her artistic skills in her coloring book until couch time was over. Charlie worked such odd hours that they had to schedule intimacy, but through many long discussions and misunder-standings, they had reached a level of acceptance and compromise. Sandy understood his desire to be a partner and to change the world. He understood that material things did not matter to her. But they enjoyed living in the city, whose standard of living was rapidly rising.

Even a small house like theirs in Myers Park was very expensive. They lived in a quaint two-story, three-bedroom house that was nestled among the tall oak trees that exploded with color every fall. They were not rich but tried to live the good life. Public schools were in such disarray that they wanted Ashley to attend Charlotte Latin, one of the top private schools in the nation. It took lots of money to have a decent life in Charlotte without moving out to one of the smaller towns, but that would require a forty-five-minute commute every day to downtown.

Charlie was from one of those smaller towns, Midland, and he despised it. He never owned a four by four and he did not hate black people and that made him something of an outsider. A stern mother with a large leather belt had raised him. His father had run off with another woman when Charlie was six, and he had become a successful corporate lawyer. Charlie always felt that somehow his own inadequacy was to blame, but he was never sure exactly what had offended his father.

The town was so small that the closest movie theater was forty-five minutes away. That was one of the reasons Charlie had started drinking. There was nothing else to do on a Saturday night. At first it was small and infrequent drinking, but in college he drank like a fish. Charlie vowed to get out of the small-town life and never go back, except, of course, for his high school reunion. His dream was to return to his high school reunion as a successful attorney with a beautiful wife and a black convertible Jaguar XK8 and rub everyone's face in his success.

Watching himself now on the evening news, he realized that his dream was quite superficial. Success carried a high price and an even higher responsibility. It would be extremely selfish to brag about his achievement in the wake of such a tragedy. After all, the money was not in the bank yet. Dr. Johnston would no doubt file an appeal. He would probably claim that the venue should have been changed and that the potential jurors were prejudiced by all of the pretrial publicity. He would file a motion to postpone payment until the appellate court tried the case. If Charlie were Johnston's attorney, he would handle it that way. Regardless of appeal, however, Charlie was still famous. He could not help feeling a little pride as the reporter asked him such easy questions.

"Look, honey," Sandy told Ashley, "Daddy's on TV."

"Yea, Daddy!" Ashley screamed and jumped up and down, then jumped in her father's lap.

The reporter asked Charlie, "What did you think of today's verdict?"

"First, I would like to thank the jury. They are the ones who had the difficult job, but they gave the correct verdict. They made sure that justice was done for Maggie. Second, I wanted to let you know that the Thomasons declined an invitation to be here today, but they did send a statement I would like to read now: 'We wanted the people of Charlotte to know the tragic loss our family has suffered. We encourage you parents to talk to your daughters. We want the politicians to help prevent any future tragedies like this. Finally, we want everyone to know that there is an alternative to abortion. That is why we are donating every penny of the settlement to the Safe House, which is a home for teenage mothers that provides counseling and education for girls in Maggie's situation.' "

Before he could continue, Charlie was interrupted by another reporter, "Does this mean that you are antiabortion?"

"My personal convictions are not important in this situation. However, my clients are against doctors who butcher teenage girls."

The anchorman stepped in at that point in the broadcast. "Sally, it sounds like things got pretty heated down there."

"That's correct, Bob. Mr. Harrigan seemed irritated when his personal view of abortion came into question. He gave a very evasive answer."

"Well, Sally, after all, he is an attorney."

"And a wealthy one at that."

Charlie clicked the remote control and threw it across the room.

"These people missed the point. I wasn't there to talk about me. I was there to speak for Maggie. I hate abortion and I think it should be outlawed. I think Maggie was stupid and a coward for not telling her parents. Maybe their relationship really stunk. But I'm not a legislator. I don't make the rules."

"They're just journalists, honey. Very few people take them seriously these days. Good old Sally probably marches in prochoice rallies. Ignore the press. Right now you are the hottest thing going and you will have many critics. The good guys always do."

"So you still think I'm hot after all these years."

"You'll just have to wait for Ashley to go to bed to find out."
Charlie jumped off the couch.

"Ashley, let's go get your bath so you can get ready for bed."

As he sat in the rocking chair with Ashley's head snuggled close to his shoulder, he thought about his wonderful life. Ashley was the light in his eyes and the spitting image of her mother. Both were so full of life. Every time Sandy put Ashley's hair in a ponytail, Charlie was reminded of their first encounter. The first time Charlie saw Sandy, he was playing flag football on Carmichael Field his senior year in college. Every Friday afternoon was the intramural tournament. He and his best friend, Chris Lemont, had a chemistry that could not be beat. They made the Falcons an unstoppable force, for a bunch of guys who could not play the real game. Chris had a rifle for a throwing arm and Charlie was quick. This particular fall afternoon at the University of North Carolina in Chapel Hill was the championship round of the tournament. The play was designed to deliver the winning touchdown with a long pass down the sideline and into the end zone, an amateur version of the flea flicker.

From the line of scrimmage, Charlie saw her. She was jogging with a friend down South Road. Her long brown ponytail was bouncing with every step. She was perfect. The ball was snapped and Charlie raced down the sideline. Into the end zone at top speed, he made the perfect catch. She looked and gave Charlie a quick smile, then turned her attention back to the road. Charlie smiled, still running, and ran face first into the goal post. Charlie was not unconscious but certainly dizzy. When she heard the thud of Charlie hitting the ground, she looked back to make sure everything was all right. When she saw that it was, she began laughing. Charlie had never seen a smile like that. Fourteen years later, her smile was just as bright and made Charlie as euphoric as that first day.

"Charlie, are you okay?" Chris had rushed to his side.

"No, I think it's broken."

"What? What? Where's it hurt?"

"My heart. She broke my heart. I just made a colossal fool out of myself and she laughed. The most gorgeous girl in the world was laughing at me. I was going to keep running and try to at least get her name."

"Who? Sandy Davis? She's in my marketing class."

"You are the man, Chris. What do you know about her?"

"Straight A's, real particular about guys who sit beside her, and real religious. She goes to that Baptist student thing on Thursday nights. I've been a couple of times."

"Well, it looks like I just turned Baptist."

Even though their first official meeting was clandestine and deceitful on Charlie's behalf, Sandy knew it. She had never seen him at one of these meetings before, and he was completely clueless about when to stand, sit, or clap. But they started talking after the service was over and soon were meeting on the steps of Lenoir Cafeteria on an almost daily basis. She showed him how to have a good time. Until that point, Charlie's idea of fun usually involved having a beer in one hand. Somehow by being around her, his taste for beer was gone. It was no great miracle and they did not fight over it. She just had so much fun without it that Charlie lost the taste for alcohol. She was exactly what Charlie was looking for.

She showed him that it was okay to fail. Charlie had always felt the pressure to measure up to his successful, absentee father, who was the in-house counsel for MicroCom and had recently moved to Silicon Valley. Even though Sandy had straight A's, she was not anxious about those types of achievements. She was far more concerned about relationships.

She also showed him how to laugh at himself. Their first official date was a double date planned by him and Chris. One Saturday evening, Charlie and Chris snuck into the planetarium and prepared a picnic on the roof. They made spaghetti, of all things. Charlie had just served Sandy her food and as he was sitting down on the blanket, he spilled spaghetti all over himself. She just laughed. Typically, Charlie would have been overwhelmed by embarrassment, but her laugh put him at ease.

"Why is it that every time I turn around you are laughing at me?" Charlie asked out of frustration.

"You are just so cute. You try to be Mr. Perfect but something goes wrong, like when you ran into that goalpost. . . ." She just kept laughing.

"I nearly gave myself a concussion because of you."

"I know. No guy has ever gone to so much trouble to impress me. It's nice, but you really don't have to." She laid a hand on his knee. "I like you with spaghetti all over your shirt."

"Well, if you think it's so cute, you wear it." Charlie dumped spaghetti on her shirt and a food fight ensued as the sun set over Chapel Hill.

Charlie went on to law school at Chapel Hill, and she got a job in the Research Triangle. They got married his second year. They had enough money to get a cheap little apartment on Franklin Street near all of the trendy campus clothing stores and coffee shops. It took them five minutes to get to Players, where they spent many late nights playing pool. They spent two wonderful years close to the poverty line before moving to Charlotte.

It was a wonderful marriage. It was not perfect by any means. But they were able to communicate and that was the key. Their first year in Charlotte had almost destroyed that bond as they both worked like dogs to get out of debt and pay off student loans. Every once in awhile, they would fix spaghetti and go in the backyard to have a picnic. Inevitably, more spaghetti ended up on their clothes than in their stomachs.

What would they do with two point two million dollars? Charlie thought. A boat? A house on Lake Wylie? Armani suits? Maybe he would just save it for Ashley's college fund; college would probably cost that much by the time she grew up.

Wherever the money went, Charlie knew one thing. He had never been this happy in his whole life. They were living the American dream, as corny as it sounded. His life seemed like a fairy tale at the moment. He watched his precious daughter sleeping as he often did and whispered a prayer of thanks for his wonderful, loving wife and his jewel of a daughter.

"Get outta my yard! If you ever come back, I'll shoot you." Walter Comstock slammed the front door as he yelled.

In his hand was a summons. It was a wrongful death suit filed late the previous afternoon by Horace and Betty Douglas. The process server raced to his car and out of the driveway. Walter Comstock's house was one of the four-story plantation-style houses on Sharon Road near Southpark Mall, the most expensive real estate in the city. He did not look like a millionaire, but he was a self-made man after all. He had built his own construction business, which, in turn, built a large majority of Charlotte. The gruff, sturdy man with the tan face picked up the phone.

"Hello, this is Martin Van Schank. May I help you?"

"You better believe you can help me. It's another lawsuit. I need to meet with you first thing this morning. These people can't do this to me. I'm 'Humanitarian of the Year,' for crying out loud. They're suing me and Paragon Group for millions of dollars."

"Whoa! Slow down, Walter. What's going on?"

"You know I've got that program to help the mentally handicapped by giving them little odds-and-ends jobs on construction sites. These people claim that my negligence led to their retarded boy's death. How absurd is that? I just received an award for helping those people."

"Walter, I will be at the office in an hour. Meet me there. We'll make this thing go away."

Hobbes was the figurehead while Reimarus was the business manager, but Martin Van Schank was the high roller of the three senior partners at Hobbes, Reimarus, and Van Schank. Van Schank had all the connections. He was younger than the other two. His jet-black hair was always moussed and he always had a cigar dangling from his mouth. He had made his way to partner quickly; he had friends on the city council, in Raleigh, and in Washington. He was someone who did not inspire a lot of trust, but he could definitely get the job done. Every sentence out of his mouth had a condition or a qualifier. That was one of his techniques for getting out of difficult situations. He had many other tricks. Associates speculated about his unsavory connections, but it was mostly gossip. Yet Van Schank seemed to do things other lawyers couldn't. Yes, Martin Van Schank had many tricks.

"Honey, here's your coffee. Big meeting today, huh?"

"Oh yeah," Charlie answered as he was shaving the remainder of his stubble. "Reimarus could want to meet about only one thing—partner!"

"Well, they really need you as a partner. You're the most famous guy at that place now. Just let me know if you're going to be late; I'm fixing your favorite."

"Steak?"

"No."

"Crab legs?

"No."

Charlie hesitated. "Jambalaya!"

"Yeah, that's it."

"Hey, my favorite."

Charlie could not imagine life without her. Sandy truly was wonderful. Of course, she was not perfect. She squeezed the toothpaste in the middle and she tended to volunteer his services at church without notifying him first, but those were very minor things. With her support, he felt that he not only deserved to be the next partner, but he would be doing them a favor. On the other hand, nobody could crush him like she could.

Early in their marriage, she wanted to skip one of the firm softball games to go to the mall. Charlie went zero for four that day, including a strikeout. *No one strikes out in softball*, he thought to himself. Since that game, they came to understand the importance of caring about the little things that the other liked. She was in the front row at every game, and he had the highest batting average that first season. Charlie went to the Parade of Homes every year and lectures at UNC-Charlotte on the style and development of the coffee table in the antebellum South. It was the little things that mattered most.

After his first cup of coffee, Charlie woke up Ashley as was his morning ritual.

"Good morning, sunshine."

Ashley just groaned. Like him, she was not much of a morning person. She inherited that and a stubborn streak from her father. Everything else, she got from her mother. Her long brown hair was tousled, and her sleepy lids would open to reveal big, emerald eyes.

He carried her downstairs, where she ate her Cheerios like a zombie. Sandy was reading the paper as Charlie finished off his eggs and his third cup of coffee. It was their morning routine, if he had the time.

"Your picture is on the front page again along with Maggie's."

"Have you started a scrapbook of all my famous cases yet?" Charlie asked.

"I was waiting until you had two."

"Oh, that hurts. What else does the article say?"

"The abortion doctor, Owen Johnston, could not be contacted for comment. Hundreds of antiabortion protestors held a vigil in front of the Downtown Women's Clinic yesterday, which had locked its doors. The celebrants sang, 'We Shall Overcome,' they prayed for aborted fetuses, and held up large posters featuring the face of the victorious lawyer and chanted his name, 'Charlie! Charlie!' Police will be on hand today should the protest continue and to provide safe access for women seeking aid at the clinic."

"No woman is seeking aid at the clinic. They want an abortion. They want a quick solution to what they see as a problem. A problem that they created, mind you."

"Not all of those women created the problem. . . ." Sandy said, trying to calm Charlie down. She should have known that trying to placate him only made Charlie more indignant.

"But the vast majority went willingly and many are repeat patients. For crying out loud, they use abortion as birth control."

"Daddy," Ashley suddenly woke up, "what's abortion?"

For a four-year-old, she was very observant and often stumped him with insightful questions. Charlie was unaware that Ashley had woken up about the time he began speaking passionately, and she had hung on every word.

"Well, sweetheart," Charlie began very gingerly, "sometimes people make mistakes, and instead of doing the right thing and taking responsibility for their situation, they want to make the problem go away without facing it."

"Now, honey," Sandy interjected, "things are not always that simple."

"Yes, dear, they are. The right choice is always simple. It may not be easy, but it is simple."

"Did that doctor kill that girl?" Ashley asked, still puzzled by the whole conversation.

"Yes, sweetheart," Charlie just shook his head. This was not a typical breakfast conversation. "The doctor killed Maggie and her baby because she was afraid of telling her parents."

Ashley began to cry. She had a tender heart and felt things deeply, like her mother.

"Not everyone in this world does the right thing, and there are bad people who just want to make money. We must pray for those people who have problems and do our best to help fix them. That is why I'm a lawyer. I want to help fix people's problems. You have to promise me one thing, Ashley. Promise you will always come to me if you have a problem. You can trust me."

Sniffling, Ashley said, "I promise I will, Daddy. And I want to be a lawyer too, so I can help people."

Yeah, Charlie thought, *that is why I wanted to be one.*

What kind of world do we live in, where a father needs to explain abortion to a four-year-old over a bowl of Cheerios? Charlie dreaded the day she would ask, "Daddy, where did we get all this money?" He'd respond, "Remember that girl who died? I won it suing the man who killed her." The more he thought about it, the sicker he got. The more he thought about it, the less it made sense.

"Hey, buddy boy!" Brad bounded into the office with two cappuccinos in hand. "My treat. Charlie! Charlie!" He chanted. "Did you see the evening news? Every wacko in Charlotte is worshiping you."

Slamming the Garcia file on his desk, Charlie shot back, "They're not wackos and they're not worshiping me! They are finally glad that someone has brought the problem to light. Did you know that there are more than three thousand abortions performed every day, and many of those are to repeat customers?"

"Hey, slow down. I'm on your side, remember? Why are you so tense?"

"You would be tense too if you had to explain what an abortion is to your four-year-old daughter." Charlie settled back into his leather chair.

"Oh man, I'm sorry. You need some time off. You can use my condo at Nags Head. Catch some rays, enjoy the beach, and get away from this circus."

"I can't slow down. Guess who wants to have lunch with me at The French Quarter today?"

"The mayor."

"Better. Reimarus."

"Oh man. He's going to make you partner, since old Burchette went south. Can you imagine him lying out in the sun? He'd be like a beached whale or something."

"I'm not the only litigator who has a chance though. Nancy got Tarheel Freight to switch to us in that dispute with Allied Brakes, Inc. Do you know how much they pay in fees?"

"No. I'm just a lowly estate planner. I'm not a big corporate raider like you guys."

"Half a million! That's not a one-time deal. That's every year. We now handle all their sexual harassment, workers' comp, and contract disputes. My deal was a one-time shot. To be partner, I have to keep producing clients."

"Hey, that's my beeper. I believe in you, man. Good luck today, buddy. Let me know how it goes." Brad jogged down the hall chanting, "Charlie! Charlie!"

Nancy Lockman-Kurtz finished first in her class at Duke Law School. Many considered her an underachiever because she stayed in the state. Most Duke graduates ended up in Washington or New York. She learned early on that the law was as much about doing favors and calling in markers as it was about the Constitution. Apparently, she either skipped ethics or had the same ethics professor who taught Richard Nixon when he was in school there. Regardless, Nancy had a way of getting new clients. Her father was CEO of Firstbank. Maybe there was some shady financing going on. Tarheel Freight about went under several years ago, but somehow it was selected to ship all the supplies to build the new business park on I-77, which was also a client of Nancy's. What she was doing was probably not illegal, but there were plenty of red flags. Some people said that she slept with all her clients, but that was probably petty gossip from jealous secretaries who were losing their figures while she maintained hers.

When Nancy arrived at Hobbes, Reimarus, and Van Schank seven years ago, she was a paragon of feminism. She rarely used makeup, kept her hair straight and plain, wore ill-fitted clothing, and pushed every sexual harassment case to its limits. At least two of the associates who asked her for dates were slapped with temporary restraining orders. When a partner asked her out, she sued for sexual harassment and won. The partner was encouraged to leave the firm and set out his own shingle, as going into private practice is referred to.

Nancy had the fire, but she needed the passion.

Then one fall morning after a trip to the Virgin Islands with some potential clients, she was a new woman. The feminist chip was gone, and now everyone wanted to ask her out. Her career took off after she discovered that she could not do battle the same way a man does; she discovered a whole new arsenal of weapons.

Charlie thought about Nancy. He had met several law students like her: cutthroats. They would cut any corner and bend every law to get ahead. He could think of at least ten friends from his first year of law school who became bitter enemies by their third year. There are so many law students and even more lawyers that competition is the motivating force behind everything. He learned early to be careful about who he trusted. Charlie shook off the bitter taste of backbiting lawyers and returned to Hector Garcia. He owned a small landscaping company that put in the lowest bid to take care of Marshall Park, but the job was given to someone else. Proving racism in such city oversight committees would be difficult, but Charlie thought it was worth fighting. Chances are the city would settle out of fear of the press. After all, he was a big gun now. No one was safe; Charlie chuckled at the thought.

Tryon Street ran north and south and intersected with Trade Street, which formed the center point of downtown. Within a half-mile radius were some of the wealthiest banks and lawyers on the East Coast. Compared to New York and Atlanta, Charlotte was a rather inexpensive place to live. As the city became the banking hub of the eastern seaboard, big business followed suit. Not long after that came the lawyers. Charlotte was now the fastest growing city in the South after Atlanta. The city had come a long way from the two Native American trading routes that formed it. The southern route to Charleston and northern route to Virginia eventually became I-77 and I-85, which met in downtown Charlotte. At the turn of the century, six different railroad lines converged on Charlotte for the burgeoning textile trade and the unprecedented growth began.

In spite of all the growth, Charlotte retained its genteel, southern charm. Lunch was sort of like a mini business party every day. Banks competed for exposure by having live bands play at their outside promenades during lunch. The Overstreet Mall was a series of shops and restaurants that connected six of the main towers in downtown Charlotte.

Samuel Baskin Reimarus and Charlie made their way through the Overstreet Mall to The French Quarter restaurant, which was a block north of Tryon on Church Street. At lunch, a line usually extended out the door. Reimarus rarely had to wait. He had pulled the right strings and helped Jacques LeTourneau acquire the loan for this prime piece of real estate.

"Bonjour, my friend and mentor, Samuel. I have the perfect table for you." To Charlie, he said, "This man is a saint. Without him, I would still be flipping burgers. He's a hero."

As they moved past the line and received many jealous looks from those who were still waiting, Reimarus said, "Jacques, this man right here is a hero. Don't you recognize him? His picture has been on the front page of *The Charlotte Observer* two days in a row."

"I'm sorry, I do not."

"That's perfectly all right," Charlie replied. He couldn't expect everyone to recognize him.

Reimarus, sitting down at a table in the center of the room that was too large for two people, said, "This man won a lawsuit for over ten million dollars. So bring us some champagne and your best Cajun smoked salmon."

"Right away." Jacques quickly marched back to the kitchen and returned with a bottle of one hundred dollar champagne. "Your meal today is on the house."

"That's okay, Jacques," Reimarus replied, "the client is paying for it."

They both laughed louder than necessary, and Charlie felt a little silly. The whole restaurant was staring at them. The display of arrogance and sucking up was obnoxious. Charlie would have much rather grabbed a bratwurst from one of the street vendors.

"Well, Charlie, how does it feel to be a millionaire?" Reimarus asked as he struggled with the cork.

"I'm not really sure. The money's not in the bank yet, so technically, I'm still a struggling associate."

The cork popped with a loud sound and champagne spilled all over the table.

"Drink, Charlie?"

"I'm sorry, I don't drink anymore. I gave it up in college."

Reimarus looked at him as if he were speaking another language. "But this celebration is for you. We can't let this bottle go to waste."

"I'm truly sorry, but I just don't drink."

"Well, your loss."

Reimarus eyed him closely as he placed the bottle back in the ice. Charlie suddenly felt very uncomfortable, as if he were in a foreign culture and had violated a custom without even being aware of it. The silence lasted only a few seconds, but it seemed like forever.

"Charlie, I brought you here today to celebrate, but also to share a proposal with you."

"Oh really? I'm all ears."

"You stumbled across a difficult case at the clinic, but you handled it like a real pro."

"It wasn't the easiest thing I've ever done. I still feel sorry for the family."

Reimarus replied understandingly, "It's difficult, I know. But the fact that you won means a lot to the parents. You have to know that."

Charlie appreciated the compassionate tone and concern in Reimarus' voice. Just as quickly as the compassion came, though, it left again.

"Now what I really wanted to talk to you about today is your future," Reimarus continued.

Charlie was stunned by how quickly the partner shifted emotional gears.

"You have been with us now for ten years. We evaluate associates at the major milestones in their careers. Some who seem to have stalled and are not moving up are invited to leave. A man cannot be happy in the same job for ten years. If the associates are producing and maturing, they are given the opportunity to step up to partner. Some make it at the ten-year mark. The ones who don't will get another opportunity at fifteen years."

Charlie thought it best to say little and listen a lot. He simply nodded that he understood the situation.

"As a partner, you would get a fraction of a percentage point of the profit of the firm. Now that may not seem like much, but all of our partners are in six figures. And you keep a larger percentage from the clients that you bring in. Understand?"

Charlie nodded, waiting for the catch.

"Do you know Nancy Lockman-Kurtz?" Reimarus asked.

Ah, Charlie thought, *here's the catch.*

"You and she are both in litigation, but I don't think you've worked on a case together. I think she graduated from Duke. Didn't you graduate from Chapel Hill?"

"Yes, sir."

"I guess that makes you rivals. However, you will have to put away your rivalry. Both of you have proven yourselves in court and in arbitration. You have had more success trying cases, but she has been very effective settling cases we had no chance of winning, plus she has brought in a few more repeat customers."

Still listening, Charlie said to himself, *This just keeps getting better.*

"The Thomasons are wonderful people, but they will probably not need our services again, except maybe to write their wills. We thrive off of repeat business."

The smell of grilled salmon preceded the food to the table.

Charlie was not particularly fond of fish, but this one simply melted in his mouth.

"How's the fish?" Reimarus asked.

"It's incredible. I don't get here much."

"Well, now that Jacques knows you're a friend of mine, you can get in any time you want. Anyway, here's the deal. Martin got a call this morning from a very important client who is in a wrongful death situation. It was tragic. One of his employees just died from cancer, and the parents blame our client. He's completely innocent, but the redneck family just wants to get rich quick. Since Burchette is rubbing suntan oil on that great big belly of his, we are in need of new litigators. I want you and Nancy to work on this case together. As we see how you handle the client and the case, one of you will make it to partner, provided you win the case. If it goes to court, you will definitely be first chair. However, a good settlement will save our client from a lot of negative press."

"Does Nancy know?"

"Sure, I talked to her this morning. You two will need to get together and meet the client very soon."

"Thank you for the offer," Charlie said, thinking that this offer really stunk. Pitting one lawyer against another when they are supposed to be working like a team was not fair. The rest of the lunch resumed with small talk, current events, and ways to spend a million dollars. Charlie did not trust Reimarus. Of course, he trusted very few at the firm, except Brad. Everyone seemed determined to make it to a corner office without concern for the casualities that lay in his or her wake. He thought to himself, *If I can make it to partner, I would not have to worry about these politics. I could just do my job.* If only it were that simple.

chapter
THREE

Office assignments were very symbolic at Hobbes, Reimarus, and Van Schank. The corner offices had windows for two of their walls and were occupied only by partners. The most senior partners were on the forty-first floor, and the youngest partners were on the thirty-ninth. Associates had smaller offices with one window-wall. The offices became increasingly larger as one moved out to the corners. So it was better to have an office on the thirty-ninth floor next to a corner than on the forty-first floor near the middle. It was a highly complicated system that all of the attorneys seemed to understand. Secretaries and paralegals were the unfortunate ones. Their offices were cubicles in the center of the building, directly across the hallway from the attorney they worked for. The only way a secretary could have a window view was if the attorney left the door open. Otherwise, they worked under the constant buzz of fluorescent lighting.

After a two-hour power lunch at The French Quarter that would be billed to Walter Comstock and Paragon Group, Charlie walked quickly past Selia, the receptionist, to his office several doors down from the large conference room. His office was next to a corner office on the thirty-ninth floor. He passed his office and peeked into Wallace J. Stoneman's corner office. Charlie thought for a minute. After this Comstock trial, he could be sitting in a corner office. It was not the prestige that excited him; it was the freedom that partnership brought with it. Associates routinely worked eighty to a hundred hours a week, and nine out of ten would eventually go elsewhere for work. Partners could afford to be more lax. No partners worked Sundays, and only a handful worked Saturdays on a regular basis. With a second child on the way, Charlie looked forward to more family time.

When he returned to his office, he dialed his home number. The voice that answered was like music to his ears. From very early in their relationship, Sandy had been the first person he wanted to tell all of his good news and bad news. He was incomplete until she knew.

"Hey, babe! What are you doing?" Charlie inquired.

"Ashley and I are stripping off the old wallpaper in the entryway. I am covered in sweat, paste, and that vinegar stuff you have to spray on the walls."

"Hmmm, I bet you look gorgeous."

"Well, you sound frisky. How was your lunch?" she asked, knowing the real reason he had called.

"It was fantastic! I'll have to take you to this place sometime. The food was incredible. Reimarus wants to give me one more case before the partners decide who will be the next one."

"What's the case?"

"Wrongful death at a construction company. I can't say too much, you know." Lawyer-client confidentiality was difficult between him and Sandy, because they shared everything. He did not like keeping anything from her, even in his job.

"You'll be perfect at that. You're the wrongful death king right now." She stroked his ego, although it needed very little at the moment.

"Well, here's the deal, I'm on the other side. Our client is being sued by an older couple whose mildly retarded son died from lung cancer. They claim that Paragon Group is responsible."

"What's the problem? Do you think it was their fault?"

"I don't know. I need to find out more about the case first, but I just got some odd vibes from Reimarus. Plus he's teamed me up with the settlement queen, Nancy Lockman-Kurtz. I don't know what that's all about." He was somewhat disconcerted by Reimarus' lack of detail about the case, but he remained optimistic.

Trying to be encouraging, Sandy said, "I'm sure you will be fine. I know you don't like switching sides like that, but try not to let it bother you."

In the Thomason case, Charlie had been the plaintiff's attorney; now he was the defendant's in the same type of case. It was an aspect of the law that had bothered him since law school. Lawyers had to be able to argue both sides of an issue with equal passion and logic. What bothered him the most was how easy it was to switch gears. In his trial procedure class taught by former U. S. District Attorney Gerald Long, he was arguing a new statute that gave drug dealers the death penalty on their third conviction. The case was an appellate decision he argued in front of the class. Roger "The Hammer" Jefferson was a two-time loser who was caught speeding outside of Winston-Salem. When the officer shined his flashlight in the backseat, the officer saw a brown paper bag that was folded over. At issue in the appellate court was the Fourth Amendment prohibition against illegal search and seizure. He argued for fifteen minutes that the officer was well within his constitutional rights to look in the bag because it was partially open. It was folded, not stapled or taped. The basis of his argument was that since no adhesive or staple was used, the bag was not legally sealed; therefore, the officer had every right to look in it.

In the middle of his argument, Dr. Long said, "Switch sides." Charlie argued for another fifteen minutes that if the officer could not see in the bag without extraordinary measures, then he had no right to pick it up and look in, even if it contained two pounds of uncut heroin. If Charlie had been arguing this case for real, The Hammer would still be free today selling drugs on middle school playgrounds. It scared Charlie. His passion for justice changed to a passion for criminals' rights in a split second, and he did it without thinking. After that class, he had sat stunned with his wife in their tiny student apartment on Franklin Street and wondered how he could be a lawyer without losing his moral center. Now that he was switching sides to defend a large company, those same feelings resurfaced. He rubbed his temples and changed the subject.

"Babe, I've got an idea. Since Monday's Labor Day, let's get outta here before this next trial starts. Brad offered me his condo at Nags Head."

With genuine excitement, Sandy said, "I'll start packing right now."

"Make sure you pack that black two-piece bathing suit." Charlie was grinning.

"Honey, I've had a baby, plus I'm pregnant. I can't wear that!" He knew she was blushing, although he could not see her.

"That's even better. Hey, I've got to run. See you later, babe. I love you."

"I love you, too, sweetheart. Bye." The phone clicked.

Charlie leaned back in his leather chair and dialed Brad's extension. "Hey, counselor, you feel like doing something after work?"

"Sure, man. How about Johnathon's around five thirty?"

"Great! I'll tell you what a power lunch is like."

"Can't wait. See ya."

It was hard for Charlie to get back into a working mind-set. He stared out the window at the miles of landscape and thought of corner offices, his wife in a bikini, Ashley running away from the waves, the despicable Nancy Lockman-Kurtz, Reimarus' snow white hair and goofy smile, and Maggie Thomason.

The vein on Walter Comstock's thick neck was sticking out and his face was beet red as he scolded Reimarus and Van Schank. In a corner office on the forty-first floor, he paced back and forth in front of the windows. Surprisingly enough, he could not be heard outside of the office.

"I pay this firm hundreds of thousands of dollars a year in legal representation and when I get sued, what do I get? Two wet-behind-the-ears puppy lawyers. Burchette was always able to smooth things over with OSHA. I need him back here now." Comstock banged his fist on the desk.

"Listen, Walter," Reimarus tried to appease him, "these are two of our most experienced litigators, and one will take Burchette's place when this is all over. Right now, all of the litigating partners are busy. One is in London and another is in Hawaii. The rest are helping some televangelist who is trying to buy Jim Bakker's old place, but it's been in arbitration for years. I will be overseeing the whole process. You are very important to us."

With a huge belly laugh, Comstock exclaimed, "My money is very important to you, and the fact that we are getting ready to do that multimillion-dollar expansion on the Charlotte Motor Speedway. What if I took my business elsewhere? Any firm in the city would kiss my feet to represent me."

Without responding to Comstock, Van Schank got up slowly and walked around behind Reimarus' desk.

"Do you mind giving us a few minutes alone?" Van Schank said to Reimarus. Normally, a lawyer would not simply leave his own office by request. It was a slap in the face to his territorial authority. Reimarus hung his head and walked sheepishly to the door. Van Schank went to Reimarus' private bar and poured two glasses of Jack Daniels.

"Now, Walter," Van Schank began quietly but sternly, "you and I both know why Burchette left for early retirement. He knew too much and his conscience was getting to him. I gave him a big bonus to ease his mind. Now I have decided to try a new strategy with you."

Comstock simply nodded to show he understood.

"I have decided to put you with attorneys who know little about you. If they feel this is just a poor redneck couple trying to get rich off an upstanding member of the community, they are more likely to give it their all. Burchette's hands were dirty.

If you continue to do business this way, then you need to trust me with your life. Because if anyone ever finds out the truth, you better take your fortune and head to the Bahamas. Understand?"

"Sure, sure." Walter stared at the carpet even harder and then helped himself to another drink.

"I don't expect you to tell me how to do my job, and I won't lecture you about the law. If you just obeyed it, you wouldn't need my services so often." Van Schank's tall, skinny frame could be very frightening. With his round spectacles, he looked like a jackbooted Gestapo officer.

Comstock acquiesced. "If you say so. I trust you. I need to meet with them soon, maybe early next week."

"I'll get Nancy on the phone for you now." Van Schank smiled. "This case could easily end up costing two hundred thousand dollars."

Johnathon's was a landmark. It had been there when North Tryon Street was the booming financial center of downtown Charlotte. During the seventies and early eighties, the financial district moved slightly south, and North Tryon Street became the stomping grounds for the homeless, hookers, and dealers. Several of the hotels had closed and boarded up their windows. They served as temporary shelters for some, shooting galleries for the druggies, and not-so-romantic settings for encounters with low-priced prostitutes. Then in the late eighties and early nineties, the republican mayor began to crack down on crime and create tax zones in poor areas to encourage businesses to return to Charlotte's quickly deteriorating downtown.

As condos were transformed out of old warehouses and a new arts district was established on North Tryon, Johnathon's remained a favorite after-hours hangout for the busy beavers climbing the corporate ladder. It was a favorite primarily because it was not new. It was one of the few places in downtown that was not. There was no neon, no bright lights, and few windows. It was all dark wood and brass. The street level was the restaurant, and downstairs was the bar and an occasional jazz band.

Charlie walked the seven blocks from NationsBank to Johnathon's, passing the new Blumenthal Performing Arts Center, the Charlotte Library, Spirit Square, and Joe, a retired Vietnam vet who lost both legs to a bouncing betty and now wheeled around downtown on a stretcher. Charlie walked in the door and down the stairs to the bar, where Brad was waiting. The businessmen and women were in the middle of their daily celebration of the five o'clock hour. Typically, he and Brad never left this early, but two days before Labor Day weekend was very slow.

As Charlie moved past the small tables through the smoke and darkness, he saw Brad stand to his feet and wave him over.

"Hey, hey, buddy-boy! Over here!" To the restaurant, Brad shouted, "Ladies and gentlemen, as I buy everyone a round of whatever you're drinking, please help me congratulate Charlie Harrigan, the hottest attorney in the Queen City."

The crowd cheered and Charlie lowered his head in embarrassment so his blushing face would not show.

"What are you doing? There are at least thirty people in here." Charlie quizzically studied his friend.

"My boy. You need to learn how to celebrate. You old married types are just too boring." Brad was not buzzed, but he was quickly on his way.

There was a time in Charlie's life when he believed that just walking into a bar was a sin worthy of hell itself, so touching any alcohol had been out of the question. In high school, he had started to get curious and drank a bit here and there. Then, his first week in a college of twenty-two thousand people and ninety percent of them drinking had sucked him in. Since he quit drinking, he had moderated his views. It seemed to him that nothing was wrong with sitting with a friend and talking, as long as he did not drink. Alcohol was a terrible problem in the legal profession. Everything seemed to center around it:

meeting clients, celebrating victories, and mourning losses. He had to be around it, though being a recovering alcoholic, he did not like it. He remembered a Sunday School teacher teaching something about the unsavory crowd that Jesus hung out with. Of course, Jesus was not seen with too many lawyers.

The bartender asked Charlie, "What can I get you?"

"Coke, please," he answered, looking at Brad's third bottle of Corona, which he was quickly draining, and an empty shot glass Charlie assumed had been filled with tequila.

"Charlie, why don't you celebrate more? You didn't even have a glass of champagne at your own dang victory party!" Brad bit down on a lime and took another drink.

"Maybe in a little bit," Charlie said, trying to placate his friend.

"So tell me all about this lunch with the head hombre." Brad fancied himself as one of the coolest attorneys in town. He drove a convertible Porsche Roadster like James Dean and frequently woke up with women whose business cards he had to read before their names would come to him.

"Reimarus took me to The French Quarter for two hours. He gave me a brief pat on the back and told me the test I must pass to become partner. I'm teamed up with Nancy."

"What a witch!" Brad's voice was quickly getting louder.

"We have to defend a guy named Walter Comstock. Reimarus lectured for an hour on how important this guy is and how much money he brings the firm. Apparently, he is a self-made, pull-yourself-up-by-your-bootstraps kind of a person. He's in his late fifties and flew A-6 Intruders in Vietnam. I guess A-6's were the first in and played decoy to draw ground fire away from the bombers. He's a tough son of a gun. He made a fortune building half of Charlotte. He gets a lot of government contracts, primarily because he is viewed as a humanitarian. He has these programs that give easy jobs to mildly handicapped people or ex-cons to help get them on their feet. He's received tons of awards. Now one of those kids he was helping is dead. The parents claim that the foreman was negligent and allowed this mildly retarded boy to do risky jobs when he didn't understand the dangers involved. I don't have all the details yet, but that's the main picture. Apparently, they are claiming that this is a pattern for Comstock."

"Man, you get all the good stuff. Everything I do is boring. Howard Brackman and Triton Partners want to buy another run-down strip mall and put in a video store, tanning salon, and yogurt shop. Have you ever noticed that every strip mall in North Carolina has a video store, tanning salon, and yogurt shop? You and I need to go into business and open a 'Tan Your Body and Eat Yogurt While Renting a Video One-Stop Store.' We'd get rich."

"Well, I don't know if it's exciting, but if it gets me to partner, that's all I care about." Charlie was halfway through one Coke and Brad asked for his fourth and final Corona.

"Just watch out for ole Nan. She may look good, but she is dangerous. I know a guy who went to Duke with her. Her senior year only one student had a higher GPA. The guy was kicked out for cheating, even though he claimed that he'd never cheated in his life. But his Social Security number was used to access the computers where the students take tests in the library, and grades were changed. He was kicked out two weeks before graduation and Nan graduated number-one from Duke."

"So what are you saying? She did it?" Charlie asked incredulously.

Brad leaned in real close to Charlie's face and whispered, "I'm saying watch your back, jack."

"Hey, I've got to get home for dinner. But can I take you up on your offer?"

"You want to go to Nags Head for the weekend? Sure." Brad took out his keys and pulled one off the key ring. "The code is 3323. Magic and Michael. Pretty smart, huh? Wait a minute, I've got a favor to ask. Be my wingman." Brad had just made eye contact with two secretaries at the end of the bar.

"Man, you know I hate that."

"Come on. You're married. I need help finding the woman of my dreams."

"Okay, ten minutes."

They walked down to the end of the bar. Brad immediately locked in on the cute blonde. The lesser attractive friend started smiling at Charlie.

"So, you come here often?" She grinned at him.

Oh, thought Charlie, *that's real original. No wonder you're pushing forty and still hanging out in bars.* "Every once in awhile."

"I see you're married."

"Actually, that's where I'm going right now. Back to my lovely wife and happy marriage."

"Not so fast, I just want to talk." She placed a hand on his knee to slow his retreat.

"Thanks, but no thanks. It's very flattering, but then again you're probably not that difficult to pick up. See ya, Brad." Brad did not answer. He was too busy falling in lust.

As Charlie left Johnathon's, a blue-and-orange station wagon with a taxi light on top pulled up to the entrance to shuttle drunken businessmen home. *Charlotte has the ugliest taxis,* he thought, and headed back south on Tryon. Passing Joe, he gave him a couple of bucks and headed to the parking garage. The drive home on Providence resembled a parking lot more than a road. Even though the city had added interchangeable lanes a few years ago to allow three lanes of outgoing traffic, it did not help. As Charlie inched forward listening to David Sanborn's latest CD, he thought about Brad's words, "Watch your back, jack." He and Nancy were on the same team. Why should he worry?

chapter
FOUR

Friday morning at five thirty, Charlie did not feel like fixing breakfast and Sandy was still in bed. Charlie kissed her and then went to kiss Ashley. He wanted to get in a couple of extra hours this morning so they could leave for the beach at noon. Myrtle Beach, South Carolina was the closest coast to Charlotte, but it was also the most crowded. A couple of local deejays voted it the tackiest beach on the East Coast because of all of the neon and T-shirt shops, and the biker week that was held every spring. Charlie wanted something quieter. Nags Head was at least six hours away. They would leave at noon.

Traveling this early in the morning had one benefit. Providence Road was wide open. He had the whole road to himself. He decided to stop off for breakfast at Sonny's Teriyaki Grill. He ate there anytime he was up early or Sandy was out of town. It was a typical small greasy spoon with a counter full of barstools and about six tables. There was already a Sonny's in Charlotte, a barbecue chain, so Sonny had to change his name to make it distinct.

Sonny's real name was Kim Il Sook. He had come to America not speaking a word of English when he was eighteen and had one change of clothes with him. He had done okay for himself. He owned this store and the dry cleaners next to it. All types of people, from accountants to street cleaners, loved

Sonny's food. The main reason for Sonny's popularity was that not a single item on his menu was fat-free. He cooked for people who loved to eat.

Charlie was rarely able to park on the street directly in front of Sonny's, but today was an exception. "Good morning, Sonny! How are you?"

"Oh fine, Charlie. You start early today. Must be big case." His English had come a long way in twenty-one years in the States.

"Well, I'm trying to leave early today so we can have a little vacation this weekend."

"Good for you. You deserve it. I saw paper. You big hero. That doctor deserve prison, you know, but DA can't find him." This puzzled Charlie, because the last he had heard, Owen Johnston had been arrested and was waiting arraignment.

Sonny continued, "Front page this morning had story. Doctor made bail. DA go to do some kind of pretrial motion and he no show."

"You're kidding me! He didn't show up for the evidentiary hearings?" These hearings decided what parts of the civil trial could be admitted as evidence. The video of Maggie probably would not be admitted. Johnston had a good shot at winning the criminal trial. The video was the big item in the civil trial. Without it, criminal negligence would be difficult for the state to show beyond reasonable doubt.

"You no worry, Charlie. You still hero. You like usual?"

"Sure, sounds good." Charlie waited to see if Sonny would get the order right.

"Okay, you got two eggs scrambled, five slices of bacon, two biscuits, grape jelly, and coffee with cream and sugar." Sonny just smiled at him. He never forgot a regular's favorite.

"You got it. Can I see your newspaper?" Charlie skimmed the article but learned nothing else. The article referred to the previous case but did not mention him by name. Johnston could simply be in the mountains trying to get away from everyone. He made a mental note to make a few phone calls at the office and see if he could find out anything else.

Charlie finished his breakfast and his third cup of coffee and made it to work by six fifteen. He closed the door of his hunter-green Chevy Blazer and headed for the elevator in the parking garage. The Jaguar XK8 would have to wait until Dr. Johnston's money came in. As he waited for the elevator, he heard high heels clicking on asphalt. He held the door while an attractive blonde in a two-piece burgundy suit got on. It was Nancy Lockman-Kurtz.

"Good morning!" Charlie attempted to be cheerful.

"Good morning," she said coldly. "I figured you would have retired with your millions by now."

She sure doesn't make it easy to be nice, Charlie thought. "Well, I'm just a millionaire on paper; it's not official yet." Trying to change directions, he said, "So I hear we'll be working together."

"Yes, I had drinks with Walter last night. I took the liberty of calling him and discussing some preemptive maneuvers before this thing gets out of hand."

Trying to be professional, he asked, "Did you clear that with Reimarus before you started working on the case?"

Grinning innocently, she explained, "It wasn't working. It was a meet and greet. I told him cocounsel would call today. I put in a good word for you."

"Thanks."

When the doors opened, Charlie headed for the Starbucks kiosk. Nancy asked him if he wanted her to wait. Riding up four floors in the parking garage had been bad enough; he was not about to ride thirty-nine floors more. He did not need more coffee this morning, but it was a good excuse to get away. She had purposely jumped the gun on this one. Instead of having a formal introductory meeting with Comstock and the partners, she went after him. It was very inappropriate.

Henry Judson sucked heartily on his Davidoff cigar and blew smoke in the general direction of his clients, Horace and Betty Douglas. They tried to be polite and not cough, but this good old-fashioned Church of God couple abhorred smoke. He was the only attorney they could afford. Henry's office was in Kannapolis, a small town in Rowan County about twenty minutes north of Charlotte on I-85. On the street across from Cannon Village was a row of mill houses that had been converted into stores and offices. Charles Cannon built a textile mill in the thirties and basically built Kannapolis himself. Cannon set up his workers in small white mill houses and named everything after himself, from the library to the bargain shopping district, which had recently been restored.

After graduating from Georgia Law School and returning home, Judson had bought one of these houses in 1960 and set out a shingle. He claimed Georgia Law was his first choice, but friends speculated he was rejected from law schools in North Carolina and Virginia. His career consisted mostly of writing wills, searching titles at the county courthouse, settling claims for friends and family in the hospital, and an occasional sexual harassment claim against the mill. Now at the age of sixty-two, Judson was a round man with several thick chins. A few strands of gray hair were slicked back over his round head. He loved to wear his red Georgia Bulldog suspenders with a blue-and-white striped suit. He spoke with a thick Southern accent and smoked Davidoff cigars incessantly.

At ten thirty, the battered and slightly rusted 1976 Monte Carlo had pulled up in front of the law office of Henry Judson. Out stepped a couple in their late fifties who looked closer to late sixties. Horace and Betty married in 1959 when he graduated from high school. Horace immediately started working at the mill. Gradually, he worked his way from driving a forklift to manager of shipping. Betty waited tables and eventually ended up working in the library. They rarely traveled, except to return to the sight of their honeymoon in Pigeon Forge, Tennessee. Finally, after twenty years at the mill, they were able to buy their own house. It was not a glamorous life, but they were happy.

After more than a decade of marriage, they had their first

child, Matthew Luke Douglas. They called him Matt. For awhile, everything seemed perfect. But by the time Matt was three, they noticed he was not progressing as quickly as the other children. It was not until he was in school that they learned Matt was mildly retarded. A freak chromosomal accident had caused Matt to be very slow. Betty quit working for several years to make sure Matt had every opportunity to progress. Their doctor encouraged them not to have other children, saying that it might happen again because of Betty's age.

After Matt graduated from high school at twenty-one, Horace found a house in Charlotte that helped handicapped adults learn to live independent lives. Matt lived at Project I Can for a year and a half and learned to ride a bus, hold down a job, and give and receive correct change. Surprisingly enough, there are people out there who will cheat the retarded out of seventy-five cents. Matt had made a C in woodshop, and he loved working with his hands. When the director of Project I Can, Frank Grady, learned of Matt's love for building things, he found Matt a job at Paragon Group. Horace and Betty made the drive to Charlotte every day for over a year to have dinner with Matt. Then one night at dinner, Matt began coughing uncontrollably. After several months, the coughing only got worse. In a few short months, Matthew Douglas was dead from lung cancer at the age of twenty-three. When no one could explain exactly what had happened, Horace and Betty responded to Judson's ad in the local Yellow Pages.

"Everything is going fine." Judson leaned way back in his overstuffed chair. "The claim has been filed in the civil court of Mecklenburg County. We will start taking depositions soon and be in trial by mid-February or early March."

"Why does it take so long?" Betty asked.

"Well now, here's the thing. Both sides have to investigate and interview witnesses," he explained, but not very well.

"I still don't understand," Horace said as he sat quietly with his arms crossed, waiting to hear something of consequence.

"We have to depose the witnesses to know what they will say on the witness stand."

"But isn't that what the trial is for? To find out what they will say?"

Judson frequently paused during the five-minute conversation and pulled out a handkerchief to wipe the sweat off his forehead.

"It's just not that simple. First of all, it's a civil case. Those usually take longer to get on the docket. Second, you're fighting a wealthy company whose lawyers will drag their feet every step of the way. The burden of proof is on us to convince the jury of Paragon's negligence. Fortunately, the threshold of proof is not as high as in a criminal case. I've got it all under control now. Y'all just need to go home and relax."

"Thank you very much," Betty said as they stood to leave. "We loved Matt very much and we appreciate all of your hard work."

Judson's big meaty hand shook her frail bony hand violently, almost shaking her whole body. Horace's hand, however, was so firm he could barely move it. At fifty-nine, Horace looked old but was strong as a horse. As the couple drove away, they discussed the meeting. For some reason, Henry Judson had not inspired them with too much confidence, and the picture of him sitting on a rocking chair on the front porch of that white mill house smoking a stogie as they drove away did not help. But he was all they could afford. At one hundred fifty an hour, Horace would probably have to dip into his pension to pay the bill and maybe even take out a second mortgage. They did not care. They wanted to see Paragon Group punished for killing their son. As they drove, Betty's frail bony hand reached over and took hold of Horace's strong tanned hand. In silence, she watched a tear roll down his cheek.

The hall was dark except for some recessed lighting above the crown molding and a light that came from an office halfway between the middle and the corner. Brad Connelly was working late on a Friday night for the first time in his life. His client had insisted that all of the papers be ready to be filed at the courthouse first thing Tuesday morning, and Brad was not about to spend his entire Labor Day weekend working. The thirty-ninth floor was quiet as lights started to pop up all around downtown. Brad's office faced west, looking up Trade Street to the federal courthouse. At the far end of the hall, he heard the sound of heels clicking on the hardwood floor.

"What are you doing here this late?" He saw the blond hair before the face registered. It was Nancy.

Trying to be nonchalant, Brad said, "I had a few loose ends to tie up before I headed out this weekend." It was eight o'clock, and all of the good action did not start until ten anyway.

"I was just seeing if there was anybody who could walk me to my car. I hate going through that parking garage at night. It gives me the creeps." He had never known her to be so vulnerable, but he really did not feel like helping.

"I'm sure that the security guards at the front desk would be happy to help. Have a nice weekend." The not-so-subtle hint was deliberately ignored.

"Come on, Brad. Be a friend." Something in her eyes flashed a kindness that was almost flirtatious. Brad softened.

As they headed to her car, she suggested that they grab a quick bite to eat since she had not yet eaten dinner. She insisted they take Brad's Roadster, because she had never ridden in one. Johnathon's was packed and densely thick with smoke. A jazz band from Memphis was raising the rafters with its own version of "Satin Dolls." They sat at the bar and waited for a table. She was patient, but she was willing to get as drunk as he wanted until she found out what she needed to know.

"So you and Charlie are close, huh?" she asked ever so innocently. "I don't know him at all, but I think we are supposed to be working together."

"He started the year before me, but he is more determined than I am. I never wanted to put in ninety-hour weeks. I'm satisfied where I'm at. I like to have fun."

"Me too."

Brad nearly spewed his screwdriver all over her at this statement. "You? Fun? You're worse than Charlie. You've only been here seven years, and already they want to make you a partner."

"Well, I'm sure Charlie will get it. He's been here longer, plus he just won that huge case. I can wait a few years. I think he deserves it." She was attractive and desirable; Brad could not deny that. But tonight, she was actually pleasant, almost like a real human being. The light reflected off the moisture on her lips, which were poised on the brink of activity. Of course, he was on his third drink and a table was still fifteen minutes away. At a certain level of inebriation, all females looked good to Brad.

"I just hope he relaxes. I don't think the partners care for those strong church boy types." It was okay to talk about Charlie; she seemed to be on his side.

"What do you mean?" This was why she had stayed around the office playing solitaire on her computer for two hours and billing it to Tramco. Information.

"Charlie sometimes has a problem with morals."

"Does he bend the law? Ignore ethics?" She was a wonderful actress.

"No. No. The problem is that he *has* morals. He didn't even drink at his own celebration. The partners think he's too stiff. That might turn off clients. Charlie's a little worried about that too."

A small table for two in a dark corner became available. They both ordered steak and beer. She drank from the bottle like a regular guy. She loosened the sling-backs on her three-inch heels and started playing footsie. After more chitchat, she returned to her purpose with calculated precision.

"So Charlie's a holy-roller?" She giggled.

Brad laughed. "Nothing like that, but he takes his ethics very seriously. He's not one of those people who sees how close to the edge he can get. Actually, sometimes I get really jealous of the guy. He's got it all: looks, family, great job, and a good reputation. Shoot. I don't know how he stays a lawyer. He sounds more like a preacher."

Pay dirt! Nancy thought to herself. "You're lucky to have such a good friend."

They finished their steak and dessert. They danced and drank and staggered to his trendy townhouse a block east of Graham Street. She did not have to go through with the rest of her charade but figured it would be fun. Then she would have Brad on her side. They promised not to tell anyone at the firm. Relationships between associates were not forbidden, but it was dangerous territory. This was not even a relationship, though. It was just a few nights until she made partner. Brad would not even remember tonight, but she would.

chapter
FIVE

With frequent stops for food and bathroom breaks, the entire trip to Nags Head took seven hours, but it would be worth it all. After driving north for two hours on Interstate 85, they headed east on Interstate 40 outside Durham. At Raleigh, the path became more complex. Highway 64 led to Williamston, where they entered the coastal plain, also known as the low country. In Williamston, Highway 17 crossed marshes and inlets until they reached Highway 158 in Elizabeth City. From there, the trip was scenic and almost a step back in time. Unlike other places near the coast, the ocean view was not visible from miles away. Highway 158 was covered with trees, and there was no hint of the beach until the scenic vista exploded into view at the Wright Memorial Bridge. The bridge led to a string of islands that covers almost the entire coast of North Carolina, called the Outer Banks. This string actually runs from Virginia to Florida, but the islands so completely cover North Carolina that they prevented settlement and economic growth in the 1700s. For years, ships tried to maneuver these dangerous banks and many failed, giving the North Carolina coast the nickname "Graveyard of the Atlantic."

Highway 158 was called Virginia Dare Trail, named after the first English baby born in the New World. It ran through beach communities named Kitty Hawk, Kill Devil Hills, and

Nags Head. The Harrigans' destination was just five miles south of where the Wright Brothers flew a heavier-than-air machine on December 17, 1903. The average twelve-mile-an-hour winds and soft sand dunes made this a perfect place to attempt flight.

Nags Head is a stretch of beach eleven miles long on an island only a mile wide. On the east is the Atlantic Ocean and on the west is the Intracoastal Waterway, a favorite of fishermen and novice sailors. Nags Head is full of Southern red oaks, some that are five hundred years old. Natural sand dunes occur all over the island and are perfect for sliding down or launching hang gliders. The largest two sand dunes are Run Hill and Jockey's Ridge.

Since the 1830s, Nags Head has been a popular tourist haunt. It was believed back then that gases, then called miasma, were being given off by the swamps and marshes of the low country, and the population became deathly ill. The inhabitants of the low country noticed that those who spent summer on the Outer Banks in the salt air and water did not contract this disease. In the 1830s, wealthy individuals headed for Nags Head to escape the miasma. Unfortunately, they did not realize this disease was actually malaria, and was caused by the mosquitoes in the swamps and not a fictitious gas. Regardless, Nags Head's resort community was born.

No one is exactly sure how Nags Head got its name. Some say that from the ocean, the island resembles a horse's head. The more romantic story is that at night, certain ill-willed men would tie lanterns around a horse's neck and ride up and down the dunes, which resembled, from afar, a ship bobbing in the ocean. These lights lured ships to the shallow ocean off the banks, and when they ran ashore and got stuck, the pirates would invade the boats, stealing their cargo and precious treasure.

It had been more than two years since they had gotten out of town on vacation, not including visiting Sandy's parents in the mountains and Charlie's mother in Atlanta. They had been satisfied to spend their vacations on the lake or fixing up their house. If this next trial proved as time consuming as the previous one, Charlie and Sandy would not have anymore time like this until Thanksgiving.

They arrived in Nags Head about seven thirty and went directly to the grocery store to stock up the condo. After they got unpacked, it was almost Ashley's bedtime, so they took a brief family walk down the beach. In Charlie's right hand was a soft, slender hand that was adorned with a solitary diamond, and in his left hand was a much smaller hand that could barely grasp three of his fingers. The setting sun behind the condos bathed the beach in an orange glow, while the horizon over the ocean was turning dark.

They walked the beach with the water rushing over their feet. For the first time in six months, Charlie did not think of Maggie Thomason or Dr. Owen Johnston. He did not worry about Walter Comstock and Nancy Lockman-Kurtz. The thought of being a partner seemed like another world. The slow pace of the coast caused him to slow down and evaluate his life.

"Honey," he turned toward Sandy and pulled her close as Ashley dug in shallow water just below the surface for sand dollars, "I really love you."

"Well, thank you. I love you too," she responded.

"No, that's not it. I know we say that all the time, but I'm serious. I could not live without you. You are not just my wife, you're my best friend."

"Thank you, sweetheart." She considered saying more, but it was not necessary. Her touch said it all. They embraced each other more firmly and kissed; long, slow, and passionate like college students again. As they headed back to the condo to put Ashley to bed, they reminisced about their first kiss.

Their first date had been a disaster by Charlie's standards, and he was unsure if Sandy would ever see him again. He summoned up his courage, however, and called her for the Fall German's Dance. The semiformal always featured big band music and plenty of waltzes, jitterbugs, and fox-trots. The sight of him dressed nicely made a strong impression on Sandy. She knew he was cute, but in a double-breasted suit, he was absolutely dashing. This date ended with a small kiss on the cheek. It was simple and sweet.

Their third date had been a different story. He was supposed to meet her at the Baptist Student square dance, but the restaurant where he worked ended up being short-handed that night. Four Corners was a tradition in Chapel Hill. The restaurant was named after the stall technique created by basketball coaching legend Dean Smith. Every item on the menu was named after a Carolina basketball star. That night Charlie was frantic. He had no way of getting in touch with Sandy, and she sat alone the entire evening.

At one thirty in the morning after he finished cleaning off his tables, Charlie ran full speed across campus to Avery Dorm. He was able to get in the dorm without too much of a problem. It happened quite frequently. He banged on the door to room 324. Silence. He banged again. "Please open up, I'm sorry for standing you up. I've got a good reason." It was a move of desperation on his part, but at the moment, it seemed necessary.

The door slowly inched open. "You smell like beer."

"Another waiter spilled it on me, honest. I couldn't get off work." He actually got down on his knees.

"Wait a minute," she sleepily said with no hint of enthusiasm.

The door opened again revealing a worn, fuzzy white terry cloth robe and bear claw slippers. Her hair was in a ponytail on top of her head. "What do you want?"

"I just wanted to bring you these." He pulled out twelve freshly picked roses of all colors.

"Where did you get these?" Sandy seemed astonished.

"Morehead Planetarium," he answered casually.

"The Planetarium!" she replied in shock. "If the campus cops find out you picked these, they will charge you a hundred dollars a rose."

"I know. I didn't think anyone had ever given you twelve hundred dollars worth of flowers before." Ah, there it was. The beginnings of a little smile. It was the same smile he had seen lying in the grass after running headfirst into a goalpost.

"Well, I guess if you risked a thousand dollars on me, I can talk to you for a little bit. I forgive you."

They walked out to the hallway that was open to the outside. They sat on the floor and hung their legs over the balcony, looking toward the baseball field illuminated by a full moon. They talked for hours. At first, it was simple conversation. They talked about family, high school, former boyfriends and girlfriends, but soon they were on a much deeper level. They talked about their hopes and dreams. He shared his fears and she shared her hurts. They connected on many levels. With their legs kicking in the breeze, it seemed like only a few minutes had passed, but then the sun began to rise over the center field fence.

He said he should probably leave to get ready for his eight o'clock class. She grabbed his arm. It was the first time she had touched him all night. It was like he was thirteen again, and a charge went through his entire body. He sat back down and she leaned into him. Her tousled, soft brown hair brushed up against his cheek and he closed his eyes. Her head turned ever so slightly toward him and their lips met. In the warm glow of the morning sun, he brushed her cheek with his hand. For a moment, time stood still. They breathed as one. They were meant to be.

Curled up on the porch swing of the condo overlooking the ocean, they had decided to watch the sun come up and relive that moment. Sandy sat snuggled up to Charlie in the same battered robe with her head on his shoulder. They sipped their coffee and watched the brilliant rays of red and orange burst over the Atlantic.

"Charlie, do you have to work so much?" She did it. She broached a subject they had dealt with many times and could rarely agree upon. Such unwavering patience was difficult over time.

"You know the answer to that. Why do you ask?"

"This is just so nice. The Thomason case consumed you for several months. Even now, I know your mind still drifts to it. I like us. I like us like this." She was not complaining. She was being honest. One thing they always agreed upon was brutal honesty.

"I do too. But if we want to stay in Myers Park and send Ashley to Charlotte Latin, this is the only way to do it. You can't be a good attorney and work fifty hours a week, not at a firm." Charlie shook his head and thought of the numerous lectures teachers gave about being whatever you want to be. It seemed to him that a person can only be what bills and circumstances allow.

"Wouldn't it be nice to live here?" The sun was almost completely over the horizon now and the water sparkled.

"Yeah, but what would we do? The only reason Brad can afford this place is because he's single," Charlie responded with a hint cynicism.

"So that's it. You want a divorce." She laughed.

"Of course not, never. I just don't know what I would do."

She sat up straight and looked him in the eyes, "What would you do if money were no object?"

"I don't know," Charlie shrugged, "I've never thought about it." He paused and thought. "See that sailboat. I'd do that."

"You've never sailed before in your life." She acted surprised.

"Well, if money is no object, I would take lessons. You, me, Ashley, and the little one could sail down to the Caribbean, north to Nova Scotia, maybe all over the world. It would be wonderful."

"Sounds good to me. Let's do it."

"You know we can't."

"No. I mean today. The three of us rent a sailboat and really see the coast. I'll get the phone book." She ran inside.

Charlie followed her into the small, but nicely decorated condo. It had a nautical motif with nets on the wall and seashells everywhere. He went upstairs and woke up his pride and joy.

Shaking her gently, he said, "Ashley, time to get up."

She moaned and stretched and after a few moments more a smile came to her face. "Hey, Daddy." She gave him a big kiss.

For the next seven hours, they did not talk about work. They learned about masts and sterns. They rubbed sunscreen all over each other. They bobbed up and down in the waves. Charlie tried his hand at deep-sea fishing. He had never particularly cared for standing on the side of a lake and throwing in a fishing line, but this was exciting. After an hour of futile attempts, he caught a two-foot-long mako shark. They came back to the condo with reddened skin and marinated the shark in the juices of fresh oranges, lemons, and limes. They had grilled mako shark and baked potatoes for dinner. Ashley was not impressed. It was just a big fish to her.

That night Charlie and Sandy acted like honeymooners again. They tickled and laughed, massaged and caressed. They slept with the windows open and the constant breeze blew in off the ocean. Their bed was bathed in moonlight.

Sunday they attended a local church and held hands. They sang and prayed together. On the walk back to the condo on Ocean Acres Drive, Charlie agreed to back off work as much as possible. In reality, he wanted to. He did not want to miss his little girl growing up. He had missed her first steps because of a client meeting in Charleston. He had to settle for the videotape. They played in the sand all afternoon. Ashley built sand castles and the waves knocked them down. She ran to Daddy crying, and they would start all over again.

Sandy tanned her body and prayed for Charlie. He had been a good provider, but there was more to being a husband. She could see him getting lost in the legal profession. That monster had devoured not a small number of marriages. He needed more of a purpose. The Thomason case had worried him, but it reenergized him also. It was not the law; it was the

64   THE TRIAL OF JOB

purpose behind the law. He was helping that couple and he loved it. The reward was not the money, not for Charlie. He loved helping that couple find closure. Sandy picked up her journal and scribbled what she was thinking. One day she would tell him everything, but for now he needed to relax.

On Monday, they decided to give their skin a break and played putt-putt. They drove golf carts and saw a movie together for the first time in over a year. He wanted to see Mel Gibson blow away the bad guys. She wanted to see Tom Hanks find his lost love. They saw Tom Hanks. They visited the Wright Brothers' Memorial and climbed sand dunes and then rolled back down. It was wonderful. They went for a final walk on the beach and headed back home. They piled in the Blazer and headed north on 158 and then west back over Wright Memorial Bridge. Ashley was asleep in twenty minutes.

With the ocean fading quickly in the rearview mirror, Charlie grabbed Sandy's hand. "I had a wonderful weekend."

"Me too," she sighed.

He looked at her face in the moonlight. "I think you get better looking every day."

"Why, thank you. You're not too bad yourself."

"I promise. I will try to work less. After I make partner, things will slow down." He did not tell her about the secret maneuvering of Nancy or Brad's words of warning. There was no need to worry her.

"It's okay with me if you don't make partner. I wouldn't mind if you went into business for yourself. Then you could help people. I saw how satisfied you were helping the Thomasons." She smiled.

"You're right. I have more fun doing my pro bono cases than I do with all of this big corporate litigation."

"You wouldn't be happy sailing. It's too isolated. You need to be where you can help people. Isn't that why you became a lawyer in the first place?"

He thought long and hard. It was difficult to remember. "You know why I became a lawyer? My father makes millions every year. He never paid child support. Our stupid attorney drained our savings account and ran off. From that day, I vowed never to be poor or taken advantage of again."

"So the helping means nothing to you?" she asked.

"I don't know. I don't know," he replied, and they drove in silence.

chapter
SIX

Tuesday morning, exactly one week after the papers declared Charlie a hero, he took his time getting to work after a long, relaxing weekend. At seven o'clock in the morning, Providence Road was already crawling, even with all of the reversible lanes heading west into downtown. He had kissed Ashley on the forehead while she was still sleeping, and he had to run out of the house without breakfast, because he and Sandy had spent a little extra time snuggling this morning. He felt alive again. After ten years of the law wearing him down, today he felt optimistic and ready to save the world again, like the first day he walked into Hobbes, Reimarus, and Van Schank. Being a lawyer often created tunnel vision; he had become so focused on his cases that he lost track of more important things. A weekend at Nags Head with his wife and daughter helped him rediscover what was important. When he became a partner, he promised to give more time to pro bono work and to use his talents to help those who did not have access to sound legal advice.

Charlie had thought very little about Walter Comstock and Nancy Lockman-Kurtz during the weekend, but now as he sat through the stoplight at Sharon Road for the third time, they consumed him. Nancy had told him that this redneck couple was just out to get rich from Walter's company. Two things bothered him. First, how did she know they were simply out for money? Second, she called him Walter. Charlie was missing a piece of the puzzle, and this greatly concerned him. They were supposed to meet with Comstock most of the afternoon and schedule depositions fairly soon. He knew nothing about the Douglases and even less about the facts concerning the case. While at lunch, Reimarus had told him very little about the civil claim. This couple was claiming that Comstock's negligence had something to do with their son's cancer; he knew that much. Reimarus had said that the risk was part of the job that everyone understood and agreed to. The facts were simple and Charlie was encouraged to handle this quickly and quietly to protect Comstock's reputation in the city. Charlie decided, however, that if Comstock was being wrongfully sued, he would fight with all of his heart against these people who were taking advantage of deep pockets. These people were probably just lazy and looking to win the lottery.

At seven thirty, Charlie had already unbuttoned the top button of his shirt. He finally reached Sonny's and parked illegally, while he ran in to get a quick sausage biscuit and a cup of coffee. Swinging the door wide open, he squeezed up to the crowded counter.

"Hey, Sonny! Did you have a good weekend?" Charlie was trying to be polite so he would get waited on more quickly.

"Yes, my friend. You want usual?" Sonny had already started cooking the bacon.

"No. I don't have enough time. I've got to get to the office. Just a sausage biscuit and coffee. I've got another big case starting today."

"You win this one too. No one beat Charlie Harrigan. The good guy always win. What you did for that little girl's family was great. Too bad about doctor though." Sonny shook his head and turned back to the griddle.

What did he mean by that? Charlie thought. *Too bad for the doctor.* Something did not fit.

Sonny handed Charlie his breakfast. "Hey, Sonny, what did

you mean about the doctor?"

Charlie's brow furrowed even more as Sonny said, "You haven't seen paper this morning? Front page. Story about your doctor."

"No. I missed it, I was running late."

"I didn't understand all," Sonny did his best to clarify the subject. "But doctor's gone. No one can find him."

Charlie's heart starting beating faster. "Is that all the article said?"

"No. No. Let me think. Something about federal court. I don't know."

Charlie was stunned by this news. "Thanks, Sonny. I'll check it out." He paid and stumbled toward the door.

Charlie was in a daze as he walked to his Blazer, wondering where Dr. Johnston was. When he reached his car, he discovered a fifty-dollar parking ticket under the windshield wiper. "This is going to be a great day," Charlie said out loud as he watched the traffic inch slowly toward downtown. He fought the traffic the rest of the way into the city and entered the parking garage off College Street.

He watched the numbers click on the elevator and thought about last week. Last Tuesday, he walked into this building a hero. If his hunch was right, he would cease being the hottest attorney in Charlotte. He got off the elevator on the thirty-ninth floor and headed for Selia's desk.

"Do you have today's newspaper?" Charlie could not help sounding desperate.

"No, sir." Selia gave a warm smile that suggested he did not want to see the paper. "There's one in the kitchen. Have a nice day."

Charlie ran down the hallway and turned left into a small kitchen. Throwing his briefcase, breakfast, and coat on the floor, he grabbed the Tuesday morning edition of *The Charlotte Observer*. At the bottom of page one under the obligatory drug-related murders and drug cases, he saw it. "Million Dollar Doctor Vanishes" was the title of the article that related the story. Dr. Owen Johnston, who was found guilty of wrongful death in the civil case of Maggie Thomason, had filed for Chapter 11 bankruptcy protection from the federal court on West Trade Street. After the indictments, Dr. Johnston's insurance company dropped his medical malpractice insurance. With no insurance carrier, he did not have the funds to pay the verdict. The article went on to say that Dr. Johnston had failed to show up for his arraignment and was assumed to have fled the country on half a million dollars bail.

Charlie crumpled up the newspaper and threw it across the room. Not feeling assuaged of his anger, he grabbed the coffeepot full of freshly brewed Jamaica Blue Mountain coffee and slammed it against the wall. The carafe made a spectacular crash and the coffee splattered all over the wall. After kicking the table over, he slumped down into a chair and put his head in his hands. *That dirty, rotten scum* was all Charlie could think. *He kills a young girl, loses a major lawsuit, and is probably in South America somewhere with thousands of dollars crammed in his pockets.* When Charlie thought of Maggie's parents, he fought to hold back the tears. Their only comfort in this whole debacle was the fact that Johnston was going to be punished and publicly humiliated. As coffee dripped slowly onto the floor, he sat feeling defeated. Bankruptcy was the last refuge of scoundrels. Sure Charlie had won a moral victory, but what was that worth now?

In a dimly lit corner office on the forty-first floor, Martin Van Schank was rubbing the shoulders of Nancy Lockman-Kurtz as he stood behind her. They enjoyed these early morning rendezvous, because the office was fairly empty and they did not have to worry about secretaries or nosy partners.

"Well, what do you think of our boy now?" Van Schank grinned icily as he bent down and kissed her on the neck.

"Well, I think that he is no longer a front-runner for partner. It just goes to show that he is not the rainmaker that this firm needs. He stumbled into the perfect case; even a moron could have won with the facts he had. But he can't produce the volume that I can." Nancy smiled and crossed her legs, kicking off her shoes in the process.

"Now we just have to get him off the case. As you know, Paragon Group pays us a lot of money every year. What you don't know is that Walter needs to be protected from the public. This case needs to disappear to protect certain interests and relationships that Walter has. Charlie's presence alone would make this case very high profile. Reimarus wanted to give the boy a chance. But I don't think he has the guts to play ball with the big boys. He's too squeaky clean." Van Schank removed his glasses and helped guide her hands to loosen his tie.

"I have the perfect plan for after work. If that doesn't get rid of him, I may have to use more drastic measures. I deserve to be the next partner. I'm just like you guys." Nancy purred like a cat stalking its prey.

"You know how jealous I get when you flirt with other men." He grabbed her arms, firmly pushing her to the leather couch against the wall.

"Yeah, you're more jealous than my husband." She laughed and tossed her hair and slowly unbuttoned her blouse.

Walter Comstock and Paragon Group would be billed for an hour and a half for each attorney during this liaison, because they did talk about the case. Van Schank would take him for three hundred and fifty dollars an hour and Nancy would bill him at two hundred dollars an hour. This little tryst would cost Comstock close to eight hundred dollars.

In his smoke-filled office in an old mill house, Henry Judson tried explaining to his clients that the case did not look good. If the truth were known, it had been seven years since he was actually inside a courtroom. His type of law was quite easy to practice. Mostly, it consisted of writing nasty letters and threatening litigation until the defendant decided to settle, then he kept one-third of the settlement. He had sued practically every insurance agency that operated in Rowan County. Most of them settled without putting up a fight and paid nice settlements to keep their names out of the papers. His highly successful and exploitative practice bought him a high-dollar bass fishing boat and a sailboat. He would soon retire and spend his days on High Rock Lake trolling for largemouth bass.

"Well, I have done a little digging and it doesn't look real good." Judson shook his head and apologetically continued, "I think we should prepare ourselves to take a good settlement if they offer one. Now I want to assure you that I would not jump at the first settlement, but we'll take them for a good chunk of change."

Horace was visibly frustrated, but remained quiet. Betty shifted in her seat, preparing for the rest of the bad news.

"Y'all want some coffee or doughnuts? It's my treat for my clients. These chocolate-covered ones are my favorite, because you get the best of both—"

"Mr. Judson," the frail little lady sounded rather intimidated, "if you don't mind, can we stick to the case? Why do you want to settle?"

"Well," Henry sat back in his chair as his stomach pushed his red Georgia Bulldog suspenders far to his sides, "these big boys in Charlotte have lots of lawyers and lots of money. I just don't know if I can keep up with them. Without some extra funds coming in, it's going to be tough dedicating all my time to this if I'm not getting paid."

"Is that the only thing stopping you?" Betty began to worry. "If that is the only problem, we can dip into our pension to help pay for whatever you need."

"No. No. That's not the only problem. Walter Comstock is spotless. He has never been cited by OSHA or the city. Besides he has won several humanitarian awards for helping the . . ." Judson stumbled for the right word, ". . . needy. Also, we will have to prove that your son's cancer was related to his work at Paragon before we ever prove that Comstock was negligent. It's a tough road. I think we ought to settle."

Until now, Horace Douglas had been stoic and reserved comment. He rose and spoke quietly and firmly like a man who would not be disagreed with. Looking Judson in the eye and speaking with a low growl, he said, "Look, I understand that you are up against a formidable opponent, but you are a lawyer and you work for me. I don't care how much money they have. I do not want to settle. I don't care about money. I want justice. I want Paragon Group to answer us in public. My son did not understand the risks he was dealing with. I can't prove this, but I would bet that there was asbestos in that old warehouse and that being exposed to it caused him to get cancer. He shouldn't have been in there in the first place, but they should have protected him."

"Yeah, but the site reports said it was perfectly—" Judson was quickly rebuffed.

"Mr. Judson," Horace was not finished speaking, "I have worked hard all of my life and I ask very little of people. Please look deeper. I believe that Matt was placed into a dangerous situation and did not know what he was dealing with. You are our only hope." Horace relaxed and sat back down.

Putting down his cigar, Henry said, "I'm sorry. I'll do my best. Paragon's liability is going to be difficult to prove, but I will try."

As Horace and Betty got in their ancient Monte Carlo, Judson looked out the window and tried to think of a way he could rescue himself. Surely, Paragon Group would pay $75,000 just to keep its name out of the paper. He was expecting to make a quick twenty-five grand. He thought some more and returned his attention to an automobile accident, a quick couple of thousand. He picked up the stationery that said, "From the Office of Henry Wallace Judson, Esquire."

Brad and Charlie left the elevator and headed down the hallway to their offices. Charlie had a one thirty appointment with Nancy, Walter, and Barry Kasick, one of Paragon's foremen. Since Charlie arrived at the office that morning, a constant parade of attorneys had come to his door offering their condolences over his loss of three million dollars. Brad had bought him lunch at The Scoreboard to cheer him up. They had tried to avoid talking about the doctor, but the conversation always came back to it.

"Did ole Hobbes say anything about your abstract coffee art that you left on the kitchen wall this morning?" Brad started laughing.

"No. Not yet, but I will probably have to pay for new wallpaper. I should have stayed in bed this morning." Charlie snickered a little and then got serious. "I can't believe it. You know that guy has to be rich, but he files Chapter 11 so they can't garnish any of his wages."

"So where do you think that snake is?" Brad was still wearing his sunglasses as they were walking through the foyer. "Hey, cutie," Brad said to Selia, who always ignored him.

"I talked to Melinda Powell in the DA's office, and she said that late Friday afternoon there was a wire transfer from Johnston's wife's personal account at First Union Bank to a bank in the Bahamas. From there, they could not trace it. The FBI was trying to get a court order, but getting those guys to talk is like getting a lawyer to give you a straight answer."

"There are over seven hundred islands in the Bahamas alone," Brad said, displaying his amazement. "That guy used the bankruptcy court to protect his cash long enough to get it out of the country."

"Which is highly illegal, mind you," Charlie added.

Brad continued, "After the money hit the Bahamas, he could have transferred it anywhere in ten minutes. The guy could be anywhere."

"Yeah," Charlie just sighed, "he's on a beach somewhere getting drunk on some tropical drink with an umbrella, and I have probably just lost the partnership."

"Maybe not, man. If you outdo Nancy, you might still get it." Brad tried to be supportive.

"We'll see. Right now, we have to meet with Comstock. I'll

talk to you later."

"How about a drink after work?" Brad asked.

"Why do you try to get me to drink? Anyway, I want to see my family. Sandy will make me feel better."

"Oh, that's right," Brad said. Then something occurred to him. "You couldn't get a drink anyway. Nan said she wanted y'all to have dinner with Comstock tonight. Maybe tomorrow after work. Later." Brad was halfway down the hall as the words clicked in Charlie's head.

Did he say 'Nan'? Charlie thought about it. Something was not right. Charlie grabbed his Paragon file and headed back to the big conference room on the thirty-ninth floor. Brad hated that woman and usually called her a witch. But just now, he had actually spoken pleasantly about her. Charlie felt as if he had walked into a play during the second act and had missed some very important information. Maybe he was just tired. He had lost a fortune that morning that he had never really possessed in the first place. That was not the worst part, however. He felt that he had let the Thomasons down, even though he had nothing to do with Johnston's flight. His victory had been for nothing. Chances were that he lost the partnership, because he had just lost the biggest client he had ever generated. Suddenly, his future at Hobbes, Reimarus, and Van Schank did not look that secure. How could things change so much in one week?

Charlie felt like a juggler who was dropping the balls one by one. As his hand reached for the polished brass handle on the solid oak door of the conference room, he had no idea that this was just the beginning. He paused before he entered the conference room and thought, *Maybe I do not want to do this the rest of my life. Maybe the firm life is just not for me.* He opened the door slowly and saw one of the most foreboding men he had ever met in his life.

chapter
SEVEN

After one hour of circular discussions with Walter Comstock, the extremely wealthy CEO of Paragon Group, Charlie had gotten nowhere. The prestigious conference room looked like a tornado had hit and scattered documents and file folders everywhere. They were on their third pot of coffee, and the vein in Comstock's neck was bulging. Charlie slumped back in his chair with his sleeves rolled up and his tie completely loosened as Comstock and his foreman, Barry Kasick, took a bathroom break. Nancy Lockman-Kurtz seemed incredibly composed and did not have a single hair out of place.

With a glib little smirk, she asked Charlie, "Why are you pushing him so hard? We're on the same side."

"He's not taking this seriously," Charlie sighed as he ran his fingers through his hair. "I just came from the other side of the bench in a civil case like this. People tend to forget that these simple, straightforward cases often have devastating effects. Remember the Watergate Hotel or Monica Lewinski? There is more that Comstock is not telling us."

"We don't have to know all of the truth in order to represent this guy. The burden of proof is on this poor Judson guy. It's been at least a decade since he set foot in a courtroom. I'm not too worried about him."

Frustrated and confused, Charlie was still dazed by the

news from the morning's paper. He stretched his legs. "How can you be so sure that Judson will take a small settlement?"

Nancy crossed her long shapely legs in her now famous trademark way and smiled, "Charlie, there is more to law than the rules. Trust me." She laughed.

Charlie shot her a quizzical look about the same time the double oak doors burst wide open and Comstock returned to the leather chair at the head of the table. Lighting up a Camel cigarette, Comstock was ready for round two. Charlie had spent the entire morning familiarizing himself with the facts of the case. This preliminary interview was designed to fill in the blanks, plan an initial strategy for the preliminary hearing in a few days, and request from Comstock all of the relevant documents. The initial strategy always included a motion to dismiss without prejudice, claiming that the facts did not demonstrate the need for adjudication and that neither party was guilty. He would also file a motion for summary judgment asking the judge to make a decision based on the facts before them, although it had very little chance of working. These tactics rarely worked, but it caused the plaintiff to work that much harder to prove the merits of his case.

After reviewing the facts most of the morning and reconstructing the history of the events, Charlie decided that Judson's clients had a valid concern that needed to be addressed, but they had a long way to go to prove Comstock's liability. He thought of how difficult Judson's job would be; one man going against all of the money and power of the great firm of Hobbes, Reimarus, and Van Schank. One thing Henry Judson did have on his side, however, was sympathy. Horace and Betty Douglas were apparently nice people who worked in a textile mill town. They had one son, Matt, who turned out to be slightly retarded. His tests at A. L. Brown High School measured his IQ at 85, which is in the range of mildly retarded. Matt progressed and was able to live in an assisted living house in Charlotte. Through the Helping Hands Program, a special county program that gave grants to businesses that hired handicapped individuals,

Matt was able to get a job on a construction crew doing simple tasks, like picking up trash at construction sites.

These facts alone made for a very sympathetic defendant. The rest of the story had several blanks. Two and a half years ago, Matt was helping clean out a building that was about to be demolished and fell through the ceiling from the attic and landed in a pile of insulation that had been ripped off the walls. The story broke down from there, but a year later Matt developed lung cancer. The Douglases believed that Comstock and Paragon Group had exposed Matt to dangerous fibers and materials that caused the cancer and killed him a year and a half later. Not a bad set of facts, Charlie thought, but lots of holes that Judson would have to fill in.

First of all, Comstock, as owner of the company, may have never met Matt Douglas. Judson would have to follow the chain of command and prove that Matt was ordered into risky situations. Also, in jobs like construction, there is a certain assumption of risk that is involved with the type of work. Judson would also have to demonstrate that the insulation and materials were the catalysts for the cancer. Charlie was glad that he did not have all of those hurdles to face. He merely had to fend off the attack of the enemy. He also had to explain all of this to his client without getting his head chopped off.

"I just don't understand why I have to pay both of you for the entire afternoon, and you keep dragging this thing out." Comstock kept his thumb on every penny that his company spent. While he had calmed down some, he was still visibly frustrated.

Charlie tried to placate his client. "It is important for us to gather all of the facts, so that we know exactly what we are dealing with. There are things that you might consider unimportant, but they may be crucial to our case."

"Hang on one second!" It was more of a command than a request. "Barry, why don't you go down to ole Charlie boy's office and get those documents and employment records that Ms. Lockman-Kurtz asked for."

"Please, call me Nancy, okay?" She smiled as Barry left the conference room.

"Now here's the deal," Comstock turned back to Charlie. "I met that kid once or twice, but Barry was the foreman on the project. Why can't they just sue him? If things get worse, I can just fire him and say that it was all his fault."

"I don't think you should fire anyone yet." Charlie got up and went to pour his eighth cup of coffee since breakfast, spilling most of it all over his suit. "If you fire someone, it makes you look guilty. The reason you are listed on the lawsuit is because of the principle of vicarious liability. Since you are the owner of the company, you are responsible for the actions and decisions of the managers under you."

Nancy added, "Besides, the threshold question in a negligence case is, how would a reasonable person act? And nothing that I have seen points to anything unreasonable."

"That's me. I'm a very reasonable person." Comstock's mood seemed to lighten a little.

"We know." Charlie finally felt like he was getting through. "Part of our strategy is to show how reasonable you are. That is why we asked for copies of all of your work with the less fortunate. I looked over the financial statements of the Douglases, and I think we will be able to show that they are desperate. They don't have much to live on, and Mr. Douglas is close to retirement age. We can show that they really need the money. Now the thing that concerns me most is the job site that Matt was working on. I . . . we need everything you have about the building you tore down, and a description of what each person was trying to do."

"I'll see to it personally that you get all of that information," Comstock finally agreed.

"My job is to protect you," Charlie continued with a lower stress level. "Since Paragon Group is a privately held partnership and is not incorporated, you are personally liable. You cannot hide behind the company. However, in the records we have here, I can't find the partnership agreement. Your partners will be equally exposed."

"I didn't think silent partners could be sued." Comstock was clearly trying to hide something.

"Well, that depends," Charlie replied. "In any case, your attorneys need to be aware of all potential defendants. It's for your own protection."

Hesitantly, Comstock acquiesced, "I'll try to get those papers to you soon."

Barry Kasick returned, not knowing that his job was close to being lost if Comstock thought it would help. They spent the rest of the afternoon reconstructing what Kasick remembered about that day and about Matt and discussing the various aspects of the pleadings. They discussed the best time to hold depositions and they talked about different strategies for protecting this poor little corporation from the threats of the terrible Douglas couple and their ruthless country lawyer.

Henry Judson was returning from an afternoon on High Rock Lake, just north of Salisbury. His wife allowed him to take these little day trips to go sailing. According to Judson, these little excursions helped him gear up for a big trial. Preliminary hearings on the Comstock civil case were to begin in ten days. He lit a cigar with his car lighter and thought about the relaxing afternoon that he had just had.

He did not realize a burgundy Buick Riviera was behind him. It had followed him up to his sailboat earlier that morning, about the same time that a phone company van had pulled up in front of his little law office. The men dressed like phone company employees had quickly entered the office, assuring the secretary that Henry Judson wanted them to check out his modem that was not working properly. In forty-five minutes, they had examined everything that they could get their hands on.

Meanwhile, the driver of the burgundy Riviera dialed a number on his cell phone, and forty-one stories above downtown Charlotte, Martin Van Schank cleared his throat and softly said, "Hello, this is Martin." His eyes squinted behind his little round spectacles.

"Hey there, buddy, it's Slade. He's headed back to Kannapolis." Slade was a short greasy man, who was usually ignored in a crowd. It made his work as a private investigator much easier. Even with his slicked back hair and a flowered shirt open to reveal his Buddha-like stomach and thick black chest hair, few people took notice of him. He was incredibly plain and quickly became part of the scenery.

"What did you find out about our friend?" Van Schank articulated each word.

"Well, I haven't talked to the phone company yet. . . ." Slade began giggling like a schoolgirl.

"Get on with it!" snapped Van Schank, who looked remarkably like Heinrich Himmler when he was angry.

"Okay, okay. Try to relax. We've got him. He got to the lake about ten and fished for awhile. Then about noon, this Caddy, a Sedan DeVille I think, pulled up and this platinum blond Dolly Parton impostor got out and boarded his sailboat. They drank and laughed like teenagers for a few minutes. Then they went below deck. About forty-five minutes later, they came out. I got some great pictures of their passionate good-bye kiss."

A sinister smile began to spread across Van Schank's thin lips. "Good. This will be the perfect insurance just in case he isn't open to settling. I'm sure his little wife would be very shocked to accidentally find these. When can you get them to me?"

"A couple of days. It'll take some time to develop them."

"Just hurry," demanded Van Schank. "What about the other thing?"

"My men are on it," Slade said, "but he's squeaky clean. The guy's a regular Boy Scout. The worst thing we've got on him is that he occasionally skips church to work."

"Keep digging!" Van Schank demanded. "I don't trust him. He could be dangerous if I allow him to stay on the case. I can't have him running to the bar association."

"I'll keep looking, but I'm not promising anything," Slade backpedaled.

"I want something soon." Van Schank slammed the phone

down and buzzed his secretary, "Where's Nancy?"

"She's in a meeting with Walter and Charlie," the secretary responded.

"Have her stop by before they take him out for dinner. I would like to speak with her." A sinister smile once again slid across his face.

Charlie, Nancy, Walter, and Barry broke from their meeting fifteen minutes after five o'clock. They decided to freshen up and meet in the lobby to go to dinner and wrap up loose ends. Charlie opened the solid oak doors of the conference room and headed down the hallway to his office. He was exhausted after a full day of trying to pull the truth out of his client. One of the more difficult aspects of his job was trying to get the people he was supposed to be helping to be completely honest. Why would a person hire an attorney if he was not going to be honest? Charlie was always amazed but never surprised.

As he turned the corner, a hand landed on his shoulder. Charlie, disoriented from hours of meetings, jumped back into the wall.

"Whoa! I'm sorry." It was the soothing voice of Samuel Baskin Reimarus. "I didn't mean to startle you, Charlie."

"That's okay. I think I'm just a little punchy from dealing with Walter Comstock all day long."

"How's that going?" Reimarus was always reassuring.

"Our client isn't making the job any easier, but I think things are going well," Charlie responded to reaffirm that he had things under control.

"That's good," Reimarus nodded in agreement. "Let's step into Jackson Broward's office. He's in Hawaii." Charlie knew that this little talk would not be a good one. "I'm a bit concerned about you, Charlie. I know that the Thomason case was a little difficult on you."

Being somewhat offended, Charlie tried not to show it. "I'm fine. I know that I got a little out of hand this morning. I will buy a new coffee pot and pay for new wallpaper. Hey, I'll even hang it myself. I just had to blow off some steam."

"I understand." Reimarus nodded his head like a compassionate grandfather. "Sometimes I need to blow off steam too. But that's not the way to do it. I think you got too personally involved in the Thomason case. I like my attorneys to have passion, but you can't lose yourself."

"I didn't lose myself." Charlie's defensiveness was gradually increasing. "I represented my client to the best of my ability. I was just disappointed. I thought for once that I had done something substantial. I thought that I had defended justice and not just billed a whole bunch of hours."

"I know that feeling. I was happy for you. It makes you feel alive. But you have other clients and other cases. You need to stay balanced." Reimarus realized that he was not getting anywhere, so he shifted gears. "Let me mention something else to you. You may want to sit down."

Charlie moved to the brown leather couch by the window. He steadied himself at the ominous tone of Reimarus' voice.

"Charlie," Reimarus pulled up a chair in front of him and spoke softly, "I know that you're a hard worker and a good lawyer. You are a valuable part of this firm, and what I am about to say will not change that fact."

"I didn't get the partnership," Charlie said in a defeated voice.

"That's right." Reimarus leaned in closer and said, "I know that today is a horrible day to tell you this, but I didn't want to prolong matters. We were counting on the settlement from the Thomason case to help determine the amount of funds that you might generate, but without that case you don't even come close to Nancy. She has brought in a lot more clients who need continual services. So her name will be added to the top of the letterhead."

"You're right. I can't argue with your decision."

"I know that you have been here longer." Trying to console Charlie, Reimarus said, "If you work hard this year and bring in some new high rollers, I will guarantee that you'll make partner next time around."

"Thank you." Charlie felt that he had to respond to such a magnanimous gesture. The thought of putting in more sixty-to seventy-hour workweeks made him want to vomit.

"I hope you're not too disappointed." Reimarus and Charlie both knew that this was a formality and that he was very disappointed. "Hang in there, Charlie. I'm proud of you." Reimarus got up and left the room.

Charlie leaned back on the couch and exhaled. His chest felt tight. He was too disappointed to get angry. In one day, not one, but two, dreams had been crushed. When he started this morning, he was a millionaire on paper and about to become a partner. Now he was just another factory line associate who was living beyond his means. He was counting on that money to pay off their cars and the credit card debt that had accumulated when Sandy stopped working.

He breathed slowly and deliberately, thinking of how smug Nancy would treat him at dinner. Of course, she was too professional to say it in front of a client. But he knew her looks. He knew that little smirk that said, "I won, you lost." He was not looking forward to this dinner. He just wanted to go home and be with his family. Sandy could make anything better. He thought about the weekend. He would love to buy a little house on the Outer Banks, nothing fancy. They could get a sailboat and travel up and down the Intracoastal Waterway. He could put all of this pressure behind him. Maybe they could run away together. Maybe someday soon. Maybe.

chapter
EIGHT

After a completely miserable dinner at the Lamplighter just south of downtown on East Morehead Road, Walter Comstock, Barry Kasick, and Charlie piled into Nancy's Range Rover. Instead of heading north back into downtown to return to the NationsBank building, Nancy turned left on South Boulevard and headed into the seedy part of town. In the backseat with Barry, Charlie was staring out the window, oblivious to where Nancy was going. He was still dreaming of sandy beaches and the sound of waves crashing on the shore. He thought of the smell of salty air on Sandy's skin. He thought of the sunrise, the smell of coffee, and the secure feeling of a worn terry cloth robe cuddled up next to him.

South Boulevard was still packed as people were trying to make it home from work. As Nancy turned right onto Tyvola Road, Charlie realized that they were headed toward the coliseum. Comstock was already a little tipsy.

"Was that the best doggone steak you ever had?" the thick-necked man blustered after a low, gurgling belch under his breath.

The force of the question jolted Charlie, "Oh . . . yeah. It sure was. Of course, we eat like that all the time."

Nancy jumped in, "Walter, I have a surprise for you for dessert."

"I love surprises! How about you, Charlie? You like surprises?"

"Not today, I don't." Charlie's gaze returned to the passing lights. "I don't think I could handle any more surprises today."

"Son, you are a wet blanket." Comstock's voice seemed to be getting louder. "Business is over with. It's time to relax. One thing I have learned is that after a hard day on the job site, you've got to unwind. You don't want to unload all this steam on your wife, right?"

"Whatever you say," Charlie agreed, trying to shut him up, but it did not seem to be working.

Nancy glanced over her shoulder to check out Charlie's expression. "Sorry about that doctor, Charlie. I know you were disappointed."

"What doctor?" Barry asked, like the good lapdog he was.

"Oh, you haven't heard?" Nancy enjoyed an opportunity to relate Charlie's pain. "Charlie won this huge case, which you probably read about. Ten million dollars. Then the doctor filed bankruptcy and fled the country. Charlie lost every penny."

"Oh man, that's tough," Comstock said. "I remember losing a major bid to refurbish an entire row of historical homes in the Dilworth section. After that multimillion-dollar contract slipped through my fingers, I found a way to make sure that would never happen again."

Nancy shot Comstock a harsh look, and he immediately changed the subject. Charlie had tried to ignore the entire conversation. It was obvious that he did not care.

"We're here," Nancy announced loudly.

Charlie looked up and immediately felt his heart sink. They had just entered the parking lot of Diamond Girls Gentlemen's Club. Once again, he felt like throwing up. His mind raced. *How do I get out of this?* He had always been faithful to Sandy and could not imagine how mad and hurt she would be if he went to a strip club. He did not want to go, but he did not want to offend his client and make a scene. He thought about trying to explain it to Sandy, "But honey, it was for business." There was no plausible arena in which that excuse would work. He had made peace about taking clients to a cocktail lounge and watch them get drunk, but this aspect of entertaining was completely foreign to him.

The skin trade in Charlotte had been controlled by the Hell's Angels Motorcycle gang back in the 1970s when most of the adult establishments were frequented by very rough or perverted people. Then in the late seventies, a gang war began between North Carolina's Hell's Angels and South Carolina's Outlaws biker gangs. Federal prosecutors stepped in with the newly designed RICO laws to stop racketeering and organized crime. Almost all of the seedy bookstores and skanky topless bars were closed in the early eighties.

In the nineties, Charlotte's booming banking industry started attracting attention. Soon professional sports began moving into Charlotte. With the professional sports, a new higher class of criminals moved in. Illegal gambling quadrupled for four consecutive years. Prostitution and the skin trade began to flourish again. This time businessmen and sports fanatics were the targets. Businessmen started using the gentlemen's clubs to influence clients and boost sales. With receipts that read something like Diamond Recreational Services, Inc., an evening at the topless bar could be written off as a business expense on the company's income taxes.

Diamond Girls had a particularly colorful history. Once a new-wave night club in the eighties, it was closed down because of the amount of drugs sold there. When the property changed hands, it was bought by a group that owned some of the biggest and nicest gentlemen's clubs in Atlanta, Orlando, and Miami. The cops believed that drugs and gambling took place in the back room, but no one had ever proved it. Prosecutors stopped pursuing the club following an incident involving an off-duty police officer. He falsely arrested one of the dancers from the club, then raped and killed her. The public was outraged. The cops left the place alone after that. It took months to rebuild the department's image.

Charlie glared out the window at the flashing neon. *I cannot do this to Sandy. I will not do this to Sandy.* The more he thought about it, the angrier he got. When Nancy turned and gave him a smirk, he almost exploded. They piled out of the vehicle. Kasick caught Comstock as he tripped over a cement parking divider. Nancy looked back over her shoulder to see that Charlie was not following them and was, in fact, dialing a number on his cell phone.

She called out to Charlie, "Hey, partner, what's the holdup? Are you coming in or not?"

Charlie would have ignored her, but he knew that she would just get louder and draw more attention to his awkward situation. "No, no. You go have a good time. I'm going to call a taxi. I have an early day tomorrow."

Nancy was not going to miss an opportunity to make her adversary look bad. "Come on, Charlie. Our clients are wait-ing. It's our job to make them feel comfortable."

Comstock punched Kasick. "I could sure use some comfort. You know what I mean?" Then he turned to Charlie and yelled at the top of his lungs, "What's wrong with you, boy? Don't you like girls or something?" The three of them laughed and slapped each other on the back. Obviously, the alcohol was taking its toll.

Charlie started across the parking lot to wait for the taxi at the McDonald's across the street from Diamond Girls. Talking into his cell phone, he tried to ignore the juvenile laughter behind him. When Comstock started up again, he could not stand it.

"Hey, boy, get back here. You work for me. You have to do what I say. Do you hear me, boy?" Comstock turned to Nancy, laughing, and when he looked back, Charlie was in his face.

"Look. You are my client. I don't work for you, and I don't have to do what you say. I've done my job, and I am going home to my wife, whom I love dearly. If you get your jollies from having drugged-out single mothers gyrating in front of you, be my guest, but the last time I checked, you had a wife too." Charlie bit his tongue, knowing he had gone too far. As he started to walk off, Comstock grabbed his arm.

"You don't talk to me that way, boy! If you ever talk about me and my wife again, I will make sure this firm loses one of its biggest clients. You don't know how much I love my wife; I just like to have fun." Comstock's nostrils flared like a horse headed down the backstretch.

Charlie jerked his arm away from Comstock's clutches and said, "You don't care about your wife; if you did, you wouldn't be here. You don't care about anybody. You were ready to sell out Barry here when you thought it would take the heat off you."

There was stunned silence from everyone. Charlie shook his head. Barry looked like a deer caught in the headlights. Comstock's red, angry face started to turn a deeper shade of purple. Nancy tried to conceal a smile, knowing this was just the ammunition that she needed.

Comstock turned to Kasick. "I was not going to make you a sacrificial lamb. What Charlie misunderstood was that I wanted to know everybody's level of liability. Next to me, you have the highest exposure."

Kasick looked suspiciously at Comstock but accepted the explanation. Nancy said, "Let's go in, guys. The honeypots are waiting." In the middle of both men, she grabbed each by the elbow and turned them around. She turned her head slightly to catch Charlie's eyes and mouthed two words, "You're dead."

As they opened the door, Charlie heard the loud music thumping. He turned and headed back through the parking lot. He felt the fine mist of the last rains of summer begin to fall. Minutes seemed like hours as he replayed the incident in his mind. He knew he had gone too far. Maybe Comstock was drunk enough that he would not remember. That was hardly a possibility. He dreaded having to face the partners in the morning.

Standing by the golden arches, the realization occurred to Charlie that maybe he had to bend his ethics to make partner. That appeared to be the way Nancy developed her vast client lists. The longer he stayed a lawyer, the more difficult maintaining his integrity would become. About that time, an ugly blue-and-orange taxi pulled up. Charlie climbed in and told the driver to take him to the NationsBank building. As the taxi pulled out into the street, Charlie laid his head back on the seat and closed his eyes.

The smell of lemon-roasted chicken filled the house as Sandy prepared each plate for dinner. Over the last few years, she had become accustomed to eating dinner at seven thirty or eight. At a quarter till, she knew Charlie would be home soon. She remembered the days when both of them were climbing the career ladder and dinner consisted of Taco Bell or take out from the House of Taipei. She did not consider these late dinners to be a matter of resignation. She truly was happy for her husband and wanted him to succeed more than he did. She knew that late dinners were part of the territory.

Ashley was spinning and dancing in the living room when she heard the car door slam. She ran to the side door. As the door opened, the little bundle of energy jumped up into Charlie's arms and gave him a huge hug. Instead of setting her down like normal, Charlie dropped his briefcase and suit coat on the floor and squeezed her with both arms. Even with his eyes closed tight, Sandy realized something was not right.

Charlie set Ashley down and told her, "Thank you for that big hug. I really needed it." Ashley smiled and demurely looked at her shoes as Charlie continued, "Do you know how much I love you, princess?"

She looked up and responded, "I sure do. You tell me every day. I love you, too, Daddy."

"I have a surprise for you, Ashley," he said, "I am going to cut back on my hours at the office, so we can spend more time together."

She screamed, "Yea!" and followed it with another big hug.

Sandy looked shocked, "Well, this is a revelation. When did it come to you?"

"In the back of a taxi." His response was cryptic.

"What are you talking about?"

As Sandy ate her dinner, Charlie related the whole story about his miserable meal, Diamond Girls, and the explosion he unloaded on Comstock. Sandy was very sympathetic and understanding. They agreed to table the discussion until Ashley was in bed. There was no reason to upset her. Sandy had the amazing ability to remain calm and discuss difficult matters with a smile on her face. She frequently served to calm Charlie down and stabilize his emotions. He was not an angry person, but fighting for what was right brought deep-seated passion to the surface.

After playing a rousing game of Chutes and Ladders, they all ate ice cream. Then Charlie read Ashley her favorite fairy tale and put her to bed. Sandy went downstairs to wash the dishes. Charlie watched his daughter sleep. It was one of his favorite activities, and it had a very calming effect on his nerves. Looking at her perky nose and angelic features, he wondered how anyone could treat their kids in the horrible ways that he saw every night on the late news. How could anyone look at a child's face and not have hope for a brighter day? How could a person look at the peaceful features of a little one and not believe in God? He brushed her hair with his hand and thought about the first time she said, "Daddy."

From the doorway he heard a whisper, "Hey. What are you doing?" He looked up, and Sandy was standing there in her favorite sweatshirt and ripped jeans.

"I'm just watching her. I guess I'm saying a little prayer, too. I'll need it tomorrow." He pulled the covers up to Ashley's neck and went downstairs with his wife.

"Do you really think it will be that bad?" she asked as she rubbed his shoulders.

"I don't know. Nancy has it in for me. She could even get me kicked off the case. Either way, my future at Hobbes, Reimarus, and Van Schank seems to be limited."

Sandy thought a minute and asked, "Why do you want to work there, anyway?"

"What do you mean?" Charlie was puzzled.

"I mean," Sandy sat up on her knees beside Charlie on the couch, "there are other firms that will not make you work this hard. There are places you can work that will help other people like the Thomasons and not defend a wealthy, unscrupulous man like Walter Comstock."

Charlie was still not out of his advocacy role. "Walter Comstock has received numerous awards and commendations for all kinds of beneficent acts of service."

"Okay, counselor, he's not on trial. It's just me here." Charlie's legal mind had frustrated Sandy early in their relationship. Now it was simply endearing. "From what you have told me, he seems very shady. I just don't trust the man. Anyway, you're ignoring my question. Why do you stay there? Even though Dr. Johnston filed bankruptcy, you still won the case. You have the name recognition to hang out your own shingle if you want to."

"I guess growing up in a hick town, I always defined success by being a partner in a big firm, driving a Jag, and living on the south side." Charlie thought for a minute. "I guess it's my way of getting back at my father for leaving us in a tiny apartment in Midland. Look at him; he's living it up in Silicon Valley and flying first-class to Tokyo. I guess deep down I'm still trying to make him proud of me."

"That man is not your father. He had nothing to do with raising you or making you into the great man you are. All he has done is give you a false view of what success is and make you work like a dog to keep up with someone who walked out on you."

Charlie interrupted her, "But he's the reason I work so hard. He got out. That's what I have wanted all of my life. He lived the dream. For crying out loud, it is so hard to admire a man that I can't stand."

Sandy's voice softened. "Charlie, you *are* a success. What you have is intangible. All he has is money and a wife who is fifty percent silicon herself. He doesn't have a family. He doesn't help people fight for justice. He helps a billionaire gobble up little upstart computer companies. Don't worry about the money, Charlie. I just want you to be happy."

"Thank you," Charlie said, "I don't know what I would do without you. You always know the right thing to say."

Charlie placed his head on her shoulder, and she ran her fingers through his hair. They sat in silence for awhile. The subject had been sufficiently discussed. She leaned over and kissed him very softly. It reminded him of their very first kiss on the steps of her dorm. They started kissing and caressing like college students again. Finally, they lost steam and fell asleep on the couch.

chapter
NINE

The red hue of dawn broke over Charlotte's skyline. The small conference room on the forty-first floor provided a wonderful view of the event. Early Wednesday morning, Van Schank had asked for a meeting of the three senior partners. He had received a call from Nancy the night before and decided to take immediate action. Luther, a genteel black man wearing white gloves, poured more coffee into one of the firm's crystal mugs that the partners used for fine dining.

The six o'clock traffic started to crowd the major veins entering downtown, but from their perch in the dimly lit conference room, J. Garrison Hobbes III, Samuel B. Reimarus, and Martin Van Schank made decisions impacting the destinies of men and businesses. These three men controlled the lives and fortunes of thousands of lawyers and clients. Van Schank took control of the meeting.

"Gentlemen, we have a situation. One of our most valued clients was treated with less than courteous behavior last night." Van Schank's narrow eyes gleamed as he made the other partners beg him to explain.

Reimarus, the consummate diplomat, chided Van Schank. "If you go ahead and tell us the problem, I'm sure we can handle it. Why are you making this such a big deal by waking me up and forcing me to get here before sunrise?"

Van Schank slyly responded, "This client is particularly valuable, and I would like to limit his amount of exposure."

Hobbes, the least tactful of the three, was getting frustrated. "Come on, Martin, what are you talking about? We all have work to do."

"Fine," Van Schank sneered at his partner, "Nancy told me that Mr. Harrigan yelled at Walter Comstock last night because they wanted to go to a strip club."

Reimarus, trying to placate everybody, said, "You know how Walter gets when he is drunk. I'm sure that was the case and Charlie was fed up. I'll talk to him and make him apologize. Besides, I've wanted to give Walter a piece of my mind once or twice before."

Van Schank tried a second time. "The problem is not the nature of the argument. It is the nature of the case. Walter is concerned that Mr. Harrigan will not be understanding of his special circumstance. He pays us a lot of money, and we have cut some corners for him. Comstock thinks, and I agree, that having Mr. Harrigan in the first chair may be a bad idea. Mr. Harrigan would not even go to a strip club; do you really think he will defend Walter to the best of his ability once he gets into the Paragon file a little deeper?"

Hobbes thought for a minute. "He *is* squeaky clean. The guy didn't even have a glass of champagne at his own celebration last week. But he would never violate attorney-client privilege, even if he found out about Paragon."

"I don't think you're seeing the big picture, Garrison." Van Schank picked up a little crystal bell to get Luther's attention for more coffee. "Mr. Harrigan's code of ethics will get in the way, and he will not defend our client as vigorously as possible if he does not believe in him. Harrigan was so successful suing the doctor because he was fighting for truth, justice, and the American way. If we do not settle this matter now, every time he comes up for partner, we will be back here having the same discussion."

"Wait a minute," Reimarus interjected, "Charlie is a good

guy. I put him on first chair in this case and gave him my word that he would fill Burchette's shoes as our principal litigator. He's the best we have. Do you really want to get rid of him?"

Van Schank drummed his fingers on the glass tabletop. "Do you honestly think that he will be a team player when he learns about our most valued clients? We had a similar problem with Burchette, and we ended up paying two hundred grand for that yacht he's got parked off St. Augustine."

The alligator skin briefcase was placed in the middle of the table, and Van Schank pulled out a file folder containing several pictures. He continued with his narrative. "You see, gentlemen, if we toss Harrigan, we can kill two birds with one stone. Our secret remains safe, and everybody involved knows and plays by the rules. We make Comstock happy. Nancy becomes first chair, and we move on to step two in our settlement of *Douglas v. Paragon Group*. Mr. Harrigan would never be a part of this strategy, but Nancy enjoys it. Our surveillance revealed Mr. Judson's adulterous proclivity. I'm sure he will amicably encourage his clients to accept a satisfactory settlement proposal."

"I agree," Hobbes said as he grabbed the pictures and studied the platinum blonde very carefully, "but how do we get rid of Charlie without facing an unfair dismissal lawsuit of our own?"

"That is the beauty of this plan. We tell him that his ethics are not up to our standards. While our boy Mr. Harrigan was shouting, he slipped and claimed that Comstock wanted to place all of the blame on the foreman, Barry Kasick. We claim that he came close to violating attorney-client privilege and threaten to bring him up in front of the North Carolina Bar Association. Mr. Harrigan does not live up to the ethical standards that we are trying to maintain."

Hobbes laughed. "I love it. You're one twisted man."

Reimarus stood and said, "I'm not doing this! I can't treat Charlie like this. If you two want to play games with this guy, just leave me out of it."

The conference door slammed and the two remaining partners sat back and sipped coffee, planning how they would execute their scheme. They would have to wait until the afternoon when preliminary motions were completed at the county courthouse. When Charlie returned from starting a case that would never be heard, they would drop the bomb. To Hobbes and Van Schank, it was all just part of another day at the office—making fortunes and losing them, making lives and breaking them, creating heroes and villains.

The morning drive had been just as slow and snail-like as every other day he tried to get to the office early. Charlie could see his building from the traffic light, but he knew it would still take twenty to thirty minutes to reach the parking lot. As he sat in his Blazer drumming his hands on the steering wheel to Elvis' "Suspicious Minds" on the oldies station, he thought about his conversation with Sandy the night before. Why was he driving himself so hard? Maybe he should make some changes. Losing the partnership had been disheartening, but he could cope. Ashley did not have to go to Charlotte Latin; Sandy could home school her and probably do better than the school system. Maybe he could cut back on his hours and stay a comfortable associate until they had the cash to start his own practice.

In the confusing whirlwind of the past week, Sandy had been his stabilizing anchor. He realized that his brief week as a millionaire on paper had not changed anything about Sandy's attitude or actions. She was just as sweet and supportive whether he was the hero or the loser. Whatever the partners had to say to him today would be all right as long as she was around.

The traffic light turned and he was moving again. By quarter till eight, he was in the parking deck. He made sure that there was no sign of Nancy or anyone else. His plan was to hide out in his office until it was time for Comstock's preliminary motions. Maybe everything would just blow over. He walked across the parking deck to the garage elevators. Fortunately, he was still alone.

He bypassed his morning *Wall Street Journal* and fourth cup of coffee. He greeted Selia and quickly went to his office and closed the door. He removed his suit coat and unbuttoned his top button. Typically, lawyers waited until after lunch to loosen their tie, but today was different. He stared out the window and thought for a minute. What should he do? Then he thought about his friend, Brad. Brad would know what to do; he had wiggled out of sticky situations many times.

Charlie sprinted down the hall and turned the corner. On the west side of the building two offices down from the corner, Brad's door was open. Charlie peeked in and no one was there. He looked down the hall and suspected Brad was just in the kitchen getting some gourmet coffee and a bagel, his yuppie version of a power breakfast. Charlie walked behind the desk and sat down in Brad's Naugahyde leather chair. As he was playing with the miniature pool table on Brad's desk, the computer beeped, and a new e-mail message popped up.

Instinctively, Charlie looked at the bottom of the screen without any intention of being nosy. What Charlie read shocked him; he felt dizzy. *Surely this message is for somebody else,* Charlie thought. He read the message a second time. "Brad, I'm sorry I can't see you tonight or ever again. You're just not my type, but at least we had fun. By the way, thanks for the info on your friend Charlie. It was a big help. Love, Nan." He read the message a third time in a state of denial. Apparently, the strip club was a setup. Nancy wanted the case to herself and Brad helped her. What did he tell her? Charlie could not believe that his best friend at the firm had helped that witch sabotage him with a client.

Charlie heard a familiar whistle coming down the hall, and in walked Brad. "Hey, buddy boy. You look like someone just ran over your puppy or something. What gives?" Brad was holding a paper cup of Kona coffee.

"I'll tell you what gives." Charlie rose to his feet and slowly made his way toward Brad. "I just found out who my real friends are."

Puzzled, Brad shrugged his shoulders. "What are you talking about, bro? You're on a different page from me. Catch me up."

"I'll catch you up, you snake." Charlie was right in Brad's face. "Let's start with traitor, betrayer. What did you tell Nancy about me?"

Brad started to respond, "I didn't say a thing—"

Charlie slapped the cup out of his hand. "Go read your e-mail, Judas. Nancy set me up last night to embarrass me in front of Comstock. What did you say?"

Studying the shine on his wing tip shoes, Brad said, "I may have mentioned what a Boy Scout you are, but just in passing. I didn't intend to say anything to hurt you. She just asked me what kind of guy you were and I was a little tipsy. I didn't do anything wrong."

"Yes, you did!" Charlie was shouting now. "You know what a cutthroat place this is and that Nancy and I were up for the partnership. You just allowed her to seduce you. Couldn't you sleep alone for one night? You belong in the ninth circle of hell with Judas and the other betrayers of friends, God, and country. See ya around."

Charlie shoved his way through the door past Brad. He was stunned to realize how shallow his best friend was. Charlie stormed back to his office and slammed the door. He thought about his best friend in college. Chris would never do such a thing. Maybe he and Brad had never really been friends. He thought for a moment. *What is going on with my life?* He felt as if he were living in a house of cards, and some giant invisible hand was pulling out one card at a time.

Eight days ago, he was a hero and a millionaire. Justice had prevailed and truth had won and he had played the biggest part. Now, his career was in the balance and he could not even trust people who claimed to be his friends. Suddenly, he felt very alone. He picked up the Paragon file and looked over the preliminary motions he had to argue after lunch. He tried to get his mind off of Brad, but he could not shake the feeling that a dark cloud was growing over the horizon.

The Mecklenburg County Courthouse was not a typical public building with dreary lighting and huge stone columns. Completed just a decade ago, it was full of windows that let in plenty of light. The foyer was large and open to the top of the third floor. On the lawn, there were a couple of news vans with journalists reporting live from the latest murder case. There was always a murder case pending. On the benches along the wall sat the usual collection of drunk drivers, people who needed a license to be a parent, and petty drug dealers. The occasional homeless person would wander in to use the public rest room and look for free coffee.

In the back corner of the foyer where the pay phones were, a greasy man in a flowered shirt went completely unnoticed. No matter how bad Slade dressed, very few people paid attention to him. He stuck an unfiltered Winston cigarette in his mouth just to feel it there. He would have to wait to light up because of the recent flood of antismoking legislation. He cursed health nuts and liberals under his breath and twirled a lighter with his fingers.

On the other end of the phone high atop the city, Martin Van Schank's eyes squinted and his thin lips broke into a smile. "Do you have the pictures?"

"Oh yea," Slade grinned. "They are true works of art. He will settle as soon as he sees these, especially the one where they—"

Van Schank broke in, "I don't want to hear the illicit details. If you enjoy that kind of stuff, fine. Just tell me that the plan is a go."

"It's all set. Don't worry your skinny behind about it, all right?" Slade assured him, "I'll deliver them whenever he gets here."

"You are not going to give the envelope to him yourself, are you?" queried Himmler's twin brother.

"Of course not. Do you think I'm stupid? I've done this many, many times. I got this homeless guy a five-dollar bottle of rum, and he's going to do it for me."

"No slipups!" Van Schank demanded.

"Don't worry. I've got it under control." Slade looked around to make sure no one was staring at him. "Now about your boy, Charlie. I got nothin'. That kid is cleaner than Mr. Rogers."

"Leave him to me." Van Schank giggled devilishly. "By the end of today, Charlie Harrigan will be a former lawyer from Hobbes, Reimarus, and Van Schank, and he will not take good references with him."

"What are you going to do?" Slade joined in on the laughter.

"Shut up, fat man!" Van Schank was tired of this conversation. He tolerated the interminable Slade. Throughout their long history, Slade had been very useful, but Van Schank did not enjoy being so dependent on a person so far beneath him. "Now go get the job done. I'll take care of Harrigan. After you deliver the envelope, I think you ought to take a vacation. In the locker at the airport is enough cash for a ticket to Mexico. Leave today."

Slade enjoyed frustrating his boss. "Not until you ask me nicely."

"Shut up and do it!" Van Schank slammed the phone down.

The loud click startled Slade, but he quickly turned to his homeless friend sitting on one of the benches. He explained that all he needed to do was follow the man in the picture, and when he was alone, hand him the envelope. The envelope was plain except for one word written on the front, "Settle!" Slade made sure all fingerprints were wiped off. Judson may suspect who was behind the plot, but he would never be able to prove it, so Van Schank was not worried about him going to the judge.

Slade noticed Judson as soon as he entered the glass doors with his clients. He followed them from a distance to civil court on the second floor. Henry Judson helped his clients into the courtroom and went to relieve himself. Slade and the homeless man were at the far end of the corridor. Slade gave his friend the envelope and showed him the target. The door to the bathroom opened as Judson was washing his hands. The bum looked around and saw that Judson was alone. He yelled, "Hey, buddy!" and threw the envelope in Judson's general direction. The bum darted out the door and down the stairwell. Henry Judson tried to catch him, but his rotund body was not as fast as the mysterious homeless man.

Judson went back in the bathroom and opened the envelope. As he pulled out the first full-color eight-by-ten picture of him and the woman who was not his wife, he felt as if he were going to have a heart attack. He splashed cold water on his face and looked again. The pictures did not change; there was no mistake, it was him. One word, "Settle!" He knew what he had to do. Judson was a small-town lawyer. He knew that he was not cut out for the big leagues, and he had just received his first and last message. He composed himself, put the pictures back in the envelope, and headed back to the courtroom. After the motions were done, he would settle this case. The oak doors to the courtroom felt as if they were made of lead. He swallowed hard and opened the door.

chapter
TEN

Charlie sat on the right side of the aisle beside Nancy Lockman-Kurtz and Walter Comstock. Charlie looked over and saw an older couple sitting at the plaintiff's table. It was the first time he had seen Horace and Betty Douglas. They did not look like money-grubbing rednecks. As Henry Judson approached the bar, Charlie actually felt sorry for them. Judson was shaking and obviously outgunned. When the trial actually started, the firm would bring along two more associates just to intimidate its opponent. Maybe the judge would quickly dismiss this case and save these nice old people the added pain of a long trial.

The bailiff called the relatively empty room to order. "Judge Carlton W. Fitzwaring presiding."

"Sit down," the distinguished, white-haired jurist said sternly, but not gruffly. Fitzwaring had been on the bench in Mecklenburg County for ten years, after teaching at Duke Law School and leaving a large corporate firm in Raleigh. After serving several years in Raleigh, he had moved to Charlotte for a higher profile jurisdiction. His desire was to receive an appointment to a federal bench and hear landmark cases. He wanted to make a name for himself, and he was going to stamp out the mountain of frivolous lawsuits filed in this country every year. He wore bifocals because he read every North

Carolina case dealing with corporate litigation, and he spent hours at his computer on Westlaw seeing where the rest of the nation was in tort reform and jury rewards.

Douglas v. Paragon Group was the case for this afternoon. The small hearing was procedural and no one expected any fireworks. The only other people in the courtroom were homeless individuals taking a nap after lunch at the soup kitchen. Charlie filed two motions. First, the motion to dismiss without prejudice simply stated that there was no legal issue in question and both parties should walk away calling it a misunderstanding. The second motion was a summary judgment. This simply asked the judge to look at the facts and impose a small fine and a slap on the wrist to make everybody happy. The issue was not serious, but the Douglases could not walk away empty-handed. Charlie really did not believe in either motion and did not expect them to work. But the corporate strategy was to flood this one-man firm with more paperwork and time-consuming motions than he had ever seen in his life.

"Mr. Harrigan, you really don't think that there is a legal issue in question?" Judge Fitzwaring despised these preliminary hearings, because they seldom contained anything valuable.

"Your Honor, you realize the number of these frivolous lawsuits clogging the court system. We have become a litigious society where people sue fast-food restaurants when they spill hot coffee on themselves or they sue the tobacco companies after smoking for forty years. My client is a businessman in good standing in the community. I am sorry for the Douglases' loss, but tragedy happens every day." Charlie could not believe what he was saying and wished he could take it back when he saw the look on Mrs. Douglas' face.

"Now, Mr. Judson, Mr. Harrigan's brief says that this lawsuit is just a shallow attempt to bilk a successful company out of thousands of dollars. Are you attempting to do that, sir?" The judge's stiff face was promising for the defendant.

Judson stood, feeling his knees almost give way. "Your Honor, we believe that Matthew Douglas was placed in situations that exposed him to carcinogens that caused the lung cancer. We feel that if Paragon Group has a special program to help mildly retarded individuals like Matt, they have a special responsibility to look out for their safety. The money is not an issue, Your Honor. You know, as well as I, that money is the only recourse in a civil case."

"I don't need a lesson on civil jurisprudence, Mr. Judson," the judge snapped. "Is that all you have to say?"

Both attorneys nodded their heads and hoped that their written briefs would suffice. The judge seemed particularly antsy today.

"I want to state for the record that I think there are far too many lawyers filing lawsuits just to get rich. I am tired of insurance companies and businesses settling with these shysters. In my opinion, we need new legislation preventing this kind of behavior." The judge was not talking to those present, as much as he was campaigning for the next level should anyone else be listening. "However, I don't think you proved your point, Mr. Harrigan. I am going to deny both motions and set one hundred and twenty days for discovery. Because of the holidays, this trial will commence the last week in February. Any questions? Good."

The judge banged his gavel and dismissed the court. Charlie tried to avoid looking the Douglases in the eyes. Meanwhile, Nancy smiled and winked at Henry Judson. He would take his clients into a small conference room and try to convince them to settle. Walter Comstock followed Charlie down the hallway and pinned him up against the large window overlooking the front lawn of the courthouse.

"Was that the best you could do?" Comstock snorted.

"Look, jack! You may be guilty. I don't know and I don't care. A kid is dead and he worked for your company. No matter how ridiculous a suit may seem, no judge is going to dismiss a case when there's a body. Deal with it!" Charlie walked off while Comstock was still talking to him.

"I don't like your attitude. You're my lawyer. You can't talk to me this way." Comstock was shouting.

"So what?" Charlie turned and threw his hands up in the air. "Sue me, jack. I don't care." The corridor was deathly silent except for the sound of Charlie's heels clicking on the tile.

Charlie took his time returning to the ivory tower that was his law firm. He meandered through the Overstreet Mall looking in the shops, watching mothers trying to corral their children, and evaluating his client. Something amorphous and intangible about Walter Comstock made his skin crawl. One thing that ten years in the legal profession taught him was that the eyes do not lie. When he looked across the aisle, there was no animosity or greed in the eyes of the gray-haired couple. He saw grief and pain. He saw the years of struggle from a hard life, and he saw people intimidated by a system that was completely alien and unfriendly to them.

Comstock's eyes were angry. They were always angry. Something about Comstock's eyes reminded Charlie of Dr. Owen Johnston; they were wealthy eyes that were not satisfied. They were defiant eyes hiding something. They were suspicious. How in the world could he represent this man? Charlie stopped at a Starbuck's kiosk and bought black coffee. He stopped on a causeway that connected two towers and stared down at the cars on College Street. How could he stand up in open court before God and everyone and claim that this pleasant couple did not have a valid claim? Did he actually say that the claim was frivolous and they just wanted money? His mind was reeling and his heart actually hurt. The weight of the entire legal profession seemed to be resting heavily upon his shoulders.

He leaned against the glass and slowly sipped his coffee. None of the partners had approached him about his encounter with Comstock, and after his little tantrum in the courthouse, he knew they would not brush the issue under the rug.

Suddenly, he understood how Damocles felt living under the perpetual specter of sudden death. One thread was about all that he had left at this point.

He drained the coffee and gazed at the bottom of the empty cup. Tossing it in the general direction of the trash can, he turned and headed back to Hobbes, Reimarus, and Van Schank. People were darting in and out of shops, but he felt gravely alone. Loneliness was bad enough, but being alone in a crowd was worse. Entering the NationsBank building, he instinctively looked for the closest exit. In case the spirit moved him and he just ran out the door, he wanted to know the quickest way. A familiar feeling hit him; he remembered the time that he broke a window in a neighbor's house while playing baseball. The long walk to his backyard with the fear of an angry mother before him was remarkably similar to how he felt now.

Charlie watched the numbers on the elevator click toward thirty-nine. The solitary rider, he looked at his reflection in the mirrored doors of the elevator. The person staring at him was not the same one who had graduated from law school ready to save the world. The reflection was that of a jaded and cynical workaholic who was not quite sure of what he was working so diligently for. The elevator dinged and the doors opened. He walked through the imposing entry under the gold letters and saw the incredible view through the window wall.

Selia said, "Good afternoon, Charlie. Mr. Hobbes has been waiting for you."

Charlie nodded because words were difficult to form around the titanic lump that was in his throat. He climbed the spiral staircase in the lobby two floors up to forty-one and headed to the southwest corner. He was ready to knock on the door, when J. Garrison Hobbes III's secretary told him to go on in. Charlie slowly turned the antique brass doorknobs and walked in.

"Charlie, come on in and have a seat. Would you like some coffee?" Hobbes was surprisingly proper.

"No thanks. I think I've reached my limit of seven cups already. My kidneys can't take the punishment." Charlie's weak attempt at humor completely missed its mark.

"Charlie, I've got something serious that we need to talk about." Hobbes stood up and moved to the front of his desk, leaning on it directly across from Charlie on the leather couch. "I have had some complaints from a client about you."

"Listen," Charlie was trying to avoid the Band-Aid being pulled off more slowly than necessary, "I know Walter Comstock talked with you and I'm sure that it was not good—"

Interrupting Charlie in midsentence, Hobbes continued, "This client claimed that you not only treated him unprofessionally, but that you also violated attorney-client privilege."

"What?" Charlie jumped up, shocked at the accusation.

"I'm afraid that I will have to report you to the bar association," Hobbes remarked, shaking his head.

"All I did was tell Barry that Comstock wanted to hang him out to dry. They are both our clients. That is not privileged communication!" Charlie protested.

"Comstock pays the bills. When Kasick left the room, Walter believed that he was alone with his attorneys. That is conditionally privileged communication. It was a special situation within that meeting. You could lose your license, Charlie." Charlie slumped back down on the couch. "However, I had to fight with the other partners. I have no desire to see you stop practicing law. You made a mistake. We are not going to report you to the bar, but effective immediately, you are no longer an associate here at Hobbes, Reimarus, and Van Schank."

Trying to compose himself, Charlie stood up and said, "Is that all?"

"How about a 'thank-you'?" Hobbes was giving the knife one final twist.

"Thank you, sir, for not reporting me to the bar. I'll go clean out my office." He walked out the door with his head down. A defeated man.

Immediately, Hobbes picked up the phone and called Van Schank. He relayed the play-by-play detail of Harrigan's dismissal. Van Schank smirked as he heard about Harrigan's pathetic thank-you. Then he called Comstock, who was elated that Charlie was off of his defense team. Soon they would put the full-court press on Henry Judson and get this case settled once and for all. Then they could get back to making the big bucks.

Charlie emptied his desk drawers into a storage box. He picked up each picture of his wife and daughter one by one. Studying Ashley's progression from infant to little princess, he wondered how he was going to provide for his family. Picking up the wedding portrait of Sandy, he felt that he had completely let her down. He had to go and face his wife as a failure, not a hero or a success. What would she think?

Remarkably, he had acquired very little personal possessions in his office in ten years. He took his diplomas off the wall and deposited them in the box. He took the Paragon file and tossed it in the garbage can. Somebody would fish it out before they emptied the trash. He took one last look out the window where eight days earlier he had gazed out over his victory. He put on his coat, picked up the box, and turned off the light.

Brad was approaching him in the hall. "Hey, buddy, I just heard what Hobbes did to you. Good thing about the bar, though." Brad was trying to be cheerful and penitent, but to no avail.

Charlie looked at the floor and squeezed past Brad, bumping him into a fake column that held an ornate flower arrangement. Brad watched his friend walk away. People started sticking their heads out of their offices, apologizing and giving Charlie their best wishes. He tried to speed up his gait without being obvious. When he reached the lobby, Selia offered a very polite, "I'll miss you, Charlie. You're one of the nice ones." But it was too little, too late.

Charlie took the elevator down to the first floor and walked across the spacious lobby to the parking garage elevator. He went down three levels and found his Blazer. Throwing the box in the back, he climbed in and turned the key. He headed north on College, turned right, and after one block headed back south. He passed Providence Road and kept going south. He was not ready to face Sandy with the bad news.

Charlie weaved through the streets just south of downtown to East Boulevard in the Dilworth section. Something seemed to tell him to pull over at the East Boulevard Bar and Grill, an upscale yuppie bar across the street from a New Age bookstore. He parked in the back but remained in his Blazer. Why was he here? He had been clean and sober more than ten years, but now it seemed like a good time to take up his old hobby. He did not want to get drunk, just anesthetize the pain a little.

Climbing up on a barstool, Charlie started with a simple Cuba Libra, what yuppies call a rum and Coke. In slow motion, he raised the glass to his lips. The alcohol raged down his throat like a fire, causing an uncontrollable coughing fit. He had had a similar experience the first time he tasted vodka as a freshman at his first college party. After he composed himself, the second drink was easier. The Cuba Libra was drained in seven minutes. Then he got a little stronger drink, a Seven and Seven.

After he had been at the East Boulevard Bar and Grill about twenty minutes, he noticed a long pair of legs in a short black, leather skirt occupy the barstool beside him. She was young and attractive, probably a paralegal or a low-level banker. She was younger than he, at least five years. He returned his attention to his half-empty glass when she tried to strike up a conversation.

"So, I've never seen you here before." The friendly girl was drinking a strawberry daiquiri.

"I don't come here much. I'm just drowning some sorrows." He was trying to be cold, but it was difficult to pretend that he did not like the attention. It was flattering.

Right now, his ego could use some flattery.

"I'm sorry," she cooed. "What happened?"

"I'd rather not talk about it, if you don't mind." The cold shoulder was obviously being ignored.

"Wait a minute! You look familiar. Did you go to Wake Forest?"

Charlie just shook his head negatively.

"Well, let me think about this. I've seen you recently." The epiphany hit her and she grabbed his arm, startling him. "You're the guy in the paper. You sued that abortion doctor."

Charlie raised his glass, "That's me. The white knight fighting injustice wherever I find it."

She giggled. "He deserved to lose. Have they found him yet?"

"Not yet. He's probably island hopping in the Caribbean. I doubt the authorities will ever find him."

She patted his arm again and said, "I'm sorry. Hey, you have really strong arms."

Charlie held up his left hand. "I have a really gold ring, too."

She laughed and slapped his thigh. "Don't be silly, we're just talking. There's nothing wrong with making a new friend."

He did not think Sandy would agree, but he said, "I guess not."

They chatted about their jobs and college years. She was, in fact, a paralegal who was still trying to live the college party life and not quite ready to grow up. Something about that carefree, hedonistic attitude was very appealing, especially to a man approaching middle age who had just lost his job. She constantly tossed her long red hair over her shoulder and crossed her legs. She was sitting very close, leaning into Charlie. His remedy worked. The alcohol and the girl had alleviated some of the pain, but a moment of clarity hit him between the drinks.

There were nine empty glasses on the bar in front of him, and at least five were his. He realized that his flirting was potentially dangerous and that he had to get out of there.

Charlie pulled thirty dollars out of his wallet and threw it on the bar. Then he stood up.

"Look, it was really nice meeting you, but I have to go." He had to run. He had to go fall into his wife's arms and hope she did not smell the strong musky perfume. He had to shake himself back into reality.

The girl swiveled on the stool toward Charlie and reached into her purse. Pulling out a business card, she placed it in Charlie's shirt pocket and patted him on the chest. "Call me sometime."

Charlie smiled and then walked off. As soon as he was out the door, he reached in his pocket, pulled out the card, and read it. Brandi Langston, Paralegal. He crumpled it up and threw it in a trash can. For spite, he kicked the can. He got into his Blazer and tried to evaluate his ability to drive home. The alcohol had not given him a buzz as much as it made his stomach churn.

He started the engine and headed home. He thought about his beautiful wife. How could he flirt like that? He thought about the beach and their long walk holding hands. He had everything he wanted. *Forget the girl,* but he could not. The smell of her perfume was strong. He was close to a line he should be nowhere near. He thought about his job, or rather the lack thereof. He thought about the booze. A decade of sobriety down the tubes. The more he thought, the more his stomach churned. He pulled over to the side of the road abruptly and jumped out. He went to the ditch and bent over, holding his stomach. He threw up his fast-food lunch and most of the alcohol.

What a picture! The once great Charlie Harrigan standing in a ditch, smelling of alcohol and perfume, covered in vomit. In a few short days, he lost the partnership and his job. He had not only let himself down, but he let Sandy down as well. Charlie leaned against the Blazer and breathed deep. He decided to go home and face Sandy and tell her everything. Sure she would be upset, but they could deal with that. Right now, he needed her more than anything else.

chapter
ELEVEN

Darkness had settled over Charlotte, North Carolina as Charlie drove through the tree-lined Myers Park neighborhood. The old distinguished neighborhood was characterized by a boulevard with large oak trees spreading their foliage like a canopy over the street. The canopy made the neighborhood seem darker than it really was. The darkness outside the Blazer was rivaled only by the darkness inside the Blazer. Charlie turned into his neighborhood feeling sorry that he was coming home so late. Sandy would not be worried, simply because she was used to the long hours. Now, they had all the time in the world. His agenda was vacant for the uncertain future.

As Charlie approached his house, he looked through the trees and saw that the lights were on. Then he looked a little closer and saw that the side door was slightly ajar. Charlie thought it was a bit unusual, but he brushed it off as incidental. He pulled into the driveway, trying to figure out where to begin his explanation of the day's events. It all seemed to be Comstock's fault. His life had been wonderful until he heard the name Walter Comstock. Charlie grabbed his coat and briefcase, leaving the storage box in the Blazer.

He walked into the kitchen and yelled hello . . . but there was no answer. Usually, Sandy was in the kitchen waiting for him, even though she pretended that she was actually working. He called out for Ashley, and again there was silence. Charlie threw his briefcase and coat on the kitchen table and looked around. A small bag of groceries was strewn across the floor. Sandy's purse was in the corner by the refrigerator with most of the contents spilled out. Maybe they were upstairs. Ashley had probably knocked over the groceries while she was playing and Sandy was getting her cleaned up.

He walked into the living room and realized that the television and VCR were gone. Frantic, he bolted upstairs, yelling for his wife and daughter. No answer. Taking two steps at a time, he realized a couple of pictures were knocked on the floor. There were spots on the floor. He ran to his bedroom and burst through the door.

Blood was all over the bed. The room was a wreck. The dresser had been ransacked and the lamp on the nightstand had been smashed. He slowly approached the opposite side of their bed. In shock, he froze at the sight of his wife's lifeless body. He wanted to move, but he could not. He stared incredulously. This could not be happening. It was a dream. He fell to his knees and grabbed her, hugging her close. Suddenly, the tears and cries started pouring forth. He brushed her beautiful brown hair now matted by blood. He pulled her body close, letting out a scream.

Suddenly, a new wave of panic overwhelmed him. He called for Ashley. He ran to her room and saw her little body curled up on the bed. She too was covered with blood. He grabbed her. She was still breathing slightly. He ran to the phone in his bedroom, but the cord had been ripped out of the wall and was covered with blood. He ran downstairs, holding Ashley, and yanked the cell phone out of his coat pocket.

It took six minutes for the first police car to arrive. Soon afterward, the ambulance showed up, and his front yard twinkled with red and blue lights. Crowds of people gathered on the sidewalk trying to look in the windows as if there were something to see. The paramedics immediately loaded Ashley into the ambulance, and Charlie, confused and torn over what he should do, rode to Mercy Hospital holding his daughter's hand. Charlie pressed the precious little hand next to his cheek and began to cry again. He also began to pray. For the first time in a long time, he asked for God to break into his world and fix his family. The ride to the hospital was only eight minutes, but it seemed like an eternity. Looking out the window, he realized his world was shattered.

Rex Armstrong was a veteran homicide detective with the Charlotte city police force. He was stocky and balding on top with a thick mustache that earned him the nickname Walrus. He was also known as one of the worst dressers on the force. Polyester jackets and ties were the foundation of his wardrobe, and they were typically covered with coffee and doughnut stains. Despite his appearance, Rex was a consummate professional whose passion for justice was not impeded by anything.

Armstrong was the one responsible for bringing in the off-duty cop who killed the stripper at Diamond Girls. His investigation was not popular within the force, but by breaking the blue wall, he earned respect from everyone. When he finally arrested the officer, two other cops were forced into early retirement because they had knowledge of the incident but did not come forward. He was not popular and his tactics were heavy-handed, but that made him successful.

He walked in the front door of the Harrigan house, putting on his latex gloves. He grabbed a rookie by the sleeve and pulled him close. "Get these stinking cameras out of here! Now!" Then he shoved the kid in the general direction of the media wolves. He surveyed the house and walked through it slowly, trying to get a sense of what had happened. He walked up the stairs examining the pictures on the floor. Stopping at the bedroom door, he reached in his pocket and popped a Lifesaver into his mouth.

"What a mess," he said to no one specifically. "So where's the husband?"

The forensics specialist, Angela DeMarco, responded, "I

believe that he is at the hospital with his daughter. She was alive when the cops showed up."

Angrily Armstrong said, "You mean he left the scene of a crime? You," pointing at a uniformed officer, "get on the horn and get a squad car to the hospital. Find the husband and tell them not to leave his side. Hold his hand while he goes to the bathroom if they have to. He is the number-one suspect right now." The cop immediately obeyed and bounced down the hall.

The forensics officer said, "It looks like he . . . whoever . . . tried to strangle her with the telephone cord. Here are the ligature marks, but apparently he couldn't do it. So he used the lamp to finish the job. Death appears to have occurred immediately at that point."

Rex studied the scene. "Any signs of sexual assault?"

"She appears to have been raped. This scene is very disorganized. Personally, I don't think the husband did it."

"What about the daughter?" Armstrong picked up the remains of the lamp after it was photographed.

"I have a call into the doctor. Last time I called, she was still in emergency surgery." DeMarco returned to the body.

"Any witnesses so far?" Armstrong asked as he brushed his hair back over his bald spot.

"A little old lady saw a big, old-model car drive through the neighborhood at a high speed just after dark. She called us to complain about 'those crazy kids' and the way they drive. We've already alerted all squad cars to look for a big car with kids driving erratically. Let me wrap up the scene for the coroner."

"All right." Armstrong grimaced. "I'll meet you downstairs."

Charlotte had become a more dangerous place in the last few years. Typically, the biker gangs stayed on the bad side of town. As the new mob and an influx of Jamaican drug rings started entering the city with automatic weapons, the violence had been increasingly random. Charlotte was the midpoint between Miami and New York, which made it perfect for drug distribution. In the late eighties, Charlotte's murder rate increased by sixty percent, placing it in the top ten per capita murder cities in the nation.

Armstrong was from the old school, which believed that most murder victims knew the killer personally, and usually it was a boyfriend or husband. His investigative technique was simple. Like concentric circles, he started with the closest relationships and worked out to strangers. He climbed into his white Chevrolet Caprice and headed to Mercy Hospital to grill his primary suspect.

Charlie sat in the surgical ICU's waiting room with his head in his hands. For the first time in an hour and a half, he breathed. Oddly enough, he had not cried since he stepped into the hospital. He was still in shock. If only he had not gone by that bar, he might have been home to save his family. The killer may not have even shown up if he had been there. His mind was flooded with all of the possible "ifs." But the fact was that no number of "ifs" would change the situation. He had blown it, and the love of his life was gone from him now. It had been forty minutes since the doctor had talked to him about his daughter.

About that time, a nurse came around the corner. "Mr. Harrigan, would you like some hospital scrubs to wear so you can get out of those bloody clothes?"

Charlie looked down, oblivious to the fact that the entire front of his shirt was covered in blood. "No, thank you, I'm fine. Have you heard anything from Dr. Stuart lately?"

"I'll go check for you." The nurse quickly disappeared again.

The waiting room was strangely silent, as if he had broken into a museum in the middle of the night. There were no screaming children, sirens, or doctors rushing around. It was all very antiseptically cold and detached. There was a uniformed cop sitting on a chair in the hall, but he hadn't said a word to Charlie, and Charlie hardly noticed him. Down the hall, he could barely hear nurses giggle about their "bogus" dates from the previous night. *Do these people not realize that others are suffering around them, while they are laughing and talking about nonsense?* Charlie thought. Then he returned his attention to the alternating black and white tiles on the floor.

For once in his life, he was helpless. He could do nothing to alter his situation or to help his daughter. The first time she had skinned her knee, he picked her up and rushed her to the bathroom. He put the biggest Band-Aid they had on her little scrape. He held her close and kissed her knee profusely. Daddy made it all better. When she forgot her one little line in the Christmas play and ran offstage crying, all he had to do was hold her and split an ice cream sundae with her after church. Everything was fixed. Now he was powerless. His daughter's fate was in the hands of an invisible doctor and some quirky nurses.

Out of frustration, he stood up and paced the floor. Upon reaching the soda machine in the corner of the room, he unloaded on it. He kicked it repeatedly, only the machine did not budge. He limped back to his couch with a throbbing foot, feeling not only frustrated but also very stupid. About that time, a dark-haired man with gray temples rounded the corner.

"Mr. Harrigan?" The man looked around the empty waiting room, realizing that this must be the father. "Would you please join me in this room over here?"

Charlie got a bad feeling. Doctors always gave good news in the waiting room. Bad news was always delivered in a private conference room. If someone had a nervous breakdown, nobody else would see. He had joined the Thomasons in a private conference room like the one he had just entered. It was dark and cramped with a table in the middle and several padded chairs around the table. Charlie noticed the inordinate number of tissue boxes that were on the table and every single bookshelf.

"Mr. Harrigan," the doctor began, "I'm sorry but I have bad news. There is no way to say this. We tried for forty-five minutes to save your daughter's life. Her breathing was very faint when she arrived. The damage was too extensive. She had several internal injuries that were irreparable. We couldn't save her."

Charlie began to cry again. The reality of the situation had started to sink in. His family was gone. Unsure of what to do or say, Charlie asked, "How about my wife? She was pregnant, you know."

The doctor cautiously placed his arm around Charlie. "I'm sorry, Mr. Harrigan, do you not remember what happened? The police said your wife was dead on the scene. I'm afraid the fetus had no chance of survival. Your wife had been dead for some time."

Exploding and throwing the doctor's arm off him, Charlie yelled, "Why do you doctors call it a fetus? It's a baby, okay! Its heart beats. I saw it on the ultrasound. That fetus is more human than you are." As if the explosion of emotion drained him, Charlie fell back into a chair and began to sob.

The doctor did not take it personally. Stuart had been here many times before, more than he desired. "I'm sorry. You're right. Please forgive me. I'll leave you alone for a minute. Would you like for me to call you a chaplain?"

Charlie's head was swimming. Everything had happened so fast. It was like a nightmare and he tried fruitlessly to gather his thoughts. Remembering the recent seminary graduate he had met when Maggie Thomason died, he said, "No. I don't need a bunch of religious clichés right now. Maybe later." He knew he would not talk to the hospital chaplain later, but he was trying to save face.

After sitting alone in the room for fifteen minutes, which seemed like an eternity, there was a knock on the door. A nurse entered and invited Charlie to take one last look at his wife and daughter. They had been cleaned up as much as possible, but it did not look like them. Their faces were bruised and distorted. He was given plenty of time alone in the ICU with his family. After he was finished saying his good-byes, he started for the door. Another nurse lightly grabbed his elbow and asked him to go to another conference room.

He was turned around and disoriented, so he simply followed orders because he did not know what else to do. After a brief death counseling session, the nurse asked him about organ donation.

Charlie stared incredulously. "Do we have to do this now?"

"Actually," the nurse explained, "it must be done right away if we are to help other individuals."

"Let me think for a minute." Charlie sighed and thought, *What would Sandy do?* Knowing her, she would want her death to benefit others. She was always concerned about others' feelings and hurts, but rarely her own. "Sure, sure. I think my wife would like that. Is there anyway I can find out who receives the donation? I may want to know some day."

"No problem," the nurse responded. "We do that all the time. Thank you very much for your help. You would be surprised by the number of people not willing to donate organs. I think it's because it's just hard to think straight at a time like this."

"Well, I don't swear to be thinking straight right now. I'm just trying to make Sandy happy."

The nurse stood up and patted him on the back. "There is someone else who would like to see you."

"No chaplains!" Charlie snapped.

"Don't worry. Dr. Stuart told me to keep him away." The nurse gave him a sympathetic smile and left.

Into the little conference room walked a stocky, balding man with a mustache and a badge hanging from a tacky polyester blazer. "Mr. Harrigan, do you mind if I ask you a few questions? I'm Detective Rex Armstrong."

"I guess not." Charlie shrugged helplessly. "I don't really have anywhere else to go."

"You made the 911 call, right?" Armstrong asked.

"Yeah." Charlie rubbed his temples trying to think back on the events of the night. Everything had happened so fast, but it seemed like light-years away. "I came home sometime after eight and found them."

"Where were you before that?" Armstrong was scribbling on a little notepad.

"After I got fired from my job, I went to the East Boulevard Bar and Grill."

Suspiciously, Armstrong asked, "Can anyone confirm that?"

"Yeah, I met some woman at the bar. I've got her card somewhere." Charlie started reaching in his pockets and realized he had forgotten where he had placed his coat. "Plus, I helped put the bartender's kid through college."

"All right. I can check that out later. Now about—"

Charlie barked at the pudgy cop, "Are you interrogating me, you jerk? Why aren't you out there trying to get the killer? My family's dead, you idiot!"

"We've got other people looking. I need to talk to you. Now just calm down."

"Don't tell me to calm down. I've just lost the most important things in my life. My reason to live is gone and you think I did it! Get outta my face!" Charlie slammed his hands down on the table and glared at the cop.

"I'm sorry to upset you. I guarantee you that this is strictly routine," Armstrong backpedaled quickly. "You're an attorney, right? Sometimes you have to ask difficult questions to help people. That's what I'm doing. Why don't you just tell me what you remember."

Charlie calmed down somewhat and related the story of finding the bodies. He actually remembered very little about the evening, which seemed suspicious. When Charlie could not produce the other woman's business card, Armstrong was curious but kept it to himself. Charlie did not even remember throwing her card away. Armstrong asked Charlie about his relationship with Sandy. Charlie said that the relationship was perfect. Armstrong asked about losing his job and his frequency of drinking. Often the loss of a job precipitated domestic violence. When Charlie started getting emotional about his wife and stopped giving hard facts, Armstrong gave up. He handed Charlie a card and said they would be in touch.

When Armstrong left, Charlie glanced at his watch. The face of the watch was covered with dried blood. He scraped it off and looked at the time, 12:35 A.M. He had been at the hospital almost four hours. He could not believe it had been that long. Opening the door, he left the room and exited the surgical ICU. Standing in the hallway, he ran his fingers through his hair and looked both ways. *How do I get out of this place? And where do I go now?*

Spotting a men's room, he went in and washed his face in hot water. He looked in the mirror and asked the reflection, *What do I do now? I have nowhere to go.* Charlie fell to his knees and cried. He splashed more water on his face and knew he had to get out of there. Charlie ran out the emergency room exit and realized that his car was back at the house. So Charlie wandered off into the darkness.

chapter
TWELVE

A dull thud woke Charlie from a deep, fitful sleep early Thursday. He had arrived home in the bleak hours of the morning. Unsure as to what to do next, the exhausted man had climbed into the backseat of his Blazer in the driveway and fallen asleep. In between night sweats, dry heaves, and nightmares, he had managed to get a little sleep. Waking in a strange place after an abbreviated, yet deep sleep, the first light of the morning sun disoriented Charlie. He almost convinced himself that the night before had been a dream. The noise that had awakened him was the sound of car doors being shut.

Police cars were parked along the street, and a large van was pulling into the driveway next to him. As Charlie climbed out of the Blazer, he looked down at his chest and saw his wrinkled, white shirt covered with blood. It had not been a dream; the nightmare was all too real.

A uniformed officer grabbed Charlie's arm. "Where do you think you're going, mister?"

"The name's Harrigan. I live here. That was my wife and daughter who were killed last night. So if you don't mind, I want to go into my house and take off this bloody shirt." He tried to slide past the officer, only to be restrained again.

"I'm afraid I'll need that shirt; it's evidence." The officer's jaw was clenched firmly, and he was not about to move.

Charlie got in his face. "You know what you need, you sorry little—"

"Excuse me, is there a problem, Officer Pendleton?" Detective Armstrong stepped between the two men. "Pendleton, why don't you secure the contents of Mr. Harrigan's Blazer?"

"Wonderful, you want to ask me more questions?" Charlie folded his arms and glared at the poorly dressed man.

"No, no. I was going to let you go into your house. Just stay away from the second floor, the stairs, and the side door. There is an investigation going on, and remember, I'll be close by, so no funny business."

"Thanks, detective. Your faith in humanity is encouraging."

Charlie grabbed the newspaper off the porch out of habit and went inside. Avoiding the second floor and the stairs, he went to the kitchen to get some water. Throwing the paper on the kitchen table, it sprawled all over the place. Charlie's double take at the paper startled him. In the bottom right-hand corner of the front page was his picture again. For the fourth time in nine days, his picture had appeared on the front page of the paper. Was the suffering not enough? Did everybody have to know his dire straits?

The story briefly recapped his involvement in the Thomason case, but said nothing about Walter Comstock. After that, the reporter gave a very detailed description of the break-in, robbery, and assault on his family. Charlie kept reading the article, not quite knowing why. He read that the husband was not ruled out as a suspect yet, simply because the police had no other leads. Charlie threw the paper back onto the table and went to the refrigerator. He passed the miniature television in the corner of the countertop, and out of habit turned on the morning news. He pulled some orange juice out of the refrigerator and then looked at the TV. On the tiny four-inch screen, Charlie saw the front of his house. Apparently filmed the night before, a reporter was standing in his front yard filling in the blanks, speculating as to why the husband would do such a thing. Charlie grabbed the television and threw it across the room. It shattered spectacularly against the far wall. Then he collapsed on the floor, put his head between his knees, and cried.

He loved her more than life itself. There is no possible way he could do this. He would kill himself before bringing any harm to his family. He sat with his back against the dishwasher for what seemed like hours. He thought about Sandy. For some reason, the good memories would not come to him. He remembered snapping at her several months ago for telling him to hurry up and get ready to go to a party, then after he did he had to wait thirty minutes for her to finish getting dressed. It was a silly spat, especially looking back now. Sure his pride was hurt a little, being told what to do as if he were a kid. Now he begged for someone to tell him what to do.

He remembered their first fight after they were married. After coming home from their honeymoon in Charleston, Charlie woke up Saturday morning to go to his usual golf game. They had spent an entire week together, and he thought she would not mind. She got upset that he did not want to spend their first Saturday at home as a married couple. She locked herself in the bedroom and cried for hours. The whole time all Charlie could think was that he could have gone and played nine holes of golf and been back by the time she was finished crying. Why was he so stupid to ever want to leave her side? Why had he not quit his job and spent more time with his family? The pain was too much; Charlie lay down on his side and cried some more, begging his memory to give him something good that did not produce guilt. The picture of the redhead at the bar kept crowding his mind, no matter how much he yelled at her to get out of his head.

Horace Douglas stepped onto the little white porch of his little white mill house. In his tattered dark blue bathrobe, holding a steaming hot cup of black coffee, he cherished these quiet moments reading the morning paper on his porch swing. After reading about the problems of the world, he turned to his Bible for solace and hope. Years ago, he heard an old-time fire-and-brimstone preacher say that he should read the Bible and the paper together so he would know when the end was near. Horace had decided that the preacher may have been a little off. When the end comes, a person is either ready or not. Reading the headlines would not help at that point. Nonetheless, the habit had stuck.

Thursday morning, he picked up the paper and recognized the face at the bottom. The attorney, who called the death of his son a frivolous lawsuit, had lost his family in a terrible crime. Horace felt sorry for the man; maybe now he understood how Horace felt about the loss of Matthew. The article implicated Harrigan in the murders and also related that his termination from the firm of Hobbes, Reimarus, and Van Schank may have driven him over the edge. Horace studied the picture closely. The eyes were honest. He could not have done such a terrible thing. Usually Horace was a good judge of character.

However, Horace believed that he had missed with their first attorney. Henry Judson was a local boy with a decent reputation. But after the preliminary hearing, they had returned to Judson's office, where the rotund man tried several times to force them to settle. He had lit another Davidoff, and cigar smoke encircled his head as he told them how long and painful the trial would be. He had tried to scare them with the wealth and influence of their opposition. He had even hinted at the fact that Hobbes, Reimarus, and Van Schank may possibly play dirty, but they were far too powerful to get caught. After all, the fat-cat lawyers were offering two hundred thousand dollars. They were willing to pay for the actual damages that Judson had asked for, but Horace was a wall.

The man and his family had lived one step in front of poverty all of their lives. Horace worked thirty hours overtime at the mill every week just to get Matt into one of the best independent living homes in the state. He really did not care about the money. He wanted a public trial. He wanted to embarrass Paragon Group and force them to make a public apology for treating his son as less than human. Money was the only language these guys spoke, and the dollar figure was meant to inflict punishment, not to make Horace rich. Horace flatly told Judson that hell has a special place for people who get rich off the sufferings of others. Horace spoke little, but when he did speak, he knew how to get people's attention.

Staring at the picture of this young lawyer, Horace thought that maybe this attorney was getting what he deserved. Then he had the odd thought that Harrigan was one who could be trusted. He surely could not trust Henry Judson to be a zealous advocate. Horace set down the paper and picked up his Bible. He arbitrarily flipped to Proverbs. One verse jumped out at him, "Do not gloat when your enemy falls; when he stumbles, do not let your heart rejoice." He immediately asked God to forgive the arrogance that had begun to stir in his heart toward Mr. Harrigan. As he was praying, he felt a strange compassion for Harrigan flooding his heart. A revelation shot through his mind like lightening.

He stood up to find Betty, and at that exact moment, the frail little woman darted out the door. She grabbed her best friend for life and said, "I think we should get rid of Mr. Judson. I got the strongest impression as I was praying that he does not have our best interests at heart. Something is not right with him, but I don't know what it is."

Taking a sip of coffee, Horace said, "I completely agree with you. I had the same thought a minute ago. He was too eager to settle, and, by George, we're paying the guy. He should do what we want."

Desperately, Betty asked, "But what are we going to do? I don't know of any other lawyers."

"I do." Horace smiled holding up the paper.

Betty was shocked. "He works for Paragon. That man wanted to dismiss our case. He can't help us."

"The person in this article is not the same one who was in the courtroom yesterday." Horace's assurance always calmed his wife. "I don't think he meant what he said. He was just doing his job, and I don't think he enjoyed it. Remember what he said to Comstock in the hallway after the hearing? He did not want to represent Walter Comstock and the Paragon Group. Besides, look at this article."

Betty read the story about Harrigan losing his family and his job, and how he had taken on a very incendiary issue with the abortion doctor and won. Horace convinced her that Harrigan fought for the underdog and that his heart was not in his oral arguments the day before. The guy had lost his job and his family. He needed something. He needed them, and now he could understand a little more what they were going through. Surely, Charlie Harrigan would champion their cause as his own, and in the meanwhile, they could help offer him some hope.

The Douglases got dressed and headed to Henry Judson's office to fire their attorney. After they broke the news to him, Judson acted relieved. He was not the least bit angry or upset. He grabbed their hands tightly and shook them furiously. He apologized profusely for his inadequate counsel and explained that he was preoccupied with other matters that had suddenly resolved themselves. After the older couple left, Judson unlocked the top drawer in the credenza behind him and pulled out an envelope. Sticking the pictures in his paper shredder, he said, "Good riddance, Hobbes, Reimarus, and Van Schank. I hope you burn for eternity."

Rex Armstrong paced the tile floor in front of the metal file cabinets. He had not slept all night. The process of interviewing neighbors was laborious, especially in the late hours of the night and the early hours of the morning, when normal Americans wanted to sleep. Such was his calling in life, to afflict the comforted and comfort the afflicted. He reached in his polyester coat pocket and pulled out a pack of cigarettes.

"Don't do it!" snapped Melinda Powell. The assistant district attorney was feminine, but also very strict and hard-nosed. The cop was on her turf now, and even though she had just turned thirty, she had quickly made a name for herself as a no-nonsense ADA who could stand up to the toughest street cop and hold her own. In fact, she had to be tough.

Campbell Law School in the low country of North Carolina was not as prestigious as her sister schools. Typically, Duke, Chapel Hill, and Wake Forest were interviewed first, and then if all of those students declined a job, an employer would consider Campbell. It really was unfair, she thought, because Campbell had quality professors and produced some of the best students, who learned to cooperate, much more so than the big three that produced serious cutthroat competition.

Powell had attended law school full-time during the day and waited tables almost every night at a redneck bar. She had picked up smoking to calm her nerves, but the habit was nasty, and as soon as she graduated from law school, she threw her cigarettes away without a second thought. She was tough that way. She had also learned to fight off the unwarranted advances of every drunk truck driver and salesman who ventured into her territory. Maybe that was why she had developed such a severe reputation prosecuting sex offenders and spouse abusers. She showed no mercy and settled only when she knew that she did not have all the facts. After demonstrating the highest prosecution rate in sex crimes for four years straight, at the age of thirty, she was moved to major crimes, the youngest ADA ever in that department.

"I don't like it." The ADA looked over the file for the fifth time. "You have no witnesses and no real motive. You can't charge the husband. Why don't you just lay low and wait for the ME to give us some physical evidence?"

Armstrong protested, "Look, if the guy spends some time in jail, I'm sure he'll confess. These cases are almost always the spouse. Strangulation is typically a highly personal crime."

"But you haven't given me a reason to believe he would want to strangle his wife and daughter." She looked at him like a teacher demanding a sound explanation for a student's delinquent homework. "Didn't they just get back from a wonderful vacation where everybody had a good time? Just follow the guy for a few days and see what happens. I've met him a couple of times. Maybe I'll just give him a friendly call and see if I can find out anything."

Trying to regain some of the machismo he lost in this debate, Armstrong gruffly said, "I'll give him forty-eight hours, and if you're still dragging your feet then, I'll go to your boss. I'm sure Guy Streebeck would love to hear that one of his ADAs refused to arrest the number-one suspect in our latest murder case." He stormed out and slammed the door.

Melinda Powell leaned back in her chair and smiled at the door. "You do that, Columbo," she laughed to herself.

Guy Streebeck was a popular district attorney approaching reelection. He had served as the county's district attorney for twenty years. One thing that had made him popular was his complete, unswerving support of the police force. Always erring on the side of the officers had caused many fights and battles at the city council, but it served him well. He had made lots of friends in blue, and one of them was Rex Armstrong. He had given Armstrong plenty of latitude to follow his gut instinct in the past, and it had proved to be the right choice in a majority of the cases.

The ADA scanned the newspaper article once again to see if she had missed anything. She had met Charlie Harrigan briefly a week ago and was impressed by his passion in the courtroom. A guy with that much passion for doing the right thing could not be guilty of such a heinous crime. After the verdict was read, Charlie hugged his clients as all good attorneys do, but his eyes had watered as if he felt the same release and closure that the Thomasons had felt. She decided then and there that she would fight Armstrong on this, but she would have to be very careful. She made a note to contact Charlie and interview him before Armstrong could get his pudgy hands on him.

Melinda Powell closed the small file on Charlie Harrigan and opened the file on Dr. Owen Johnston that was twice as thick. The FBI had traced a wire transfer of funds from the downtown branch of First Union National Bank to a bank in Nassau. After a little pressure, the Bahamian bankers turned over the wire transfer records, which showed that after two weeks, the remainder of Johnston's money ended up in a German bank in Panama. From there, it was impossible to get any further information. Powell had interviewed the wife, whom Johnston had left behind, but got nowhere. She had talked to every employee except the newest nurse at Johnston's office, who had conspicuously disappeared the same time Johnston did.

After interviewing the nurse's roommate, Powell encouraged the FBI to tap the roommate's phone. In ten days, there had been one phone call from the young, blond nurse who said she was fine and would be gone for awhile. She was having a wonderful time although her "man" was a little old. In the background, a ship's horn could be heard, along with waves crashing and a variety of languages being spoken. Obviously, the nurse had called from a public phone near the coast in a tourist town, but that still left hundreds of options. The FBI tried to convince Melinda Powell that they had more important things to do, but she was not going to give up that easy. She was a fighter.

chapter
THIRTEEN

Once the police had given him the okay, Charlie had spent several hours cleaning up his house as best as possible. He had called his mother and stepfather. His mother would be there soon, and he expected his stepfather had a softball game or something urgent to attend to. He left a message with his father's secretary, who assured him that he would be in touch. Charlie assumed that his message would simply be one of the many pink message slips piled neatly on the right-hand corner of his father's desk. Sandy's parents were going to call a quick prayer meeting at their church in the mountains of Old Fort and drive down tonight.

In between cleaning and phone calls, Charlie had very little time to think. He never realized all of the minuscule duties a person has to take care of when he loses a loved one. It was apparently not enough that his heart was in a continual state of breaking, he had to act like a business manager and call insurance companies, find a nice funeral home, and ward off reporters who smelled a juicy story. The insurance adjuster would have to get back to him. Charlie really did not care. He had more important things to deal with, like desperately trying to find a reason to wake up tomorrow.

In an attempt to return some normalcy to his life, Charlie showered and shaved, put on a starched shirt and suit, and walked out the door with his briefcase. It was three in the afternoon; he was not sure where he was going, but he had to get out of the house. It felt haunted to him. He continually imagined his wife coming around the corner in her bathrobe or his daughter bounding down the stairs, but every time he looked, no one was there. He had to get out. He felt like he would go crazy at any second.

Charlie climbed into his Blazer and headed west on Providence. He was not actually sure why he was headed to work. He simply wanted something familiar, anything that would make him feel at home. He had made this drive every day for ten years. There was something minutely comforting about it. In the past ten hours, he had talked to many people, all of whom were strangers. Everyone wanted something from him. This one wanted an interview; this one wanted a blood sample; this one wanted organs. He simply desired a familiar face who did not want something else, because Charlie had absolutely nothing left to give. Of course, he could not go to the office; he was not welcome there.

In the afternoon, Providence was relatively empty, so he arrived downtown in no time. Suddenly, he saw the sign for Sonny's. He swerved into the little gravel parking lot beside the dry cleaners. As he turned off the engine, he realized that without his family or the firm, Charlie really had no friends in this city. Kim Il Sook might as well have been his best friend for all intents and purposes. The stark realization hit him. He was, in fact, entirely alone in this cold world. It took a few minutes for Charlie to compose himself and get out of his car.

Charlie walked into an empty diner. A young Korean girl was wiping off tables, and "Love Me Tender" wailed on the jukebox. Charlie sat on a barstool next to the counter. The young girl brought him some water and went back to her duties. Charlie mused over the fact that maybe he *was* completely alone in the world. Either the girl did not speak English or was very shy, but she just looked at the floor and walked off when Charlie greeted her.

Finally, the walk-in refrigerator opened. "Whew! Very cold. Very cold." Sonny was rubbing his arms, trying to start the circulation again. "My friend, Charlie. How are you doing? I've missed you last couple of days." He noticed Charlie's eyes. They were blank and lifeless.

"Not good, Sonny." Charlie placed his head in his hands. "I lost my family last night."

Without a word, Sonny took off his apron, poured two cups of coffee, and came out from behind the counter to sit beside Charlie. They sat in silence for a long time. They would sip their coffee and then set it down, gazing into the blackness in the cup. The harder they looked into the coffee, the blacker it got. Both men had known blackness in their lives, but Sonny held his tongue, waiting for Charlie to break the silence.

The silence continued. Elvis gave way to Patsy Cline, who gave way to Phil Collins. The jukebox was the only sound in the diner for more than an hour and almost a whole pot of coffee. Finally, Charlie sighed, "I don't know what to do or how to feel. I just feel lost."

"You *are* lost." Sonny glanced out of the corner of his eye and quickly looked back down. "Your wilderness journey just beginning. It never gets easier . . . but you learn to survive."

Confused, Charlie looked at his only friend in the world. "You're just a barrel of sunshine, aren't you? What in the world does that mean, 'my journey is just beginning'?"

"Do you know how I came to America?" Charlie negatively shook his head, realizing he actually knew very little about Sonny, except for his culinary talents. "I was in Korea when the war began." Charlie nodded to encourage Sonny to continue.

"January 4, 1951, Seoul fell to communists. My family lived in the city of Wonju near the thirty-eighth parallel. As four hundred thousand North Koreans broke through United Nation's front, they hammered the allied force of two hundred thousand. They destroyed everything in their path. They went from house to house. When gunfire got near our house, my father shoved me into back of closet and tried to hide my two older sisters and mother when soldiers kicked door in. They pull my family outside. I crawled to a window and watched. Soldiers lined my parents up in front of house and shot them. I never saw my sisters again. The soldiers dragged them off screaming. I can only imagine the horrible things they did to them. But I know they did not die quickly, they may have lived many days or even years in slavery."

Listening to the narrative, Charlie could not believe it. He had no idea Sonny had been through such a horrific event. Tears welled up in Sonny's eyes and matched the ones running down Charlie's cheeks. Charlie suddenly realized that probably everyone has a horror story; we just never take the time to find out.

"What did you do?" Charlie asked.

"I ran back into the closet." Sonny wiped his eyes and got up to make a second pot of coffee. "I must have stayed in closet four hour. When I finally came out, city mostly empty and many houses on fire. A few children were sitting along road crying. I just started running. I headed south because I knew Americans were south."

"How old were you?" Charlie asked. For the first time in many days, he was not thinking about himself, and it actually made him feel slightly better. His mind was engaged and not flooded with guilt and despair.

Sonny thought for minute. "I was six."

"How in the world are you still a Christian? Didn't you blame God?" Charlie defiantly said.

"I didn't. I blamed Buddha." Sonny smiled at Charlie's embarrassed reaction.

Charlie was uncertain how to respond. "Oh, I'm sorry, Sonny. I thought you were a Christian. You wear a cross around your neck and you keep a Bible on your little desk over there, so I just assumed . . ."

Sonny gave Charlie a reassuring smile. "I am a Christian now . . . but I wasn't always. My family was Buddhist. I didn't become a Christian for many years later. For a long time I lived on streets with other children. We begged for food, and many times, Americans fed us. Eventually, some people found me and put me in a Buddhist orphanage. They taught me to be good and seek the ways of Buddha, the Golden Mean, and maybe the same thing would not happen to me that happened to my parents."

"I don't understand," Charlie said.

"The Buddhist monks told us that Korea was being punished for their sins. Allowing Americans into our culture, Buddha was punishing us. They convinced me that my family deserved their fate, but Buddha had smiled on me and chose me to help purify Korea."

Charlie interrupted the story. "Did you seriously buy that?"

"I didn't know. They fed me and gave me shelter. It looked like Buddha was protecting me. But I wasn't happy. Trying to live at peace with everything and everyone made me feel fake, because of rage in my heart. You know, we Asians don't share our feelings easy."

"Nothing's stopping you now." Charlie actually chuckled.

"I started searching, reading all great religions. One day I was sitting on a park bench in downtown Seoul, years after the war. My head was shaved; I was barefoot, wearing an orange robe. This old man saw me reading a New Testament. This missionary came up and asked me if I understood the story. I asked him 'why the man had to die?' and he explained it to me. Then I asked him why my parents had to die. He and his wife met with me once a week for six months. The monks punished me for meeting with them, but they were so nice, I kept going. Finally, I left the orphanage and they adopted me and brought me back to America."

"Wait a minute!" Charlie stopped the narrative. "What did they say? Why did your family have to die?"

"They didn't say." Sonny knew the cryptic answer would only frustrate Charlie, but there was no other way.

"What is that supposed to mean?"

"They just told me that the man who died would help me understand if I got to know Him." Sonny stood up and went back into the kitchen to get ready for the dinner rush.

Desperate for a solution, Charlie asked, "So what's the solution? How do you deal with the pain?"

"Like I said, your journey just beginning." Sonny patted him on the shoulder. "You are not ready for the solution."

"Look, Sonny, I'm real sorry about your family. If anybody can understand what I'm feeling, it's you. But honestly, you haven't really helped me." Frustrated, Charlie swiveled in his chair to leave.

"Charlie, I'm always here. Come by anytime and I will walk with you on your journey. God be with you." Sonny waved and went back to marinating his chicken.

"Thank you, Sonny." Charlie looked quizzically at the cook. Under his breath, Charlie whispered, "Whatever."

Pushing the glass door open wider than necessary, Charlie thought, *God be with you. God should have been with me yesterday. He should have been with my family yesterday.* What were all of Sandy's prayers for anyway? They sure did not work. Maybe the killers prayed to Satan, maybe they had a direct line. The one time in his life that he needed God, God refused to show up. Charlie was tired of being sad. He was not passive and refused to sit by and feel sorry for himself. It was easier to be angry.

Maybe God was punishing the Koreans for something. Maybe God was punishing him. Charlie certainly had not given God much serious thought since high school, except for Christmas and Easter, but he was not a bad guy and went to church most of the time. Why did God want to punish him? What did he do to God? Charlie was fighting for the little guy; he was doing God's job. So why was God absent the one day Charlie needed Him most?

Martin Van Schank pulled out a bottle of brandy from the private bar in his office. Around the table sat Walter Comstock and Nancy Lockman-Kurtz. J. Garrison Hobbes III was on his way down to celebrate. There was quite a bit of obnoxious laughter and backslapping. The mood was celebratory because the case was apparently in the bag, and Comstock had just received a new contract.

The revitalization program in downtown Charlotte was in high gear. New companies were moving in and the poor people were being shoved out. Through Comstock's connection, Paragon Group had been offered the contract for a new complex of government offices to be built in an old department store on North Tryon Street. The good citizens of North Carolina would pay for the project itself, to the tune of almost twenty million dollars. Overall, Paragon Group would earn an estimated two million dollars off the project, and Hobbes, Reimarus, and Van Schank would get at least four hundred and fifty thousand dollars in fees. So everybody was happy.

Comstock did not mind paying fees for contracts. It was part of his deal, but he refused to pay for any lawsuits. They had agreed that the firm would swallow whatever expenses were necessary to settle any cases. None of the other partners knew about this deal, primarily because their ethics would not allow them to make such agreements. Lawyers were merely representatives and were not to become unduly entangled in the affairs of their clients. But Comstock and Van Schank's relationship went deeper than that.

"I wish I could have seen that boy's face when you fired him. It would have made my day," said Comstock, the worst dressed in the group, as he leaned back in his chair.

Hobbes smiled, his bald head gleaming. "What was really priceless was the look on his face when he thought that he was going to have his license yanked because of that little argument he had with you. I thought he was going to lose it right there."

They all laughed. Then Comstock asked, "Could they really take away his license?"

Hobbes said, "Not really, but he was on a fine line, and if we pressed, we could probably have had him suspended."

　　　　　　　　　　　　　　THE TRIAL OF JOB

Comstock replied, "That would have been the icing on the cake."

Nancy, who had been a spectator to this point while rubbing her foot on Van Schank's leg, asked, "So when does this new deal take place?"

Van Schank eyed her as if to say "mind your own business," but instead replied, "Well, the contract has not been officially signed yet, but I have it on good information that the city will give us the contract. From there, it is just a matter of getting all the partners on the same page and we'll be in business again."

Instead of remaining silent, Nancy pushed even further. "That is something I don't understand. In preparing the case against the Douglases, I kept coming across references to limited partners, special partnerships, and once even a secret partner. The funny thing is that there are absolutely no partnership agreements in the Paragon files."

Hobbes and Van Schank looked at one another while Comstock took another drink of brandy. Hobbes said, "Some of our more valued clients are handled exclusively by partners, and their files are off-limits to secretaries and paralegals. Once you officially become a partner, we will show you where all of those files are kept, but for now you shouldn't worry."

Comstock abruptly changed the conversation. "What if those old rednecks decide to hire a new attorney? We owned Judson. How are you going to ensure that the lawsuit does not make it to trial?"

Van Schank smiled and replied, "I have informed some of my associates about the recent developments with our friend Henry Judson. He promised them that he would stay in touch and help us if he heard anything. Plus, my associates are going to follow the Douglases for a couple of days to see if they contact another attorney, and then we will go to work on him."

Nancy, who was more lost than ever, tried to be funny. "Why does it have to be a him? What if they hire a female attorney?"

Van Schank took off his little round spectacles and smiled as he said, "Then that will make my job that much easier now, will it not?"

Nancy was offended by that statement, but she was not going to let it show. She wanted to be included as one of the guys, which meant that jokes about, against, or directed at women must be laughed at and not taken personally. All three of the men had a hearty laugh at Nancy's gender's expense. They decided to move the meeting to a place where they could have prime rib and even more alcohol. At that point, they would lay out concrete plans to solidify their next million-dollar deal.

chapter
FOURTEEN

The old gray stone church was packed with people dressed all in black and navy blue. Charlie sat in the first row with his mother and in-laws, thinking of a million other places he would rather be. What truly astonished him was the sheer number of people crammed into the Baptist church. He had no idea his wife had touched so many lives. Where were all these people when she and Ashley were alive? He glanced over his shoulder to see if he recognized any of the faces.

He wanted to pay his respects to his wife and daughter, but he felt so conspicuous grieving before such a large audience. The only thing worse than being in the front row during a funeral was standing in a receiving line during the wake the night before. The South had inherited a tradition from the Irish called a wake. In many places, it was a cross between a funeral and cocktail party. Spectators stood around eating food and talking about the latest weather reports, while others stood in line to talk to the survivors. Meanwhile, those grieving stood for hours, unless a person was over sixty. Then he could sit, while all types of well-intentioned sympathizers tried their best to comfort those who could not be comforted.

As he had stood in line, Charlie barely heard anything that was said to him. He did not really want to. Instead, he thought about the receiving line at their wedding. It had been a small affair at the ancient Episcopal church on Franklin Street in Chapel Hill. The building was small and intimate with hardwood floors. Both had just graduated from college and did not have a lot of money, so the event was a basic no-frills ceremony, except for an enormous number of candles. Sandy had insisted that the only light in the church come from candles, and the incandescent glow made for a beautiful setting. Of course, these types of wishes had made the wedding coordinator angry.

The overweight woman with too much time on her hands was being paid to organize their wedding, but she acted more like a czar than a coordinator. When it was time for the receiving line at the reception, she actually forced one of Charlie's friends to go to the back of the line, because he had "cut in." At that, Charlie got fed up. He ran to the band and asked them if they knew any calypso music. They started playing "The Girl from Ipanema." Charlie exploded out of a storage closet with a broom in his hand and yelled, "Limbo!" The hall erupted in shouts and laughter, everybody started dancing, and the poor wedding coordinator frantically tried to preserve her precious line. When she snapped at Charlie for his stunt, he invited her to leave quietly or else not get paid. Sandy was somewhat embarrassed, but secretly she enjoyed Charlie's prank. She never publicly approved of his spontaneity, but privately, it was one of the idiosyncrasies that drew her to him.

The reception was a hit with all of their friends. Even Sandy's very conservative parents went under the broom once. After they left the reception hall, the newlyweds took Charlie's beat-up Toyota to the Hilton in downtown Durham. They were so hungry, the happy couple ordered Domino's pizza and watched "Jeopardy" on their wedding night. At the Raleigh-Durham airport the next morning, Charlie had a big surprise for Sandy. They boarded a plane for Bermuda. They had never been out of the country before, and Charlie had saved nickels and dimes for years just for this moment. Five hundred miles off the coast of North Carolina, they played in the sun and white sand.

The pastor said something that struck Charlie, and suddenly he was back in Charlotte, attending his family's funeral. No sun, no white sand, no wife—just pain. The pastor had said something about God's ways being higher than ours. Charlie thought, *If this is higher, I would hate to see what lower looks like.* Charlie tried to pay attention, but his mind wandered to his wife and daughter. He was desperately trying to remember what Sandy looked like. He focused and concentrated on her face, but it was blurry. He grabbed his chest. Why could he not remember her face? He was terrified that he would forget her. He tried to picture Ashley. In his mind, he could see a little brown-haired girl dancing in the backyard by her swing, but he could not see her big green eyes. He breathed slowly and deeply. He had to get out of there.

Charlie did not notice the other guests who were at the funeral. In the middle on the left side under the stained glass window of the Good Shepherd, Horace and Betty Douglas watched and prayed reverently. In the very last row, Slade kept his eye on the Douglases. He had actually put on a coat and tie for the occasion. He was not worried about being respectful; he simply did not want to be noticed. He had two more friends in a car outside to follow the couple after they left.

On the right side near the front, sitting on the aisle, was Melinda Powell. She had come on her own because Charlie was a colleague, but she also wanted to keep an eye on Rex Armstrong. Armstrong stood quietly at the back of the church and made mental notes of all who were present. He wanted to make sure that Charlie did not try to skip town. In the next to the last row on the right side sat Brad Connelly. He tried to see his friend. He wanted to talk to him and repair their friendship, but he would have to wait for another day. He realized that he had been used by Nancy Lockman-Kurtz and felt terrible. Little did he know that Charlie's fate at Hobbes, Reimarus, and Van Schank was predestined, regardless of his actions.

As they piled into black limousines, the first cold rain of fall started to drizzle. As they rode in one long line with their lights on, Charlie thought about how absurd this tradition seemed. Why did they do such unusual things when people died? Why wait until a person has been robbed of life and breath to show how much you care? He noticed all the cars pulling off to the side of the road and thought, *My family is gone. I have all the time in the world.* These people did not have to get out of his way; he was not in a hurry to get to a hole in the ground. Charlie returned his attention to the rain splashing off the window. The drizzle had turned to torrents, and heaven itself seemed to be grieving along with the powerless little humans here on earth.

After the burial, the Harrigan house was full of relatives. Charlie's mother, in-laws, and assorted cousins were milling around the first level, sorting out food that friends had brought by. Casseroles of every shape and flavor lined the table: chicken, macaroni, broccoli, and sweet potato. Somehow, casseroles had become the food of sorrow. Charlie went upstairs to dry off from the soaking he received at the graveside. He refused to allow anybody else upstairs, because bloodstains were everywhere.

He had been the one who found the mutilated bodies, and he did not want anyone else to know exactly how violently their loved ones had died. He sat on his bed with a towel around his neck. He picked up a picture of the three of them on a picnic. The picture was beautiful, but it was not quite right. Sandy was prettier than this picture; cameras could not capture the sparkle in her eyes. Every time they saw each other after being apart for awhile, she would get the same gleam that he had seen the first time they met on the football field. No picture could do her justice. He set it down and went back downstairs.

In the kitchen, his mother-in-law, Barbara Davis, and sister-in-law, Caroline Warfield, were preparing the food. They were busy about their work, while his niece and nephew watched cartoons. It seemed very surreal to him; all of these people were going about daily routines while ignoring the obvious elephant in the room. Finally, somebody broke the ice as Charlie was pouring himself an iced tea.

"The funeral was lovely." Caroline tried to smile. "Sandy would have loved the music."

"Oh, I agree," Barbara added. "I thought the pastor did a wonderful job. He was so uplifting."

Charlie had difficulty critiquing a funeral and felt it inappropriate. "I think she would have enjoyed the music more if she had been alive."

Suddenly, the room thickened with tension. No one dared talk for a few moments. Finally, Caroline said, "Charlie, we didn't mean we enjoyed it. Funerals are hard on everybody. The pastor has to give the family some hope, and I think he did that."

Barbara agreed. "Yes, Charlie, like the pastor said, 'God works everything together for good for those who love Him.' "

"So God did this." Charlie was incensed. "Is that what you're telling me? God killed my wife for some higher good somewhere?"

"If you're a Christian, Charlie, you have to believe that God is in control and that He has your best interests at heart." Barbara should have known better than to try to argue God with a lawyer, but it was too late. As the voices got slightly louder, Jim Davis came to his wife's aid.

"Well, if God is in control of everything, then He's brutally cruel. If He's a good God, then He somehow forgot about my family for one day," Charlie argued. "You can't have it both ways."

Jim chimed in, "Charlie if we accept everything good from God's hand, then we must accept everything bad too."

"I don't understand you people. Is God good or bad? Are you actually trying to tell me that we have absolutely no power? God is just some kind of cosmic chess master who takes pawns at will?" Charlie was getting frustrated.

"I thought you were a Christian, son." Jim tried to force the conversation back on Charlie.

"Apparently not the kind of Christian you are. A loving

God would not do this purposely. So either He isn't all-powerful or He isn't loving. In either case, I'm not sure I like the options." Charlie was getting disgusted with the conversation.

Caroline tried to console Charlie. "Maybe God just loved them so much that He wanted them to be with Him in heaven. After all, nobody could say anything negative about Sandy. Maybe it was just their time." Caroline was seriously outgunned in this type of argument.

"God loved them so much that He took them, huh?" Charlie grunted. "I guess that means God hates me so much that He destroyed my life."

"Charlie," Barbara said, "there is a bigger picture that God has in store for you. He's working everything—"

Charlie interrupted, "If I hear that verse quoted at me one more time, I am going to slap somebody up against the head. Do you know how many times I heard that at the wake and at the gravesite? What is He working? How is it good? Why did He choose me to work on all of a sudden? I wasn't bothering God. I kept all the commandments. For crying out loud, I quit drinking years ago. I am the most moral lawyer in the city. What else does He want?"

The rest of the family looked at Charlie in stunned silence. For three days, Charlie had been isolated and talked to no one about Sandy or Ashley. The first time he was with people he knew, he exploded. Finally, Caroline broke another awkward silence.

"Charlie, you are not the only one suffering here. All of us are hurting. I'm sorry if God doesn't help you at this time, but that is your fault. Knowing that God is in control gives me some comfort."

"I'm sorry for shouting. I just want some answers. So how can you explain this? Out of all the houses on this street, some stranger picked this house at random, raped my wife and killed her, and choked my daughter. Where is God in that?" Charlie asked.

"I don't know that God gives us the answers," Jim said in a conciliatory manner.

"Well, then what's the point of believing in Him? Where is

He when you need Him the most?" Charlie threw up his hands and walked out the side door. He hopped into his Blazer and headed back into the city, not sure of where he was going.

The phone on the cluttered desk rang. Rex Armstrong ground his cigarette into an ashtray and picked up the receiver.

"Armstrong here!" he growled. "Talk to me."

"He's on the move again. We're about four cars back." Bryan Paxton, the plainclothes detective, had been sitting with his partner, Kevin Schmidt, in an unmarked Oldsmobile across from Charlie's house for four hours.

"Maybe he's going to see his girlfriend." Armstrong loved prodding his detectives.

"What are you talking about?" Paxton asked.

"Well, I just found out the name of the red-haired girl from the bartender at the East Boulevard Bar and Grill. It seems that she is a regular and gives her business card out frequently. I'm going to try and track her down. If little miss ADA wants a motive, I'll give her a motive."

"So what are you thinking, boss?" Paxton talked into his cell phone as he turned a corner slowly, trying not to arouse Harrigan's suspicions.

"What I think is that this guy has a little chippy on the side who was pressuring him to get rid of the wife. They wanted to run away together. Suddenly, the guy loses his job, so they meet and discuss their plan. They decide to get rid of the family and make it look like a robbery. That's why only two things were taken. Harrigan was running out of time." Armstrong was proud of his re-creation of the case.

"So why all the violence? Why not just shoot them?" Paxton was uncertain about this theory, but did not have any alternatives.

"Maybe he thought killing them would be easy, but as he started choking her, he realized he couldn't do it, so he grabbed the lamp."

"What about the rape?"

CHUCK CHITWOOD

"I don't know, Paxton. Some couples are like that. Do I have to do the thinking for both of us? For crying out loud, you boys and that ADA live in some Pollyanna world where everybody is nice and neat and the bad guys are always bad. Let me tell you something. I've learned that everybody is capable of horrible violence if pushed far enough."

After the brief lecture, Paxton tried to compose himself and act professional, not like a chided second-grader. "So what's next?"

Armstrong said, "You stay on Harrigan. I'm going to chase down this girl after I get a hold of Harrigan's insurance company and bank. I've decided to freeze all of his assets and insurance payments, just in case he and the girl decide to make a run for it."

"Okay," Paxton half-heartedly agreed. "We'll check in later."

"All right." Armstrong ordered, "Don't lose him."

chapter
FIFTEEN

Charlie picked up the bottle of Smirnoff vodka for the seventh time. He looked carefully at the red label and the clear liquid. He tore the plastic off the top and unscrewed the cap. He did not want to lift the bottle to his lips but could not seem to stop the motion in his arm. On a whim, he had run into the liquor store after getting a pepperoni and extra-cheese pizza from Domino's. Even though he had no taste for food, he was forcing himself to eat something. For the last six days, his diet had consisted of fast-food grease and Chinese takeout. His stomached churned constantly; somehow he had reverted to his collegiate ways of dealing with stress.

The night that he learned his father would be in Hong Kong on business and would not be at his graduation, he ended up drunk in the wooded arboretum on campus. It was his first and only lapse back to the bottle after he met Sandy. Everything in his life seemed to be an attempt to please an absent father. The man who gave him the name Harrigan also gave him an incredible sense of accomplishment and drive, but none of the love and support that he really needed. Charlie had started at the open-air bar, He's Not Here, on Franklin Street and worked his way down to Hector's. He woke up with the worst hangover of his life. Now that same little demon was whispering in his ear to relieve the pressure and blow off steam.

When the bottle touched his lips, he spewed the liquid all over the living room carpet. At that moment, he wanted nothing more than a drink. He felt that the only solace he could find was in inebriated numbness, but he could not destroy everything Sandy had helped him build. After the glorious fog of alcoholic oblivion woreoff, he would still face the same situation with nothing changed. He had been sober for so long. But he knew that if he took this drink, it would be the first of many with no end in sight. If he fell again, it would be the last time. He would not stop until it killed him. This was no way to handle a problem, no matter how big. He screwed the cap back on the bottle and placed it on the dark oak mantel over the fireplace. It would remain there as an option of last resort, just in case he needed it.

Charlie looked around and surveyed his house. Sandy would have hit the roof if she had seen the mess. Five days' worth of mail littered the living room, along with several pizza boxes and Styrofoam containers of half-eaten Chinese food that had started to give off a putrid aroma. The view into the kitchen was no better. Five days' worth of newspapers were strewn about the floor. Half-empty glasses and coffee mugs were on the countertop and the kitchen table. In the entryway, shoes were scattered everywhere and clothes lined the stairs. He had tried to avoid the second floor as much as possible, so most of his clothes were piled on the steps. He had tried to sleep on the couch, but sleep was fairly impossible.

He sat on the large stone fireplace and decided to go through the mail. After all, life goes on, he told himself unconvincingly. Not just life, the very tedious and monotonous aspects of life had to go on. Did the credit card companies not understand that his wife had just died and he did not feel like paying bills? Apparently not; the bills and daily grind kept forging ahead despite Charlie's resistance.

He opened his Visa statement, which had a balance of $3,784; his MasterCard was not much better. His electric bill was about $200, and the phone was a third larger. Eventually, he reached the bill from Hartley Brothers' Funeral Home. Those guys did not waste any time. The total cost of the funeral, interment, and two caskets ended up being $10,684.32. The least these guys could do would be to round off the change, but that would be too humane. In the last paragraph of the letter, the Hartley Brothers had apologized for asking for payment, but Charlie's life insurance had denied payment of the claim. Charlie was puzzled and frantically began searching through the other junk mail.

Finally, he came to a letter from his insurance company. The police had informed them of the ongoing investigation and had asked them to suspend all insurance payouts until further notification. The company graciously apologized for the inconvenience. There were similar letters from NationsBank and Wachovia Bank. All of Charlie's assets were frozen. He had nothing to live on except his last paycheck from Hobbes, Reimarus, and Van Schank. He could cash that, but he would still simply spiral further into debt. He had no job, no access to his savings, no insurance, and no way to stop the exponential compounding of his debts.

Sitting on the floor and staring up at the bottle, Charlie realized that his only one recourse remained to clear his name. Somehow, he had to find the real killers. He could do nothing about that tonight, however. It would have to wait until morning. In the meantime, he could not stay in his haunted house one more night. Everywhere he looked, he saw ghosts. He heard voices calling for "Daddy" or "Honey," but when he looked, no one was there. He imagined Ashley calling out from her bed, "Daddy, I need a glass of water." It was the little things that stuck in his mind. He remembered the spat he and Sandy had about the ugly yellow vase on the dining room table that her crazy Aunt Sophia had given her. Why was he thinking about that? There were so many better memories he should be replaying, but they just would not come to him.

Frustrated, Charlie ran upstairs and grabbed a garment bag. He threw a couple of suits, shirts, and ties in along with some toiletries. He decided to stay in a hotel for awhile. It would have to be the cheap kind that took cash. The picture on his nightstand caught his eye: he, Sandy, and Ashley in Carowinds with the children's roller coaster in the background, which was appropriately named Scooby-doo. It was Ashely's first and last roller-coaster ride. By the end of the day, she had fallen asleep in his arms on the way back to their car. It had been a perfect day. He threw the picture in the garment bag and ran down the stairs and out the door.

He sat in his Blazer and cried again. His eyes were puffy and red, and his unshaven face was awash in saline. He decided that this would be the last time he cried for awhile. He had to do something, and becoming an amateur detective might get his mind off things. He wiped his eyes on his sleeve and started the engine. He headed to some cheap motels just across the South Carolina border off I-77. He did not see the black Oldsmobile parked down the street pull out behind him.

The condo was on the seventh floor and looked out over one of the many harbors on Lake Norman. The largest man-made lake in North Carolina had become prime real estate for young urban professionals who wanted to avoid the rapid population growth and overcrowding in the city. Melinda Powell liked the location in Davidson, built up around the Presbyterian college that had given the town its name. She had all of the benefits of small town life and was only thirty minutes from her office, except in rush hour when it took her more than three times that long.

The lake was calm and serene, making her evenings like miniature vacations. After dealing with abusive fathers, murderous boyfriends, and drug dealers all day long, not to mention the shark-infested waters of the political landscape, this was her sanctum. The biggest crime committed in Davidson in the last five years was when some honor roll college kids decided to play a practical joke and steal the mailbox from the front of the post office. It was a traumatically scandalous event that caused the expulsion and arrest of two of Davidson College's best students. That was plenty of excitement for her.

After watching the last remaining sailboat meander around the lake, she returned her attention to the file on her lap. There were at least three sets of unidentified fingerprints in the Harrigan house. But they could have been from guests or family. There were no signs of forced entry. The fact that the first floor had not been bothered at all gave her some problems. To Armstrong, this was proof that the missing television and VCR were Charlie's way of trying to make it look like a robbery. For some reason, he had run out of time to mess up the rest of the house.

Melinda was not convinced that Charlie was the perpetrator. It just didn't make sense. Their friends had reported no marital problems. In fact, they had just returned from a romantic weekend at Nags Head. Armstrong believed that Charlie snapped after losing his job. He went berserk, which would explain the disorganized crime scene, but it did not answer all the questions. Why attempt to strangle her and then hit her with the lamp? Charlie was bigger than she was, and athletic; he could have overpowered her easily. Why was the telephone cord ripped out of the wall? Maybe she was reaching for the phone after the encounter and the murderer flew into a rage. Maybe she had consented to sex in an attempt to save her life.

Even with all the unanswered questions, Guy Streebeck wanted Melinda to convene the grand jury to indict Charlie Harrigan. He was their prime suspect, and Streebeck needed a conviction. His election was just a year away, and the district attorney could not afford to have a murderer running loose. When Melinda raised the possibility that Atlanta's latest serial killer had moved north, Streebeck shut her up. He needed a quick conviction to stabilize his support.

Drug-related violence and the recent death of two police officers in a housing project had caused tremendous erosion among Streebeck's conservative voter base, which had grown to see him as too lenient. In his opinion, even if Harrigan was innocent, they could prosecute him, and if they found the real killers later, just let him go. The conviction would be front-page news for several days and that was all Streebeck needed. Rex Armstrong was an ardent Streebeck supporter, so he was not following other leads at the moment. He adopted the DA's strategy and had made peace about possibly prosecuting an innocent man.

The file contained interviews that attested to Charlie's violent outbursts. He had smashed a coffeepot against the kitchen wall at his firm. According to Armstrong, he shoved his best friend up against the wall on the day he got fired. One of the partners, Van Schank, had related a number of violent episodes and erratic behavior that led to Charlie's dismissal, including a public shouting match with a client. Charlie Harrigan was being portrayed as a man who could not control his emotions.

To Melinda, the case still stunk. It had too many holes and relied on witnesses' interpretations of a few isolated events. Such character testimony is easy to blow out of proportion in a courtroom. Simply take the five worst moments of a person's life with some inflammatory adjectives, and a monster is created. She had done the same thing on occasion when the evidence was not sufficient, but she knew the person was guilty. Latrell "Ice Daddy" Herman had been a ravenous drug dealer who used twelve-year-olds to provide drive-up window service at his crack house. When one of the boys was found shot to death, talk on the street was that the boy had been skimming some money from Latrell. All evidence against Latrell was circumstantial and left plenty of room for reasonable doubt. But after she painted a picture of this slave-driving monster corrupting many neighborhood children, the jury was not about to let him go even if he was innocent of this particular crime. He was definitely guilty of something.

It was a tactic that worked all too often, but she was not ready to use it against Charlie Harrigan. She had decided to look into matters herself. She would begin with the little old lady across the street who had reportedly seen a "big, old, blue car full of kids playing their radio too loud" that night. She would have to work fast if she were going to exonerate Charlie Harrigan. Somebody had to have seen something that night. She decided to interview the neighbors one more time and try to get a better description of the blue car. In a yuppie neighborhood full of foreign sedans and sport utility vehicles, an old-model car would be conspicuous.

Melinda made some notes on a legal pad and closed the file. She had worked enough for a Saturday night. Trying to relax, she made herself a hot chocolate and put in her favorite Humphrey Bogart movie, *Casablanca*. Since there was no realistic opportunity for romance in her life at the moment, Ingrid Bergman's troubled decision between Paul Henried and Bogie would have to suffice. By the time Bergman walked into Bogie's life again at Rick's Café American, she was asleep on the couch . . . exhausted.

After a restless night's sleep on a lumpy mattress and an ultrathin pillow at the Palmetto Motel just off the interstate, Charlie woke early. He showered and shaved. He put on one of the suits he had pulled out of his closet, a starched shirt, and a silk tie. He had decided to go to church and give God another chance. He just had so many questions. How could God bring any good out of this situation? Is God really so selfish that He would take Ashley from him because He loved her more? Does a Christian have to blindly accept everything from God's hand without question, like a mind-numbed robot?

The more questions he asked, the fewer answers he had. Charlie leaned on the bathroom sink and stared into the mirror. He had bags under his eyes and his brow was furrowed, making him look like an old man. His eyes were red and irritated. His stomach rumbled. It had been days since he had had a decent meal. Driving to the Shoney's right on the North Carolina line, he devoured a huge breakfast of bacon, eggs, grits with butter and sugar, and biscuits with gravy. He almost felt like a human again.

As he drove, the morning sun heated up the interior of the Blazer. Sunday morning was peaceful. He had missed going to church the last couple of months because he was working so hard, but he was actually looking forward to the comfort and familiarity that Sunday morning worship offered. He thought about the little white country church that his mother had taken him to in Midland. Wooden floors and wooden pews made it difficult to fall asleep as a little boy, but he always seemed to be able to.

While the preacher did get rather loud from time to time, no one could doubt his sincerity. He was not a hellfire-and-brimstone preacher, but he was resolute in his belief that contemporary culture and much of contemporary church had compromised the uniquely high truths of the gospel to accommodate popular worldviews and the fallen nature of mankind. To him, truth was simple—not easy, just simple. True Christians were few and far between; everybody else was just a spectator. Charlie could picture the old Pentecostal preacher with a handkerchief in his hand wiping the sweat and tears off his face. In his opinion, Charlie would probably be a sinner, but at least the preacher would never make him feel like one.

Charlie turned off I-77 to the 385 loop and headed toward Matthews. Just off the loop, a large glass edifice rose triumphantly over an empty field. The towering cathedral was home to the fastest growing church in Charlotte. The Solid Rock Church was one of those independent charismatic churches that were quickly replacing old-time Pentecostal churches like the one he grew up in. At nine thirty in the morning, the parking lot was packed. Slamming the door of his Blazer, he could hear the music before ever entering the building. To Charlie, it sounded like some of the concerts he had gone to in college.

Charlie slipped in the front door and into the back pew, trying not to draw attention to himself. He did not want to attract any looks or sympathy; he just wanted answers. The service was loud and raucous, much like a pep rally. After forty-five minutes of music, finally, the preacher got up to speak. Charlie had gone to church that day in the bargaining stage of the grief process; if God would give him an answer, Charlie would find a reason to move forward with his life. Up to this point, Charlie had not seriously considered ending his own life, but he had considered spending the rest of his life in his bathrobe in a comatose state of despair on the couch watching game shows.

The pastor, Billy Rae Higgins, stood behind the pulpit in what looked like one of Van Schank's thousand-dollar Armani double-breasted suits. His hair was pulled back in a pompadour and he wore shaded glasses. The man looked like a cross between an attorney and a used-car salesman. Something about the shaded glasses bothered Charlie. He thought, *Jim Jones preached behind shaded spectacles, did he not?* The preacher came out with both barrels blazing.

Reverend Billy, as his flock affectionately called him, announced boldly, "This is the year of the Lord's favor!" The crowd burst into a spontaneous throng of applause and shouts, "Amen, preacher!" "Hallelujah!"

He continued, "In Luke 4, Jesus proclaimed to the church that this was the year of the Lord's favor. If you are on God's side, you are favored by God. I get criticized for driving a Lexus and wearing nice clothes, but God gave'm to me. I have faithfully served God since I was seventeen, when I preached my first sermon, and every step of my journey, God has shown me favor. Luke also tells us that God is a good God and gives good gifts. He says if you earthly fathers being evil know how to give good gifts, your Father in heaven is good and will give you better gifts. My brothers and sisters, I am living proof! Hallelujah!"

Another round of cheers and acclamation broke out; Charlie expected to see the wave at any minute. He thought, *If God is like my father, that explains things. I guess I'm being aban-*

doned for a second time. The analogy fell short for Charlie, but he continued to listen to the orator, waiting, longing for a word of hope or encouragement.

Pulling a handkerchief out of his pocket to wipe off his forehead, Reverend Billy continued, "Now some of you have no earthly idea what I am talking about. I can see it. You're looking at me like I'm speaking French or something. Some of you don't believe. You're like my critics who don't understand.

"God has shown me what this passage in Luke means. I have lived in the favor of God all my life. I have never been sick. I had a little cold once when my faith wavered, but God has given me healthy children, a wife that is still good lookin', and blessings you could not imagine. Some of you pray for healing, but you are still sick because there is sin in your life. Some of you are in debt because you haven't given to the church. When you give to God, He will give back to you. If you're sick, get the sin out of your life! If you're running on empty this month, have more faith! Jesus said that you do not have, because you do not ask. I'm telling you people to ask God and He will open up heaven and pour out health and blessings on your life." Applause erupted into a spontaneous song of celebration. An old man started to run the aisle. A couple of ladies started to spin around at the front of the church.

Charlie sat perplexed. God was doing this to him because of his sin. What sin? He had flirted with the girl at the bar; he had liked the smell of her perfume and had briefly imagined being close to her, but that was it. He had had a few drinks, but he had just lost his job. Could God not understand that? Sure, he was not the ideal Christian, but he was no sinner. He had lost his job primarily because he would not go into a strip club. If anything, he was fired *because* of his morals.

Charlie felt more like a sinner after the sermon than he did before he walked in the church. He had gone to church for answers to his suffering and discovered that his suffering was all his fault. Either his lack of faith or his abundance of sin had apparently enraged God, and He therefore destroyed Charlie's life. Charlie could live without his job and being a successful partner, but he could not live without his family. During the final prayer, Charlie slipped out of the church back into an abysmal existence. He thought about the words of Reverend Billy Rae Higgins, "You do not have because you do not ask." So Charlie sat in his Blazer in the parking lot and asked God for answers. All he got was silence.

chapter
SIXTEEN

Room 27 at the Palmetto Motel was a wreck. The sheets were balled up in a pile on the bed. Every towel and washcloth was on the floor. The chairs were overturned and the Gideon Bible was in the garbage can. The drapes were drawn tight and the door was chained shut. Charlie, wearing his sweatpants, was curled up on the lumpy mattress. He did not want to move. Any sort of movement made the pain worse, and light made his head pound. His plan was to lie still for as long as possible.

Suddenly, there was a loud banging on the door. "Housekeeping," said the voice. Charlie tried to ignore it, but he heard the maid trying to find the right key to unlock the door. The door opened but was quickly caught by the chain. "Housekeeping, can I come in?"

Charlie threw the pillow on the floor and walked to the door. "The door is chained, or couldn't you tell? Now get out of here! I'm trying to sleep! Aren't there other innocent guests who you can bother besides me?"

He slammed the door shut and immediately heard a soft whimpering through the hollow paneled doors. Charlie grabbed a shirt and threw it on over his bare chest. He unlatched the door and ran down to Room 28. The door was open and a black woman was sitting on the bed sobbing. She was probably younger than she looked, but the effects of a hard life had taken their toll on her face. Charlie eased gently through the doorway.

"Ma'am?" he said gingerly, walking on eggshells. "I'm very sorry for yelling at you. I uh . . . I'm . . . it's a really bad time for me right now. I'm just going through some difficult things—"

His apology was abruptly interrupted as the maid's tears turned to anger. "You don't know nothin' about bad times. My thirteen-year-old boy is trying to get into a gang. I work two jobs to buy him food and clothes, because his daddy's in prison for drugs. He stands on the corner of Nations Ford Road at Yorkmont selling guns to anybody that gives him a hundred-dollar bill. This gang guy got my son in his back pocket. Calls him Little Maxie. I can't afford to buy my baby shoes, but dis vulture done bought him those Michael Jordan shoes for a hundred and twenty dollas." She slouched back onto the bed and burst into tears.

"I'm truly sorry." Charlie was unsure of what to do next. He sat down on the bed next to her but did not touch or look at her. "I know what it's like to lose your family."

She looked at him as if to encourage him to tell his story.

"My wife and daughter were murdered. The cops are blaming me. There are no other suspects. I lost my best friend, my job, and I am in debt up to my ears."

"You the guy in paper. I recognize it now. I read about you." Her glare softened ever so slightly. "Nobody could do what dey said you done."

"Unfortunately, the cops don't agree with you. Frankly, I don't think they're looking at anybody else." The awkwardness of the situation caused Charlie to stand up and pace.

"I wondered why de cops were here. Two guys been in dat big black car since I got here early this mornin' 'fore the sun came up." Charlie peeked through the curtain and saw one man in the car she was talking about. Another man was walking across the street to Krispy Kreme Doughnuts.

"That's just great." He threw his hands in the air. "Maybe I am a sinner. Maybe God is punishing me for my sin. They might as well throw me in jail. I'm already in a prison all my own."

"God don't punish nobody." Her sympathetic eyes turned back to rage. "What you talking about? God is the only one who's been with me. I couldn't trust my husband to stand by me, but God ain't never left me. Why you talking crazy?"

"So how do you make sense of it?" Charlie turned off his emotions and switched into litigator mode, grilling his witness. "According to the sermon I heard yesterday, God is allowing your son to get involved in gangs because you aren't praying hard enough. Maybe if your husband wasn't a drug dealer, God would protect your family."

"I don't know where you goin' to church, but I can't pray no harder. I pray the whole time I clean these rooms and wait tables. God, He has protected me and my family. Jail was the only thing to keep my husband from gettin' shot. He owed Big Daddy Jake money he done stole. Cops stopped him for speedin' and caught him with smack as Big Daddy was chasing him down South Boulevard. I can't make sense of it all, but I know God's in control." She stood up and returned to her work.

"How can you be so sure of Him?" Charlie asked.

She shrugged her shoulders and said, "I don't know, I just can."

He turned to leave and handed her a business card. "My name's Charlie Harrigan. Look, I am really sorry for yelling at you. I'm really glad we had the chance to talk. I haven't had a real conversation in days. If you ever need an attorney, call my cell phone number. I'm not at the firm anymore, but if there is anything I can do for you, please don't hesitate."

She smiled at him and wiped her eyes. "Thank you, Mr. Harrigan. I'm Daisy Maxwell. Maybe you can help me with my boy some day. I'll be praying for you. That ain't enough though. You can't just lay in that room feeling sorry for yourself. You won't find God at your own pity party."

"Thank you," Charlie said and walked out the door. He leaned on the iron rail and looked at the interstate. He glanced down at the Oldsmobile. He ran down the stairs and walked right up to the window of the undercover car. "Hey, guys. Look, in case you lose me, after I shower and shave, I'm going to go back to my house and systematically go to every pawn shop I can find to look for my TV and VCR. I'll start close to my house and work my way out. I'll probably eat dinner at Sonny's Teriyaki Grill, and then come back here to spend the night. Tuesday morning, I'll probably go to the DA's office to find out about the investigation." Handing them a card, he said, "Here's my cell phone number in case you lose me. Happy hunting."

Charlie smiled and ran back upstairs to Room 27. Bryan Paxton slammed his hand down on the steering wheel. Kevin Schmidt called Armstrong to tell their boss that they had been made. They waited for twenty minutes until a new team showed up, then went back to headquarters for another fruitless meeting to discuss the fact that their weekend of following Harrigan had proved nothing. There was no redhead. No money. He talked to no one. Paxton and Schmidt decided they were following an innocent man, but Armstrong warned them that if they ignored Harrigan as a suspect, they would lose their badges. Paxton suggested they split up. He would stay on Harrigan, but Schmidt would assist Charlie in the pawnshops. If they got fired, it would be for doing the right thing.

Melinda Powell stopped her red convertible Mercedes at the gas station on the corner of Providence and Sardis Road. She had spent the entire day going door-to-door in Charlie Harrigan's oak-lined neighborhood. Random murders were not unheard of in Charlotte, but in this upper-middle-class picturesque neighborhood, it never happened. The murder caused an uproar because the people who considered themselves respectable citizens of the Queen City felt that this crime had crossed over from the wrong side of the tracks. If the truth were known, a majority of the people wanted Charlie to be the killer. If he was innocent, then anyone was a potential target. If Charlie was guilty, this would be an isolated incident and they could all feel safer. The paper and local news broadcasts hounded the slothful progress of the police investigation.

The ADA, deciding to take matters into her own hands, realized that the district attorney would not approve of her free-lance investigation. So she called Guy Streebeck complaining of female problems. The DA did not want to know the details and did not ask any questions. He told her to get some rest and take as much time as she needed. Starting early in the morning, she was hoping to catch potential witnesses before they went to work. Surprisingly enough, half of the houses were already empty. Many of these people dropped their kids off at day care at seven and did not return home until six or seven in the evening. *Poor Sandy Harrigan was all alone*, Melinda thought. She never had a chance. She could have been followed from a grocery store or even the gas station without anyone noticing.

However, the Harrigans' elderly, nosy neighbor, Gilda Wurtzner, had been home across the street. She was a frail little lady who enjoyed sitting in her rocking chair on the front porch and watching everybody else's business. In the police report, she recalled an older model, large, dark blue car that was playing loud music that night. She had tried to call the police to complain, but was placed on hold. Melinda was far less intimidating and more patient than the police had been. In the midst of the conversation, Gilda remembered that the music was loud and obnoxious, like the Mexican restaurant her children would take her to. Mexican music was certainly uncharacteristic for this neighborhood.

Melinda thanked Gilda, and said she needed to be on her way. Finally, she had a break. She had looked at Sandy's receipts and noticed that she had filled up with gas at a station on the corner of Sardis and Providence about six o'clock on the night she was murdered. Melinda drove to the station, walked in the glass doors, and waited in line at the counter behind a woman who desperately needed a nicotine fix. Behind the counter was a teenage guy with a bad case of acne and a little red vest.

"Welcome to Gas-n-Go. How can I help you?" He was not

very convincing about his desire to offer assistance.

"I'm Assistant District Attorney Powell. Can I ask you a few questions?" The title was so ominous that few people ever declined her request. She placed her credentials on the counter.

Kyle Lightner told her that he worked weekdays from four to eleven. He was a freshman at Central Piedmont Community College and was working his way through school. Apparently, he had been working the night Sandy Harrigan was murdered.

"Do you remember seeing this woman that night?" Melinda held up a recent picture of Sandy. Kyle just shook his head.

"How about an old blue car? Maybe some Hispanic guys?" Melinda held her breath as Kyle rolled his eyes searching his brain.

"Yeah. There were some guys in here trying to buy some beer." When he saw the woman smile, his chest swelled up with pride. Trying to impress her further, he spoke more confidently, as if he were taking part in the investigation, "This kid was obviously not twenty-one, so I had to take his fake ID. We're supposed to turn them in to the police. I think the guy cussed me out in Spanish—"

"Where's the ID?" Melinda demanded, forgetting to be polite.

Kyle grinned sheepishly. "Can I get in trouble if I tell you something?"

Trying to be patient, Melinda placed her hands on her hips. "It depends. If the information you give me is useful, then I might be inclined to forget how you acquired this information. However, if you keep wasting my time, I may just have you arrested right now for obstruction of justice and interfering with an ongoing investigation."

"Okay. Okay. It's in the office with the other fake IDs. We're supposed to turn them in to the police. But a couple of us here keep them and sell the IDs to high school students to make a little extra money. These rich kids in this neighborhood will pay anything for some cheap beer."

"Well go get it!" she ordered.

Feeling more like a freshman than ever, he tried to look important. "I'm not supposed to leave my post. What if somebody drives off without paying?"

Melinda got right in his face and spoke softly, "Do you see this badge? If anybody drives off without paying, I'll get the license number and make sure they get the gas chamber. Understand?"

Of course, North Carolina no longer used the gas chamber, but Kyle did not have to know that. He was sufficiently scared by the power of the law, and he would have crawled on his stomach over glass to get the fake ID if she had asked him. After this experience, Kyle would be a very cooperative witness at trial, if it went that far. The name on the ID was Manuel Noriega, but Kyle confirmed that the picture was the person who asked for the beer.

She smiled to herself as she walked back to her car. Finally, a real lead had surfaced, and it was corroborated by two different witnesses. If Armstrong had been a little more diligent and not simply followed his emotions, he would have found this connection a week ago. She rubbed her hand along the hood and picked up the first yellow leaf of fall that had landed there. Summer was officially over, and winter was on its way. She hoped she could find some answers soon. She had a face; all she needed now was a name.

Horace Douglas sat in his beat-up Chevy truck, feeling completely perplexed. He had been looking for Charlie Harrigan's house for three hours. He rarely came to this side of Charlotte, but usually he was good with directions. With impatient drivers honking their horns behind him, he looked at the road signs. He sat at the corner where Providence Road crosses Providence Road West. He did not know which way to go. He wondered who designed these streets. He had been on Providence and suddenly without turning to the right or left, he ended up on Third Street. As he circled back around, he went through the intersection of Queens Road and Queens

Road West. Eventually, he passed through the intersection of Sharon Road and Sharon Lane. He decided that something happens to these city folks when they put on a tie; it cuts off the oxygen to their brain. In the early years, Charlotte's roads had been laid out by necessity, not by design, so the same road crossed itself on occasion, or one road may have three different names, depending on the part of town.

By now he was thoroughly confused and turned around. Horace pulled a quarter out of his pocket and designated a right turn as "heads." He turned left onto Providence Road and headed to Sardis. The businessman behind him yelled out the window and blew his horn like an angry teenager. Horace just laughed to see a grown man behaving like a juvenile. Finally, he found the street that the phone book listed as Charlie Harrigan's address. He marveled at the big beautiful houses in Myers Park. These houses were two and three times larger than his little white mill house. He was too old to be jealous, but he wondered if the occupants appreciated their level of comfort. He started whistling the old gospel song, *I've got a mansion just over the hilltop* . . .

He found the house number that was listed in the white pages. He pulled into the driveway behind a black Porsche. A man in a navy blue, double-breasted suit was standing at the front door writing a note. Horace got out of his truck. He was wearing faded jeans and a red plaid shirt, which had several old oil stains from working on his truck.

"Excuse me," Horace said, trying to get the man's attention. "Is Mr. Harrigan at home?"

"Why do you want to know?"

"I'm looking for an attorney. My name is Horace Douglas, and you are . . . "

"Brad Connelly." He extended his hand. "I used to work with Charlie. I haven't been able to find him since the funeral."

"It's a terrible, terrible tragedy." Horace stuck his hands in his pockets.

"He didn't do it, you know," Brad said.

"I don't think so either. That's why I've come to talk to him. Your law firm represents the man who killed my son. Now that Charlie doesn't work for you anymore, I want him to represent us. I think he understands now what it means to lose a child."

"You're the one suing Walter Comstock!" Brad was astonished. "Look, I'd like to see that guy get it myself. If anybody can do it, Charlie can."

"That's why I want him. I don't think that he really believes in that Comstock character, but if he believes in my cause, he will put up a good fight against your big firm."

"You know that they have six attorneys trying to get Comstock's case dismissed?"

"Are you one of them?"

"No," Brad backed up, "that's not my field. I do easy real estate stuff."

"Well, I need to be moving on soon. Do you know where Mr. Harrigan is?"

"I've got one more place to check." Brad looked at his watch. "It's about dinnertime. Charlie may be at his favorite greasy spoon. If you want to follow me there, you can. I'll drive slow so that bucket of bolts won't fall apart."

Horace chuckled. This attorney was harmless. "If that little matchbox car gets in my way, I'll just drive right over top of it."

The Porsche and Chevy headed against the flow of outbound traffic back toward downtown. They pulled into the crowded gravel parking lot at Sonny's Teriyaki Grill. Brad could see Charlie sitting at the counter talking to Sonny. He had spent six hours and gone to forty pawn shops without a single trace of his electronics. He would start again bright and early the next morning. He did not realize Charlotte had so many pawn shops.

About the time Sonny was pouring Charlie another cup of coffee, he heard the door chime ring as Brad and Horace entered together.

Looking at Charlie, Sonny said, "My friend, looks like you have company."

chapter
SEVENTEEN

Sonny's Teriyaki Grill was full of accountants and lawyers who needed a quick dinner before heading back to their offices for a few more hours of frantic paperwork. Something about the atmosphere made Charlie feel at home. He was in an expensive suit, and except for Sonny, no one knew who he was. The anonymity within the familiarity was comforting. For the last two weeks, his entire life had been lived in the newspaper. His victory against Johnston, the doctor's bankruptcy and disappearance, the death of his pregnant wife and daughter, the funeral, and the ongoing investigation into every last aspect of Charlie's life. The media had convicted him long before there was any evidence. Pretty talking heads with plastic smiles related the fact that Charlie was the only suspect in the murder of his wife and daughter.

He had finally found some solitude, then Horace Douglas and Brad Connelly walked into the grill. Though he would have preferred to, Charlie realized that he could not ignore them, so they grabbed a small round table by the picture window facing the street. A couple of tax attorneys had been sitting there, arguing over the latest changes Congress had effected in the tax code. Sonny's daughter came to the table and offered to take their order. Two black coffees, a patty melt, and coconut cream pie for Brad would serve as their dinners.

CHUCK CHITWOOD

Horace Douglas broke the ice. "Mr. Harrigan, I am really sorry to hear about your family. I can certainly sympathize with your situation, but I can't really begin to understand the violation and sudden emptiness you must feel."

Charlie's jaw dropped in amazement. Almost choking on his food, he looked at Horace and said, "Thank you. I mean that. You are the first person who said that he does not understand what I am going through. I mean, I know you lost your son. I'm truly sorry about those things I said in court; I was trying to do my job." Horace simply nodded as if he understood Charlie's position. "I'm sure your loss was terrible. But thank you for not saying you understand what it is like to come home one day and have your whole world shattered, your wife violated, and everything you hold dear violently ripped from you."

"I wouldn't dare say that. Our situations are very different. Mr. Harrigan, Charlie, that's what I wanted to talk to you about. . . " Horace began, but Charlie interrupted him.

"Look, if you want this conversation to be protected, you better not say a word in front of this clown. He'll go post it on the Internet. He probably has his own Web page—www.Judas."

Brad finally gathered the fortitude to open his mouth. "Hey, Charlie, maybe we should talk first and then I'll leave and you two can meet. Do you mind, Mr. Douglas?" Horace agreed and excused himself to the jukebox to see if there were any Platters or Everly Brothers instead of the deafening racket that was currently playing.

"Make it quick!" Charlie snapped and directed his attention back to his patty melt, which was the most important thing in his life at that moment.

"Okay. This is the truth. I don't care if you believe me or not, but I have to tell you." Brad sounded honest, but he sounded sincere to every girl that he hit on. "Nancy hit on me and I enjoyed it. I can't lie. For some bizarre reason, I found her attractive. She's really softened her image recently."

Charlie looked up, raising one eyebrow, and Brad realized that he was quickly losing his audience. "Here's the bottom line. I was drunk and I didn't realize she was using me. I just told her that sometimes our strengths can be our biggest weakness. You're a Boy Scout. You don't cut corners, you're idealistic, and you are a lawyer for noble reasons. You want to help people and you won't bend the law or lower your values. She took that and set you up. I didn't know anything about that. I'm really sorry, man. It's not the same without you and I'm sorry that I had a part in that."

Charlie sighed.

"Look, she did everything else. She went to the strip club to provoke you. I'm sure if you would have gone in, she would have told Sandy somehow. She wanted you off the case bad, but I don't think she was the only one. She's been spending a lot of time in Van Schank's office lately. I've heard talk that he is taking first chair if the Comstock case goes to trial." Brad was scrambling to keep this drowning conversation afloat.

"I know you probably won't forgive me now, but I *am* your friend. I know I'm a sorry excuse for one. But I really want to make it up to you." Giving up, Brad stood and walked to the door. He looked back, but Charlie was still studying his patty melt. Brad pushed the door open and walked into the darkness.

Horace gave Charlie a few moments to meditate on the conversation and then broached his concern carefully. "I won't take up much of your time. I don't think you killed your wife and I also don't think you enjoyed what you said in court. I believe that you really think our case should be heard. I read about you winning that other case against the abortion doctor, and we want you to represent us. I fired that shyster, Henry Judson."

"Why?" Charlie's curiosity was piqued.

"All he wanted to do was settle. He was pushing it on us." Horace was getting visibly frustrated. "I don't care about the money. No amount of money can replace Matt. I want Walter Comstock punished. You're the only one who can do it. You know how he operates, and I don't think you like him any more than I do."

Charlie felt as if this man were reading his thoughts. How did this old guy know that he hated Comstock?

"If you don't mind some free fatherly advice, I don't want to be condescending, but I have learned a little bit in this life." Charlie nodded consent. "The healing will begin when you stop looking inward for the answer. I do know one aspect of what you're going through. You're questioning God one day and doubting Him the next. You want to know the whys, but there are no answers. The only way to fix this is to help others and look for the answer outside of yourself. Since Matt died, I have been volunteering at a home for retarded children. I push the wheelchairs and talk to the parents. I know what they are going through. 'God, why couldn't my child be normal? Why can't he just play baseball? Why can't she just be a normal girl?' By helping them, God is helping me."

Charlie's eyes were full of tears, but he was forcing himself to hold them back. "Tell me about Matt."

Horace pulled a napkin out of the little metal container beside the salt and pepper. "Matt was mildly retarded, which means that he was just really slow. He graduated from high school when he was twenty. He was making progress. That's why we found that house in Charlotte. It gave him a sense of accomplishment and independence. He could count correct change. He could take the bus and hold down a manual labor job. He loved building stuff with me in the woodshed, so we found him a construction job. After they completed a project, we would drive around town and he would point out all the buildings that he built. He was so proud to feel like an adult. To him, *he* built the big buildings; nobody else did. He was always good-natured and sweet. He always had a smile, and at night when he said his prayers, he prayed for everyone who had teased him that day. He asked God to make everybody nice and make them understand that God loves everyone."

Both men dabbed their eyes and looked around, feeling embarrassed by their public display of emotion. Charlie hesitantly asked, "So how did he die?"

"Lung cancer." A hint of anger replaced the sorrow on Horace's face. "He went downhill in six months. The last two months he lived at home with us. He wasn't strong enough to leave the house. One day the crew he was on was renovating an old mill to turn it into condos and offices. He fell through a spot where they had dug up the second-story floor. He slipped and dropped straight through the old insulation to the first floor. He was okay, but he was covered in the stuff. I think it may have been asbestos or something. That's why it killed him so fast."

"If it was asbestos and Comstock did not take the necessary precautions, this case is a no-brainer. I wonder why Judson wanted to settle so bad," Charlie said, scratching his chin.

"I don't think he's spent much time in court. He was probably scared; your firm has hundreds of lawyers."

Charlie tensed a little. "It's not my firm. And yes, they have four hundred in Charlotte alone." He hesitated and took a big gulp of water. "You should sue them for everything they're worth. But I don't think I'm your man. I'm really sorry. Right now, I don't think I would be very effective. I'm not thinking too clearly. I sincerely am sorry. Please forgive me."

They sat in silence another minute. Finally after an uncomfortable interlude, Horace stood and said, "Please think about it. I really don't have anyone else to turn to, and I think you need me as much as I need you." Charlie shot him a curious looked as Horace walked off with his gray head hung down and his chin in his chest. Charlie watched him climb into the old pickup with dents and rust spots on the fender. He did not realize that Horace was praying for God to comfort his heart and change his mind. Charlie sat like a statue and stared out the window until all the businessmen had returned to their offices and he was alone.

The club was dark and full of cigar smoke. The Hunter's Club was the oldest private country club in the city. Although it did not exclude blacks from membership, every member seemed to be white, Protestant, and extremely wealthy. The thirty-six-hole golf course designed by Arnold Palmer surrounded a clubhouse that was reminiscent of a medieval feudal castle. The billiard room could be reserved for private meetings, and Martin Van Schank enjoyed conducting business here, drinking brandy, smoking Cuban cigars he had obtained illegally, and playing pool.

A dark mahogany wainscoting circled the room, and shelves of antique books and first editions lined three walls. The fourth wall contained stuffed heads of wild animals killed by club members. Several multipoint bucks and even a few bison were symbolic of the fierce nature that it took to arrive at the Hunter's Club. The only women allowed in the place were the waitresses. They were tastefully dressed in miniskirts and tuxedo jackets. One such waitress racked the billiard balls again so the three men could play cutthroat, which seemed an appropriate game for Van Schank, Comstock, and their third silent partner.

It was highly unethical and illegal for attorneys to be in business with their clients. Van Schank's name appeared on one contract, which was locked away in a safe-deposit box. In all other documents and contracts, he was referred to as the silent or secret partner. Their third partner had a similar concern for privacy and knew that if he were found out, he would lose everything.

After the waitress left, the men got down to business. Van Schank slowly pulled back his cue and scattered the balls, sinking two high stripes. The point of cutthroat was to clear the table of the opponents' balls while keeping as many of one's own on the table as possible. Undercutting and sinking opponents had been the secret to their success.

"The city is going to zone more of Graham Street for condos and private apartments. They are intent on pushing crime out of the downtown area, and they think if enough yuppies move into that northeast section behind Discovery

Place and the I-Max theater that more private security firms will help force out the trash." The other partner related the specifics of the latest closed city council meeting.

"How can you be so sure?" Van Schank questioned.

The partner took another drink of brandy. "Have I ever been wrong? The city council is a bunch of robots. The council is far more concerned about other things, and they will trust me on this one. The only foreseeable problem is the possible appearance of impropriety."

Van Schank was the leader of the unholy trinity. One had the muscle and the other had the connections, but Van Schank had the brains to make it work. Van Schank was concerned. "I think we need to stop meeting like this for awhile. We need to stay out of the public eye. It's a good thing we got rid of Henry Judson. That trial would have focused too much attention on Paragon Group. We need to keep our future communications to cell phones just to be safe."

Taking a huge puff on his cigar, Comstock asked, "So what's the lowest bid so far? How much is this one going to set me back?"

"What does it matter?" the partner sneered. "Whatever it is, you're not paying the whole thing. Thompson Brothers' bid was eight point four million in six months."

"I can't tear down all those old warehouses and build condos in six months," Comstock huffed.

"You idiot!" the partner snapped. "Don't you get it yet? We make money on both ends. When we go over time and over budget, we just pocket the rest. We'll have that much extra interest from the money saved to repay the overdrawn account."

Comstock slammed his pool cue on the green felt and got in the partner's face. They were nose-to-nose. Comstock barked, "Don't you dare call me an idiot! You owe me your life! I should have let you die in the jungle over there."

They were snorting and shoving when Van Schank stepped between the two to take a shot at the cue ball. "Gentlemen, do we really have to do this every single time? Walter, go take a drink and calm down."

"I've got the most exposure here. I have more to lose."

"I understand, but nothing is going to happen." Van Schank was on a roll, five balls in a row. "If you two would just worry about your own parts, I will take care of the rest. We will save money on manpower. One of my guys in the Atlanta office just told me about a carpet mill that is closing in Dalton, Georgia. We've rented a truck to ship all the illegals up here. They'll work for one hundred dollars a week. We will save thousands on payroll and invest it offshore. We'll draw up some dummy payroll records and show a loss. Voilà! I foresee an easy two to three million cleared off this deal. Capitalism is a beautiful thing!" He sank the last of his opponents' balls and laughed. "Boom! You're dead!"

chapter
EIGHTEEN

The morning sky was overcast, and rain was imminent. Charlie thought that maybe Providence was teasing him with the knowledge that at any second he would be soaked in the deluge. At this moment, it seemed like a trick that God might play on him. Of course, God was probably not so petty as he imagined, but it seemed to fit the pattern of his life in the last few weeks.

For the first time in several days, Charlie decided not to put on a suit. He had determined that trying to act normal did not provide him any comfort at all. Quite the opposite, the pretense of normalcy made him that much more pathetic. Dressed in blue jeans, hiking boots, an L. L. Bean flannel shirt, and a light Carolina blue windbreaker, he drove to the west side of the city. He had effectively combed the pawnshops on the east side and was now moving west into Fourth Ward. The north and south seemed less likely targets, so they could wait until later.

He drove through parts of Charlotte that he had never seen before. He had been in the city ten years and had never been to these neighborhoods. Out of curiosity, he headed to Nations Ford Road and Yorkmont, the streets mentioned by the cleaning woman at the Palmetto Motel. On the northwest corner was a liquor store. On the northeast corner was a gas station with several older black men walking around with brown paper bags wrapped around bottles. On the southeast corner, two rough-looking women, one white and the other black, smoked cigarettes. Finally, on the southwest corner was an abandoned building with large sheets of plywood covering the windows and the front door hanging off the hinges.

Three young black boys sat on the steps listening to music. Charlie guessed that one was Little Maxie, Daisy Maxwell's son. Why were they not in school, he wondered. He made a U-turn to take another look, but this only raised the hopes of the two women at making a quick twenty bucks. He decided to park at the gas station and purchased some stale coffee and hard doughnuts for brunch. He kept his eyes on the three boys as he was paying for his food. Sure enough, he watched as a beat-up Grand Prix with tinted windows pulled into the parking lot and stopped. One of the boys ran up to the car and took something from the driver. He darted up the steps, and in a couple of minutes, the boy returned with a briefcase, which he handed to the driver, who quickly sped off. No doubt Charlie would hear of another drug-related murder on the news tonight.

How terrible, he thought. That poor woman worked two jobs. She rarely saw her son and had little power to stop him from becoming a career criminal. He watched for a few more minutes and saw two more cars drive up. To these cars, the boys brought only small brown bags. Charlie assumed that these were drugs. Perfect, the one-stop gun, drug, and hooker shop. What a world.

It did not take long for Charlie to find what he was looking for. At the fourth pawn shop in a Hispanic neighborhood, Big K Pawn, Charlie was walking through an aisle of used VCRs when he stopped dead in his tracks. He saw a Sony four-head VCR just like his. It had the same scratches on the display where Ashley had hit it with a little metal car. The meticulous perfectionist pulled from his back pocket the insurance papers that contained all the serial numbers to his electronic equipment. The numbers matched.

He grabbed the VCR and searched frantically for the television, but did not find it. He ran to the counter. An obese lady in a flowered dress and a hair net sat on a small stool that must have been incredibly well built to handle the load. She was polishing a double-barreled shotgun. He set the VCR on the counter and pulled out a wad of cash and a business card from Hobbes, Reimarus, and Van Schank.

"I'm an attorney working on a case." Placing a twenty dollar bill on the counter, he said, "Do you keep records in that computer there of who sold you the equipment?"

She was unfazed by the fact that he was an attorney. "Have you heard of the Right to Privacy Act? You can keep that puny little twenty."

Puzzled, Charlie said, "It has nothing to do with what you do for a living."

"How 'bout the right to bear arms?" she snarled.

"Which I can see you are a strong advocate of." Frustrated, he continued, "Look, I have reason to believe that this VCR was stolen, and I need to find out who sold it to you."

"Look, pretty boy!" She stood up and was at least five inches taller than Charlie. "You got two choices. You can buy the blasted VCR or you can leave here in an ambulance. I run a legit business and I don't mess around with no lawyer types. You understand?"

"Fine. How much?" He was down to his last roll of twenties.

"Four hundred bucks!" She plopped back down on the stool that creaked but did not give way.

"That's outrageous!" He slammed the countertop, shaking everything on it. "A new one doesn't cost that much."

"Son, have you heard of supply and demand?"

"I don't have four hundred dollars." He tried to look vulnerable, hoping maybe that would work.

"What do you have?" she smiled.

Charlie counted out two hundred seventy four dollars and eighty-seven cents. It was all the money he had to his name. The rest was frozen by banks and insurance companies.

"There! You happy?"

"Yes, I am. We're having steak tonight." She stuck the money in her bra and went back to cleaning her gun. "You have a pleasant day now and do come back. We have some golf clubs. I'll make you a good deal."

Charlie ignored the hacking laugh and went to his Blazer. He tried to get through to Armstrong, but there was no reply. He decided to head back downtown to the Law Enforcement Center. He turned off of Trade Street into the parking garage. As Charlie entered the building, the officer who had been following him all day walked up beside him. Bryan Paxton took him to a conference room and took a statement and the VCR into evidence. After four hours of waiting, Paxton and Kevin Schmidt obtained a subpoena for the computer records.

Charlie rode in the backseat of the police car as they headed to the pawn shop. He felt odd looking through the wire mesh that separated the front and back seats. After wrangling with the cops to no avail, the large woman acquiesced. In five minutes, they learned that Umberto Callabro had pawned the VCR for fifty dollars eleven days ago. They also learned his address. The apartment complex was not far, just off West Boulevard. An elderly woman with several young toddlers running around her frail legs answered the door. Callabro was not home. He was already in jail for shoplifting.

The three men headed back to the Law Enforcement Center and then to the Mecklenburg County Jail. Umberto Callabro was waiting arraignment for shoplifting a hundred dollars' worth of compact discs from a store at Eastland Mall. The twenty-two year old was a petty thief who worked as a part-time bookie for cockfights and fenced stolen merchandise for the poor Hispanic section of town. He refused to answer any questions. Finally, Paxton told him that they might erase the charges if he would tell them how he got the VCR. Callabro agreed. Things were finally starting to look up for Charlie Harrigan.

* * *

The phone rang at eleven thirty that night, startling Melinda Powell out of a deep sleep. She had been finishing up some paperwork on her couch, and the fatigue and exhaustion had overwhelmed her. When the ringing shattered her peaceful dreams, she awoke disoriented for a moment. The police officer on the other end of the phone told her that they had caught an individual who had some information that she might find useful, but he wanted a deal before he said a word to anyone. She tore off her pajamas and threw on a smart-looking suit with few buttons that hung on the back of her closet door for circumstances just like this when she needed to get dressed fast.

Jose Florez was seventeen years old. His father was an illegal alien who worked on different farms in and around Mecklenburg County, and when he was at home, the father was usually drunk and abusive. The children of the growing number of illegal aliens dropped out of schools at early ages and took minimum wage jobs. For fun, companionship, and protection, they joined gangs. The Diablos or Devils was the Mexican gang that had recently joined the foray of violent gang activity in Charlotte. The Jamaican gangs specialized in trafficking cocaine through Charlotte from Miami on its way to New York and Memphis. The Diablos' specialty was heroin, among other forms of larceny.

The Diablos had a strenuous initiation process that consisted of two parts. The first part was the gauntlet. The initiate walked through the entire gang while they punched and kicked him. If the person took the abuse without crying or asking them to stop, he proved himself tough enough to be in the gang. The second part was more dangerous. The initiate had to prove he had the guts to break the law. There were two choices. He could either carry out a hit on an enemy of the gang, which usually resulted in drive-by shootings, or else he could get himself a real woman. In other words, the gang member would pick out a woman at random and rape her, thereby "proving" his masculinity.

Jose Florez decided to join the gang because of the amount of teasing he was subjected to because of his accent and inability to read English. When he dropped out of school, he decided to retaliate against the entire world. He did not really want to rape Marianne Hurst. After a couple of beers, the three guys in the old blue Dodge parked and strolled through Eastland Mall picking out Marianne for no particular reason. They followed her home. Jose followed her at a distance from the parking lot, but as she opened the door, Jose bolted up the stairs and pushed her inside the condo. With a switchblade at her neck, he forced her back to the bedroom. As he shoved her on the bed, he did not notice the small box she grabbed off her nightstand.

Marianne pressed the panic button and a shrill alarm pierced the air. Jose panicked and punched her in the face, giving Marianne an awful black eye. He bolted out the door to see the blue Dodge tearing out of the parking lot. An overweight private security guard responded to the alarm. He drove a little golf cart. The cart caught up with Jose, who could not make it over the eight-foot-tall privacy fence. The police were there in six minutes.

The shaken but grateful victim made a positive identification of Jose Florez before she was taken to the hospital to have her face X-rayed. The cops immediately booked him for attempted rape and battery, then he told them that he had information they might want. However, he had seen enough American television to know to ask for the district attorney to cut him a deal. The seventeen-year-old kid sat stoically in the interrogation room smoking a cigarette and trying not to show how scared he was. This was the third cigarette in an hour and a half of waiting for the DA. The door opened and Melinda Powell walked calmly and confidently into the cage with the wild animal.

"I hear you have something to say." She pulled the chair from under the table and sat across from the potential rapist.

"You the DA?" he growled.

"I'm the assistant district attorney." She handed him a card. He immediately threw the card on the ground.

"I want the DA! I don't want to talk to no woman!" He folded his arms and leaned back on the two rear chair legs.

Melinda stood up slowly and walked to Jose's side of the table. In one swift move, she grabbed the chair and held him perilously close to falling, then whispered in his ear, "You're a big man, aren't you? You're so macho you rape innocent women to show just how tough you are. Just wait until I throw you in prison with a whole bunch of men who haven't seen a woman in fifteen years. I know a couple big fellas named Bubba and Duke who will love your lean, thin body and your smooth, dark skin. I don't care about you and I wouldn't lose one second of sleep if I threw you to the wolves. The DA doesn't want to talk to you. I'm the last person who's going to listen to you, and you've got five seconds to start talking or else you're going to get what you were about to give that nice lady and nobody's going to care." She could bluster and bluff as well as any of the men who worked in the DA's office.

Jose was sweating and visibly shaking as the front two legs of his chair landed on the floor with a loud thud. It echoed in the little chamber. "Okay. I'll talk," the teenage voice cracked. "Just don't send me to jail."

"I can't guarantee that." Melinda tried to keep from laughing. She never saw herself as the tough guy, but she was adept at playing the role. "It depends on whether or not you give me something good."

A tear started rolling down the cheek of this streetwise kid. "I didn't want to hurt her, but it was an initiation for a gang. My friend joined the Diablos a couple of weeks ago. I just wanted to be like him."

Melinda nodded her approval so he would continue his story.

"Anyway . . . he comes to me a few days ago and shows me the newspaper. Says he's famous now. He's all bragging about it. That lawyer's wife that was killed. He had just gone to get her like the rest of the guys in the gang. They tried to buy some beers and spotted her. They followed her back to her house. He followed her inside and forced her upstairs with a knife. He sent the kid away, but then the wife started fighting back. He tried to choke her but ended up smashing her head. He killed the kid too, because she was a witness. That's how he got in the Diablos."

"Does your friend have a name?" Melinda tried to remain calm.

"What do I get?" Jose folded his arms, feeling the renewed sense of power.

She thought for a second. "I want you out of the gangs. I can reduce the charge and send you to this little boot camp up in the mountains. You're seventeen, so I charge you like a kid and seal your record. When you've done one year at boot camp, I have your record expunged, so it will look like you never committed a crime. The catch is that you have to give me the name, testify in court, and promise me to stay away from gangs forever."

"Sounds cool to me." Jose breathed a sigh of relief. "Enrique Alvarez."

chapter
NINETEEN

At times, the judicial process can move at a rapid pace. Enrique Alvarez was sixteen years old and was sitting in a conference room with his public defender, Delbert Watkins, after spending the day in the county jail with drunks, drug addicts, and wife beaters. The predawn raid on the apartment that Alvarez lived in was nothing less than spectacular. Guy Streebeck had tipped off the media and orchestrated the entire raid to maximize his political exposure. The lead story on each local news broadcast that night would be the arrest of a suspect in Sandy Harrigan's unsolved murder. Twenty police cars with flashing blue lights surrounded the building. Camera crews caught the whole thing on tape.

Bryan Paxton and Kevin Schmidt wore black windbreakers with "Police" printed on them in bright yellow letters. Underneath, each one wore a Kevlar vest. They banged loudly on the door twice yelling, "Police! We have a warrant!" Before Juanita Alvarez's drunken boyfriend could get up from the couch, the battering ram shattered and splintered the flimsy wooden door. The flashlights mounted on the assault rifles cut the darkness, sending everyone into a panic as the cops pushed Ms. Alvarez and her boyfriend to the floor. With little kids screaming in Spanish, the cops took fifteen seconds to find Enrique's room. The shouting startled him out of a deep sleep, and he awoke to find flashlights blinding him and the barrels of three assault rifles pointed at him.

The picture of ten armed police officers in full battle gear escorting one sixteen-year-old to a squad car seemed like overkill. But it made for beautiful footage. Guy Streebeck and Rex Armstrong held a press conference in which they took credit for the swift arrest in this unsolved multiple murder. Streebeck bragged that his intuitive investigative techniques had discerned that this crime was gang-related all along. Charlie was exonerated with no apology or remorse. Then Streebeck related how crime statistics had dropped during his term as district attorney and that he was developing a new task force to fight gangs in the Queen City.

Finally, Streebeck ended by declaring that Enrique Alvarez would be tried as an adult and that they would seek the death penalty. He vowed that nothing would prevent him from using the full force of the law to bring justice to this situation. Armstrong followed the DA with a detailed description of the arrest and thanked the officers who had worked so hard to track down the criminal. No one would ever know that Charlie Harrigan and Melinda Powell did the legwork that gave the cops the breaks and snitches that they needed to catch Alvarez.

Delbert Watkins had the unenviable job of being a public defender. After graduating from East Carolina School of Law, he sold shoes for eight months to pay off student loans. There was an overabundance of lawyers in a market that was already saturated. He was a third-rate student at a second-rate school. He was the soft, pudgy type and looked more like an accountant than a lawyer. He wore off-the-rack suits and polyester ties and still drove his Honda Civic. He took a low-paying civil servant job to do something, anything, in his field of study.

He hated his job and despised the people he represented. They were scum, derelicts, and the refuse of humanity that God had forgotten. They injected chemicals into their veins, they beat the ones they claimed to love, and they killed each other for the most banal of reasons. He wanted them to go to prison; he would feel much safer if every single one of his clients was either behind bars or six feet under. But he was still practicing law. If he stayed in the trenches for a couple of years, he would apply for a position in the DA's office when something opened up. His approach to defending the indigent was simple. Plead them down to Class D felonies and get them a couple of years. He refused to work past five, and he did as little research into his clients' lives as possible, because nobody really cared.

He sat across from Enrique Alvarez and found it hard to believe that this baby-faced teenager had killed two people. Alvarez was stoic. He showed no emotion and looked at nothing. The dingy, pale white walls seemed to be closing in. The only color in the room came from the metal conference table and chairs, one of which Enrique was handcuffed to. Years before, a defendant had been handcuffed to a wooden chair. He had ripped a leg off the chair and attacked an attorney for no apparent reason. Delbert knew this and felt a little nervous, but he made a conscious effort to breathe slowly and smoothly.

"Enrique, I don't think there's much I can do for you." Delbert swallowed hard. "If you plead guilty to manslaughter, breaking and entering, and robbery, you will probably do ten to twenty years, but at least you won't die."

"I don't want to go to no prison, man." Enrique glared at his attorney. "I didn't do nothing. You got the wrong guy, you pig."

"Look kid, I'm your attorney. That means I'm on your side. I don't like it any more than you do, but the DA has two witnesses against you. You bragged about killing the lawyer's wife to your friend, Jose. Two Diablos were arrested yesterday, and they're going to rat you out and plead to misdemeanors. The fence that you sold the VCR to is prepared to testify. Everybody's out to get you. You better accept this deal." Delbert fell back into his chair and ran his fingers through his curly hair.

"I can't go to prison, man." A hint of desperation came from Enrique's voice. "I'll act crazy or somethin'." He cocked his head like a chicken and started howling like a dog.

"Shut up, kid!" Watkins yelled and then hoped that his client would not attack him. "Insanity rarely works. This is not television. It's real life! Why don't you accept the deal? The jury's going to nail you."

"Look, man. There's five people in that car. Me, Tino, Kiki, Juan, and Jorge. Anyone of them could've done it. It wasn't me." He tried to look innocent and vulnerable. For a second, it almost worked. He could be very convincing pretending to be an innocent, misunderstood poor kid. Watkins caught himself thinking that he might be able to win with this kid. This case could propel him into the spotlight. For an attorney, any publicity is good, because there will always be people on both sides of the law. More fortunes are made from the unscrupulous people trying to wiggle out of something than from the righteous trying to defend the truth.

"Well," Delbert gave up, "it's your funeral, but if you want to go to trial, we'll do it. I'll put you on the stand and you can tell your sorry story, but nobody's going to buy it. It's your word against theirs. But I'll tell you what. If you can keep that innocent baby face during the whole trial, you may have a shot. But I'm not promising anything."

"I'll take my chances." Enrique leaned back in his chair and crossed his arms.

Charlie slept until noon that day in his cheap little motel. Daisy Maxwell brought him a couple of doughnuts and coffee as she was making her rounds. He was sucking the cream out of the center of one of the doughnuts and listening to his arteries harden when the anchorwoman on the news said that there was breaking news in the Harrigan murder. He watched intently as a perky reporter stood outside a run-down apartment complex on Rozzelles Ferry Road flashing her million-dollar smile.

"I'm standing in front of the Windsor Court Apartments where the police made a predawn raid, arresting sixteen-year-old Enrique Alvarez, who is now in the county jail and charged with the unsolved murders of Sandy and Ashley Harrigan. District Attorney Streebeck has assured us that Alvarez is being charged as an adult and the death penalty will be pursued vigorously. Mrs. Alvarez refused to talk to us, and Charlie Harrigan was unavailable for comment."

He was actually laughing. In a fit of uncontrollable emotion, he fell back on the bed and laughed. Finally, justice was done. It was the only good news he had heard in three weeks. He desperately needed to smile. He decided to get involved with the case. Charlie brushed his teeth and put on jeans and his favorite ivory sweater. He laced up his brown leather hiking boots and started out the door to the DA's office when he heard the perky reporter continue with her coverage.

"In our continuing coverage of this story, we have been asked to announce that Reverend Billy Rae Higgins is holding a candlelight prayer vigil tonight to help put a stop to the violence in this city. Reverend Billy, why are you doing this?"

The preacher cleared his throat and played with the little gold chain that held his tie in place. "Violence has become a blight on our city. The rampant sin in Charlotte has brought God's judgment down. So we are having a time of prayer and repentance to put an end to the violence. I would also like to announce that we are receiving gifts and contributions to help the Harrigan family in this time of need. So just make your checks out to Reverend Billy Ministries and I'll make sure that the money gets where it belongs."

"Thank you, Reverend Billy. I will be following this story all the way through the trial, so stick with us. Back to you, Susan." She smiled and tilted her head ever so slightly.

Only one thing could have taken the joy out of this moment, and Reverend Billy Rae Higgins had done it. Charlie stared at the big-haired preacher with shaded glasses and became furious. He did not ask for their help and did not want their money. According to the gospel of Billy Rae, Charlie was a sinner, or at least an unfaithful Christian. He walked over to the television and kicked the little table that supported the nineteen-inch screen. It wobbled and eventually fell over. The cord pulled out of the wall and the television hit the floor, cracking the picture tube and setting off small sparks. Charlie thought, *Too much television is bad for you anyway.* He walked out the door.

Thirty minutes later, Charlie pulled into a parking garage off of Fourth Street. The place was full, but Charlie finally found an empty space on the fifth level. He got out of his Blazer and had a wonderful view of the skyline. Back in high school, he and his friends would drive into the city at night and park at the top of these garages to make out with their girlfriends. Back then, there were only five or six towers. Now they were popping up everywhere. Charlie looked at the tallest tower. The NationsBank building was by far the tallest; it was the crown of the Queen City. He used to stare out his window looking down on the world far below. Thirty-nine stories above the earth, he seemed to be above the problems of the plebeians. His dream had been to gradually move higher and higher. Now he was king of the plebeians.

It was an intoxicating dream that, at the time, seemed to overshadow everything else. Yet suddenly, his dream seemed incredibly shallow and superficial. His dreams now had become far more practical. If he could just turn the clock back three weeks, he would have spent more time with his family. He would have stayed away from Walter Comstock when Reimarus made him that ridiculous deal. Maybe he would have quit his job and worked out of the house. If he had been there, things would be different. Maybe they would not be . . .

A chilly, late September breeze caught his face. He folded his arms and headed downstairs and across the street into the big triangular-shaped, pink granite city building. The city council definitely leaned toward modernizing Charlotte, instead of following more conventional styles of architecture. At the security guard's desk, he called Melinda Powell's secretary, who immediately invited him up to her office.

The office was much smaller than his office had been. A row of metal file cabinets lined the wall behind the desk. A set of metal shelves containing legal books and binders went all the way to the ceiling. There were two wooden chairs in front of the desk. Apparently, the rank of assistant district attorney did not merit the perk of glamorous furnishings. The place was functional, not fashionable.

"Charlie, please come in." Melinda rose and pointed at one of the uncomfortable-looking wooden chairs. "I've been trying to contact you, but your phone seems to be disconnected or something."

He folded his hands in front of him and looked out the window in the general direction of the NationsBank building. "I've been trying to keep a low profile. I haven't been home in weeks to pay bills or anything. I guess they cut off my service. Let me give you my cell phone number; I have kept that current now that my assets are unfrozen. Anyway, I want to help. What I mean is that I want to help you with the Alvarez trial. It has to be unofficial, I know, but I really want to feel like I had a part in nailing him."

"You did!" Melinda tried to encourage the man who seemed as if he were lost and trying to find his way. "You found the VCR and brought in a solid witness. We're giving Callabro a slap on the wrist. He pleaded to misdemeanor larceny, and got three years' suspension for his testimony against Alvarez. That's a big help."

"Sure, that's wonderful. But I want to be in on the case. Even if you just need some extra research or you want to have an audience to practice your opening arguments. Your office practically destroyed my life. I think you owe me something."

She rolled her eyes in consternation. "First of all, that was Guy and Armstrong who were pushing so hard. They've been watching too many Sunday night movies or something. They wanted a quick arrest and Guy wanted to protect his electorate. Do you remember when that saleswoman from Oregon was shot in the back at the University Hilton while she was here for a convention? Nothing like that had ever happened at University Place, but it was just another random gang initiation. Businesses pulled their conventions out of Charlotte, the city lost money, and Guy almost lost his office. They don't want gangs. In all honesty, they wanted you to be the killer."

"Gee thanks. That's what I really needed to hear." Charlie frowned.

"Second, if I may finish, please." She was somewhere between being sympathetic and frustrated. "I never believed you could do something like that. I've seen you in court. Your professional ethics are too high to be for show. You have to believe it and live it. I spent my nights and days off trying to clear your name. You will probably never get an apology from Guy, so please accept mine."

Charlie slumped in his chair, wishing he could just hide behind it. "I'm sorry; I didn't realize that. I'm not quite in control of my emotions these days. Please forgive me."

"Don't worry. I deal with people in terrible circumstances every day. Unlike some people here," she nodded to the office across the hall, "I'm not just climbing the political ladder. I care about the victims, and I try to help whenever I can. Now about your offer, I guess I could find you something to do. Since you're still unemployed, I guess you have the time."

Charlie grinned to acknowledge his unfortunate employment situation.

The assistant district attorney outlined the entire case against Alvarez. They were going to throw a myriad of charges at him to make sure something stuck: two counts of capital murder, sexual assault, burglary, breaking and entering, and murder in the perpetration of a felony. Most of these charges were to impress the jury with the weight of the crime. Melinda had tried to make a case with Streebeck to charge him with three counts of murder since Sandy was pregnant, but he wisely convinced her not to make a slam dunk case a political nightmare by obscuring the issue. She could fight abortion on her own time, Streebeck told her.

Melinda would open with Charlie Harrigan. The grieving husband and father would be an image that no attorney could counter and no jury would forget. She thought she might even be able to win with him alone, but she was not about to count on it. She needed a sympathetic jury. Then she would put up the fence who bought the VCR and television from Alvarez. Although the television was still unaccounted for, it was not necessary. They had arrested Tino and Kiki on some accessory charges, but she was willing to drop the charges to misdemeanors if they gave up their friend. They had been in the county lockup for only six hours. After three days, they would break. The other two accomplices could not be found. They were probably illegals and headed down to Atlanta or up to Richmond. They would find a new gang and continue where they left off.

The star witness was Jose Florez. He would be the last to testify, and he would make a tremendous impact on the jury. The Saturday night after Enrique made it into the Diablos, the two had stolen a couple of forty-five-ounce cans of beer from a gas station. They were drinking them out back of the store beside a Dumpster. Alvarez had looked in a trash can and pulled out a copy of *The Charlotte Observer*. Holding it up, he bragged about being famous and being a real man. It was at this time that he talked Jose into joining the gang. Jose had run the gauntlet barely flinching. But he was scared and intoxicated when he attacked the young lady. Now he was scared of jail, and he was convinced that the ADA was his best friend in the world. She got him a cell by himself and a television. She brought him pizza to keep him happy while he was waiting to testify.

The prosecution's case should take no longer than three days. Most prosecutors made the mistake of getting caught up in details and forensics that the average juror does not understand or care about. Speed and rhythm are the keys to success. All she had to do was to tell a reasonable story and assign blame. Her jury would probably be half white and half black. They would know the story already; they just needed somebody to blame. She was giving them Alvarez on a silver platter.

chapter
TWENTY

Fourth Street was a one-way that headed north into down-town, past the east side of the Mecklenburg County Courthouse. Nine o'clock workers would be late because of the traffic jam. On the west side of the courthouse, the outbound Third Street was silent. News vans had parked on the side of the road, taking up one lane of traffic and creating a blockage in the artery. The green lawn in front of the courthouse was covered with cables, cameras, and pretty people primping, while each one was waiting for the accused. Each police car that passed under the covered walkway caused a hush that quickly diminished when they realized there was no news.

The trial was still months away and this preliminary hearing for Alvarez was strictly for show. A series of typical, yet useless, motions would be heard. Dismissal, reduced charges, release to own recognizance, and a lowered bond were all doomed to fail miserably. No elected judge would be so lenient on an accused double murderer who was a considerable flight risk; it would be political suicide. Besides, judges have families too, and they do not want killers on the street any more than anybody else does.

The parking garage was full, so Charlie had parked at the Adam's Mark Hotel just south of Marshall Park. If he got towed, he was within walking distance of the police station. He was not worried. He darted across Morehead into Marshall Park. His black suit, blue shirt, and red power tie made him feel somewhat normal. Just a few weeks ago, he had stood in this court wearing his lucky tie that he wore at the beginning of all trials. The lush green grass of the park and the gold, orange, and deep burgundy leaves on the trees had a calming effect. The morning had been chilly, but now the sun's rays heated up everything in their path. He felt good. He felt normal, somewhat. He finally had a bright spot in his walk through Hades.

He knew this was just a preliminary hearing that would take fifteen minutes at the most. He laughed at the army of reporters crowding the front lawn all saying the same thing. For Charlie, this was the day that God would begin executing His justice. Even the heavens agreed. The sun had burned off the past few dreary and misty, overcast days. Maybe God would finally do something on Charlie's behalf. He wished that North Carolina still used the gallows. Lethal injection seemed like such a peaceful alternative for such violent criminals. There was actually a spring in his step. As he came to the courthouse, he climbed every other step to the door.

The lobby was buzzing with activity. Occupying its benches were a variety of vagrants, deadbeat fathers, future divorcees, and small-time drug dealers. Paralegals puffed their last cigarette on the steps outside before spending all day checking titles in the clerk's office. Security escorted the media to the third floor, where criminal court was, and Charlie followed in behind the parade.

The courtroom was sleek and modern. The gallery consisted of beige theater-style seats. The two tables in front of the bar were natural wood color that fit the minimalist decor. The jury sat in two rows in a small box on the right side of the room, and a three-tiered edifice rose in the front. Clerks and stenographers occupied the first two tiers, but the third tier was reserved for the judge, flanked by the American flag on the right and the North Carolina state flag on the left. It did not inspire the same fear and reverence that the federal courthouse on East Trade

Street did, but it was ominous in its own right. The empty, minimalist feel left very few places to hide. The clean, straight lines made the room appear much larger than it was.

Charlie stood at the double doors and scanned the crowd. Every seat was full. Fortunately, all cameras had to wait outside on the lawn, but the reporters sat in the back row with their cell phones in hand, balancing laptop computers on their legs. He spotted Melinda Powell sitting at the right-hand table. When she glanced around the room, she caught Charlie's eyes and waved him forward. His stomach was upset and nervous. He had not eaten breakfast that morning because he did not want to see it a second time. After all the waiting and not knowing, the judgment day had arrived. Melinda pointed at a row of chairs behind the table that backed up to the bar.

"I checked with the judge to make sure you could sit here," she spoke in a low tone. "How are you holding up?"

"I'm ready. I want you to throw his rear in jail. I'll lead the parade when he takes that walk down death row."

"We've got a long way to go to get there. Guy told me to take second-degree murder and life if they offer it. So don't get your hopes up." Her conciliatory manner was an attempt to calm his nerves. "I know you want this; just be cool. Remember, I'm the prosecutor here. You're a witness and still a member of the bar, even if you're unemployed. Just keep a low profile. The last thing we want is some kind of mistrial."

Taking a deep breath and gripping the chair tightly, he said, "Okay, I'm just . . . it's just that this is important. Justice is the only thing I have left. The only bright spark in my miserable existence is that the guilty one will get what he deserves. You're my only hope, Melinda."

"Thanks, Charlie." She rolled her eyes. "I didn't have enough pressure with the cameras, my boss breathing down my neck, and a violent murderer who may have friends bent on revenge. Knowing that you're placing your last remaining shred of hope in life on this trial is just the right amount of pressure I need."

"I'm sorry." Charlie realized that she was as serious as he. "For a litigator, I haven't been too good at expressing myself lately. What I mean is that I really need this to make sense, to give me a hint of resolution, to know there's a God somewhere, anywhere."

"I understand, Charlie. Believe me, I know how important these trials are for victims. I have convicted worse offenders with less evidence. Don't worry. This is a marathon, not a sprint. The case will still take weeks after today, so don't invest too much in this proceeding." She turned back to her briefcase and pulled out a yellow legal pad, scanning her notes for the seventh time in the last two hours.

Standing in front of the cameras, Delbert Watkins cleared his throat and ate up his fifteen minutes of fame. He wore khaki pants, blue blazer, and a tie with some sort of mud brown stripe. Only a public defender would dress in such a haphazard way to appear before a superior court judge. The reporters, desperate for anything, swarmed around Watkins like sharks going after raw meat. Watkins loved it. His purpose was to use this sudden spotlight to catapult him into private practice.

He swaggered and blustered in front of the camera without really saying anything. He talked boldly about the Constitution and a sound defense being the right of each citizen. He disassociated himself from the criminal, saying that his was a constitutional calling for the people and that his client was presumed innocent. He sounded like a person who had watched too much "L. A. Law" as a teenager. Every legal cliché dripped from his mouth, but he sold it. He would go home, watch the news, and then start advertising in the Yellow Pages as "former public defender as seen on TV."

Delbert paused to collect his thoughts and then went into his defensive mode. My client has been falsely accused. They caught the wrong guy. There were four other people in the car and one of them was the actual murderer. No eyewitnesses came forward to pinpoint my client at the crime scene. Finally, his last big gun was the race card—prejudice. People who speak broken English are railroaded through an unfair system that they do not understand. He was on a roll. Of course, he knew he would lose the case, but he sounded good. He walked away from the cameras imagining the offices of Delbert Watkins, Attorney-at-Law.

"Sit down!" The gavel slammed on the judge's wooden podium. Judge Lorna Jefferson was far too practical to wait for everyone to rise while she took her seat. The spectators were barely out of their seats when she commanded them to sit back down. The middle-aged black woman with thick, black-rimmed glasses had a reputation for being a no-nonsense judge. She had a strict interpretation of the law. She always gave the maximum sentence under the state's sentencing guidelines. Police could not stand her because she was a stickler for due process and individual rights. She wanted justice, but she refused to live in a police state where cops run roughshod over the Bill of Rights.

As a thirteen-year-old girl, she had accompanied her father to the fast-food counter at Woolworth's in Greensboro. When they were refused service, the very first sit-in began. Lorna had grown up with heroes who defended civil rights and who were willing to violate civil rights to accomplish equality. After receiving a minority scholarship to Wake Forest University and then Wake Forest School of Law, she vowed to end racism and injustice in both extremes, liberal and conservative. She resented whites who thought that Wake Forest lowered its standards for her, and she resented blacks who accused her of denying her people and wanting to be white.

When a young black boy thought that calling her "sista'" would give him a break because she understood institutional racism, she hit the ceiling. Not only was he sentenced to a boot camp-style training school until he received a diploma, but he was also charged with contempt for calling her "sista'," and was given two hundred hours of community service in a drug rehabilitation center. Then when the white district attorney let a giggle slip, she slapped him with contempt. He spent one night in jail and had to appear before the North Carolina Bar Association before he could try another case.

Prosecutors and defenders feared her equally. The only ones who loved her were the people, and they were the only ones she felt responsible to. Many people thought she was a good candidate for a federal judgeship, but she never really showed an inclination to leave Charlotte. She had no real desire to punish white-collar criminals and tax evaders; she wanted to improve the life of the average person. For Lorna Jefferson, the Constitution was a fiercely personal and practical document. In her office on one side of her law school diploma was a copy of the Bill of Rights and on the other was a copy of the Ten Commandments.

"Ms. Powell." The judge put down her pencil and removed her glasses. "I believe this is your show. I have the charges before me. Do you have anything new to add?"

"Your Honor." Melinda rose in her fitted, red two-piece suit. She refused to try to wear women's suits designed like men's clothing. She wanted to look feminine, unlike her radical feminist counterparts who stayed with dark colors and straight lines. She placed her fingers lightly on the table. "Only this. The People would like for you to deny any sort of bail. This is a capital crime and the defendant is a considerable flight risk. He is not in school and has no job. We think it would be very irresponsible for the court to take that chance."

"I don't need a lecture on responsibility. I raised two daughters who are both attorneys, worked forty hours a week processing tobacco, and went to law school in my spare time. I know about responsibility. I just need the facts. Is that all, Ms. Powell? Hmmm." Her face showed neither frustration nor anger; it was simply a matter of fact.

Melinda nodded and carefully sat down, trying not to make any noise or draw attention to herself.

"Mr. Watkins," the judge swiveled quickly in her leather chair, "please stand." Watkins was startled and he bounced out of his chair. A few reporters snickered at the display as his body was still jiggling. "I hear you've been trying your case in front of the cameras already."

Watkins started, "Well, actually, Your Honor—"

"I'm not finished." Silence permeated the courtroom, and all eyes were on Watkins to see if he dared open his mouth. She let him hang for a few seconds before continuing. "As I was saying, where I'm from, trying your case in front of the cameras before going to court is seen as extended jury tampering. Is it your intention to plant thoughts in the minds of potential jurors who might be watching the evening news? Hmmm."

Watkins gulped hard and looked unsure whether or not he could speak. When she said nothing, he quietly began to explain, "Actually, Your Honor, I was just answering a few questions as I was coming to court. I couldn't even get through the crowd of reporters. The only way to get around them was to answer their questions."

Judge Jefferson looked over his head into the gallery. "All of you reporters do me a favor. The next time Delbert Watkins comes near you, please make an opening so he can make it into the courtroom without any impediment." The gallery muffled their laughter, knowing she would throw them out into the hallway and laugh about it later with her clerks. "Now, Mr. Watkins, neither side is to talk to the media. This investigation has been covered enough. Let's keep the trial in this room. Hmmm."

She paused, waiting for nods from both tables. "Okay, Mr. Watkins, the floor is yours."

He shuffled papers and tried to regain his composure, which was badly shaken from her first salvo. "I have a motion to dismiss here that I would like to show you—"

"Denied. Next." She took her pen and made a check mark in her file.

"Your Honor, his mother needs him at home. She's on

welfare and he does odd jobs to help support her."

"What kind of jobs? Hmmm."

He furiously looked through papers, legal pads, and file folders.

"Denied. If it were that important, you wouldn't have to look it up. Next."

"We would appreciate it, Your Honor, if you would reduce bail to ten thousand dollars. His mother could afford the five percent to go to a bondsman. Enrique is desperately needed at home."

"Isn't his mother living with a man she is not married to? Hmmm."

"Well, ah, sort of—"

"Denied. Shacking up is not a healthy environment for young people to learn good moral values. I'm denying bail of any kind. Now sit down." She put her glasses back on and ran her pen up and down the file as if searching for something. Then she looked at the ADA. "If that is all of the preliminary motions, I am setting the trial date for December 1, and I'm blocking off two weeks on my calendar. Is that enough time, Ms. Powell?"

"Yes, ma'am," Melinda agreed, realizing that her chastisement was just for appearances of fairness and was not personal.

"Mr. Watkins?" The judge glared.

Watkins was already shaking his head before she looked at him.

"If that is all of your business before this court today, then we will stand—"

Her gavel was in midair when the double doors burst open. A long-haired Hispanic man in an olive suit was walking and digging into a briefcase making all sorts of noise. "Your Honor, Your Honor. If it may please the court—"

"Young man," the judge was furious, "this building better be under nuclear attack for you to barge into my courtroom and disrupt this proceeding."

The man stood anxiously behind the bar as every eye peered at him with curiosity. "Counsel for the defendant, Your Honor. May I approach the bench?" She waved him up and told the rest of the lawyers to remain in their seats. The reporters were looking at each other in amazement. Preliminary hearings never have any fireworks; most attorneys could do this in their sleep. The judge and the young man gestured and spoke quickly back and forth. Wide eyes and furrowed brows accentuated the staccato exchange. The judge nodded and motioned for the man to take a seat to the left of Alvarez.

"Go ahead," she gestured ambiguously, "introduce yourself to the court and make your motion."

"Your Honor. My name is Hector Calderone. I work for the Free Legal Clinic representing clients who cannot afford to hire attorneys. Enrique Alvarez is one of my clients. I defended him on a previous drug charge. I ask that this case be dismissed, because my client's Miranda rights were violated. When they asked if he wanted an attorney, they should have contacted me and not just given him a public defender."

A collective gasp went through the courtroom. The gavel slammed immediately, quieting the response to the sudden revelation. Sandy's family, the Davises, looked at each other incredulously. Alvarez looked back and forth between his two attorneys, bewildered by the turn of events. Charlie's jaw dropped and he forced himself to remain seated. Melinda, initially dazed, quickly regrouped and jumped to her feet.

"Your Honor, the State requests a recess. Please." She tried to hide her desperation, but it was impossible.

"There will be no need for that, Ms. Powell." The judge caressed her gavel and looked around. She spoke slowly and deliberately. "Mr. Calderone, I appreciate the work you do for the needy and the self-sacrifice that is involved. I do want to tell you, however, that we do not do things that way in my courtroom. If I ever see you again, you better be on your best behavior. I don't appreciate your turning my courtroom into a circus. In light of this new information, though, I must agree with you. Mr. Alvarez's rights were violated when he was arrested, and in light of that fact, young man, you are free to go. However, Mr. Alvarez, let me admonish you. God has seen fit to give you a second chance at life. Don't mess it up. Get a job. Go to school and get out of the gangs. I'll be looking out for you, and if I ever see you in this court again, you'll be sorry. Court dismissed." The gavel slammed.

chapter
TWENTY
ONE

The courtroom was in chaos. Judge Lorna Jefferson stormed down the steps and out the door behind the bench to her private chambers. The reporters started dialing their cell phones frantically and rushing out of the courtroom to find their cameras. They tried not to look anxious, so they walked with a rapid gait. Jim Davis stood and started shouting, "You can't let my daughter's murderer go free! This is insane!" The deputy sheriff struggled to restrain him.

Barbara Davis and Caroline Warfield hugged each other and wailed loudly. Delbert Watkins' head was spinning. His fifteen minutes of fame were over. He leaned against the table with his hands thrust deep in his pockets and watched Alvarez being led out of the courtroom by his new former attorney. Melinda Powell was close to hysterics. She rushed to the clerk, grabbed the transcripts, and pushed her way into the hall behind the bench. She banged on Judge Jefferson's door, but there was no response.

In thirty seconds, the courtroom had cleared out. The news would wait for no one. The clerks and stenographers packed up their briefcases like it was any other day. The bailiff secured the doors that led to the holding area, the jury room, and the judge's office. Charlie sat defeated. He was alone again. No justice. No hope. No answers. He was still sitting on the row directly in front of the bar and behind the prosecution's table. His elbows were on his knees, and his head was in his hands with his fingers woven through his hair. Life could not get any worse.

Charlie was in shock. The thug who killed his wife and daughter just walked out of the courtroom a free man. They had more evidence against him than O. J. Simpson, and he still he got off on a technicality. In the blur of the predawn raid on the Alvarez apartment and the quick arraignment, the police failed to realize that Alvarez had been arrested a year earlier with two nickel bags of heroin. He apparently had been holding them for his mother's boyfriend, Pepe Hernandez. When he learned of the arrest, Pepe had sent the attorney from the free clinic who had represented him on several drug-related charges.

Hector Calderone was a brilliant attorney who graduated first in his class from Virginia School of Law. He moved to Charlotte to be with one of his heroes, a civil rights legend from the sixties, Sidney Weinstein, who fought for the underdog. The clinic represented all kinds of underprivileged and disenfranchised people who were being oppressed by the white, wealthy, corporate-owned democratic process in America. To them, every cop was dirty and every judge was prejudiced. Hector pleaded Alvarez to a misdemeanor, and as a minor had his record sealed. Technically, the cops were clueless to this fact, but Alvarez, being just sixteen, did not realize he already had an attorney. Once again, Calderone had successfully vanquished the tyrannical power of the enemy, and he and Weinstein would have a couple of beers after they closed the clinic to celebrate.

Charlie was astonished. How much could one man take without cracking? It simply was not fair. The bad guys go free and the good guys get punished. He stood slowly and felt his head swimming. Nausea hit him again. He had not thrown up in six days and finally felt like he was pulling things back together. Now this. He stepped up to the prosecution's table. Melinda was still trying to track down the judge, but she had left in such a hurry that all of her files were still open on the table. Charlie flipped through the Alvarez file one page at a time.

On the right side of the file was a daily activity log. Each person who viewed the file signed his name on the log and noted what action he had taken. On the left side was the actual case in chronological order, with the arrest record on the bottom and the responses to Watkins' motions on top. Charlie came across one interesting page as he looked through the file. Alvarez and his mother were illegal aliens. Their father brought them across the border six years previously and had followed the seasonal work around the country. He had picked oranges in Florida, worked in carpet mills in Georgia, harvested peaches and tobacco in South Carolina, and most recently worked construction in Charlotte, where he had died.

The lawyer wheels in Charlie's mind started spinning. If Hector Calderone found out, he would call in the feds. The INS would pick up the Alvarez family and deport them before Melinda would have a chance to perfect an appeal. Only one recourse remained. Charlie had one shot at justice. He was determined to make things right. He ripped a sheet of yellow paper off Melinda's legal pad and grabbed her pen. He copied the Alvarez address out of the file. He looked around the room. The two clerks left were talking about college football and did not notice Charlie was still there. He folded the yellow paper and stuck it in his coat pocket. He ran out of the courtroom and down the stairs.

Charlie headed out the rear entrance of the courthouse and crossed Third Street back to Marshall Park. The sky had become overcast while he was in the courtroom. It was almost noon, but it looked more like dusk outside. He reached his Blazer. There was a fifty-dollar parking ticket on the windshield. He crumpled up the ticket and threw it on the ground. He squealed his tires and swerved onto Morehead, almost hitting a Volkswagen. He headed uptown and parked illegally in front of NationsBank. He ran in to use the ATM. He took out the maximum two hundred dollars. As he returned to his

Blazer, he took the second parking ticket and threw it on the ground. Charlie sped off and made an illegal left turn onto Trade Street toward the west side.

Nancy Lockman-Kurtz was tucking her shirttail back into her skirt as Martin Van Schank poured them a couple of champagne cocktails. They had briefly discussed Comstock's latest successful bid and had arranged for more cheap labor from Dalton, Georgia. Van Schank did not love Nancy, but right now he needed her, and because of his relationship with her, he was forced to share some of his dealings with Comstock. However, he did not tell her the extent of his involvement. She had always been unethical—that is what made her a great attorney—but she had never done anything blatantly illegal. After today, she would be a criminal.

She had been willing to take a few chances to reach the heights of the legal profession. In two weeks, an official ceremony would take place welcoming her as the newest and youngest attorney to ever become a partner at Hobbes, Reimarus, and Van Schank. It had cost her greatly to get there. She had slept with two other attorneys and at least one Fortune 500 client. Finally, the realization hit her that she could procure the same type of entertainment from several unscrupulous establishments and bill the client for the costs under the heading, "Miscellaneous Legal Fees." She thought Martin Van Schank was different. He seemed to care about her. Their encounters were not sordid, but simply convenient. They had been on vacation to Cozumel and Belize from time to time, and he continually promised her that the divorce was coming, but something always stood in the way. She could wait to marry him. Her divorce was at least two years away. Right now, business was her main priority. To Nancy, that is what the law was—a business. It was a way to make lots and lots of money and she was very good at it. The only one better seemed to be Van Schank.

Van Schank brushed his hair straight back in place and

pulled his suspenders back over his pointed shoulders. He looked out the window and thought briefly.

"What are you thinking?" she cooed.

He pivoted slowly on his heels and looked at her out of the corner of his eye. "I was just wondering how much I could trust you. Now that you are going to be partner, you will be privy to information of a more, how shall we say . . . sensitive nature."

She pulled her legs underneath her and sat up attentively. "Martin, I care about you more than anyone else. You can trust me."

"Yes, yes. But you've had several trusting relationships in the last couple of years. Do you trust them the same way you trust me?" These barbs were wonderful little ways of keeping control of the relationship.

"That was business. This is romance." She tried to pout, but it did not work. She was too cold-hearted to be wounded by the truth.

"I need people I can trust implicitly. I would hate to destroy you should you ever feel the need to betray me." Suddenly, his joking tone became very foreboding.

"Look, if you have some scheme and you need an assistant, I'm yours. I live in the gray areas, so nothing you say can shock me." Her eyes were dancing, and he knew she was on his side.

"Ever since Burchette left, I have needed a litigator to assist me. He left a huge void, and not just because of his size. He was a gross specimen of humanity, but he was a twisted genius. Hobbes, Reimarus, and I keep our dealings separate for a purpose. I have some clients they know by name only. Oliver Burchette was my confidant and kept my name out of the spotlight. That Boy Scout Charlie would never have made partner. He's a straight arrow. You see, the law is not set in stone. Men, who keep changing their minds, wrote the law. Take prohibition, for example. One day it's illegal to drink and the next it's perfectly innocent. I need someone who is willing to take risks in those areas." He paused to take another drink.

"Did you hear about the guy who killed Charlie's wife? Got off on a technicality." She was actually grinning.

"Poor sap." Van Schank exhaled. "It just doesn't pay to do the right thing. Justice doesn't work that way; the law is a farce. But . . ." He put a finger on his chin and started back to the window. "But we can use it to our benefit. If you will be faithful to me, I'll make you rich beyond your wildest dreams. Call your secretary and have her bring the Paragon-Graham Street file up here. I'll show you what I mean."

She flitted around the office like a cheerleader, not realizing the unholy alliance she had just made. Something had happened to her at Duke School of Law. Her first semester she was a die-hard feminist who chose the law to level the playing field between men and women and stomp out sexual harassment. Then a senior gave her a copy of the final exam for her Wills and Estates course during her spring semester. The competition was so difficult that she took it. Two of her classmates turned to drugs, and one attempted suicide. The backstabbing was rampant, and this senior was willing to provide her with answers in exchange for a relationship. She was a legal genius in her own right, but this gave her the edge she needed to reach number one. He actually got her on the Law Review at the beginning of her second year. She learned quickly that her gender could be a weapon or an obstacle.

As the sun set, a chilly wind swept in across the city. Clouds gathered quickly, blocking out the light. It would be a starless night, blacker than black. Charlie wrapped his dark trenchcoat around himself tighter. The heater was on full blast, but the Blazer was still cold. The windshield wipers slapped the droplets out of the way so he could see. He sat in the parking lot of the convenience store on the corner of Yorkmont and Nations Ford Road. On the opposite corner sat a vacant building. Charlie spun the radio dial until he found some blues on the public-supported jazz station. He was waiting for the sun to complete its descent so darkness would provide some cover.

As the drizzle intensified, he decided that sitting in the parking lot might be too conspicuous. He decided to circle the block and watch for any cops or innocent bystanders. His fingernails dug into the steering wheel, leaving little crescent-shaped indentations as he thought about Enrique Alvarez. That punk kid killed his wife and daughter for no reason—just to get into a gang. He violated his wife. He destroyed Charlie's pristine paradise in one swift moment. They had followed Sandy from the gas station. He had jumped out of the car and probably forced her into the house as she was going in the side door entering the kitchen.

Charlie circled the block. His heart was racing as the thunder began to rumble. There were no hookers, no drunks, no homeless wanderers. As he passed the vacant building for the third time, the door opened and two little black boys leaned against the doorjamb. He cut left across traffic and skidded into the gravel parking lot. The tall, lanky boy ran up to the window.

"You Little Maxie?" Charlie tried to sound tough, but these kids actually intimidated him.

The boy shook his head and ran up the steps. The shorter of the two ran to the Blazer. He was cute. He was a little boy trying to hide behind a big scowl. He would be right at home playing with GI Joes or a water gun, but he was lost. He was in a grown-up world playing with real guns. Charlie took a deep breath and pulled a bill out of his left pocket. The portrait of Benjamin Franklin was spread grotesquely across the new currency. He handed it to the boy, who did not smile and did not say a word.

Lightening popped somewhere close, startling Charlie. He looked out the rear window. He checked for cops and witnesses, but he was alone. As he turned back to the driver's window, Little Maxie was there, startling him a second time. He was drenched, his white T-shirt clinging to his body, and he held a briefcase. Charlie pushed the little silver button and the window rolled down. The boy shoved the briefcase into the window and ran back in the building. Charlie slammed on the gas, spraying wet gravel along the side of the building. He raced along Nations Ford Road to Interstate 85. He headed south at breakneck speed, going nowhere in particular.

Adrenaline coursed through his veins, and the rain was torrential. He pulled off on Woodlawn Avenue and drove into the car wash behind the Texaco. He found safety from the rain and relative privacy. He placed the briefcase on his lap. Opening it slowly, as if it contained a bomb, the glimmer of blue metal caught his eye. It was a simple .38 caliber revolver. The gun was heavier than he had imagined it would be. Actors wave them around effortlessly on television, but the real thing is cumbersome. Beside the gun was a box of Black Talon bullets. The last attorney general had gotten the hollow point bullets outlawed because she convinced the world that there were safer bullets already on the market. He put six bullets in the chamber and waited.

He pulled his alligator skin wallet out of his back pocket and flipped through his pictures. Sandy was gorgeous. Her eyes danced and her smile sparkled. She had always hated having her picture taken, and as a result, Charlie had relatively few pictures of her. The picture in front of him was taken on their honeymoon in one of those little booths at the beach where the machine takes four snapshots for a dollar. It was now his most precious possession. Even so, pictures were so one-dimensional. She had been his best friend and now he was alone. A clap of thunder shook the metal roof, and he flipped to the next picture.

He turned to Ashley's picture—riding her first horse. She had been scared of the beast at first, but after they trotted around the corral, she began laughing. Her face was the angelic perfection of innocence and light. Tears streamed down his face uncontrollably. He wiped his face with his sleeve, but it was immediately wet again. He would never again rock her to sleep. She would never jump into his arms when he walked in the door after a hard day. Her smile would never eradicate everything black and ugly about the world he lived in.

chapter
TWENTY
TWO

The deluge continued throughout the evening. Charlie drove through puddles and streams of water. The heavens had opened up and poured their wrath down to the earth below. Charlie meandered his way through the back roads and eventually found his way to Windsor Court Apartments. He parked in a clearing behind the apartment complex where people dumped their trash along the privacy fence. The fence was falling apart. He stuck the gun in his belt and climbed out of the Blazer.

He was immediately soaked to the bone and the aired chilled him. His shoes sunk two inches into the sloppy mud. The blackness was shattered sporadically by flashes of lightning. The darkness and the rain comforted him. He was sure no one would be looking out a window during such a horrible storm. He had driven by earlier, before the rain's strength increased. Little black and Hispanic kids had been running freely all over the complex, so he was thankful for the rain. At least the elements seemed to be on his side.

He had thought this through. He could claim posttraumatic stress disorder and no jury would convict him. After all, the world would not mourn the death of Enrique Alvarez. In fact, the world would probably cheer. No one would miss him. His life was worth little compared to Ashley's potential or

Sandy's benevolence. Of course, Charlie did not care if he went to prison. He had no reason to think he would have any sort of meaningful life now anyway. God had taken the best things from Charlie, so he had nothing to lose.

As Charlie climbed through the fence, his heart pounded. He weaved through apartment buildings, looking for G6. Finding it, he sneaked around back. His rage was uncontrollable. Apartment G6 was on the first floor. Charlie peeked in the window. A Hispanic man with no shirt and a dragon tattooed on his shoulder was holding a baseball bat in one hand and a bottle of beer in the other. Charlie watched. He must be the boyfriend, Pepe Hernandez. The boyfriend drained the bottle of beer and threw it wildly across the room. He was yelling in Spanish.

Charlie moved carefully to get a better look. Enrique Alvarez was curled up on the couch. The boyfriend grabbed the bat with both hands and swung with all his might, smashing Enrique's rib cage. His mother was crying and grabbed her boyfriend, who threw her off into the wall, shattering a mirror. Charlie was gripping the gun tightly and cocked the hammer. He watched . . . confused. He hated that kid, but for a second, a flash of sympathy raced through his heart. Enrique gathered his strength to defend his mother and exploded off the couch to attack the boyfriend. The screaming could not be heard over the torrential rains. The bat connected with Enrique's jaw. His mother was bleeding but pulled herself up and ran back to the bedroom. Apparently, this was a common occurrence in the Alvarez household.

Rain washed the tears off Charlie's face. He could not do this. He released the hammer and suddenly felt a tug on his trenchcoat. He spun quickly, knocking someone down. He pointed the .38, and then his eyes focused. The little boy was no older than six or seven. He yelled, "Please don't shoot!" in between cries and wetting his pants. Charlie collapsed to the ground. He was sobbing profusely. "I'm sorry! I'm sorry!" Charlie was sincere, but the little black boy did not care. He ran for his life. Charlie gripped the mud and cried out to God for help. He was not a killer. He was hurting. He needed help. He stood slowly and let the rain wash the mud off his face.

Suddenly, a gunshot eclipsed the thunder, echoing through the apartment complex. Charlie looked in the window and could see only the mother, holding a small-caliber pistol. Dogs began barking and doors started opening. Porch lights and outside lights came on all over the complex, and suddenly Charlie was exposed. He stuck the gun back into his belt and ran toward the fence. He tripped and fell twice in the slush and mud as he made his escape. He rushed through the broken fence, scratching his face on a rusty nail. He climbed into the Blazer and sped off. He was covered in mud, and tears from his eyes mingled with the blood on his cheek. He headed south to Lake Wylie to get rid of the gun and realized for the first time just how close he had come to taking a human life. Nausea hit him again.

The storm blew out to the Atlantic during the night. Rays of light pierced the clouds and glimmered off the wet pavement. The ground was quickly collecting red, orange, and yellow leaves as fall marched headstrong into winter. Charlie had fallen asleep on his couch. In terror and panic, he had returned to his house after hearing the gunshot at Windsor Court Apartments. Exhausted, emotionally drained, and scared, Charlie had fallen into a deep sleep. The brightness of the sun disturbed his blissful slumber. He slowly sat up and stretched.

He was covered from head to toe in mud. It was caked to his wrinkled trench coat, his Giorgio loafers, Armani suit, and silk shirt. The ivory couch was stained and probably irreparable. He retrieved a plastic garbage bag from the kitchen and stuffed his clothes in it just in case. He looked at the couch. Sandy would hit the roof twice if she could see the disarray her *Southern Living* show home had become. He took a shower and decided it was time to fix some things. He would start with the living room, then pay bills, and then hire professional cleaners who could get mud out of the couch and blood out of the carpet.

The water streamed down his face, washing off the mud and caked-on blood. He looked in the little Sharper Image mirror attached to the shower wall and shaved for the first time in two weeks. The stubble had started to itch and it frustrated him. That is why he never grew a beard; he could not persevere through the scratchy phase. He stepped onto the bath mat a new man. This water was cleansing, somehow washing away the evil that had gripped him the day before. He looked up and thanked whoever had intervened to keep him from crossing that line, the point of no return. Maybe Sandy was watching him, maybe it was God after all. At this point, there was no way to be sure who was watching, who cared, and who did not. All he knew was that he was exceedingly thankful.

He turned on the tiny television in the bathroom and the morning news was showing live video from a very familiar spot. Charlie turned up the volume as he brushed his teeth. The reporter flashed a smile at the camera and attempted to look genuinely sorrowful, but it did not work.

"Susan, police officers tell me that a domestic dispute led to a murder here at the Windsor Court Apartments last night."

"Excuse me, Kim. Isn't that the home of the young man accused of the Harrigan murders?"

"Yes, Susan," she replied, tossing her hair. They had rehearsed the perfect questions to ask, but they looked believably spontaneous and insightful. "Yesterday afternoon, Enrique Alvarez was released on a technicality. This morning he is in the hospital in a coma with several broken bones and his mother's boyfriend is dead."

"Kim, is there any indication that a distraught family member was trying to get revenge after the charges against Alvarez were dropped?"

"Well, Susan, the police are not answering any of those

questions at this moment. But the Harrigan case has gone unsolved for three weeks, and now the alleged killer is released. I guess that the drama isn't over yet. Back to you, Susan."

Charlie turned off the television and decided that it would be best to head this off and not wait around for the police. He would run by the district attorney's office and run a couple more errands. He had to make some things right in his life. He had to start living again, in spite of the pain. He had to make sense out of his survivor's guilt and grief.

He dressed casually, jeans and a lamb's wool sweater. It was not cold enough for a jacket, but the blistering summer heat had given way to brisk autumn days. It would be a perfect day to play football. He had spent many fall afternoons, like this, playing football with Chris Lemont after classes. After they started dating, Sandy would be a regular spectator on the sidelines when she had finished her lab work in the graphics department in the journalism building. He grabbed his car keys and wallet. On the floor, he noticed a little, purple butterfly hair clip. Ashley had been wearing them the last time he saw her. He stuck the clip in his pocket. He thought of her smile and the way her *l*'s sounded like *w*'s. He smiled and thought, *Minute by minute, I can do this.*

Melinda's desk was covered with case books, legal codes, and Supreme Court reports, opened to every case dealing with Miranda rights. The Alvarez file was strewn over a folding metal card table that doubled as a workstation for cases she was trying. A secretary, who had difficulty walking around in the small office, and a clerk, who had formed a crush on the ADA, were pouring through cases trying to find grounds for appeal. Enrique Alvarez was a free man, and the only way to charge him was if the police found new evidence completely separate from anything found while Watkins was representing Alvarez.

All of the evidence that had been obtained while Alvarez's rights were being violated by not having his first lawyer present was like poison. None could be used in court. Not finding anything that would help them, Melinda Powell finally decided to give up. She ordered her helpers out of the office. She had not slept all night, and everywhere she turned she found dead ends. There was no legitimate way to touch Alvarez. Of course, where he was, he could not hurt anybody, but that did not satisfy her.

She was losing. First, Dr. Owen Johnston skips the country with a twenty-year-old nurse and goes to play on a beach somewhere. Now a cold-blooded murderer swaggers out of the courtroom as if he were royalty. Justice was taking a major hit in the Queen City. While Streebeck and the other ADAs seemed to be more concerned about politics, she seemed to be fighting the bad guys alone. Was justice such an antiquated notion? Had the Warren Court destroyed the legal system in this country? At what point do the victims have rights equal to the accused? She sat on her desk and looked out the window.

A courier in a gray uniform appeared in the doorway with a package. "I'm sorry to interrupt your meditation or whatever. This is the Audio Central delivery. You need to sign for it."

"Thank you very much. No interruption. Hopefully this will make my day. I need a break."

The tape was a digitally enhanced reproduction of the phone call from Emily Turney, Johnston's nurse, to Remmie Fox, her former roommate. Melinda had a hunch that with a name like Remmie, she might have a file. The former dancer turned cosmetologist had a couple of arrests for possession of a controlled substance and solicitation. She was more than willing to help Melinda and record her phone calls, but so far there had been only one. The sound technician rerecorded the tape using several different channels. The background noise was enhanced and the level was raised, while the actual conversation was lowered. Melinda placed the tape in her little boom box sitting on the windowsill. She closed the door and listened intently. There were bells, horns, birds, and crowds of people speaking a melodic foreign language that was difficult to discern but sounded something like Spanish. There was nothing unusual on the tape, and the Spanish language "narrowed it down" to over two thousand miles of coastline.

There was a barely audible, gentle knock on the door. The stoop-shouldered, dark-skinned cleaning lady wanted to empty the wastebasket. She was whistling a lilting tune that made it impossible for Melinda to hear, and she was about to sternly rebuke the well-intentioned cleaning lady when the little woman turned and said, "Isn't Creole the most beautiful language?" Her eyes were closed and a big smile was on her face. "Every time I hear somebody speaking my native tongue, I am twenty again with my husband, dancing on the beach near Bayeaux before he was killed in the riots."

Melinda jumped off her desk, startling the poor little woman out of her dream state. She grabbed and hugged her miracle. "You understand this?"

"Of course. It's Creole, but there's a little Spanish in it. There is a little bit I that don't understand. In Haiti, we have mostly French influence, but further south the Creole is mixed with Spanish or Portuguese."

Melinda's eyes started to sparkle. "That narrows it down to a couple of islands. Guadeloupe or Martinique. Well, what are they saying?"

"It's several different people, saying different things."

Melinda closed the door and offered the cleaning woman a seat and a Diet Coke from her tiny refrigerator.

"Would you mind listening to this tape and telling me everything . . . everything no matter how insignificant?"

"Sure. If that's what you want." The lady was confused, but rather enjoyed being noticed by one of the bigwigs.

She listened hard, trying to be as helpful as possible. "Well, it begins by saying . . . 'I love you, too. I'm sorry, let's never fight again.' They fade out, I can't tell, but the next people say, 'Come on, man. One-shot deal. You got to take it.' 'How much we talking?' 'Not here.' "

Melinda had nothing useful yet and was about to lose

hope. There was one distinct conversation left on the tape. The lady continued. "The man says, 'I'm so glad we came here. Cayenne is so beautiful. Maybe we should charter a boat for the afternoon and sail around the harbor. Whatever you want, my sweet.' "

"Where's Cayenne?" Melinda rifled through her drawers, desperately searching for an atlas. She searched frantically over every island and inch of coastline. "French Guyana. Where is that?"

The cleaning lady smiled. "It's on the coast between Brazil and Suriname. It's a beautiful land, not spoiled by too many tourists. I visited family there once. My ancestors were brought over as slaves and scattered all over the Caribbean."

"Thank you. Thank you," Melinda said profusely. She hugged the cleaning lady again until the little woman complained that Melinda was hurting her. She finally had a break and things were looking up.

The cleaning lady opened the door to leave just as Charlie was poised to knock. Melinda invited him in and shared her good news about Dr. Owen Johnston. She had identified the city where he was hiding, and now the only question was whether or not he had moved on. Charlie hated to rain on her parade, but he carefully shared his intention to avenge his wife and daughter.

"I really didn't do anything" he groveled apologetically. "I bought the gun illegally and had planned on using it, but I couldn't go through with it. I saw what happened. Then I drove to Lake Wylie and threw the pistol in the water."

Melinda had seen many grieving spouses in her life and understood the need for revenge. "Charlie, there's really no need to share this information. The cops pretty much figured out what happened. There's no mystery there. Pepe Hernandez has a long track record. Prosecuting you for a handgun violation would serve no purpose. You're not going to do it again, are you?"

"No way. I'm not a criminal. I'm just angry." He sat down

and paused briefly. "I do think that there is something I can do to pay for my sins, however."

She was intrigued and saw his wheels turning. "What did you have in mind?"

"If I can give you the gun dealer, could you do something to protect my witness and help his family?"

She placed her elbows on her desk and leaned on the backs of her hands, curious about Charlie's proposal. "I'm not sure, but I think we can make a deal."

chapter
TWENTY
THREE

Purging his soul to the assistant district attorney relieved some of his guilt, but Charlie felt as if there were more he should do. He had slept on his couch, which the cleaners had attacked the day before, and he had spent the majority of the previous night cleaning and straightening. He left the Smirnoff vodka bottle on the mantel. He had decided that every morning he would test himself before life could test him. Every morning, he would embrace the pain and refuse the anesthetic. Every morning, he would muster the willpower to see another day.

The sun gleamed through the orange and red leaves. It was one of those warm fall mornings that reminded him of summer. Charlie fixed himself a healthy breakfast. A bowl of oatmeal and a glass of milk would be his new routine. He had decided to do things differently. His life was not changing, so he decided to change his life. He had gained ten to twelve pounds in the last month and was becoming soft all over. He pulled on a warm-up suit and decided to start jogging again. Years ago, Charlie would run three to four miles every other day. When Ashley was born, he had become too busy feeding her and dressing her every morning. Plus, the time he spent jogging was time away from the apple of his eye.

Charlie had decided that today was the day of new beginnings, and the warmth of the sun seemed to agree with his decision. He turned on the television and channel-surfed while lacing his Nike cross-trainers. Somewhere in the outer limits of cable access, he found a curly-haired pompadour, thick face, and shaded glasses. The man was wearing a sharkskin suit with a black shirt and white tie. He was crying. Charlie watched intently as Reverend Billy Rae Higgins pleaded with his satellite congregation.

"I don't want you to miss your blessing." Reverend Billy dabbed his eyes with a handkerchief. "I suffer when my flock is hurting, and many of you are hurting from credit card debt." Charlie looked at the stack of bills on the kitchen table and returned his attention to the television.

"Now if you people would give to God, God will give back to you. When you build God's church, God will build your house. Now don't give to those dead, lifeless churches. You better give to a place that has power and is getting something done. We're helping unwed mothers, we're fighting abortion, and we're still raising funds for Attorney Harrigan, who so tragically lost his family. Make your check out to Solid Rock Ministries and I will give it to him personally. Mr. Harrigan, Charlie, wherever you are . . . I love you and feel your pain."

The crash was spectacular. The electricity sparked and snapped. Shards of glass scattered over the living room. The green miniature marble obelisk that Sandy had bought from Pier One was the only thing within arm's reach, and Charlie had hurled it at the television. Reverend Billy Rae Higgins had never spoken to him and knew nothing about him. Charlie looked at the sun bouncing off the tiny slivers of glass.

He jogged out of the front door and started down the tree-lined sidewalk. Birds were still chirping and squirrels were furiously gathering acorns for the winter. He breathed deeply and it felt good. He felt rejuvenated and young again. The sun smiled on him as he picked up his pace. He concentrated on his feet, trying to block out thoughts of Sandy, Ashley, Enrique Alvarez, blood, and carpet stains. Instead, he focused on the leaves that were beginning to cover the sidewalk. Sweat started to pour down his face, as if cleansing all of the fat and impurities out of his system. For the first time in a long time, he did not feel like he had a truck parked on his chest and acid swirling around in his stomach. His body stopped hurting. Now it was just his heart.

After a shower and shave, Charlie unwrapped a starched shirt and got dressed in an olive four-button suit. He grabbed a briefcase and a couple of yellow legal pads and climbed into his Blazer. He headed southeast on Providence and exited onto the 385 loop which almost completely surrounded the city. At Interstate 85, he headed north into Cabarrus County and turned off at Cannon Boulevard in Rowan County. He drove through the mill town of Kannapolis. Out of all of his years in North Carolina, he had never been here. Of course, few people went to the little towns. Most of the traffic headed in the opposite direction.

Kannapolis reminded him of his hometown. Midland was much smaller, but it still had a Dairy Queen. A vast majority of small-town Southern kids grew up in Dairy Queen. The downtown area of Kannapolis was one of those completely refurbished villages that had been turned into a factory outlet. He parked his Blazer and explored some of the outlet stores. It was half an hour before lunch, but he decided to have an ice cream cone as an appetizer. He was a single man, plus he had jogged two miles that morning, and a double scoop of double fudge would be his reward. At the ice cream shop, he walked back to the rest rooms and opened the phone book that was resting on a shelf by the pay phones.

His morning of new beginnings and reconciliations featured Horace and Betty Douglas. He had declined their initial offer and was fairly rude at their first meeting at Sonny's Teriyaki Grill. He at least had to apologize for his behavior. In the back of his mind, every new step he made was evaluated on the basis of what Sandy would think. She would definitely be upset with the way Charlie had treated Horace. The phone book listed the Douglases' address as 7210 Central Avenue. The old man behind the counter told him that it was a block behind the store and north about two miles. It was a little white house that would be difficult to miss.

Charlie turned north onto Central Avenue. To the left, a set of railroad tracks ran parallel to the street, and to the right, an endless row of white houses stretched as far as the eye could see. Each one essentially looked like the next. They were small with little front porches surrounded by trees. Charlie drove slowly, reading the numbers on the mailboxes. Finally, he reached 7210. He pulled in the short gravel driveway, got out, and walked to the front door. It was almost noon, and it was actually getting hot outside. There would not be many more days like this before spring. He knocked on the door. There was no answer.

With nothing pressing to do, Charlie decided to sit down on the front porch swing and watch the traffic, which amounted to six cars and a stray dog. Five minutes after twelve, a train whistle blew, jolting Charlie out of his peaceful rocking reverie. The train originated in Alabama, dropped off cotton at the textile mill, and would pick up sheets and towels to take to a local distributor in Charlotte. Charlie watched the locomotive slow down and remembered when he was a kid in Midland. He and his friends would run beside the trains when they came through town and then pretend that they traveled off to exotic places. Every fantasy game seemed to include leaving the small-town life for the promise of bigger and better things.

Apparently, that is what his father did. Charlie remembered coming home from first grade and seeing a set of luggage by the door. His father never told him why he left. His job took him west, and he kept getting farther and farther away. The only thing his mother told him was that his father was too big for the small-town life, and that to be a success, he had to get out. There was no hint of abuse or affairs, just a lack of passion as far as Charlie could remember. His mother was strong for him and never talked much about it. She remarried when Charlie was in high school. A local refrigerator repairman just could not take the place of his father, so when Charlie went to college, he rarely returned home. The wheels on the behemoth brought back a flood of feelings he had not thought about in years. He had always longed for the "Leave It to Beaver" family, but for the most part, his family had simply been several individuals who shared a common living space.

Charlie was about to leave when a dented, rusty blue pickup pulled into the driveway behind the old rusted Monte Carlo. Betty was driving, and Charlie cringed as she came perilously close to scraping his right rear quarter panel. Horace actually jumped out of the truck with a smile on his face. For a man of little emotion, Horace was very animated.

"I knew you would come. I knew you were the man to help us beat those guys. You're the only one who can do it!" Horace grabbed Charlie's hand firmly and shook it profusely.

Betty moved a little bit slower. "God has answered our prayers and has brought you to us. Thank the Lord!" She raised her hands and hugged Charlie, who was overwhelmed by the emotional display.

"Look, I just came by to apologize . . . "

Betty was pushing Charlie through the front door. "Horace has only an hour for lunch, so I'll go pour you boys some tea. Charlie, please stay and eat with us. I pick up Horace every day, and we have homemade soup and a fresh garden-grown salad. I would be crushed if you didn't join us."

"Have a seat on the couch, son. I need to wash my hands. That mill's a grimy place." Usually, the term "son" infuriated Charlie, but from Horace he did not seem to mind too much.

The house was small, but quaint. It smelled of mildew and old people. Lace curtains from the sixties hung on the window, and a little nineteen-inch television sat on a homemade wooden crate. Then Charlie looked at the floor. It was all hardwood. Pine floors were throughout the house. It had cost Charlie four thousand dollars to put hardwood floors in his kitchen alone. Apparently, in the forties when these houses were built, hardwood floors were not a luxury item. They were a necessity. The couch had a homemade quilt draped over it, and a wooden rocking chair sat in the corner. Charlie was inspecting the wooden crate when Horace returned.

"I know it's not much to look at, but that is the first thing that Matt made in wood shop. He was so proud when we actually used it in the house. He would sit on the couch and smile at it all evening long."

"I didn't know retarded people could do things like that." As soon as the words escaped his lips, Charlie realized what he had said and tried to make it sound more politically correct. "What I mean is, I didn't know he was capable of this level of work."

"Oh, Charlie, I know what you mean. Matt was just mildly retarded. Very slow, is all. His motor skills were fine. Of course, he would never be a rocket scientist, but with excellent training, he could have had a very full life. If you met him on the street, you wouldn't be able to tell anything different about him."

"Lunch is on!" Betty called from the kitchen. "Honey, don't forget your Geritol!" Horace looked embarrassed, and glanced at Charlie out of the corner of his eye to see if there was any reaction. Charlie pretended to be studying a framed poem with a picture of footprints beside it.

They sat around a small round table in a tiny breakfast nook. The tea was strong, sweet sun-brewed tea that one can get only in the South. Charlie picked up his spoon to attack the potato soup and noticed that both of the Douglases were watching him. They were holding hands, and Betty's other hand was stretched out toward Charlie. He had not prayed for a meal since his last breakfast with Sandy and Ashley. As they began eating the thick, cheesy soup, Charlie tried to explain why he had stopped by.

"I just wanted to apologize for the way I treated you at the diner, Mr. Douglas. I was really rude. I'm trying to make amends with everyone I've offended so I can move on. I didn't come by to take the case. I don't think I can practice law anymore."

"First of all, call me Horace." He set his spoon down carefully and looked Charlie in the eye. "I don't trust people who use titles. Second, you're our only hope. I read that you lost your job at that big firm. So I know that you're free. The one concern I have is that I don't know if you could legally represent us, seeing as you worked for Comstock first."

Charlie shifted in his chair. "Technically, I didn't do much on the case. Hypothetically speaking, if I took the case, it wouldn't be an issue as long as the judge thought I could be objective. But since I'm not taking the case, you don't have to worry about it."

Horace quickly countered Charlie. "But if we're going to fight a big company with wealthy lawyers, we need one of our own, but I can't afford a whole firm. You know how they work. But more than that, you have conviction. I read about you suing that abortion doctor, and I saw the passion that you had for doing the right thing on the news. That's why I was so shocked that you called our case frivolous."

"Once again, I'm sorry for that." Charlie studied the chunks of potato swimming around in his soup. "That's just a technique. I didn't enjoy it either."

"That's what I mean. You were meant to fight for the little man, the side of justice. Your heart wasn't with Mr. Comstock. Your heart was with Matt, the same way it was with that girl."

"Charlie," Betty said, touching his hand again, "I wouldn't presume to give you advice, but I do know about losing people you love. I buried a son and a husband. You don't do your loved ones any justice by giving up or quitting."

"You mean Horace isn't your first husband?" Charlie looked amazed.

"We've been together thirty-nine years. I'm a couple of years older than Horace. I'm not telling you how many. I married my high school sweetheart the Saturday after graduation. He was a second lieutenant in the army. In 1957, three months after we were married, he was sent to Israel. There was a skirmish over the Sinai Peninsula with Egypt. Omar was killed by what they call friendly fire. Two weeks later, the Israelis withdrew. You hear about war heroes, but when someone is killed in a police action, nobody cares. I was crushed, but then I came back home to my parents and this kid right here had graduated high school and turned into a good-lookin' man. We were married in 1959 and I got a second chance at life." As if she anticipated a question that Charlie dare not ask, Betty added, "There are times I do still miss him. But Horace is the most wonderful person in the world, and we've had a wonderful life. God helped me through the whole thing."

Horace brought the conversation back to the point. "Charlie, I think you can beat those guys, and I think you need us as much as we need you."

Charlie set the glass of tea on the table and reflected on Hobbes, Reimarus, and Van Schank; Nancy Lockman-Kurtz; Walter Comstock and Paragon Group. Those tigers would chew up this little old couple and spit them out and then trample on the remains. He knew how they operated. He knew their style. And he was the only one who could beat them.

"If I took your case, it would be difficult. I have no staff, no paralegals, and no help. They have over eight hundred attorneys throughout the Southeast. One man can't fight an army."

"Son," Horace leaned in real close to Charlie, "one man with virtue outnumbers countless immoral hordes."

"Let's get started." Charlie opened his briefcase and pulled out a yellow legal pad.

Horace began the sad story. His son was twenty-three years old when he died of lung cancer. Unlike many people who die a slow, agonizing death, Matthew Douglas contracted the disease and went downhill fast. Horace traced the problem back to a fall during a remodeling job when Matt landed in a pile of insulation and materials that were demolished during the renovation. Horace believed that Comstock's company used individuals on special government programs to do menial tasks and skirt the minimum-wage law. Apparently, Matt and others were involved in some fairly risky work that they were not aware of. Horace's inclination told him that they may have been removing asbestos but were not told by the foreman.

Charlie listened intently and took copious notes. He started drawing lines and flow charts that connected names of individuals with concepts like vicarious liability, assumption of risks, and imputed negligence. Paragon was a privately owned company and not incorporated. So Walter Comstock was vicariously liable for the actions of his managers and foremen, even if he never visited specific sights. Charlie placed a question mark by imputed negligence. He would have to prove that by commission or omission, Comstock was negligent in supervening his employees' safety. Charlie drew an arrow to the words *passive negligence*.

All he had to do was prove that Comstock's inaction led to Matthew Douglas being exposed to a known carcinogen. The issues seemed to be very simple and clear-cut. Charlie searched his brain for a reason not to take the case, but nothing came. As a matter of fact, this type of case was why he had entered the field of law in the first place. He wanted to fight for truth wherever lies reigned; he wanted to speak for those who had no voice; he wanted to punish those who hurt the innocent. Meeting Maggie Thomason had changed his life and invigorated his career after years of litigating contract disputes between two fat cats. Finally, he had the chance to do what he was trained for. Sandy had been right all along.

Charlie looked at Betty, whose eyes started watering. "I'll do it."

chapter
TWENTY
FOUR

The greasy man in the orange shirt with pink and yellow flowers chewed on the end of a cigar, but did not light it. He was in a bowling alley in Kannapolis. He had kept an eye on Horace Douglas and Charlie Harrigan ever since their first meeting at Sonny's. As the burgundy Buick Riviera drove past Henry Judson's office, the driver laughed himself silly. The blinds were closed and the driveway was empty. Apparently, Judson had taken an early retirement and was probably getting drunk on his boat somewhere on High Rock Lake.

Henry Judson had been a mediocre lawyer at best and was looking for quick settlements with little work. In three afternoons of surveillance, the greasy man owned him and Judson caved quickly. He was not a strong man, and Slade did not expect any resistance or retaliation. Slade dialed the number to Martin Van Schank's direct line with one hand and drank a Turbo Dog beer with the other. He tipped up the dark brown bottle and drained almost all of it in one swallow.

"Hey, Marty, how's my favorite shark?" Slade spilled beer on his large belly and tried his best to savor every last drop so it would not go to waste.

"Where have you been? I haven't heard from you in days. I don't pay you a thousand dollars a week to goof around, and what is that I hear? Bowling! You're bowling on my dime? I'm going to fire your sorry round rear."

"Wait a minute, buddy. I've got information you are going to want. Guess who just hired your old protégé, Charlie Harrigan?"

Van Schank waited with baited breath. He had followed the downward spiral of Charlie Harrigan and enjoyed the demise. The death of the little girl had made him a bit sad, but he got over it.

"Here it is." Slade knew that Van Schank was impatient and hated these little games that he played. "Our friend Horace Douglas has not given up the fight. It looks like good ole Charlie is going to pick up the case against Comstock."

"This is great!" Van Schank slammed his hand on the desk. "I can't get rid of that loser. I get him fired and he's still in my face. Stay on him, Slade. Forget about Douglas. Stay on Harrigan. I want to know every step he takes. Bug his house. Spy on his friends. I don't want to know everything you do. I just want results. Get me something that I can bury that Boy Scout with. Now how 'bout the other deal?"

"My boys got a couple of Ryder trucks and drove to Dalton, Georgia. They have about twenty-five or thirty illegals, who have had some experience doing construction work. That was a brilliant idea you had—calling the INS and reporting the carpet company and then picking up all of their cheap labor when the owner panicked and laid them off. Man, I admire you." Slade was beaming at the manipulative nature of his mentor and ordered another Turbo Dog.

"You'll like this even better. Hammerstan Carpets is one of my clients. I sent the original group of Mexicans in his direction in the first place. He doesn't know that I'm the one who turned him in. So now he's paying me eight hundred dollars an hour to keep him out of hot water with Immigration and Naturalization Services. I can't lose. Even if my clients go to jail, I still make money." Van Schank's laugh was sinister and evil. He enjoyed controlling people like chess pieces. He had to find a way to get control of his newest adversary.

"You're my hero, you sorry dog." Slade hung up the phone, drained his second beer, and headed back to Charlotte.

Charlie sat at the counter of his favorite greasy spoon and flipped through the thin file Horace had given him. Upon firing Henry Judson, Horace, rightfully so, had demanded the working file on the case and all information pertaining to Comstock and Paragon Group. Charlie was amazed at the dearth of information. Had this man done anything at all? When Charlie was at the height of his litigation at Hobbes, Reimarus, and Van Schank, he had one case for Tyger Construction whose documentation occupied one whole room at an annex on South College that they called the pit. Twenty-four boxes contained almost all of the evidence, except for nine long round canisters that contained maps and aerial photographs of the zoning site in question.

J. Garrison Hobbes resented anyone who made a mess of his pristine castle in the air, and litigation was known for massive amounts of evidence. He wanted the file room to be nice and neat. Any file folder more than two inches thick was to be filed in a separate locked room away from traffic, so that anyone who happened to walk past the file room would be impressed by the organization of the firm. File clerks were constantly replacing folders that were bent, torn, or coffee-stained. Hobbes refused to look like every other firm that piled folders everywhere and had wrinkled papers and documents. In court, the neatness and efficiency caused fear in the hearts of lesser-prepared attorneys.

By contrast, Henry Judson's files were chaotic. All of Charlie's files at work had been exactly alike. On the right hand side, the papers were filed in chronological order, with the most recent motion and counterclaim on top. On the left side was an inventory of the file's contents, and a sign-in sheet for every person who touched the file to record what action he had taken. Correspondence between the two parties always had its own separate file, arranged in the same manner. Judson did not even hole punch the documents and affix them to the folder. What documents he had were just crammed into the file. There were pleadings, some correspondence, and motions, but no countermotions and no affidavits. The file was sparse. What had this man done to help his client?

Sonny walked up to the counter and poured Charlie a cup of coffee. "So, my friend, how's the journey?"

"What is it with you and this journey? Are you ever going to explain it to me?" Charlie was getting frustrated, but Sonny was his only friend in the world, so he kept calm.

"I will tell you later. You not ready yet." Sonny smiled sympathetically at his friend. "You got a new case? Good. Get back in the swing of things. Looking inward never solve anything. You got to look out."

"Yeah, it's actually the last case I was on at the firm before they fired me. The other guy hired me."

"The old man who came in here with that other lawyer few days ago?"

"Yeah, that's him."

"He has a good face. You can trust him. He's in the right, you know."

Charlie looked in amazement. "How can you be so sure? You've never met the guy."

Sonny grinned. "Charlie, I know people. Their eyes tell the secrets of their soul. Like the other guy, who was with him, he was genuinely sorry. You should have talked to him."

"Wait a second. I just came in for a patty melt with extra onions, not advice. You're not a bartender or a priest."

"Very funny, my friend. Last advice. You are going to have to trust again. Maybe not today. It will be slow, but a little trust here builds to bigger trust. You can trust the old man and I think you can trust your friend." Trying to lighten the subject, Sonny changed directions. "You going to start your own firm? Harrigan and Associates?"

Charlie chuckled. "I don't think so. This is a one-shot deal. I kind of owe it to them; after all, I stood up in court and called the death of their son frivolous. It's my way of making amends. Sandy was big on always setting things right."

"If you need office, the second floor above the laundry is vacant. I rent it to you at a good price. Three rooms, a kitchenette, and full bathroom. I lived there many years until I could buy a house."

"How do you do it, Sonny?" Charlie studied the blackness of his coffee. "How do you wake up every day knowing you will never see your family again? Knowing that the people who killed them were probably never punished? So many loose ends in your life and so many 'what ifs' facing the future? How can you be so optimistic?"

Sonny stuck the spatula in his apron and leaned on the counter. "I wasn't always like this. I hated my missionary parents who adopted me; their God was weak and couldn't stop the enemy. I hated the North Koreans; the Devil owned them. I hated Buddha or God or whoever lost control of the universe at that time. In the States, I joined the army as a young man to kill people. It just made me more angry. In 1963, nobody cared about Vietnam yet. But Kennedy sent Green Berets and Special Forces to wage underground war and teach sabotage to South Vietnamese."

"I had no idea that you were in the military, much less a Green Beret. For cryin' out loud, you're a hero." Charlie was amazed at this mild-mannered cook.

"I wasn't a hero. I wanted to kill people. I wanted to drown my pain. I cursed God every day, because I hated the mess He made of this world. Anyway, the NVA controlled Hanoi, and we went in and blew up communication links, armories, and assassinated officers. One day, we were supposed to blow up radio tower on a hill on west side of Hanoi. Sniper in tower wiped out all of my men. I had been drinking the night before, drowning my anger. I led them into an ambush because I didn't have enough information, but went ahead anyway. I watched all six of my men get machine-gunned down by one sniper. I got shot in the shoulder. I walked and crawled for miles until I collapsed. I spent next four years in a POW camp somewhere. I had no idea where I was."

"Wow," Charlie gasped in amazement at the horrific life of Kim Il Sook. He saw this guy almost every day and had no idea who he really was.

"I was one hundred and six pounds when I got out, lost forty-two pounds. I had a glass of water and a piece of bread every day. Every other day, we had a bowl of rice. I was marched hundreds of miles through the jungle, digging tiger pits. I knew that someday my fellow soldiers would be marching through the jungle and fall into these pits, being impaled on bamboo spears. The physical torture was not as bad as the mental torture. We were told we would be killing our friends and innocent people, not NVA. I lived in a cube four feet by four feet with a pile of straw and a blanket. There was one bowl for my personal functions that they emptied once a week. I cried myself to sleep every night.

"That's when I could sleep. Most of the time, I woke up screaming, reliving the deaths of my family and my squad. But there was this guy in a cube next to me. We were taken out and locked up at different times, so we never saw any of the other prisoners, so I never met him. He just told me his name, Ralph Potter. He left seminary where he wanted to be a chaplain and enlisted in the marines. This guy sang hymns and quoted the Bible out loud every night. I know that he sang 'Amazing Grace' every night for two months straight. The more I listened to his singing, the less angry I felt. I started to look forward to the song, and then he started teaching me the words and what they meant. He told me the story behind 'Amazing Grace,' how this slave trader cried out to God to save his life during storm in the Atlantic and he went on to be a preacher.

"One day, he told me about how Jesus suffered unjustly. I realized something about his God that started making sense. Buddha didn't understand my pain. He was above it. But this God voluntarily came down and joined my pain, so He could understand and help me through it, not necessarily fix it. One night while Ralph was singing 'Amazing Grace,' this was after they put electrodes on my body and poured water over me, I started singing and crying. The pain briefly lifted and I felt peace. In my mind, I swear to you I heard the words, 'You'll be all right, son.' Ralph told me I had become a Christian. Everything my missionary parents had tried to teach me made sense. They had told me about the cross, the soldiers, and the trial, but not about God's suffering. If the Creator suffered, then He knows the suffering of His creation . . . and yours too, Charlie."

Water filled Charlie's eyes. He was mesmerized by the strength Sonny possessed to live through terror most Americans never dream about, and he still wore a smile. All of the Vietnam vets Charlie met were either alcoholics, or were like the paraplegic in front of the NationsBank building who was addicted to crack. The movies portrayed Vietnam heroes as Rambos or psychotic killers. Sonny was an average guy with an excruciatingly average job, but he enjoyed his life. "I don't know what to say," Charlie fumbled for words. "I had no idea you lived through all that. I'm sorry."

"Why? You didn't know."

"That's what I mean. I'm sorry for not knowing you better. Is there anything I can do?" Charlie searched for the right thing to say, but it would not come.

"Yes." Sonny patted Charlie's shoulder. "When the time is right, you will share your story with someone else who is on a journey, who needs your friendship. If you don't share it, you might as well explode because the anger needs to be released. When the time is right, you need to release that anger to God."

Sonny's wisdom was at times too cryptic and oriental for Charlie's taste, but the tone of his words was soothing and confident. Charlie had learned a great deal about Kim Il Sook that day and knew he could trust his wisdom. Somewhere in the back of the kitchen a bell rang and a cook shouted, "Order up!" Sonny grabbed Charlie's patty melt and hash browns, placing the food in front of him.

Before he went on to the next customer, Sonny said, "You want the answers all at once. It doesn't work like that. It comes a little at a time. Helping that couple is the best thing you can do, because if you are always looking inward, you will miss a piece or two of the puzzle."

Charlie pulled a napkin from the little metal dispenser. He dabbed his eyes and straightened his tie. Controlling his emotions made him a great litigator, and he was a little embarrassed at almost losing it in public while Sonny told his story. Clearing his throat and draining the cup of coffee, he returned to his stoic demeanor, but in his mind, he replayed the story over and over. He compared his story to Sonny's. He looked for hints and clues. Then he thought about helping other people. Maybe Sonny was on to something there. A burst of energy hit him and he devoured his food, even the last extra onion. Charlie shouted across the grill to Sonny.

"Sonny, let me take a look at that space you have for rent!"

chapter
TWENTY
FIVE

October 1st hit Charlotte with cold winds from the Blue Ridge Mountains to the west. Fall was in full force and the colors were at their zenith. The Tarheel football team was two and two, but doing considerably better than the Panthers. Most of Charlie's possessions were in boxes in ministorage. He had moved his favorite recliner, television, and coffee table into one of the small rooms above Sonny's Teriyaki Grill. He would have a difficult time staying in shape with the aroma wafting up from the kitchen. The walls were covered with pictures of Sandy and Ashley. From infant to toddler, the pictures of Ashley showed the brief history of her precious life. Sandy's pictures were arranged according to hairstyle: the college ponytail, the professional bob, and the return to long hair when she quit her job.

In the other room, he had set up a metal card table and four chairs. This was his workstation. Books on civil procedure, torts, cross-examination techniques, and rules of evidence sat on the floor against one wall. Next to that stack was a collection of textbooks on lung cancer and the pulmonary system that he had checked out from the downtown branch of the public library. The third stack was considerably smaller: a Bible with his name embossed in gold that his church had given him when he was growing up and a copy of his favorite John

Grisham novel that he kept close by for inspiration. *The Firm* was considerably more worn than the Bible. On the metal card table was his IBM ThinkPad and the Douglas file, what there was of it.

Charlie had agreed to work for a percentage of the verdict if he won. Typically in a tort case, he received one-third of any judgment. After Charlie's assets were unfrozen, he had paid all of the past-due bills and credit card debt. In one afternoon, he wiped out all the savings that he had. Sandy's will was still in probate court, and insurance refused to pay anything until the court had settled her matter. They had not thought much about the future. Her will was in the process of being written when she was killed, so the government would end up claiming the bulk of her estate. Charlie was forced to put his house up for sale, because he was essentially working for free.

He grabbed his briefcase that contained the first motion he would file as a self-employed lawyer. He was about to go up against his old firm for the first time. His motion was simple, and he planned on keeping things simple. Hobbes, Reimarus, and Van Schank would clobber him with mounds of paperwork, but the judge would look favorably on Charlie's self-restraint by not engaging in the paper war. He learned a long time ago that lawyers, especially litigators, always try to impress the wrong people. The judge and the jury are the ones who count, but most lawyers spend their time trying to impress other lawyers.

Sure enough, Nancy Lockman-Kurtz filed every motion her twisted little mind could imagine. Charlie knew the tactic well; they had trained him and he was an expert. Nancy probably had three associates, four paralegals, all of their secretaries, and a couple of interns researching motions. She probably just reviewed the final drafts and signed her name. But Charlie was prepared. He had predicted all of the motions except one. The obvious one was the motion to dismiss, because the facts were not there. The motion of demurrer stipulated that all of the facts were true, but Charlie's case was still deficient; therefore, the judge should dismiss. The bill of particulars required Charlie to provide more details to establish the validity of his pleadings. The motion for summary judgment was standard but rarely granted in cases like this.

The one that shocked him was the motion for sanctions. Nancy wanted the judge to reprimand Charlie for bringing a frivolous lawsuit and fine him. The motion hinted that jail time would be appropriate, since Charlie himself had called it a frivolous lawsuit. It was an attempt to make Judge Carlton Fitzwaring sympathetic to Paragon Group. Fitzwaring was a frequent guest lecturer at law schools across the Southeast, and his favorite topic was the litigious society we live in, a society in which insurance companies would rather settle than fight for the truth and where people manipulate the system to get rich quick.

Every year in the United States, over twenty million lawsuits are filed in state and federal court. Many of those lawsuits lack any merit, but those who file know that three-fourths of those cases will be settled before they ever go to trial. Henry Judson had made a very comfortable living without ever seeing the inside of a courtroom. The North Carolina State Legislature labored diligently to limit frivolous lawsuits, and it was working. In the wake of the four point two billion-dollar settlement against the breast implant industry, corporate lobbyists contributed thousands to reelect sympathetic judges and congressmen.

North Carolina is actually a good place to get sued. It has fewer lawyers per capita than any other state, and seventy-five percent of all potential jurors believe that settlements are too large. The Northeast and West are by far the best places to sue, because juries are far more willing to grant large cash rewards. Charlie had an uphill battle ahead of him. Now he had the added pressure of losing the case before it ever reached the trial stage. For the first time since his rookie year, he was actually nervous before he went to court. After his first four or five appearances, the nerves had worn off and Charlie realized that the courtroom was a job like any other. He got to know the judges, and the image of the unapproachable jurist wore off quickly.

He went downstairs where Sonny had fixed his favorite breakfast. They had worked out a deal that Charlie could eat for free and pay a reduced lease for free legal advice. It sounded good to Charlie. He liked the food and was getting to know Sonny very well. He took the deal, knowing that he was on the losing end. Charlie picked at his food, but was not able to eat much. He downed four cups of coffee and headed off to meet his clients.

The Douglases were waiting for Charlie in the lobby, sitting on a bench and leaning back against the pink Georgia granite wall. Betty reached out and hugged him. Her hair smelled like his mother's after she got a perm. Horace grabbed his hand and patted him on the back. Charlie tried to exude the confidence that Horace obviously had in him, but his knees were shaking and his heart was pounding. As usual, Charlie had parked at the dry cleaners and used the rear entrance to avoid people. As he greeted his clients, he looked out the glass front doors and saw the lawn filled with cameras.

Were they there to witness the return of Charlie Harrigan? The last few weeks of his life had been lived on television and in the newspaper. Charlie and his clients walked to the second floor and entered a small anteroom next to civil court. In the small space with no windows, Charlie described the series of motions that would be filed, and explained that this pretrial session was just a formality. He tried not to let his nervousness show; in fact, he was as nervous as the Douglases were.

Charlie had no desire to arrive in the courtroom early, so at twenty-five after nine, they entered the room, walked down the aisle, through the bar, and sat at the table to the left. The courtroom was empty. Three reporters sat in the row behind the bar. A couple of bored attorneys, who staked out the courthouse looking for clients, sat in the back row and ate M & M's or peanuts out of their briefcases. The courtroom seemed excessively large, and the twenty rows of seats seemed unnecessary. Nobody wants to watch a civil trial.

Charlie settled into his seat and looked across the aisle at his enemies. Nancy Lockman-Kurtz had brought her entire entourage. Four young men in blue pinstripe suits sat to her right. Each one had a varying shade of burgundy stripe or print tie. They looked like uninspired backup singers. Nancy shattered the mundane with her bright red power suit. The skirt was of questionable length for trial purposes, but judges tended to like it. An air of confidence hovered around her.

Charlie could smell her perfume across the aisle. He opened his briefcase and pulled out the file with his copy of the various motions. A picture that a stranger had taken for him at Nags Head was clipped to the inside lid of his briefcase. Charlie was holding Ashley in his right arm and Sandy clung tightly to his left. He remembered how tight she used to grab his arm, as if she would lose him. He closed the lid. Horace pulled something out of his pocket and reopened the briefcase. Charlie started to say something to his client, who at the moment had overstepped the boundaries of familiarity. He looked and saw that Horace had placed a picture of Matt Douglas next to the picture of Charlie's family. No words were said. None were needed.

"All rise," the bailiff cried out while the clerks and stenographers ignored him and went about their business. Judge Carlton Fitzwaring strode into the courtroom triumphantly with his black robe flowing behind him. He placed his bifocals on the edge of his nose, read something quickly, and then took them off.

"Please sit down. Let's begin. Mr. Harrigan, I was very shocked indeed to see your name on the change in representation that crossed my desk. Now please forgive me—as I get older my memory fades—but last time you were in my court, weren't you at that table?" He pointed to Nancy and smiled.

"Yes, Your Honor, but there have been several changes

lately. Primarily, J. Garrison Hobbes told me that my services were no longer needed with his firm."

"Yes. I seem to remember him saying something about that when we played golf a couple of weeks ago. It had something to do with the way you handled the client that Ms. Lockman-Kurtz is representing." It was not unethical for judges and lawyers to fraternize, but it made Charlie feel very insecure at the moment.

"With all due respect, Your Honor, I have a feeling where this is headed. I'm not here to talk about myself. I had only met with Walter Comstock a couple of times and learned very little. There's no conflict of interest here. Henry Judson was not effectively representing my clients and he was ignoring their wishes in handling this case."

"Now let me interrupt you. My memory is still playing tricks. Last time you were here, you claimed that Mr. Judson's case had no merit. I believe you called it frivolous."

"That's exactly the word I used, Your Honor. I can't reveal too much about that motion because it has to do with work product at Hobbes, Reimarus, and Van Schank. Generally speaking, that type of motion and language is the first line of defense."

Nancy shot up out of her seat and the battle was on. "Your Honor, he cannot hide behind the work product of a place in which he does not work."

Charlie stared straight ahead. "Work product has to do with where I was employed at the time, not currently. Besides, Your Honor, I have discovered new information that leads me to believe my initial impression of the merits of this case was wrong. Mr. Comstock was not very cooperative in his own defense. The Douglases have informed me that they have excellent grounds to demonstrate imputed negligence in the wrongful death of Matthew Douglas."

Nancy was not finished. "Mr. Harrigan is wasting the court's time. He should be sanctioned. He is simply mad that I was made partner and he got fired. Now he wants revenge. It is shocking how he is manipulating the legal system for his own purposes."

Charlie glared. "And you are the expert on manipulation. Aren't you!"

"Quiet!" Fitzwaring's face was red. "I have half a mind to throw this case out before it becomes a circus. But your tenacity, Mr. Harrigan, would not let it go. I'm not going to give you grounds for appeal. Listen to me, both of you. This is my court. Stay in your seats and play nice or I'll throw you both in jail for contempt. According to your brief, Mr. Harrigan, I do think you have introduced some new information that Mr. Judson did not file in his original pleadings. I'm not going to dismiss the case or offer a summary judgment. This case needs to be heard. However, Mr. Harrigan, if you don't prove causality in Paragon Group's behalf, I may sanction you and force you to pay the court costs for both parties."

"Your Honor—" Charlie stood up.

"Sit down! How many times do I have to repeat myself? If you are committed to your cause and your case has merit, you have nothing to worry about, okay? No dismissal. Ms. Lockman-Kurtz, please address your demurrer motion."

"May I stand, Your Honor?" He nodded and noticed the legs. "Mr. Harrigan is assuming facts that are not indicated in his pleading. The fact that Matthew Douglas died of lung cancer may be true, but the pleading only hints at the causal connection between my client and theirs."

"Your Honor," Charlie started to stand, but thought better of it. "That's what discovery is for. I'm not required to set forth all the facts of my argument. I've had this case only a few days, but I have my suspicions about how Comstock killed my client—"

"Your Honor, prejudicial!" Nancy snapped.

"There's no jury." Fitzwaring ran his fingers through his wiry gray hair. "Who are you two performing for? If you're doing all this to impress me, I'm really touched, but it is not necessary. Ms. Lockman-Kurtz, please refrain from antiquated tactics. If he doesn't prove his point, file a motion of nonsuit."

"Your Honor, there's no causal connection. I'm very sorry for the Douglases, but he just died. It happens." Nancy protested to no avail.

"If what you say is true, then this should be a slam dunk for you. Finally, the bill of particulars has got me curious. You are correct, Mr. Harrigan, in saying that you do not have to state all of your facts now, but you do have your work cut out for you. You do realize that you are assuming a lot of givens to approach the threshold for negligence."

"I understand, but the facts are there under the surface." Neither side had scored with the judge today and they both knew it.

"Keeping that in mind, here's how the trial is going to proceed. There will be two parts. First you must prove that Mr. Douglas' lung cancer was associated with work he was doing with Paragon Group. If you cannot prove the first part, then the case will be dismissed and the sanctions will be imposed. The second part of the trial will deal with the claim of negligence on behalf of Mr. Comstock. Understand?"

"Your Honor, you're tying my hands." Charlie forgot to ask and stood to his feet.

"This is my last warning, Mr. Harrigan. Keep calm. Court dismissed." Judge Fitzwaring quickly escaped out the back door to avoid conflict. He told his secretary that he was not to be disturbed.

Nancy shot Charlie a grin. The judge had just made Charlie's case twice as difficult. The five attorneys from Hobbes, Reimarus, and Van Schank would spend the rest of the morning reviewing the judge's rulings and then have lunch together. Walter Comstock would be billed close to a thousand dollars an hour for all of these attorneys replicating efforts.

Betty grabbed Charlie's sleeve as he was packing his briefcase. "What does this mean?"

"Not here." Charlie nodded toward the door, and they went back into the anteroom. He closed the door and made sure the hallway was empty, protecting against eavesdroppers. "Overall, today was good. Fitzwaring cuts no slack and I figured he would give me a hard time, but I was ready for that."

"What about the last thing he said?" Her eyes welled up with doubt.

"The bill of particulars? Simply put, we don't know all of the facts yet, and to satisfy the defense, he has divided the trial into two phases. First, we have to prove that the lung cancer was caused by something Matt came in contact with at his job."

Horace thought hard and came up with a layman's answer, "That shouldn't be too difficult to prove. He really didn't do anything but work and go to church with us."

Charlie paced next to the window with his arms folded. "That's not the problem. The problem is strategy. You two won't be allowed to testify until the second part of the trial, because you can't really speak to carcinogens. In other words, we might lose the jury during the first part, because it will be professional, scientific testimony. Civil juries are notorious for not being smart enough to follow expert testimony. They tend to ignore the evidence and punish the side that takes the most time."

"Maybe you should join us for church on Sunday. We could pray for wisdom."

"I'm afraid that I'm too busy for church, Horace. I have an uphill battle to fight. They have eight hundred attorneys; I'm all alone."

chapter
TWENTY
SIX

Charlie sat at his metal card table drawing flowcharts that diagrammed the power structure of the Paragon empire. The cold autumn wind blew through the windows. The traffic noise from people rushing home to their happy families had died down hours ago. Sonny's Teriyaki Grill shut down about seven every evening, because all the attorneys and government workers had gone home. The building was empty and quiet. The only sound was the wind creaking through the windows and cracked weather stripping. He looked through the window at the lights in the tower downtown. Somewhere on the fortieth floor of the tallest tower, an unholy cabal of attorneys plotted his demise.

The television in the corner was on MSNBC. The talking heads were discussing the latest scandal in the White House. At first, Charlie was intrigued by the political drama, but lately, he had become bored by the duplicity and mudslinging. The nation was in dire need of a hero, but none was forthcoming. He had resigned himself to pour through the mounds of documents that Nancy had provided for discovery, but he was finding very little useful information. Most of it was meaningless tax data.

Suddenly, he heard footsteps coming up the stairs to the tiny apartment. Had he forgotten to lock the front door? He realized that he was alone in downtown Charlotte and nobody would discover his body for days, unless Sonny happened to stop in to check on him. The footsteps got louder and louder until they stopped on the top step and paused. There was a knock on the flimsy wooden door. Charlie scrambled for anything resembling a weapon. He snatched the Smirnoff bottle from a makeshift bookcase he had created from fruit crates.

"Charlie!" The voice was familiar and authoritative.

Charlie walked to the door slowly. The floor creaked beneath him. He flung the door open and instantly slammed it shut. "Go away!"

The doorknob turned and the man entered. He wore a black double-breasted suit and an Irish wool sweater. His Pierre Cardin designer glasses framed his distinguished face and salt-and-pepper gray hair. He pulled a Macanudo cigar from a gold case. "Mind if I smoke?"

"Yes. Go smoke in the street." Charlie continued examining the towers.

"Stop acting like a teenager. You're a grown man now."

"What are you doing here?"

"I came as soon as I heard."

Charlie snapped up and stood toe-to-toe with his father, who seemed to tower over him. "You just barely missed the funeral by a month. At least you did better than my wedding day."

"I just got the message about Sandy ten days ago. Then I lost a day crossing the International Date Line."

"Oh yeah, that International Date Line causes lots of problems. Did the International Date Line get in the way of your marriage and family too?"

"Look, I know I was a bad father, but don't you think it's time to move on—"

Charlie grabbed the cigar and crumpled it up. "You weren't a bad father. To be a bad father, you have to be around and make stupid mistakes. You weren't even there to screw up. You weren't a father at all."

"I just thought that you might need somebody now. I felt bad."

"That's wonderful. I'm glad you feel bad. I hope you feel bad in your Gulfstream jet all the way back to La-La Land. I hope you feel bad in your ZR-1, cruising with the top down, hitting on college girls. I hope you feel bad when you realize that I don't need you. I need a wife and a daughter. I need another child six months from now. I need a God who can turn back the hands of time." Charlie walked back to the window. "You know, come to think of it, out of all the things that I need right now, you're the only thing I don't need."

Charles Harrigan, Senior, was stoic. "Are you done?"

Charlie glared with a look that lay somewhere between rage and heartbreak. "Are you?"

"You are an adult now." He spoke slowly and distinctly. "It's time for you to put the past behind you and deal with this like a man. I am here for you now, and I am truly sorry for deserting you. Midland was killing me. I had to get out and make a life for myself. Your mother refused to join me. She's the one who kept you in that small town with no future. That's why I was so happy for you when Garrison Hobbes hired you. That firm is about the best there is in the Southeast."

"So that's what this is about. You're disappointed in me for blowing it. I had a shot at the big time and screwed up. Now all I can handle is one frivolous case against my former employer, and I'm probably doing that just for revenge. You want to know where you went wrong raising a son who's a failure. Is that it?"

"Of course not, you know that's not the truth—"

"I don't know anything about you or what you think. All I know is that my mother raised me to have high morals, to believe in God, and to respect my fellow man. Midland taught me that honest work has its own rewards, and those corporate sharks you represent, who feed off the little people, will pay someday. Why don't you go join Hobbes, Reimarus, and Van Schank? You'd fit right in with their moral code."

"I'm here to help." The last attempt at reconciliation fell flat.

"Well, you can't. Thanks for stopping by. I'll look forward to seeing you again in another five years or so." Charlie opened the door for his father and stared at the floor.

Charles Senior hung his head and walked quietly down the steps. He opened the bottom door onto the street. Charlie could see the limo parked outside. His father looked up the stairs and said, "I won't see you again in five years. My doctor doesn't give me that long to live. Have a nice life." The door slammed.

A few minutes later the limo pulled away. Charlie sat on the top step, dazed and bewildered. Suddenly, he felt sorry for a man whom he had lived his whole life to hate. Yet the desire to live up to his father's success had driven him to excel. The man had created any number of complexities and contradictions for him. Now Charlie was forced to add another. Forgiveness and hate. Remorse or revenge. The absent father was suddenly present.

Charlie arose from his stupor a little after nine. He had plowed through documents late into the night, because sleep was evasive. The startling encounter with his father sent him into a whirlwind of confusion. He had never considered that he would ever have any sympathetic feelings for the man. But as he was shaving, clearing the stubble from his face, he realized that he could not escape the image of his father in him. He decided that soon would he contact his father again, but he had other fences to mend first.

He showered and dressed quickly. Jeans and sweaters had become his new uniform. He reserved the suits for court appearances. He pulled on his hiking boots and grabbed his sunglasses. Breakfast would have to wait, because he had not planned on sleeping so late.

The sun was bright and the roads were clear. In the last couple of days, it was as if he were looking at Charlotte for the first time. Everything seemed different. He noticed people and things he had never noticed before. As he turned and headed west on Trade Street through downtown, he realized the large number of people who wandered around town with seemingly nothing to do. He realized the number of people sleeping in doorways and parks. When he resided on the thirty-ninth floor, he never noticed these people. Living downtown, he realized the number of sirens that were responding to people who were suffering all around him. He had grown to love this city; as a boy living in Midland, Charlotte offered salvation to a small-town kid who dreamed of greater things. Now the Queen City was vastly different from the one he had known just a few short weeks ago.

He turned north over to Graham Street and scoped out Comstock's latest endeavor. He parked at the very back of the Discovery Place Museum's parking annex. From a safe distance, he observed the construction workers. Barry Kasick was the foreman on this crew. He was barking orders from the back of a monster pickup truck. The men were gutting an old warehouse and grain mill that had been closed for thirty years. It had been a crack house and home for squatters, but the city council bought it and sold it to a consortium of private investors to develop upscale condos with an old-time feel.

Paragon Group got the bid. The teams were ripping down Sheetrock and insulation. On the side of the building, a group of Hispanic men were sandblasting paint and rust off the frame. A couple of young guys, apparently handicapped like Matt, were picking up trash and throwing it in a Dumpster. It was a flurry of confusion, and rubbish flew everywhere. There seemed to be no order to the operation, but the tornado of work quickly stripped the building to its steel frame skeleton. Across the street at a convenience store, several of the men took a break. A few went around back and drank beer out of brown paper bags. Charlie would come back later and start there.

Charlie put the Blazer in gear and headed to I-77. Turning

south, he was in South Carolina in a few minutes. He pulled into the Palmetto Motel. He scanned the rooms and saw Daisy Maxwell pushing her cleaning cart out of Room 28 as she moved on to the next room. Charlie climbed out of the Blazer and bolted up the stairs, full of energy. He stepped into Room 29 and blurted out, "Hey, Daisy!"

The frightened woman jumped and grabbed her vacuum cleaner. "Jesus help me! Back off, jack. I'll beat you with this vacuum cleaner with Jesus' help. I ain't got no money!" She started screaming. "Help! Help me! Rape!"

Charlie ducked down and looked for anyone who could hear the shrill screams. "Daisy. It's me. Charlie Harrigan. I was a guest here not long ago. I griped at you and you yelled at me. The attorney?"

She lowered the vacuum to the floor and studied his face. When she realized that she knew the man, she grabbed her chest and fell back on the bed. "You scared the snot outta me. You know how many times I been robbed? Don't sneak up on people."

"I'm sorry. I'm sorry." Charlie pulled up a chair next to the bed and sat down. "I've been thinking about your situation. My friend is one of the district attorneys. If Little Maxie is willing to give her the name of the person he works for, then she'll help you two. There is a small fund that they have to help people. She has a friend at Appalachian State University in the mountains. You can work maintenance there. They have insurance and benefits. One job, Daisy. No more waiting tables. Max will be able to start over."

She looked suspiciously at him as if to say, *What do you get out of this?* "I don't know what to say. Are you for real?"

"I'll be honest. I bought a gun from him." She showed no emotion. "The guy who murdered my wife and daughter got off on a technicality. I wanted to kill him, and I remembered your telling me about your son. But I threw the gun away. I just want to make things right now. I'm doing this for you, but I'm also doing it for myself."

"What do I do?" Daisy was tired from the years of abuse and hard labor. She had moved all over the South following one man or another. Now she was ready to be her own woman.

"I'll call the ADA and then we'll go pack up some of your stuff. We'll pick up Max and drive to the ADA's office. He'll never see the man until you come back to testify. Chances are, he'll plead to a lesser charge and Max won't need to testify. Please, let me help."

Daisy jumped at the chance to start over. She locked the door and turned in her apron. They drove north, back into Charlotte, and ended up at some run-down apartments on South Boulevard. Charlie looked at the busy street, bars, and thugs cruising the road and thought, *How could people raise children in this area?* They were almost guaranteed to be criminals. The apartment was smaller than Charlie's new home above the grill. The thirty-inch television sat directly on the floor with a Nintendo next to it. In the back bedroom, two mattresses lay on the floor. The clothes were piled on the chocolate brown carpet in the closet. Two pairs of hundred-dollar tennis shoes were lined up neatly against the baseboard. The little apartment was a study in extremes. It didn't take Daisy long.

Charlie drove slowly past the abandoned warehouse with no sign of Little Maxie. Leaves covered the street in an area where the street cleaners seldom traveled. Charlie headed south on Nations Ford Road, but watched his rearview mirror. He backed into a gravel driveway beside the Deuce's Wild Club, a bar known for drug-related shootings. They waited and watched. Sure enough, within fifteen minutes a late seventies-model green El Camino drove up and Max ran out to meet it. The driver handed him something and Max disappeared into the building. Forty-five seconds later, Max reappeared with a battered briefcase, much like the one he had given Charlie. The El Camino sped away.

They waited and watched two more cars. They were scared of drawing attention to themselves, but nobody seemed to care that a white man and a black woman were sitting together in a parked truck. There was a knock on the driver's window. A blond woman with matted hair, dark circles under her eyes, and yellow teeth was smiling.

"Hey, honey. You looking for a . . ." She saw Daisy. "I'm sorry, you're already taken." As she walked off, Charlie noticed the scars on her arms from years of drug abuse. She walked aimlessly from storefront to storefront, waving at each car driven by a lone man. Charlie felt he was watching the living dead.

When he returned his attention to the warehouse, the door was opening. Little Maxie and his young friend came out and headed across the street to the convenience store. Charlie looked at Daisy, who had tears streaming down her face. "This is it. Are you ready?" She nodded and clasped her hands around the cross on her necklace.

Charlie pulled out slowly and drove well below the speed limit. He studied the warehouse and saw no movement. He looked at the convenience store. The doors opened and each boy had a case of beer. Charlie slammed on the gas pedal and the Blazer jolted. The boys were waiting to cross the street, and Charlie pressed on the brake, squealing the tires. Smoke from the burning rubber came from the rear tires. Daisy threw the door open and grabbed her son, who started screaming. Charlie slammed on the gas again and spun around the gravel parking lot of the old warehouse heading back to the interstate.

In his rearview mirror, he saw the other boy run inside. Seconds later, the garage door opened and a shiny black Cutlass Supreme ripped out of the building and raced down Nations Ford Road. Charlie started to panic. Max was screaming and Daisy was wailing. The Cutlass was gaining ground as Charlie headed down the on-ramp. He looked in the mirror and saw the Cutlass sideswipe a Yugo as it forced its way onto the interstate. The Yugo ran into the median, hitting the retaining wall.

Charlie wove through the three lanes of traffic. In a matter of minutes, he was doing seventy. Then three tractor-trailers blocked all the lanes. Charlie veered sharply from the outside lane, cutting in front of two cars, and swerved onto the I-277 loop around downtown. Normally, he enjoyed this little trip around Ericsson Stadium and the scenic skyline, but not with a muscle car of killers behind him. A black man with sunglasses and black hat leaned out the window with a pistol. Charlie jerked the car off the loop and onto Morehead Street as he heard the shot.

Charlie dialed 911 on his cell phone. Within seconds, two Mecklenburg County deputies appeared from side streets and caught the chase. Lunch hour was quickly approaching, and Morehead would be packed with lawyers and accountants heading toward their power lunches. The operator was keeping track of Charlie's movements, and she told him to turn right on Kenilworth. As he did, he noticed several police cars fall in behind him and block off the street. The black Cutlass turned the corner and squealed its brakes. The deputies closed in behind, blocking any escape.

Charlie kept driving. He wove through the city streets until he reached the county building. Finally, in the parking garage, he breathed a sigh of relief. Daisy was praying and Little Maxie was spouting every profane word he could think of. Charlie looked at Daisy, who realized that Max had no choice. If he ever went back, they would kill him, so his life was back in her hands.

Charlie smiled. "I told you that it would be easy."

She smiled. "I thought you were a lawyer, not a race car driver."

"All in a day's work."

chapter
TWENTY
SEVEN

Charlie hit the streets early. The mornings were cooler now, and he wore sweatpants and his favorite Carolina sweatshirt. Granted, he did not like jogging in the city. He enjoyed the tranquil oak-lined streets of Myers Park. At this time of year, the sidewalk would be covered with spectacularly colored leaves. Reds, yellows, oranges, and browns of all shades would blanket his old front yard. Occasionally, a brilliant purple leaf would stand out among the rest. He ran two miles south before he hit his first trees. He would circle through Dilworth around the old Methodist church with its tall steeple. Then he would head back to his apartment for a shower and a highly fattening breakfast. After a month of neglect, his body was taking shape again, though Sonny was not helping any.

He took a detour in Dilworth and stopped at Bruegger's Bagel Bakery. He decided that a bagel would be much healthier. He grabbed a copy of *The Charlotte Observer* and sat down to enjoy his sparse nourishment. He scanned the front page. "Big Jake" Johnson was indicted for selling guns and drugs after an anonymous tip. The cops chained the doors to the abandoned warehouse. The story mentioned the high-speed chase, but did not mention his name, Daisy, or Max.

Melinda Powell had called her friend in Watauga County and put the two on a bus that night. When the Greyhound pulled into Boone, North Carolina, Daisy and her son started their new life. Max would be on house probation and a curfew. He would go to school and come straight home for nine months. Daisy was given a day shift at Appalachian State, cleaning offices and classrooms. It was menial labor, but definitely a step up from the Palmetto Motel.

Charlie thought about the chase. He was stupid for pulling such a crazy stunt. These were drug addicts and gunrunners—professional thugs—and he had gone up against them alone. If Sandy and Ashley were alive, he never would have attempted it. Sandy would have yelled at him for being so reckless and stupid, but deep down in places only she knew, she would regard Charlie as a hero.

Halloween, their senior year at Chapel Hill, Charlie had pulled a similar stunt. Franklin Street was packed with all kinds of drunks parading around in costumes. The street was closed to traffic. They were walking back to Player's for a game of pool after having lattes at the Carolina Coffee Shop. Charlie saw a football player shove his girlfriend into the alley by the Rathskellar Restaurant. He recognized the tight end as the recent all-conference award recipient. Without a second thought, Charlie darted into the alley where the drunk football player was slapping his tiny girlfriend. Charlie grabbed a trash can lid and jumped between them.

The first fist smashed Charlie's nose. The second one knocked the breath out of him. He quickly composed himself and swung the metal lid viciously. The direct blow to the head knocked the tight end to the ground, unconscious. The girlfriend started kicking and stomping the boyfriend, payback for nine months of abuse; after every game, he would get drunk and relive his miraculous feats of strength on her face. Sandy showed up with the campus police. The football player spent two years in jail and lost his shot at the NFL. Charlie was never charged.

At the hospital, Sandy had chastised Charlie for not thinking. He had let his emotions get the best of him. Charlie tried to defend himself by saying he was just helping, but she was not going to lose this one. Years later, as they viewed the Victorian houses of Bermuda from a horse-drawn carriage on their honeymoon, Sandy confided in Charlie that she was secretly proud of him. He was a hero. He was rash and stupid, but acting quickly may have saved that girl's life. After her confessional, Sandy had described several safe ways that Charlie could change the world, including becoming an attorney.

Charlie turned the page and scanned the rest of the morning's paper. On page eight of the Metro section, he saw a story about Enrique Alvarez. The story said that the teenager, accused of killing a lawyer's wife and daughter, died in a coma after being beaten by his mother's boyfriend. The mother shot the boyfriend in a domestic dispute, and now she was being deported back to Mexico. She had lived in the U.S. illegally for nine years. Charlie felt little consolation.

The rush-hour traffic was lining the street outside the picture window. Charlie slurped the last remaining drop of coffee from the Styrofoam cup. He realized just how close he had come to killing Enrique Alvarez himself. Now he knew that if he had pulled the trigger, none of his grief would have subsided. With Alvarez dead, there was no one to direct his hate toward. His tear landed on the napkin in a perfect little circle, next to the brown ring left from the coffee cup. So much violence and so much death—none of it made sense.

The world was spinning out of control, yet drivers were yelling at each other because one person wanted to turn left and was holding up traffic. Had people lost all perspective on reality? Charlie looked around the bakery and realized that he was the only one left. All the secretaries were headed to work. The clerks were in the back cleaning up after the morning rush. He was alone. It was too much. He could not face the next fifty years by himself. The future seemed useless. Any victories seemed empty without Sandy to share them with. He did have work to do now though, and Charlie decided to bury himself in that. He threw his trash into the recycle bin and headed out onto the sidewalk. He walked at first, but quickly starting running. He ran aimlessly without a distinct direction, but he ran with every ounce of strength within him.

Charlie studied the diplomas on the wall of the tiny office. Dr. Keith Alford studied medicine at Johns Hopkins and completed his training at Duke Medical Center, where he specialized in oncology. After Horace and Betty took Matt to the county hospital, they were told he needed special care. They found Dr. Alford at University Hospital next to UNCC. He was, in fact, an excellent oncologist, but he was also the only one that their HMO would pay for. Alford, himself, was a staunch opponent of managed care, but he realized that many HMO members did not receive adequate cancer treatment and many ended up in hospice care. So he added his name to the list.

Dr. Alford's office was dark blue and burgundy. On the opposite wall from the diplomas were pictures of a happy family. Two boys and a blond wife hugged their loving father and husband. Charlie sat back down on the couch and pulled out his wallet. The pictures of Ashley were becoming worn and crinkled because they were handled so much.

The door opened and a relatively young man entered. "Coffee?" The man was bald on top, but the hair around his ears flowed into a beard, giving him a very distinguished, Trapper John look. He placed his long white coat on the back of the door after handing Charlie a paper cup.

"So, Mr. Harrigan," he sat down and moaned, "I'm sorry it's taken so long to get you in here. My secretary has been trying to fit you in. I just got back from Chattanooga. I spoke at a conference there. When I got back last night, one of my patients needed emergency surgery. I was going to take a nap, but since you're here . . . what's the problem? You're not suing me, are you?"

"Nothing like that. I represent the family of one of your former patients, Matthew Douglas."

"Yes, tragic." He looked down.

"The short version of the story is this. We are suing the construction company for wrongful death, because we believe that they exposed Matt to carcinogenic materials negligently. First of all, I need to know if you can help, and second, I need to know if you can testify."

"Let me get his file. I don't mind testifying if that's the truth."

"The Douglases believe that an accident on a job may have put Matt in contact with asbestos, cadmium, ceramic fibers, or some other material used in insulation that causes cancer. I've been doing lots of research into asbestos litigation. It would be open and shut. All I would have to do is show that the owner was negligent and we win. It's that simple. You would barely have to do anything."

Dr. Alford placed the file on his desk and opened it slowly. "I'm afraid it's not that simple."

Charlie looked puzzled.

"There is no trace of asbestos in the toxicology reports. Nothing similar to it. I haven't seen a case related to asbestos in five years."

Charlie slumped back into the couch.

"Wait a minute. All hope's not gone. There was an excessive amount of silica in Matt's bronchial tubes."

"Silica? Wait, what are you saying? He had sand in his lungs?"

"Well, not really. Sand is made from crystalline silica. Many industries use crystalline silica every day. Primarily, you have four groups of workers exposed to the stuff: coal miners, underground workers, metallurgy and foundry workers, and quarry workers."

"That doesn't help me. Matt worked construction."

"Hang on a second. It's not a lost cause. Take foundry workers, for example. You got this guy who's shaping metal. Let's say he's repairing an old boat that has rust. How does he get the rust off?"

"Ah . . . I don't know." Charlie could tell that Alford was thinking hard and leading him somewhere.

"Sandblasting." Alford seemed to be enjoying this discussion, as if he were investigating a crime. "What happens is that as the sand blasts the rust, it tears apart into minuscule particles that are breathed into the lungs."

"That's the same way you might take paint off buildings, right?" Charlie had clued into Alford's direction.

"The silica dust is so fine that the hairs in your nose won't keep it out. It's easy to prevent. All you have to do is wear a mask and wash your hands and clothes real good. Your biggest problem is going to be connecting crystalline silica to lung cancer."

"Isn't it obvious that breathing tiny particles of sand can kill you?"

"Well, yes, but it's not an obvious connection to lung cancer, like nicotine. That's been proved. The results of the silica studies on cancer are inconclusive. However, we do know that crystalline silica breathed over years can cause silicosis."

"What's that?"

"Silicosis is a fibrous scarring of the lungs. It usually is the result of a prolonged exposure to the dust. Now, we do know that metallic particles are cancerous. That's called pneumoconiosis. Somehow, you would have to prove that crystalline silica causes lung cancer or malignant neoplasms. The other problem you face is that the average age of death from silicosis or pneumoconiosis is sixty or sixty-one. Matt was what, twenty-three?"

"What if he was exposed to sandblasting eight hours a day for a couple of years? Would that do it?" Charlie was hopeful, but realized the cards were stacked against him.

"I'm an oncologist, but I'm not a specialist in respiratory diseases. Look, the Douglases are wonderful people and Matt was the nicest guy, but to be honest with you, I think you're fighting a lost cause."

Charlie stood up and squared his shoulders as he handed Alford a newly printed business card. "That's me. I specialize in lost causes. All I need from you is a commitment. You don't have to testify whether or not silica causes cancer. All you have to do is testify to what you know. Are you willing? It will mean several depositions, meetings, and practice sessions."

"If you're willing to fight for the kid, I'll do what I can. It's a terrible way to die and nobody cares about it, because the people it kills aren't politically correct. Typically, white men who have worked hard in manual labor jobs all of their lives are the victims. The ones who built this nation suffer. Somebody has to care about the Matts in this world. I doubt I can help much, but I'm in, if you want."

"Thank you for your time, Dr. Alford. Your willingness is all the help I need." Charlie shook Alford's hand and left the office.

In the elevator, he could feel his chest tighten and his breathing increase. He thought, *There is too much to prove. There are too many connections. There are too many unknowns.* He had no doubt that Walter Comstock was negligent, if not dirty. But Alford was right. The case was a loser. In a civil case, the threshold of proof was much lower than reasonable doubt, but it still had to be logical and rational. The elevator doors opened, and he walked quickly into the fresh air.

Charlie loosened his tie and tried to slow his breathing. He leaned up against his car and looked at the octagonal-shaped hospital covered in mirrored windows. Matt had died here. Charlie knew what it was like to sit by the bedside of a child in the last moments. He had ridden with Ashley to the hospital and held her tiny hand as she struggled to breathe. Matt's breathing would have been labored. A machine would have aided his lungs. Horace and Betty would have been sitting by either side of the bed holding his hands.

A wave of resolve crashed over Charlie. He erased all doubts from his mind and decided he would fight for this couple. Whatever it took, he would do it, and if he lost, it would be because of Comstock's innocence and not Charlie's lack of preparation. He got into his Blazer and turned north on Highway 29. He would drive through Harrisburg and Concord to reach Kannapolis and report on his meeting to his only client. As he pulled out, the Buick Riviera followed six cars back. Slade picked up the cell phone.

"He just met with the doctor that treated the Douglas boy. Should I tell Van Schank?"

"Why don't you wait and follow him. If he keeps pushing, you may have to apply some extra pressure."

"I have to tell Van Schank if I touch him."

"What Walter and Martin do not know will not hurt them. I didn't say kill him. I just said if he finds out anything, a little pressure might be applied. Understand?"

"Capeche." He hung up the phone and dropped back a few cars, but he never lost sight of the Blazer.

chapter
TWENTY
EIGHT

The library at UNC-Charlotte closed in ten minutes. Charlie sat at a table with piles of books, photocopied articles, and information retrieved from the Internet. A couple of young romantics were giggling in a study carrel in the corner and a few students had desperate eyes, as if their research papers were due first thing in the morning and they were just getting started. In the ten hours since he had left Dr. Alford's office, Charlie was no closer to proving that crystalline silica caused cancer than when he started. He was never good in biology, and he hated chemistry. Judge Fitzwaring had given him an uphill battle.

Each year in America, more than two hundred fifty people die from silicosis. More than one million people are exposed to silica on their jobs, and one hundred thousand are in the high-risk category for contracting the disease. By far, the victims are hard-working, manual laborers and predominantly male. These workers do everything from removing paint and rust from buildings, to cleaning foundry castings, mining through rock, crushing stone, working with clay, and etching and frosting glass. Silicosis dates back to the first century and the great building programs of Caesar Augustus. The most shocking part of Charlie's research was the fact that silicosis is one hundred percent preventable. With proper oversight and training, no one should ever contract silicosis.

The one missing link that Charlie needed was a direct connection to lung cancer. The research findings proved cancer in rats, but that was the extent of the studies. Britain and Scandinavian countries had outlawed the use of crystalline silica. Australia was quickly limiting its use in construction jobs. The Department of Labor in the U.S. listed crystalline silica as a potential carcinogen. He found no one who would make a causal connection, however. The vast majority of the research and litigation was being carried out in California.

Charlie put the photocopies in his briefcase and stacked the books neatly on the table. His footsteps echoed throughout the empty library. He despised California, primarily because his father resided there. Now every aspect of his research led him west to California. Charlie walked out the glass doors into the cold night breeze. The rush of air blew away the fatigue for a second. It was refreshing, renewing. He scanned the well-lit parking lot and noticed a lone burgundy car at the far end, parked in the darkest section. Campus security drove by, and Charlie returned his attention to his keys.

He took North Tryon back toward his apartment. With nothing to return home to, he took his time looking at the neon-strip-club and fast-food signs. He passed car dealers. He wove between the cruisers and noticed a car weaving behind him. Turning right onto Sugar Creek Road, he noticed the other car went straight. Charlie decided he would be safer on the interstate, although he was probably just overreacting. Charlie drove the interstate and the loop around Charlotte for an hour, thinking about the car chase from days before. It was a really stupid stunt; then again, taking this case was proving to be a less than intelligent move.

He pulled off the shoulder on the south end of the loop and looked at the skyline. He plotted strategy; he cross-examined himself to discover the weak points of his case; he thought about depositions. He could not go into these depositions blind. He needed more information. He needed help. There was too much information for him to handle on his own. He would have to mend some bridges and ask for help. He stepped on the gas and drove into the night.

Charlie arrived at the restored Victorian house on Shamrock Road a mile west of Eastway Drive at nine in the morning. He was very impressed by the cleanliness of the I Can House. Charlie had expected a run-down, depressing environment, but from the looks of things, the house was taken care of very well. He walked in the front door and saw a receptionist who was smiling from ear to ear. Charlie assumed that the receptionist was probably one of the residents.

"Howdy! Can I help you? My name's Hattie. What's yours?" She never stopped smiling as her head tilted from side to side.

"My name's Charlie," he said, looking around for a real secretary. Not finding one, he said, "I'm here to see Mr. Grady."

"He's right down there." She pointed vaguely in the general direction of the hallway.

Charlie walked carefully, peeking into rooms with open doors and listening at closed doors. As he reached the end of the hallway, a door swung open and a large black man came bounding out. The man was not looking and almost ran over Charlie.

"Who are you?" The shirt was stretched tight across a muscular chest, and his tie was way too short. The short sleeves would have ripped if he flexed his biceps.

"I'm Charlie Harrigan. Could you help me find the director? We have a meeting at nine."

The man stormed past Charlie and stomped down the hall. When he got to the reception desk, he stopped and folded his arms, glaring at the demure Hattie. She cowered at the giant. "What did you do wrong?"

"I sent the man back to you." Her smile quickly faded.

"Who did you send back to me?"

"That man." She pointed at Charlie, and he thought about ducking in a room to get out of the way.

"How do you know he went to my office? Maybe he was a thief. Or a drug dealer. What if he was a killer walking in here off the street? You just let him loose in your house."

She was trying to hold back the tears. "I'm sorry."

"Don't be sorry. We've done this before. Use the phone. Just pick it up and press my number. You call me, and I will come out and get the man, okay? Next time, let's do it right, okay, Hattie?"

She smiled and nodded. She picked up the phone and practiced. The man stomped back to the office, waving at Charlie to follow him.

Charlie leaned around the corner and told Hattie, "I assure you that I'm not a thief or drug dealer."

"I don't know that." She returned her attention to the phone.

Charlie entered the cramped office. Metal filing cabinets covered one wall, and a corkboard with job notices and contacts covered the opposite wall. Behind the little wooden desk, Frank Grady looked as if he could split the thing in half. Charlie sat gently on a metal folding chair, hoping it was cleaner than it appeared.

"I bet you think I'm pretty cruel, don't you?" The man had not yet introduced himself or offered Charlie a greeting.

"I thought she would burst into tears any second. I don't know, but it seems like you could be more gentle."

"That's exactly the problem." The man started lecturing Charlie. "From the moment people realize a person is retarded, they treat that person with kid gloves. No one holds them responsible for their actions, and they keep them from experiencing the consequences. The result is that they never learn. I've shown her how to buzz my office thirteen times. If she doesn't learn, one day she will invite the wrong person in, and something serious could happen."

Charlie felt very small in his little chair. "I guess I'm not very familiar with the mentally challenged."

"So that's your excuse. Do you avoid the mentally challenged? Are they a nuisance? I bet you looked for another person before asking Hattie for me."

Charlie thought for a second. The man he now assumed to be Mr. Grady did not seem like a compassionate person and might be frightening as a witness. "Do you operate on donations, Mr. Grady?"

"You're an attorney, right? You lawyers are all the same. Always wanting money."

"Would you like for me to go back out front and try this again the right way?" Charlie stood up and walked to the door.

"No. I'm sorry." His voice had little regret. "I have to be so firm with my clients all day that I forget how to turn it off. People who condescend to the mentally challenged make my job harder, and I get a little passionate. They want to be normal, more than anything else. Hattie was a mess when she got here. She's smart enough to realize that her parents never punished her, so she would break the dishes and her sister would take the blame. Now, she cleans her room every morning and works at Wal-Mart in the afternoon."

"You're the boss. If you say so, I believe you." Trying to get the conversation under control, Charlie said, "So is that how you dealt with Matt Douglas?"

"Oh man, you're that attorney." He looked at his calendar. "I get so busy, I don't make long entries into the calendar. No, Matt was very obedient and teachable. His situation was different. I had to teach him that this world is not a nice place. His parents and church were wonderful. Apparently, the students in high school treated him fine. There's always jerks, but he came here completely trusting. Like many handicapped people, he needed a healthy skepticism."

"Do you think he ever learned it?"

Frank looked at the clock. "You want to go for a ride?"

They climbed into an old Ford van that was bright yellow with dark tinted windows. They stopped on Eastway and got a couple of chicken biscuits and coffee at Bojangles. Grady talked the whole time about working with the handicapped. He played college football at Clemson in the seventies and could have turned professional until he was in a drunk driving accident. His best friend, who was the passenger, ended up with brain damage. He never fully recovered. Frank had suffered a broken leg and now walked with a perpetual limp. He gave his life to helping the less fortunate. His penance uncovered a passion for helping others. Many of the lessons he learned in football helped his clients to become independent and overcome their doubts. The discipline he learned as an under-appreciated linebacker served him well in this position.

They drove past several construction sites. On weekends, residents from the home would pile in the van and look at the buildings Matt had worked on. The other patients applauded and cheered as if Matt had built the entire building. He was one of the success stories. At the I Can House, Matt learned to count correct change for the bus, buy his own lunch, and come home and wash his clothes. He was a leader among the group, and the other patients looked up to him.

Frank Grady had never met Walter Comstock. He simply responded to a flyer produced by the city manager's office, which described a special program, called Helping Hands, that allowed special-needs individuals to perform small tasks on construction sites. Paragon Group was one of the companies listed. Grady handled the entire transaction by phone and figured that if the company was willing to help the underprivileged, it had to be legit. From Grady's running monologue, it was obvious that he carried a lot of guilt. They sat at the convenience store, looking at the Graham Street renovation project.

"So what should you have done?" Charlie spoke carefully.

"I should have realized that because of the nature of the program, Matt was not considered an employee as much as an intern. Therefore, he was not being paid minimum wage and Comstock was not paying FICA. I can't prove this, but it looked to me like Comstock was using the program to get cheap labor."

"Do you think that Matt was ever in danger?"

"I assumed that he was doing things like picking up trash, carrying equipment and supplies, maybe digging holes. But then he started describing things like sanding, ripping walls with a reciprocating saw, and sandblasting."

"Sandblasting?" Charlie perked up. Finally, a connection had been made.

"Yeah, Matt loved it. He called it a gun. He would tell me how he would shoot the gun all day long."

"Did that ever concern you?"

"Sure, I was worried that he didn't understand how dangerous that could be. I went to the site one time and got run off. But I didn't see anyone watching out for him. He came home day after day covered in dust."

"Are you saying that the company did not provide enough protection for Matt because he was retarded?"

"Keep in mind that if you saw Matt on the street, you couldn't tell he was retarded. It just took him a lot longer to catch on to things. The foreman may not have realized that Matt needed very detailed, explicit instructions."

"Even if he were in danger, wouldn't inspectors or somebody catch it?"

"That's what I thought." Frank started rubbing his face with his giant hand. "I called the city manager, Josh Donovan, and he told me that he would take care of everything. That's the last I heard from him. If Matt were in danger, I figured Donovan would spot the problems. I tend to get overprotective of my clients, so I just figured I was being paranoid. If Matt's death was related to his job, that means that I'm partially to blame."

"Frank, are you willing to help me?"

Frank looked up.

"I need all the witnesses I can get. We have a tough case. Anything you can tell me will help."

"I'll do whatever I can."

chapter
TWENTY
NINE

The frigid winds of November blew in like a hurricane, stripping the trees of the remaining vestige of foliage. Brown leaves covered streets and sidewalks, while the skeletons of once vibrant oaks lay bare throughout the city. For four weeks, Charlie had plunged himself into investigation and discovery, preparing for the upcoming depositions. He sat among the stacks of legal pads and flowcharts scattered over the floor of his little apartment. On Monday morning, he would question the defense witnesses at his old law firm. He imagined the snickering and jokes that all contained the punch line, Charlie Harrigan. He dreaded seeing his former bosses and associates.

He had established several things over the past few weeks during his investigation. Mecklenburg County and OSHA had very few safety violations for Paragon Group. As a matter of fact, Paragon Group was apparently the safest construction company in Charlotte. Of the accidents and incidents, only one person had filed a complaint. Brian Beckley worked at Paragon Group for four years before losing part of his leg when a brick wall collapsed. The case was settled out of court and was under seal. A few others that were injured received adequate worker's compensation payments and had never complained. It seemed to Charlie that Paragon's records were too perfect; they lacked the normal accident reports that one would expect.

His case had several other holes. His biggest problem was that he found no one willing to claim that silica actually causes cancer. Many were willing to say that off the record, but they were hesitant to come forward and testify without any concrete evidence. The primary research on crystalline silica was being done in California. It was becoming increasingly obvious that Charlie would have to face his father and ask for his help. Being an influential lawyer in Silicon Valley, Charles Harrigan, Senior, had many contacts and had represented many people who now owed him markers. He could be a big help to Charlie.

Matt had worked under Barry Kasick. Apparently, he had been involved in activities that exposed him to abnormal levels of silica. Why had he been operating a sandblaster in the first place? Were the dangers explained to him? How much did Comstock know? Why had OSHA not red-flagged a retarded man operating dangerous equipment? Did crystalline silica cause lung cancer? Every path Charlie went down led to the same inevitable question. If he did not prove that one question, he not only lost the case, but he also faced sanctions by the court. Under the Federal Rules of Civil Procedure, if he knowingly filed a frivolous lawsuit, he could be fined, lose his license, or both.

Charlie had purchased a dry-erase marker board from an office supply company and put it on his credit card, which was quickly reaching its limit. He had hung the marker board on the wall that overlooked Davidson Street, and on the top half, he had drawn a calendar in blue, listing every major trial date. On the bottom half, in green, he had traced a line of argument and witnesses. A large red question mark occupied any spaces where there was a gap in the logic or a missing piece of the puzzle. He had too many question marks.

He rubbed his eyes and paced around the room, trying to shake something loose in his brain. When he pulled his hands away and his eyes focused, he was face-to-face with Sandy's bridal portrait. She had her hair pulled up, but little brown ringlets fell along her temples. He remembered being shocked that his conservative girlfriend had shown her entire back to the audience on their wedding day. He grabbed the picture and fell to his knees. It was too much. The case was impossible to make. The apartment felt like solitary confinement. Life was too hopeless to go on. Charlie sat with his back against the wall and thought of his wife and daughter until he fell asleep on the floor.

Sunday morning, Charlie was up early and hit the city streets for a three-mile run to the center of downtown and back. It had taken him a while to get back into some semblance of routine, but the jogging cleared his mind and made him feel like a part of the human race. He was beginning to work off all of the calories that he had put on eating fast-food three times a day.

He had agreed to go to church with his clients, basically because he had nothing else to do and he enjoyed Betty's Southern fried chicken. After his run, he ate a light breakfast which consisted of a bagel and coffee. After showering and dressing in slacks, a turtleneck, and a blazer, he headed north to Rowan County and ended up at the row of white mill houses. Charlie offered to drive the Douglases to church, afraid that the old Chevy pickup would be as dirty on the inside as it was on the outside.

They drove past the large textile mill, past the lake, and into the country. After passing a couple of pastures full of grazing cows, they arrived at a little white building, the Moose Road Church of God. Charlie fully expected to see a moose right in the parking lot. The church was narrow and had a ragged old cross to the side. He thought that he might donate some money someday to buy a better cross, because the one in the courtyard was ugly and detracted from the quaint beauty of the church.

Charlie elbowed Horace as they were walking through the parking lot and quietly said, "Hey, Mr. Douglas. To whom do I give a contribution if I would like to help you guys buy a nice, new cross for your courtyard?"

CHUCK CHITWOOD

"That's mighty nice of you, but you've got it all wrong, son. That is a fairly new cross. One of the members made it that way."

"But it's so ragged and takes away from the beauty of this quaint little country church. If you had a creek running alongside the church with a couple of deer in the meadow, it would be picture-perfect."

"That's not the point. The cross is supposed to be ugly. As a matter of fact, it's grotesque." Horace saw that Charlie was puzzled, so they stopped just underneath the cross as the sun cast the cross' shadow on Charlie's face. "The Romans invented the cross, the most cruel way to kill people. When Jesus lived, there were over twenty thousand crucifixions. There's nothing special about the cross itself. It's what happened on the cross that gives it significance."

Charlie thought about the Solid Rock Church and the large gold cross behind the platform that shimmered under the spotlights.

Betty leaned over and grabbed Charlie's arm. "You know, Charlie, when I think of the cross and the fact that God chose to suffer, I know He understands how we feel losing our only son."

"We're late." Horace glanced at his watch. "And there's some people I want to introduce you to, Charlie. I'm sure I can help you find lots of new business."

"I'm not looking for any new . . ." His words trailed off as the Douglases headed toward the front door. Alone in the courtyard, Charlie stared at the jagged pieces of wood with three iron spikes driven deep into the planks. He thought, *Why would God choose this?*

When Charlie entered the church, the hardwood floors and wood benches reminded him of the little church his mother had taken him to in Midland. After he graduated from high school, he had never gone back. As Charlie looked for a seat, he realized that the music had already begun. It was passionate and emotional, but seemed sincere. Horace and Betty were sitting in the second row. When Horace saw Charlie, he waved for him to join them. Charlie opted for the back row, in case he wanted to make a quick exit and wait out the service in the courtyard. God and church had not been a friend to Charlie the past couple of months.

From various well-wishers, he had been told that his wife or he was under the judgment of God because of their extravagant lifestyle. He had heard preachers say that he did not have enough faith or that his own rebellion caused his suffering. He had been told that God loved his wife and daughter so much that He took them to heaven. Somehow, losing his family was apparently God's will, but Charlie was not allowed to question God about it. Either he was a rebel or a sinner for questioning God's purpose. Charlie had asked God many times for answers, but he found only a deafening silence.

The songs were powerful and stirring, but not necessarily the best music he had ever heard. The people waved their hands and clapped vigorously. Memories flooded Charlie's mind, as if unleashed from some dark cavern. The little country church in Midland had had the same religious fervor. The songs sounded familiar. He remembered his mother crying and praying for hours as he was growing up. His mother was extremely strict, but only because her love for him was so vast. Somehow those memories had been forced to a rarely used corner of Charlie's mind. After the music, a young girl got up and sang the same song Sonny had listened to night after night in the POW camp. "Amazing grace, how sweet the sound, that saved a wretch like me." For a moment, the airy, lilting voice took Charlie to a place of tranquillity.

Pastor Roy D. Yeates was old and slightly pudgy. His suit was probably one he bought in the early eighties and he wore white shoes. He was quite a comical character who apparently did not take himself too seriously, but he took his job very seriously. As he read from the Bible, he spoke with power. As he preached, he pounded the pulpit and spoke urgently. His topic sparked Charlie's interest immediately, "The Trial of All Centuries." Charlie sat on the edge of his seat and intently followed the logic in Pastor Yeates' argument.

He spoke of Jesus. He said that God gave up His divine power and became completely human. He taught thousands of people for three and a half years, amassing a large following. Eventually, the people wanted Him to become a political revolutionary and overthrow the Roman government. The part that captured Charlie's imagination was the arrest and trial of Jesus. Of all the things Charlie had heard about Jesus, even from Sandy, this was the first time someone had told him about the trial.

Pastor Yeates raised his voice. "It was a travesty! A miscarriage of justice! If you think life has been unfair to you, let me tell you about the trial of Jesus. The Jewish Sanhedrin arrested Jesus. There were at least eight violations that made Jesus' trial illegal. It took place at night, instead of the daytime. It was not held in public in the Temple. They rushed the case through the system too fast. They bribed witnesses. The court did not give witnesses a solemn oath. The accused was forced to testify against Himself. They failed to dismiss the case when witnesses did not agree. Finally, the accused was brutally beaten. These things violated the very standards of law and justice in Palestine."

Charlie felt himself getting mad at how an innocent man was treated and realized he understood such a miscarriage of justice. He thought of Enrique Alvarez. Pastor Yeates continued, "When the Jewish high court realized that they did not have the power to enforce the death penalty, they shipped him to the Roman governor, Pontius Pilate. Jesus was shuffled between two different leaders, Pilate and Herod. Neither one found Him guilty or deserving of the death penalty. Pilate finally caved in to public pressure and had an innocent man put to death."

Charlie sat stunned. He thought about how powerless God must be if He could have been killed by common man. It was no wonder that his prayers had gone unanswered. It was no wonder that all of his wife's prayers failed to protect her. He thought about how to quietly sneak out without drawing attention to himself in this small church and quickly realized that it would be impossible. He decided to wait until the end and slip out unnoticed. Then the preacher said something that caught Charlie's attention.

"And He did it all for you." The preacher's voice quieted almost to a whisper, and Charlie returned his attention to the front. "The power of Jesus Christ is not that He can do miracles, although He can. The power of the God we worship is that He voluntarily gave up His power, put on our shoes, and walks through the hard times with us. He experienced every drop of pain imaginable. His friends betrayed Him. The people He loved turned their backs on Him. He was tortured in the worst way imaginable and died, because that is the world we live in and He wants to be part of our world. Nobody killed Him. He gave up everything for you!"

Sonny's words starting making sense to Charlie. He felt his heart beating and his eyes filling with tears. He held onto the bench in front of him, trying to keep his emotions in check. The preacher quoted the Book of Hebrews, saying that the Author of our salvation was made perfect through suffering and that He experienced everything we do, therefore, we can approach Him boldly. He quoted the Book of John saying that in this world we have troubles. That is part of this life. It does not make sense and there often is not a deeper meaning. Suffering hurts. The preacher finished his talk by reading Isaiah 53. He was despised and rejected by men, a man of sorrows acquainted with grief. Surely, He bore our infirmities and carried our sorrows. He was pierced, crushed, and bruised for us. And by His stripes we are healed.

The pastor invited anyone who wanted to, to walk down front and pray. Charlie did not move. He sat in the last row, weeping into his hands. Every painful memory played through Charlie's mind, like a movie on a large screen. The betrayal by his best friend. The blood stains on his bedroom floor. His wife's broken and bruised body. His daughter's lifeless body filled with tubes. The large casket and the small casket at the front of the church. His house that had become a haunted mausoleum. The years ahead of him without the two people he loved most.

A familiar hand touched Charlie's shoulder. Horace sat down next to him and put his arm around Charlie without saying a word. They sat and cried together for a long time. Even after everyone else filed out of the little country church, they sat in the back row. Finally, quietly and carefully, Horace spoke, "Suffering never makes sense; don't try to understand. It's always wrong. Jesus chose to suffer so He could understand everything we feel on this planet. If you ask Him, He will come in and join you in your suffering, and eventually you'll find peace."

Charlie was unsure. He had left the praying to others most of his life and had only talked to God in moments of rage or desperation. But that morning through the tears, the pain, and the unanswered questions, Charlie asked God to join him on his journey. For a brief second, he felt his heart lift ever so slightly. Something told him that Sandy would be very happy at this moment, wherever she was. Horace hugged him. Charlie could not remember the last time a father figure had hugged him. He felt safe.

"Charlie, you have to take it one day at a time. Even though you have given your heart to God, there will still be hard days in front of you. But if you trust Him, He will be there each and every day."

"I want to trust Him so badly. Something has to change." Charlie wiped his eyes and smiled. "I just need enough strength to face tomorrow."

chapter
THIRTY

Charlie Harrigan watched the numbers on the elevator click past in silence. He was alone on this trip to the thirty-ninth floor. The last time he had been in this elevator was the day his life fell apart. Now he was back, the adversary walking into the lion's den. The bell dinged, telling him that he had arrived at his old law firm. He uttered a quiet prayer and asked for strength. The majestic foyer looked much larger now that it was not his. He walked slowly and deliberately, trying to hide his nerves. He had been a litigator for ten years. He had done thousands of depositions. He had gone up against some of the most prestigious firms in the Southeast, but he had always had the power of Hobbes, Reimarus, and Van Schank behind him. This time, he would face his most formidable opponent alone.

He walked to the receptionist desk. "Good morning, Selia. How are you doing?"

"I'm fine, Mr. Harrigan. How may I help you today?"

"You know very well why I am here. Van Schank's probably going to tape the deposition and throw a firm party, watching my performance for the slightest snafu."

She looked through the appointment book very professionally. "Oh yes, here it is. You have a deposition in the large conference room. You'll have to wait a few minutes; the partners are pulling together some last-minute items. In the meantime, please put this on."

Charlie looked at the visitor's badge. It was obviously meant as an insult. "You've got to be kidding. Everybody here knows me."

"It's new firm policy. With so many lawyers and clients, we have gone to a system for identifying all nonemployees for our safety." She smiled and tilted her head.

Charlie pinned the unusually large badge on his lapel, walked across the Persian rug, and sat down on the leather couch. He waited ten minutes. Eventually, Samuel Reimarus came around the corner. He grabbed Charlie's hand, squeezing it vigorously.

"My stars, Charlie Harrigan. You're a sight for sore eyes! It is so good to see you. Take off that stupid badge. You look like an idiot sitting there."

"Thank you, sir. I didn't think it was necessary. How's the firm?"

Reimarus pulled him closer. "It's different, since you and Brad left."

"Brad left?" It was news to Charlie.

"Yeah, shortly after you. He and Nancy had a shouting match. He knew that since she's a partner now, she would have him canned, so he beat her to the punch. He quit. It's very tense here. Don't tell anyone I'm saying this, because I'll deny it, but I think you have them scared. Nancy and Martin have done a lot of prepping with their deponents."

"Really?"

"Another thing. I voted for you to stay. The other senior partners had their own agenda. Personally, I think we lost a great lawyer."

"Thank you. That means a lot to me."

"You know who else would be happy to see you? Oliver Burchette." Reimarus started to walk off and caught Charlie's quizzical stare. "You know, he handled all of Comstock's litigation until his second heart attack. I think he would enjoy seeing you again."

"I'll give him a call."

Selia interrupted, "Mr. Harrigan, you may go in now."

"Good seeing you again, Samuel."

"Good luck in there, Charlie. Remember who you're dealing with."

Charlie swung the heavy oak doors wide open and immediately saw the grim face of Nancy Lockman-Kurtz standing at the head of the long table. The chairs on the right side of the table were completely empty. The left side of the table was full. Immediately to her left were no less than six associates, brought along to sharpen her pencils and look intimidating. Bronson H. Kadison, M. Ross Trafaldt II, Megan Reese-Warfield, Alexander H. Wythe III, and two others Charlie did not recognize all had yellow legal pads in front of them, poised to take down every word with their Mont Blanc pens. It seemed ridiculous to Charlie, because the stenographer sat at the far end opposite Nancy, typing every word.

Next to the attorneys, Walter Comstock sat with his arms folded around his barrel chest. He was not happy to be there and would be less than cooperative. Charlie decided to depose Comstock last to make him even more angry. He knew that he would learn nothing from Comstock anyway, so he might as well have some fun. Next to Comstock, Barry Kasick sat staring at the floor. It was obvious that he had been severely warned about his answers, because he never looked Charlie in the face. Kay Merritt sat beside Barry. She was the office manager in charge of personnel and payroll. Joe O'Reilly and Dake Warner worked closely with Matt on the same crew. Charlie noticed immediately that Brian Beckley, the former Paragon employee who had been injured on the job, was not present. Charlie made a mental note to gripe out whoever appeared most vulnerable.

"Well, Charlie. Come on in and sit down." Nancy smiled and gestured to a lone chair in the middle of the table. "Would you like some coffee?"

"No, thank you." Charlie looked through his briefcase and studied his files, realizing that all eyes were on him. "Actually, I would like to get started. I don't want to waste anybody's time."

Charlie had learned finesse the hard way. He had gone into his first deposition with both barrels blazing and gotten nowhere. It did not take him long to realize that drama was reserved for the courtroom. A successful litigator has a friendly, casual demeanor. He takes his time and asks simple questions and lulls the deponent into a comfortable position. Then he throws him a curve ball, catching him off guard. Inevitably, the more friendly Charlie appeared, the more trust potential witnesses placed in him.

Nancy cleared her throat. "Mr. Comstock is ready. The rest of you may leave. I figured you would want to start at the top and work your way down."

Charlie's head was buried in a file and he ignored Nancy. As the last deponent was about to leave the room and close the door behind him, Charlie leaned back, "Okay. Mr. Kasick. Can you come back in here, please? Mr. Comstock, you may wait in the break room with the others." Charlie kept studying the file, but could feel Comstock's eyes burning a hole in him. The door slammed shut. Charlie did not flinch. On the inside Charlie was laughing. Grown men could act so immature when their egos were at stake.

"Let's go on the record." Charlie nodded to the stenographer. "Mr. Kasick, how long have you worked at Paragon Group?"

"Eight years."

"How many as a foreman?"

"Six."

"Do you have a family?"

"Two little boys, four and six."

Nancy leaned over and whispered something in Kasick's ear, apparently telling him not to volunteer any information.

"Have you ever committed a crime?"

"Object!" Nancy blurted. "That's irrelevant!"

"Relevancy is not an issue here. You know that." Charlie placed his pen carefully on his legal pad. "Are you planning on objecting to every line of questioning?"

Nancy squirmed and pouted. "Fine. I want my objection noted."

"Mr. Kasick. Why were you arrested?" Charlie also learned early on that he should never ask a question that he did not know the answer to. There is too much potential for damage if a witness is unpredictable. Charlie decided to test Kasick's honesty early on.

"In college, I was arrested for possession of marijuana. It was a stupid, kid thing."

"Anything else? More recently?"

Kasick looked around desperately for help and found only blank gazes. "Ah . . . um, a couple of years ago, an undercover cop almost busted me in a massage parlor, but he let me go if I promised to stop going to those places. How did you find out about that?"

Charlie ignored the question and moved on to the next one. Melinda Powell had contacted the police chief to dig up everything they had on Paragon employees.

"What's your wife's name?"

"Suzanne."

"How long have you two been married?"

"Twelve years." Kasick was almost in tears.

"Who hired Matt Douglas?"

"Kay Merritt. She's in charge of all personnel matters."

"Whose idea was it to hire mentally challenged people?"

"I heard it first from Walter."

"What reason did he give for hiring the handicapped?"

"He wanted to give back to the community."

"Was that the only reason?"

Barry hesitated and Charlie made a note on his legal pad. "Mr. Kasick, lying under oath is a crime."

"I don't remember."

"What are the OSHA requirements to protect workers from silicosis?"

He thought hard and Charlie said, "I know Nancy prepped you for these depositions, so don't act like you have to search your brain for the answers."

The associates looked at one another as Nancy pretended to be bored. Charlie had done his homework and realized that Barry Kasick was the weak link and knew something. He struggled with his conscience trying to work for Comstock.

"People are supposed to wear masks, wash their hands and work clothes frequently, rotate responsibilities so that the same person is not always working in dangerous areas."

Nancy flinched at the word *dangerous*, but there was nothing she could do.

"Aren't you supposed to assign individuals on-site to observe and stop work in dangerous areas? What about safety training before undertaking a job?"

"I think those are requirements."

"Did you train Matt on the dangers of sandblasting?"

"Somebody probably . . . "

Charlie blurted out, "Did *you*, Mr. Kasick? Did you warn him that inhaling the dust could kill him?"

"No."

"Did you monitor the amount of silica in the air?"

"No." Kasick was against the ropes and pleading for help with his eyes.

"Where did Matt learn to operate the sandblaster?"

"I told one of the other guys to show him."

"Were you aware that Matt's IQ was significantly lower than that of the average person, and he needed more thorough explanation?"

"Yes, I guess."

"Yes, you were aware of his special needs or yes, you gave him further safety training?"

"Uh . . . I was aware."

"Do you think Matt's death could have been prevented?"

"Don't answer . . . " Nancy started.

"Yes," Barry said without thinking.

"I think we should give Mr. Kasick a break." Charlie had drilled him for two hours straight and caught Barry with rapid-fire, machine-gun type questions. The tactic had served Charlie well over the years. The questions came from every angle, mixing up the subjects and not allowing the deponent time to think about the answers. Charlie proved from the start that he would know if Barry lied. After all, Barry was not a good liar.

Kay Merritt was next. She was a hard-edged lady with black hair sprayed stiffly to her head. She swaggered confidently into the room. Charlie instantly evaluated her potential as a witness. She was too hard for juries to sympathize with. Nancy would have to work on Merritt to make her sympathetic, soften her dress, hair, and makeup. He had little to lose with Kay Merritt and decided to knock her off balance with the first question. She sat down and took a drink of water. Before she swallowed, Charlie shot the first arrow.

"Are you and Walter Comstock having an affair?" She coughed and spewed water over the table.

"How dare you?" Nancy stood up. "You can't come in here and attack everybody."

"You know you can't limit discovery. It goes to her credibility as a witness."

"No, of course not." Kay straightened her dress and sat up, sufficiently offended.

"Has Mr. Comstock ever sexually harassed you or made you feel uncomfortable?"

"Well, he hasn't harassed me."

"So he's made you feel uncomfortable?"

"Well, yes. Sometimes his temper gets out of control."

"Would you call him an ethical business man?"

"As ethical as anybody."

"How do employees get paid at Paragon?"

"They come by the office on Friday afternoon and pick up their checks."

"Do you pay some people in cash?"

"No, that would be impossible to keep track of."

"Are there some people who get paid in cash?"

"Not that I know of."

She looked genuinely sincere, so Charlie made a note that Kay Merritt was probably out of the loop if anything shady was going on.

"Did you know Matt Douglas?"

"Oh yes, he was very friendly."

"How much was he paid?"

"I think it was three or four dollars an hour."

"Isn't that way below minimum wage?"

"Yes, but he was hired more like an intern under that program, not like a real employee."

"Did he understand everything about his check?"

"I had to explain the difference between net and gross."

"Did he understand it the first time?"

"No, I explained it almost every Friday the first couple of months he worked."

"What did he look like when he came to your office?"

"It looked like he was covered in snow. His hair would be covered with dust or something. It would be all over his clothes."

"You ever ask him what he had been doing?"

"No, several of the guys looked like that."

"Was Paragon a safe place to work?"

"As far as I know."

"Did you and Comstock ever entertain the idea of having an affair?"

She was startled again. "Yes, but nothing ever happened."

Charlie's hunch had paid off. Kay demonstrated that she could be honest if backed into a corner, but she would be a fairly useless witness in a trial. Charlie had deposed her to find out if there were in fact two separate companies operating at Paragon. If there were, he didn't think she knew anything about it.

They broke for lunch. Charlie would depose the other employees and come back to Barry the following morning. He would make Comstock wait in that little break room at least a day and a half. Comstock seemed like a person who lost control of his emotions when he was angry. If Charlie made him mad enough, he may learn something.

chapter
THIRTY
ONE

When they broke for lunch, Charlie was sure that his former associates would dine at the Top of the Tower Restaurant, spending lots of money on lobster, filet mignon, and Robert Mondavi wine. Charlie settled for a five-dollar patty melt, fries, and coffee at Sonny's. He was reviewing the background files on the next deponents at the crowded counter when he heard the bell ringing as the door opened. Sonny refilled Charlie's double-sized coffee mug for the third time and told Charlie, "You got company, friend. Don't go backward, Charlie. It makes the journey twice as hard."

Charlie looked at the door. Brad Connelly was looking for an empty spot near Charlie. He was wearing jeans, a J. Crew sweater, and his camel overcoat. He approached Charlie slowly and deliberately.

"So is this the new dress code at Hobbes, Reimarus, and Van Schank?" Charlie returned his attention to the file, pretending he did not know about Brad's job. He wanted to see how honest Brad would be.

"Well, it's *my* new dress code." Brad leaned on the counter beside Charlie, squeezing next to a disgruntled civil servant.

"What do you mean?"

"I tried to tell you two months ago, but you wouldn't listen. I quit the firm three days after they fired you. I've just

288   THE TRIAL OF JOB

been handling a couple of my old clients while I've been looking for a job." Brad waited for a reaction, but received none. "Apparently, Garrison's PR machine has spread plenty of bad recommendations about me and no firm will come close to me. The only firms that even considered me advertise on television. I did it for you, you know."

"You didn't have to," Charlie sneered.

"Yes, I did. Those sharks used me to get to you. You were my only true friend at the firm, and I wanted to make it up to you." The civil servant sitting next to Charlie paid for his lunch and slowly headed back to his mundane job, so Brad grabbed the vacated seat. "I admit it; I was wrong to let Nancy use me. You know me; I can't resist a pretty face no matter how ugly her character is. But that's not me anymore. I swear I've changed. You have to believe me. I was at the funeral. At the graveside, I sat in my car and watched from a distance. I slipped into the trial and sat in the back row. Please forgive me, buddy."

Sonny walked up. "May I take your order, Mr. Connelly?" He wrote quickly and looked at Charlie. "Dessert for you? Apple pie? Coconut cream pie? Humble pie?"

Charlie glared at Sonny and shook his head. "Brad, I just felt betrayed. Plus with everything else that happened, the thought of you reminded me of how much of a garbage pit my life was. But I've changed too; I don't have anything else in this life. I've got to hang on to any friend I have."

"Thanks, man. I couldn't live with myself if I believed that you wouldn't forgive me. I'll do whatever it takes to make things right."

Charlie looked out the corner of his eye and sipped his coffee. "I've got an idea. I'm going up against Nancy, but I can't do it alone. Since you're out of work, why don't you help me? I need someone to do background checks on potential jurors."

"I'll do anything to get back at Nancy and the whole gang. I'm your man."

"I'm working on contingency, so there's no money coming in. I'm in debt again until my house sells."

"I don't care." Brad was genuinely excited. "I've got an idea. Why don't we start our own firm? Harrigan and Connelly, Attorneys at Law."

Charlie set down his mug and thought. "I was really thinking about getting away from the law after this case. I don't think I can handle the snakes and sharks anymore."

"Think about it. The world needs lawyers like us, if only to keep the snakes in check. Besides, what are you going to do with your life?"

"I was thinking about moving to the Outer Banks, buying a boat, and sailing up and down the East Coast."

"With what? You've got no money."

"When the house sells, I will be able to leave all this behind."

"Okay, you can't say yes, but don't say no. Think about it. When can I get started?"

"Right now. I'm in the middle of depositions, but I can give you the juror list and you can start your research."

They shook hands and headed upstairs to Charlie's tiny apartment. Charlie filled Brad in on the case against Paragon Group and showed him the dry-erase board and all the holes that he still had to fill. Brad's specialty had been wills and estate planning, but research was research—anybody could do it. Charlie had made a little progress in the depositions, but he still had a long way to go. Brad's apology and help gave him a second wind as he headed back to the afternoon's depositions.

This time Charlie did not even stop at the receptionist's desk; he barreled right through the lobby into the conference room and sat down as if he owned the place. The stenographer was in place, but Nancy had not yet returned from her hundred-dollar lunch. One of the associates Charlie did not know was there, so Charlie decided to take this opportunity to make a point.

Charlie started barking out orders, "Well, Comstock has representation here. Why don't we proceed with Mr. Dake Warner?"

The associate looked like a cornered animal. "I don't think . . . I mean, I can't do that."

"Of course you can. You're an attorney, right?" The green lawyer nodded his head. "Well, run get Mr. Warner and we'll get started."

In two minutes, the attorney was back with the muscular, rock-jawed man, but he was frantically dialing Nancy's pager number on his cell phone.

Charlie began, "On the record, Mr. Warner, how many years have you worked at Paragon Group?"

"About five."

"Did you know Matt Douglas well?"

"As well as any of the other guys, I guess."

"What were your responsibilities on the crew?"

"Well, I trained the new guys on the crew, and I double-checked their work to make sure everything was right when they were done."

"What were Mr. Douglas' responsibilities?"

"Well, at first he just gathered trash and scraps. He ran errands and he did little things like that. He even went to get us beer a couple of times." Warner laughed at his feeble attempt at humor and quickly realized that no one else had cracked a smile.

"Did the foreman ask you to train him for any special jobs?"

Dake Warner looked uncomfortably at the associate, who merely shrugged his shoulders. "Well, he thought we were not making good use of him, because he just sat around a lot of the time. So he told me to teach him to run the sandblaster and help on the demolition crew."

"What do you mean the demolition crew?" This was new to Charlie, and he tried to delve as deep as possible before Nancy returned.

"Comstock basically divided his company into four teams. I'm on demolition. We go in and clear the site and get it ready for the next crew. The framing crew does all of the basics. The exterior crew does the brick and roofing. The finishing crew does all the inside stuff like molding, you know?"

Charlie knew that Nancy would never allow potential witnesses to talk so freely. "Did Mr. Douglas understand everything you taught him right away?"

"Oh no, it took several times."

"Did he understand the dangers of running a sandblaster?"

"Basically, but I had to keep reminding him."

"Did he wear his mask the whole time he was running the sandblaster?"

"I don't know. Sometimes, maybe?"

"Did you tell the foreman you were having trouble getting Matt to comply with safety regulations?"

"Yeah, but he said if that retard don't know any better, it's his own fault."

The oak doors burst wide open, slamming against the wall. "Stop this right now! I want you to strike this whole deposition. You questioned my client without me present." Nancy was fuming, waving her arms, and cussing under her breath.

"Actually, I'm deposing your client's employee and you had representation. This guy."

The young attorney wanted to crawl under the table but remained in his seat. Nancy continued ranting, "I'm going to call Judge Fitzwaring and see what he thinks about this!"

She picked up the phone and was dialing, when Charlie said, "Unless you're sleeping with him too, he won't listen to you, since an attorney was—"

Charlie ducked quickly. The phone barely missed his head. "Okay, let's take a recess; I really don't mind."

After a thirty-minute recess, Dake Warner proved to be less forthcoming than before. Nancy yelled, cussed, and screamed at him for twenty minutes and then yelled at Joe O'Reilly, in case he decided to be as honest as his friend. Charlie backed off the questions for awhile. He asked relatively innocuous questions and threw in a zinger every now and then, but got nowhere. By eight o'clock that night, he had finished with Warner and O'Reilly, having learned nothing else.

The depositions of Paragon employees continued for a week and a half. Walter Comstock was there every day, waiting his turn. Charlie could call any employee at any time. Nancy had to make sure every potential deponent was available, or Charlie would file his own motion of sanctions that Ms. Lockman-Kurtz was interfering with discovery. At the end of a week and a half, Charlie finally called for Comstock. Comstock walked into the room with the blood vessel in his neck already throbbing. When Charlie said that he had no questions for Comstock, he thought that blood vessel would explode. Charlie collected his things and exited the building quickly.

He knew that he would learn nothing from Comstock. If Charlie could keep the man angry enough, he would make a great witness whether he said anything or not. The jury would be afraid of him. Charlie drove back to his little office, where Brad had been researching the two hundred and ten potential jurors. With the Thanksgiving holiday so near, they would spend a month getting to know their jury pool, and try to find any scientist who could connect crystalline silica to lung cancer.

Charlie knew what would be going on at Hobbes, Reimarus, and Van Schank. They would find the best doctors from Duke, Bowman-Gray, Emory, Virginia, and the best New England medical schools and pay them $10,000 a piece to demonstrate that there is no connection between silica and cancer. Charlie would not even depose these men. Nancy would have hired private investigators to research the potential jurors, and she would have two hundred and ten separate files including pictures, background information, and anything incriminating. Of course, they would not contact the jurors personally, but they would come close.

Then Nancy would hire a professional jury-consulting firm at five hundred dollars an hour. They would select the best jury for the defense. She did not need the help, given North Carolina's reputation for stingy rewards. As the trial approached, Nancy also would hire behavioral psychologists to sit in the courtroom during voir dire and the trial. They would study the body language of the jurors and make recommendations that would influence how Nancy would question a witness. If the jury started folding their arms and frowning, she would lighten up on a sympathetic witness. If their eyes started darting around the room, they were bored and she would go on an attack. If they were sitting up straight, they were very interested and she would forge ahead, making the most out of that witness.

The process was all very scientific, but a jury of twelve people is the most unscientific thing on the earth. Juries are notorious for missing the main points. In complex civil matters, they get lost in the science and business and vote for the plaintiff because the defense attorney seemed mean. Juries have been known to punish prosecutors for dragging out a case and wasting their time. No jury consultant or psychologist can predict with any certainty what will happen behind closed doors.

Each year, over five million people are summoned for jury duty for one hundred and twenty thousand trials. Seventy-five percent of all jurors believe that verdicts are too large and sixty-six percent believe that there are too many lawsuits.

Charlie's potential jury had fifty blacks, one hundred and thirty seven women, and ten union laborers who always vote against corporate America, ninety-six college graduates, fourteen small business owners, and about half blue-collar workers.

The average juror in America is a white, college-educated woman between the ages of thirty and fifty. Women are notoriously stingy when it comes to jury awards and tipping waiters. Charlie had worked in both professions and knew it was true. Charlie wanted all ten union members, and he knew that the small business owners would love to stick it to the big guy. He and Brad split over the blacks. They may punish the CEO, but may not be willing to reward white plaintiffs. White-collar workers and college-educated people frown on giving large sums of money to anything, unless it 's for dolphins or spotted owls.

None of the juror information that Brad and Charlie gathered would mean a thing, however, unless they could demonstrate that the silica was the cause of Matt's death. The research was scarce but some had started coming in.

"Hey, Charlie, look!" Brad handed him a paper he printed off the Internet. "This guy at Chapel Hill has proposed that silica causes cancer. Dr. Daniel Goldberg has proved it in rats. But it looks like the rest of the research is out west, UCLA, Berkeley, and Los Alamos National Laboratory in New Mexico."

"I guess that means one thing," Charlie said gravely.

"What's that?" Brad asked curiously.

"Oh, man, I really didn't want it to come to this. But I guess now is as good a time as any to forgive."

"What are you talking about?" Brad's face displayed the fact that he was totally in the dark.

"There's one person I know out west who has all the connections and could put us in touch with those people, but the last time I saw him, he told me he was dying and I didn't say a word. I didn't even ask him why! I feel horrible, but I just don't know how I can forgive almost thirty years of abandonment." Charlie was studying the cross where four floor tiles came together.

"Oh, your dad. I'm sure he'll understand your feelings, but sometimes you just have to bite the bullet and do it." Brad headed toward the kitchen. "If you wait for your feelings to change, you'll still be sitting here while Comstock walks away with a victory."

Charlie picked up the phone and dialed long-distance. "Hello, Marie. Can I talk to my father?"

"Oh, Charlie, he's been wanting to talk to you. Hang on." Charles's second, much younger wife took the phone to Charlie's father, who was soaking in a hot tub.

"Hello, Charlie. I'm so glad to hear from you. I was afraid that you would just try to forget about me." The voice was not strong and confident as Charlie remembered it.

"Dad, I admit that seeing you was not easy, but I could never forget about you. Believe me, I've tried. But you're always somewhere behind me, pushing me. Not a single day has gone by that I haven't thought about you for some reason or another."

"I don't have long left. The doctors gave me six months."

"What is it? Isn't there anything they can do?" Charlie was overwhelmed with a sudden flood of sympathy.

"It's Lou Gehrig's disease. There's nothing they can do. Imagine that. I come out west, get a good tan, jog three miles every day, and avoid red meat. I've done everything right, and now I'm going to just waste away. Ironic, isn't it?"

Charlie felt the lump in his throat getting larger. "I'm so sorry. I wish I could say something."

"Well, there is one thing you can say. I can't make up for all these years, but you could say that you forgive me." Charlie had never heard his father speak so gently and contritely.

"I'll try, Dad. To be honest, it won't be easy, but I swear I'll try."

"Charlie, I want us to be a family, even if it's only for six months. I'll do whatever it takes to prove that I do love you."

"Actually, I did call with the intention of groveling and asking for your help. Two things. First of all, I need you to talk to your friends at UCLA and help me find a couple of doctors out west there. I need scientific proof to win this case."

"I'll do even better. I'll pay the consulting fee and plane tickets to North Carolina. What's the second thing?"

"Why'd you leave?" Charlie held his breath waiting for the answer to a question he had been asking all his life.

"Charlie, I'm a great lawyer," the voice faded slightly, "but I'm not a great man. Small-town life was killing me. The gossip. The morals. Everyone judging everyone else's actions. I wanted to make money and I knew I couldn't do it there. I decided that you would be better off without a father than with a guy as bad as me."

Charlie felt a huge lump in his throat. "Well, you're wrong.

I needed a father who was present whether he was good or not. I've been trying to make up for whatever it was I did wrong—whatever I did to make you leave—all my life."

"Charlie, you've always been so much better than me. You didn't have anything to live up to. You had everything I wanted, but I gave it away." He tried to regain his composure. "So can I join your legal team?"

"Sure thing, Dad. I'd be honored to have you."

chapter
THIRTY
TWO

Charlie was sitting in his tiny apartment watching the Christmas Day parades and eating Chinese food out of small boxes. He had held depositions that accomplished very little. He and Brad had waded through the two hundred and ten names on the juror list and had drawn very few conclusions. His father had located three doctors willing to testify and had received signed affidavits from all three. At least something was beginning to happen.

At this time of the year, most of Charlotte shut down and Charlie would accomplish little discovery until after the New Year. The thought of celebrating Christmas had no appeal to Charlie. He had spent most of Christmas Eve watching videos of the ghosts of Christmas past and remembering the good times.

He picked up his Bible and thumbed through the Christmas story. He had read it many times to Ashley, but now wanted to read it for himself. As he read, the beautiful story he had learned as a child seemed quite different. Two young people under the veil of shame of an illegitimate child with no family in Bethlehem face a cold winter's night. The hope of humanity lies in the worst of conditions. Herod the Great attempts to destroy the hope by killing all of the baby boys in the town. The story was fraught with heartache and despair, but in the center of it all was a baby, the promise of brighter days. Charlie set down the Bible and thought about Mary and Joseph, on a journey. There was that word again—journey. Would his own journey never end?

Suddenly, Reimarus' advice flashed across his mind in a Christmas epiphany. At the time, Charlie had not given it much thought. Knowing he was facing a marathon of depositions had crowded every corner of his brain at the time. Looking back over the minuscule amount of useful information he had uncovered, he had started to get depressed. Now, though, he realized that he may have one more shot at uncovering something that would make sense of this case.

He ran to the bedroom and rifled through a file cabinet, looking for his address book. He remembered the words of Samuel Reimarus, the one partner who had not wanted him fired, "Oliver Burchette would be happy to see you." Charlie almost kicked himself for not jumping on this sooner. Burchette had handled Comstock until his second heart attack. Charlie flipped the to "B" section and dialed the number for Oliver Burchette. After five rings, someone answered the phone.

"Merry Christmas!" the slightly gruff voice shouted.

"You're starting kind of early, aren't you, Oliver?"

"It's a day of celebration. Who's this?" Burchette was slightly lucid, but would be so for only a few more minutes.

"Charlie Harrigan. Your old friend from Hobbes, Reimarus, and Van Schank. Samuel Reimarus said that I should give you a call. I left the firm a couple of months ago, and I'm now trying a case against Walter Comstock. Reimarus suggested that you might be able to help me."

Burchette thought for a minute. "I'm not sure how much I can tell you, but shoot . . . I don't care if I lose my license. I'm retired. What can they do to me? I have a feeling I know what he's talking about, but I can't tell you over the phone. We need absolute privacy. Can you come down?"

"I thought you would never ask. I want to see that new

boat of yours. I need to get out of Charlotte anyway. I don't feel very festive."

"I understand. Look, I was actually going to take my boat out tomorrow. Can you get here about noon?"

"Sure. No problem."

"I've got a thirty-foot Catalina named *Easy Money*. It's docked at Camachee Cove on Harbor Drive. You can't miss it. Anybody on the docks can point you to my boat. We can head up the Intracoastal Waterway to Matanzas Bay. I'll tell you the whole story."

"Is that why you retired so abruptly?"

"You got it, partner. You're involved with some very dangerous characters and you don't even realize it. Hey, I can't wait to see you again. I'm tired of looking at all of these old people down here. They're really depressing."

"I imagine they're pretty tired of looking at you too. See you tomorrow."

Charlie quickly packed a small bag and headed down the stairs. He climbed into his Blazer and weaved through the streets to Interstate 85. The streets were deserted; there was not a single police car in sight, so Charlie took some liberties with the speed limit. The Buick Riviera had a difficult time keeping up with him, but it remained inconspicuous.

The three-and-a-half-hour drive southwest to Atlanta was desolate. The rolling hills were bare and the trees stood naked in the sky. Except for an occasional peach orchard, the land-scape was empty. When Charlie reached Atlanta, he took the loop around the city. After a quick dinner, he would spend the night with his mother and stepfather celebrating the holidays, then wake up early in the morning and finish the drive. This little side trip to Atlanta would take him five hours out of the way, but his mom would be devastated if Charlie did not show up. He had promised her he would come, though the last thing Charlie wanted was to participate in anything that resembled a traditional family Christmas.

He pulled off the Windy Hill exit to his favorite restaurant. Any trip to Atlanta always included the Three Dollar Café for the best hot wings in town. The sports bar and grill had been closed all day because of Christmas, but it opened for dinner for all of the men looking to get away from in-laws or wanting to play darts, or who just wanted to stare at the cute coed waitresses in their Atlanta Braves baseball caps. Charlie simply wanted a large bowl of hot wings. A redhead named Megan took Charlie's order and flirted a little to ensure a nice tip. Charlie ignored the flirtations and returned his attention to the Blue and Gray football game.

Sitting in the far corner, Slade hid behind his menu and studied every move Charlie made. This trip had not been on Charlie's schedule and was out of character. Over the past two months, Slade did nothing but study Charlie. He broke into the flimsy door of Charlie's apartment several times to sift through Charlie's research and report back to Van Schank and the other business partners. Slade worked for all three in different capacities. None of the men knew exactly what Slade did for the others. A less attractive waitress approached Slade's table and had to keep herself from laughing at the ridiculous Hawaiian shirt.

"What may I get for you today, sir?" she asked, trying to suppress a giggle.

"Actually, sweet cheeks, I'll take any dark beer you have, but would you mind if that redhead over there waits on me?" He gestured in the general direction of Charlie's table.

"Humph. Well, first of all, my name's not sweet cheeks. And second, this is my station."

"Go file a sexual harassment lawsuit. I don't care. Here's a twenty. Can she bring me my beer?"

The waitress stormed off and Slade laughed. Being obnoxious was one perk of his job of investigating the underbelly of people's lives. Before long, Megan arrived at Slade's table with a tall glass of Killian's Red.

"Will there be anything else for you this evening?" She did not trust the man who asked for her; he looked like a pervert.

"You see that guy over there you just waited on? Me and some friends are giving him a surprise birthday party. I've just got to make sure that he doesn't go home right away. Would you casually find out where he's headed and come tell me?" Slade slipped a hundred-dollar bill into her apron. She did not want to help the greasy man, but she was a college student and had bills to pay. When Charlie's food was ready, she delivered it to his table and struck up a conversation with the lonely man. After a few minutes, she returned to Slade's table.

"Are you sure that you two are friends? You don't look like you have anything in common."

"Of course, I normally wear suits too. I'm in disguise. What'd he say, sweetheart?"

"Well," she looked at him, and against her better judgment said, "he's headed to his mother's house tonight, and then tomorrow he's going to St. Augustine. I think he's going to miss his birthday party."

"Thanks, sweetie." Slade threw another twenty on the table and patted Megan on her rear. She gave him a death look as he scooted out the door.

In his car, Slade dialed the direct number for Martin Van Schank. "Martin, Slade here. Your boy is going to St. Augustine."

There was silence on the other end. "Oh, no. Burchette's going to spill his guts. You've got to get down there and talk to Oliver. Tell him we will pay whatever it takes to keep him quiet. He can't tell Charlie what he knows. Do it!"

"Whatever you say, boss." Slade hung up and dialed another number. "Slade here. Guess where Mr. Harrigan is headed?"

"Tell me. I don't play games."

"He's going to see your old friend, Oliver Burchette."

"Why?"

"I guess since Oliver was the only litigator for Walter, Charlie thinks he's got some inside information."

"Take care of him."

"Martin wants me to buy him off."

"I don't care what Martin says. Take care of him, and I'll take care of Van Schank."

The phone clicked and Slade heard the dial tone. He started the engine and pulled out of the parking lot about the time the manager ran out of the restaurant to find the man who was harassing the waitresses. He was too late. Slade was already on his way to St. Augustine.

Charlie arrived in St. Johns County shortly before noon. It was sunny and seventy-two degrees in St. Augustine, much different from the cold, gray overcast climate of Charlotte in winter. He admired the city. It was beautiful and immaculate. No wonder Burchette wanted to retire here. Outside of the tourist areas, much of the Old World charm still remained. He drove through downtown past the Mission Nombre de Dios, the first Catholic church in America. Through three hundred years of history, the church was still strong.

He arrived at Camachee Cove. It was the day after Christmas, and the harbor was dotted with white sails. The last time Charlie had seen the beach, he was at Nags Head with Sandy and Ashley. He parked and walked onto the docks. He strolled in and out of the various moorings and decided that there had to be a system. Maybe the boats were in alphabetical order, but that was probably too simplistic. He found an old man hosing off a fishing boat and asked if he could point Charlie to *Easy Money*.

The man gestured to the very end of the cove. Charlie walked to the southern end of the harbor, where only three boats remained docked. *Easy Money* was the first one he came to. It was fifteen minutes after twelve and Burchette was nowhere in sight. Charlie climbed on board and leaned against the rail, soaking in the tranquillity of the water. Knowing Burchette, Charlie assumed he had gone to buy some beer for the trip. He waited half an hour.

For all of Burchette's shortcomings, he was a man of his

word. He was a glutton, arrogant, greedy, and frequently crude, but he took his job seriously. Charlie started to get worried. He opened the door and looked below deck, calling Oliver's name. There was no answer. Charlie moved slowly toward the bedroom. The door was slightly ajar. Charlie eased it open. He let out a gasp. Oliver Burchette's body was slumped over his desk. The gun was to his right and behind him. Charlie looked carefully; the apparent suicide note was covered with blood. The pen was sitting by Burchette's right hand. Oliver was left-handed. Charlie knew that all too well because they had attended a bar association banquet one night and bumped elbows the entire evening. Something was wrong with this picture.

Charlie felt himself getting sick as images of his wife flashed through his head. He darted up the stairs and leaned over the rail gasping for breath. He forced himself to hold back the impulse to throw up. He reached in his pocket and dialed 911 on his cell phone. Within minutes, the cops were there. The boat would be off limits for days, and Charlie would not stay around to search for whatever information Oliver had. He waited a few hours for the police to contact Oliver's wife. Then Charlie dialed the phone, trying desperately to think of what he could say.

Charlie identified himself as Oliver's friend and associate, but he didn't need to. He had met Burchette's wife at an office function, and because he had been so different from the other attorneys, she remembered him. He expressed his deep sympathies and explained that Oliver was going to meet with him that morning. Charlie told her that he thought someone had killed Oliver and tried to make it look like a suicide. Mrs. Burchette listened and cried. Finally, Charlie mustered the courage to ask if she may have known why anyone would want her husband dead. She agreed to talk to him and mentioned that several odd things had happened that day, like a number of hang-up phone calls. Maybe that person was after her now.

Gladys Burchette agreed to meet Charlie as soon as possible at Café Cortesse Bistro and Coffee House, which was about halfway between them. Charlie reached downtown and turned onto San Marco Avenue. He immediately saw the elegant bistro. He waited on the front porch and eventually saw Oliver's wife drive up. She got out of the car. They hugged, and she just cried in Charlie's arms.

"I don't know what to do; I'm really scared. After I hung up the phone, I noticed a man sitting in a car across the street from my house. Do you think he's after me, too?"

"I don't know what's going on. Let's go inside." Charlie led her into the foyer. They sat at a dark table in the corner.

"It's good to see you, Charlie."

"I'm sorry it's under such terrible circumstances. I'm truly sorry about Oliver."

"He's been acting funny since you called yesterday. It's like the way he acted before he had his second heart attack, looking over his shoulder, griping at people for no reason."

"I didn't mean to stir up problems. One of the lawyers at my old firm seems to think Oliver had some information that might be useful in a case. Maybe it has something to do with that."

"When he left this morning, he told me to put this in our safe-deposit box." She handed Charlie a thick expandable file.

"What is it?" Charlie looked curiously.

"It's the novel he was writing, a legal drama."

Charlie nodded so she would continue.

"After we had been retired a couple of months, he started telling me that some of the people he represented were not necessarily good folks, you know what I mean? He mentioned that one client and a lawyer had developed this scheme to make money. So he decided that it would make a good novel."

"Do you think this is what he wanted to tell me?" Charlie flipped through the pages. "Are there any other records or journals where he may have written something down?"

"Before we left Charlotte, he hired these people to take several boxes of stuff and have it shredded professionally. He

---

said he wanted nothing to remind him of the firm, that he was finally out."

"Can I keep this?"

"Sure. Use it if it can help you find out who killed my husband."

"Are the cops saying anything?"

"They still think it was a suicide, but they promised to look into it."

Suddenly, she stopped. Her face became white and her hands started shaking. "That's the man. The man who was sitting in the car across from my house."

Charlie looked and saw a very familiar face, one he had seen before but could not quite place. He jumped up, knocking over the glasses on the table. Charlie raced toward the entrance, shoving his way through people. Slade noticed him and headed for the door. Charlie dove and grabbed Slade's legs. Charlie smashed a fist into Slade's face repeatedly, until he was violently ripped away from the man. The manager grabbed Charlie and held him by his arms as Slade ran across the street, jumped into his car, and disappeared into the night.

chapter
THIRTY
THREE

Brad sat across from Charlie at a tiny table in the corner of Johnathon's. The owner of the St. Augustine restaurant where Charlie had attacked Slade said he would not press any charges as long as Charlie agreed never to return. Charlie had told the police that the man at the restaurant was probably Oliver Burchette's murderer, but the police had no leads other than a vague description. The only set of prints on the boat, other than Charlie's and Burchette's, belonged to someone who had been in the military. The Pentagon had sealed that particular file, and they could not reveal the identity of the person behind the fingerprints.

Charlie finished the last chapter of Burchette's manuscript and handed it across the table to Brad. Charlie watched Brad's face as each revelation registered. The story was irresistible, and it took Brad just fifteen minutes to finish. They looked incredulously at one another as the saxophone player started warming up for his second set of the evening.

"Do you think all of this is true?" Brad took a bite of his steak.

"His wife said that he was writing this book based on his experiences at the law firm. It's hard to tell what's true and what's fiction."

"A secret cabal of dirty lawyers and businessmen, who planned a get-rich scheme while they served together in

Vietnam, now working in government and law in Charlotte."

Charlie set his sweet tea down on the table. "I think Comstock flew A-6's in Vietnam."

"Our murderer is a mystery man who must've been on some black-ops squad in Vietnam, because the Pentagon won't even give his name to the police. That means he must've been a Green Beret or something."

"That's marines. He wouldn't have anything to do with the air force."

"Wait a minute." Brad scratched his head. "I think the marines have planes too. Weren't A-6's the first ones in?"

"Yeah, Comstock brags about that."

"And they always send the marines in first. So we have the possibility of a secret cabal."

The waitress approached the table. "Would y'all like anything else?"

"I'll have a Corona with a lime," Brad said.

"I thought you were a changed man."

"I am, but I still like a beer every now and then."

Charlie waved the waitress away. "He's fine, just the check. Look, Brad, I need you completely sober if we're going to win this thing. No lapses of judgment, okay? Nancy's capable of anything. Back to the story."

"Okay, fine," Brad agreed reluctantly. "You've got a lawyer, the mayor, a hit man, and a CEO all in Nam together, who decide to bring some drugs back home and use their respective businesses to launder the money. How does that fit with Comstock? Plus, Mayor Humphreys is a World War II vet, isn't he?"

"Yeah, he is." Charlie thought. "What if Oliver knew something about one of the attorneys at Hobbes, Reimarus, and Van Schank? He and Van Schank did all of Comstock's litigation before his retirement. You know what? I remember seeing a partnership agreement in Paragon's file. There was a reference to a secret partner, or essentially a silent partner."

"Do you think big ole Oliver knew who Comstock's partner is?"

"Even better, do you think Van Schank is his partner? Comstock isn't smart enough to launder drug money."

"Think about it. How many times has Comstock received government contracts? Refurbishing Graham Street? The Dilworth renovation? All we have to do is connect all this information to Matt, and you've got more than passive negligence, you've got criminal collusion."

Charlie was standing, pacing around the table, drawing attention to himself. "Wait a minute. Wait a minute. The program!" He slapped the table and all heads turned in his direction. Charlie sat down and lowered his voice. "Comstock received a government grant to hire disabled people. Because they were hired as interns, he didn't have to pay minimum wage, vis-à-vis low bids. He saves money on employees and always gets the lowest bid."

"Somebody on the inside keeps him abreast on the bidding war. Everybody skims a little off the top."

"And they pay hourly fees out the wazoo to Van Schank."

"Our own little cabal."

"Now we just have to prove it." Charlie placed his elbows on the table and listened to the soulful wail of the saxophone.

"I can't believe you almost got caught. You idiot!"

"I'm sorry; I didn't think Burchette's wife would recognize me." Slade apologized profusely. "Anyway, they don't know who I am and there's no way to find out."

"It doesn't matter. You're getting fatter and sloppier the older you get. I talked to Van Schank, and he's worried that Harrigan may start delving into Burchette's past and discover what he knew."

"I searched the boat and I've been through the house. Nothing's there. The man kept no records."

"Did he have a safe, safe-deposit box, or a storage facility elsewhere? Did he have a lawyer who might have something?"

Slade tried to justify himself. "There's nothing that can do us any harm."

"Still, we want you to send Mr. Harrigan a strong message. If he doesn't back off this case, he will suffer."

"What kind of message?"

"I'm sure you can think of something."

"Why don't you just encourage your partners to settle with him?"

"That's the plan, but I think he needs some added pressure that will help convince him to settle. I don't want to know what it is. I just want it to be effective. Capeche?"

"Capeche." Slade hung up the pay phone and drove to the twenty-four-hour Wal-Mart.

Finding all the materials he needed, he drove to the Myers Park section of the city. For hours, he drove through the streets, watching all the lights go out one by one. He made several passes by the Harrigan house until he was sure that no one was around. He parked two streets back and pulled on a dark blue jogging suit. Placing wire cutters, matches, lock-pick kit, and knife in his coat, he threw the knapsack containing a gallon of gasoline over his shoulder. He started jogging down the sidewalk. When he got to Charlie's house, he looked around and darted behind the house. At three in the morning, no one would notice him.

Cutting the wires that connected the security system, he opened the door to the basement. He found exactly what he wanted. Charlie stored his lawn mower and other equipment in the basement. Slade moved all of the equipment next to the gas furnace in the corner. He had other methods to make arson look like accidents, but this was the easiest way. He poured the gallon of gas all over the floor and walls near the furnace. With one match, the basement was an inferno. By the time anyone discovered the fire, the complete interior of the house would be engulfed in flames. Slade escaped out the back door and darted through two yards without detection. Mission accomplished.

The shrill ring jolted Charlie out of a deep sleep. He struggled to open his eyes and grabbed the phone.

"Harrigan here."

"Charlie, turn on channel nine. You got to see this." Brad's voice was desperate.

Charlie fumbled for the remote and instinctively pressed nine. It took a couple of seconds for his eyes to focus on the blazing fire. "No!" Charlie screamed.

"Man, I'm sorry! I can't believe it! Now your house."

"What happened?"

"The news said that the fire started by some flammable fumes near your furnace."

"This is no accident, Brad. This was a message." Charlie stood up. "We're getting too close and somebody's getting nervous."

"You better contact the DA and let him know what's going on. This thing might get worse before the trial's over."

"Oh, man." Charlie sat down on the foot of his bed.

"What?"

"I've got to go and see if anything is left. I packed up everything but left most of it there. My wedding album, Ashley's baby book, everything Sandy ever gave me, it's all gone. This can't be happening. I can't do this anymore. It's too hard. I might as well settle this thing and get it over with."

"You want me to come over?" Brad asked compassionately.

"Meet me there." Charlie hung up.

He threw on some clothes and drove furiously against the morning rush hour traffic. He prayed the entire way that something could be spared. When he arrived at his house, the fire chief had to restrain him. The decision had been made to let the house be consumed by a controlled burn, because so much of it had already been destroyed. The firemen, who had been in the house, reported that nothing was salvageable except a few things they had grabbed as they were looking for survivors. On trips in and out of the house, the firemen had brought out four boxes before the heat had become unbearable.

They put the boxes on the sidewalk near Charlie's Blazer. He sat down on the ground, tears flowing profusely. The boxes were singed but still intact. He opened the first box. As soon as he turned back the lid, he eyes immediately locked on Ashley's baby book. He opened it and there it was. His finger twirled the lock of brown hair from her first hair cut. He put the box in the back of his Blazer and opened the second box. This box contained all kinds of things he had found in Sandy's closet. There was a shoe box full of letters they had written to each other in college.

Among the things was a bag he did not remember. He opened it and found a present wrapped in green and red paper. Sandy loved Christmas and would have all of her shopping done in July. She would get excited like a little child. He unwrapped the present. In the gift box, he found a Bible. Opening it, he found a picture that was taken his senior year in college at the Fall German's Dance.

On the inside cover was an inscription, "To the love of my life, you have given me everything I ever dreamed of. Most people look their whole life and don't experience the joy you've given me the past ten years. You are my hero, and I love you more than you can even imagine. But as much as I love you, there is Someone who loves you more. If you will trust God, He will take care of you no matter what happens. Trust Him like you trust me; He will never leave you."

For once, Charlie really felt like God answered his prayers and that maybe God was on his side. Sandy had spoken to him from beyond the great divide. He held the Bible and wept again. He was her hero. She would not be proud of the way he had given up on living. He resolved not to give up and not to cry anymore. Sandy had come through for him again. She was still the catalyst, the spark that drove him to dream big dreams. Now more than ever, he was going to nail Comstock, even if it killed him.

Melinda Powell examined the two pictures. They could be sisters. Two blondes, both in their early twenties, killed three months apart. The pathology and crime scenes were very similar, except for the fact that the bodies were on opposite sides of the city, a junior at Queens College and a Dairy Queen employee in Indian Trail. No one would have noticed the similarities two years ago, before the cooperative effort between city and county was established by the district attorney, Guy Streebeck.

"Rex, do you have any leads?" Melinda's voice cracked.

"I got nothing. One person heard a scream, but that was it. The Dairy Queen girl was leaving her job around midnight and disappeared for two weeks until her body was found in a drainage culvert. The coed was jogging down Queens Road and was never heard from again. Her body was found in a Dumpster."

"Guy is desperate for an indictment. The media is eating him alive in the headlines, "Serial Killer on the Loose." Are there any suspects we can take in to custody and throw the news hounds a bone?"

"Listen, lady," Rex screamed into the phone, "there's nobody. No fingerprints. No DNA. No fibers. This guy is a professional. The bodies were clean."

"As soon as you find out something, let me know."

"You got it, lady." The phone clicked.

Melinda slammed down the phone and returned her attention to the pictures. They were horrific, but she could not look away. This was the part of the job she hated. Fighting for the victim and the innocent seemed like a losing battle. There would always be more perverts and idiots than heroes and champions. The worst part of it was the waiting. The serial killer would have to strike again before they could establish patterns and an accurate psychological profile. She may have to wait three more months.

There was a knock on the door. She closed the files and slid them in her bottom desk drawer. She opened the door. It was Charlie Harrigan.

"Hey, Charlie, how are you doing?"

"Not good, did you see the news?"

"Yes, I'm sorry." She motioned for Charlie to take a seat. "I don't know how much one guy can take."

"Well, I can't take anymore, but I actually discovered Someone who could help me. I finally understand that God does care and looks out for us. I was so repulsed by religion and some of the things I've seen that I had really been ignoring God, even though I called myself a Christian."

Melinda paused momentarily and pulled out a file. "Speaking of repulsive religion, have you ever seen a penny of the Harrigan Family Fund?"

"What are you talking about?" Charlie was completely clueless.

"Reverend Billy Rae Higgins has been raising money for you and some other families of violent crime in the city, but so far no one has seen a dime from the funds. I'm preparing to indict him for fraud, embezzlement, and tax evasion."

"God helps those who help themselves, right?" Charlie snickered and thought about the flashy pulpiteer. "I may have some more indictments for you. I'm not sure of anything yet, but I wanted to let you know so you would be aware of what I am doing."

He told her the story of the apparent suicide of Oliver Burchette and the inconsistencies. Burchette was left-handed, but the pen was found by his right hand. He left a note about crimes he had committed, but he wrote a novel about being duped into fraudulent practices. He and Charlie were supposed to have a meeting, and Burchette had something very important and confidential to tell Charlie. Charlie gave the ADA one of the twenty copies of the manuscript that he had made and stashed all over the city.

Melinda thumbed through the pages, speed-reading the print. "How much is true?"

"I don't know. That's what I'm trying to find out. Comstock may not just be guilty of negligence and wrongful death. He may be criminally negligent. Don't show this to anyone else. Somebody in local government may be involved."

"You've got my word. This goes in my private safe in this office. Here's what I'll do. I'll snoop around the edges quietly and let you try the case. If we make a big deal of this now, everything might blow and no one gets justice. If you keep him preoccupied with the lawsuit, he may not notice that I'm asking questions."

"Sounds good to me. Thanks, Ms. Powell." Charlie stood to leave.

"It's Melinda, okay? You make me sound ancient."

"Sure." He reached for the door and turned back. "Oh, by the way, any word on the good doctor and his whereabouts?"

"The girl's roommate has received a couple of calls, apparently from the same place. They may have settled in South America. I'm working on an extradition order in case we can pinpoint their location. I'm not giving up—not yet."

"Neither am I." Charlie walked out and closed the door behind him.

chapter
THIRTY
FOUR

Snow brought the city of Charlotte to a standstill in the middle of January. Icy roads and overly optimistic drivers caused accidents and dented fenders all over the city. With just two or three snowfalls a year, Mecklenburg County is frequently caught off guard when the skies do open up. Meanwhile, the street cleaners, who double as snowplow drivers, were on strike for better pensions, retirement benefits, and insurance. The early morning rush hour crept slowly through the slush, while the safety inspector, Mark Ashton, yelled into his phone.

Charlie sat on the couch and watched the young, stressed-out man ranting and raving, stopping only occasionally to take a drag on an unfiltered cigarette. The phone was tucked snugly under his chin, with the smoldering butt in one hand and a cup of black coffee in the other. The dark-haired, dark-skinned man had been on a fast track to success, but somehow he had gotten stuck along the way, much like the thousands of cars on Independence Boulevard waiting for a disgruntled employee to start his snowplow.

"Fine! Tell them we will set up an arbitration after they get the blasted roads cleared! The sooner they get it done, the quicker they will get what's coming to them! That's all I can do right now. Nobody else is here. Josh must be caught in traffic himself. You'll be the first person he calls when he gets in." He slammed the phone down and talked to no one in particular. "I'd give them what's coming to them. I'd fire them all and pay high school students minimum wage to do their job. Maybe we could train monkeys to do such a mindless job. Nobody's in the office who can make decisions, and for some reason, I'm the one everybody wants to yell at. How'd you get here so early without getting stuck in traffic?"

Charlie sat up, realizing that the inspector was talking to him. "I live only a block and a half east of here. I just walked. Listen, if you are too busy to talk, I can come back later."

"We might as well talk now. Nothing is going to get accomplished today anyway. Let two inches of snow fall and these people act like it's the apocalypse." He took another long drag. "Heck, it might be the apocalypse. I don't know. So what can I do for you, Mr. Harrigan?"

Charlie had spent most of the month trying to uncover the safety records of Paragon Group. The construction company had a remarkably clean record. The Occupational Safety and Health Administration had been able to tell Charlie little. OSHA had red-flagged Paragon only twice in five years. One was for Brian Beckley's accident. There was some sort of claim that was dropped for no apparent reason. The other red flag had been for lack of safety supervision. By and large, OSHA based its inquiries on information from the local city and county inspectors. The safety inspectors were part of the city manager's portfolio, along with land development and managing city employees.

A Republican mayor appointed Josh Donovan city manager. He did such a good job restoring the elegance of downtown Charlotte that the Democratic mayor who followed left him in place. He was an eloquent speaker with a handsome face. He knew how to inspire people to get behind his vision, but he always let Mayor Humphreys get the credit. Most importantly, he knew how to get things done cheap. He saved the city thousands by awarding contracts to the right companies. To the public he was a hero, but to his subordinates, he was a tyrant.

"The reason I am here is regarding a lawsuit against Paragon Group. My clients are suing the company in a wrongful death claim. I just need some information from any safety inspections or warnings that your office may have on the company."

Mark Ashton looked at Charlie. "Paragon Group? They have the best record of any construction company in the city. Why is anyone suing them?"

"Remember the mayor's program to help the handicapped? Apparently, Paragon hired some people who were mentally challenged and gave them simple tasks. My clients believe that Paragon allowed their son, who was part of that program, to perform some tasks that are relatively dangerous. He simply did not have the mental capacity to understand the risks." The facts of the case were public record, so Charlie could share some of the details.

"I don't know how I can help you." Ashton shrugged his shoulders.

"Well, first, you could let me see their safety records, and second, you could answer some questions."

"I don't think I can show you their file, privacy rights, you know. But I will try to answer your questions." He crushed the cigarette butt in a small tin ashtray.

"All I have to do is ask the judge and he can compel you to give me those records. It's part of discovery. You could be interfering with a—"

"Do all attorneys take a class on threatening litigation, or is bullying people something that comes naturally?" He left the room and headed down the hall dragging his feet. "So what are your questions?"

"Have you ever inspected Paragon?"

"All the time."

"How are jobs assigned to a particular inspector?"

"Basically, it's random. Whatever site is due inspection, the next person in line gets it. Sometimes Josh calls me and sends me to a certain place. I've been here the longest."

"Are you aware that Paragon has a program to help handicapped individuals?"

"I'm sure it's in the file, but I never saw any."

"Really?" Charlie scratched his head. "Do you know a foreman at Paragon named Barry Kasick?"

"Never heard of him." Ashton pushed open a door and flipped on the light. He opened a file cabinet and grabbed a stack of files. "Here you go. Paragon's safety records. There's a conference room right there you can use to review these. I can't let you take them out of the office though."

"Anybody else ever inspect Paragon?"

"Probably. I don't know. Check the signatures." He opened a file and pointed at the bottom of one of the pages.

"OSHA pretty much waits for your red flags before they get involved, right?" Charlie looked suspiciously at Ashton.

"Basically. Sometimes complaints bypass us, but usually they'll go with our recommendations."

"How many times a year does the average company get red-flagged?"

"Four, maybe five times."

"How about Paragon?"

"I don't know off the top of my head. Check the blasted files. That's what you wanted to see, right?"

"Fine." Charlie sat down at the table and spread out the mountain of files.

He searched for several hours. Out of more than fifty inspections of Paragon, Mark Ashton's name was on more than forty. Sure enough, Paragon had received two red flags in five years and only six in ten years. The files on Paragon were relatively thin and immaculate. There were few recommendations or updates to make sure Paragon was complying with those recommendations. Charlie looked through all the files for a fourth time. This time he focused on the names of the Paragon employees. All of the foremen were mentioned, except Barry Kasick. Somebody in that building was helping Paragon Group keep its record squeaky clean.

It was almost lunchtime when Charlie finished with the safety files. He took them back to Mark Ashton's desk. Ashton looked frazzled. His tie was loosened and his sleeves rolled up. Charlie decided not to bother him again. He walked down the hallway to the city manager's office. The secretary told him to wait. Five minutes before noon, she told Charlie that Josh Donovan would see him briefly.

Charlie and Josh shook hands. Josh Donovan was a charming man. He smiled and was very cordial. He offered Charlie a seat and a cup of coffee.

"So what can I do for you?" He looked at his watch and then back up at Charlie.

"I'm looking into safety violations at Paragon Group for a lawsuit I'm trying."

"I don't really know anything about that." Donovan glanced out the window at the increasingly heavy snowfall. "I pretty much let the inspectors handle things themselves and then come to me if they have problems."

"You sign off on all inspections, don't you?"

"Sure, but you know how government works. Unless the inspectors tell me there's a problem, I don't read all the small print looking for things." He leaned back and crossed his arms.

"How are inspectors assigned to construction sites?"

"It's random. Whatever comes up, the next guy goes out."

"Do you ever assign specific inspectors to certain sites?"

"No, I don't have time to micromanage people like that. Like I said, my inspectors are competent. But as I remember, Paragon is one of the safest companies we have in the city. Mr. Comstock has received several meritorious citations over the years."

Charlie paused and reluctantly asked the next question. "Why does Paragon Group do so many government projects, like Graham Street?"

"Are you accusing me of something, young man?" Donovan stood up and put his hands on his hips.

"No, it's just too big of a coincidence that they seem to always have the lowest bid."

"Here's how business works." Donovan's voice was full of righteous indignation. "Paragon is safe, which means fewer lawsuits. Fewer lawsuits mean cost-effective business. Cost-effectiveness means lower prices. The city council goes with the best and the safest. I'm sorry, but I have a lunch appointment." He opened the office door for Charlie.

Charlie stood to leave and scanned the diplomas on the wall next to several military commendations. Then a picture of an oddly shaped plane caught his attention. "So you were in the air force, huh?"

He looked at Charlie. "Air force is for wimps. I flew for the marines. A-6 Intruders, the first ones in. We cleared the way for everybody else."

"A-6's are hard to forget. They have that little nose thing on the front that makes them stand out." Charlie took a few steps so he could closely study the picture.

"That's the fuel line. When they built the plane, they had no place else to put it for quick refueling, so they stuck it on top of the nose."

"So you were in Vietnam?"

"Yeah, about the time you were messing up your diapers, I was flying air strikes into Hanoi. See that Purple Heart? I got shot down behind enemy lines. They had to send in some Green Berets to rescue me. One of the other pilots circled my downed plane seven or eight times, covering me with gunfire until the Green Berets got there."

"How awful." Charlie stood there amazed.

"There are worse things in life." Donovan looked at Charlie, obviously frustrated.

"Would you be willing to testify to everything you've told me?"

"That's one of those worse things I was talking about." The door slammed in Charlie's face.

Martin Van Schank was swimming laps in the Olympic-size pool at the private athletic club in the First Union Tower. The club was state of the art, and only the wealthiest executives and attorneys were members. Since the city had all but shut down, he decided to exercise and relax. Later, he would get a massage from one of the young aerobic instructors. He had completed his twentieth lap and was coming up for air when he saw a worn pair of white wing tips on the edge of the pool. His eyes followed the ugly shoes to the light blue pants and eventually the Hawaiian shirt, open to reveal a thick gold chain.

"I thought I told you that you were not to contact me in public." Van Schank's voice echoed through the natatorium.

"Relax. Nobody's here. The place is empty." Slade shouted at the top of his lungs. "Hey, I got free drugs here. Anybody want some? See, what'd I tell you?"

Van Schank climbed out of the water and stood inches from Slade's face. "If you do anything stupid to get us caught, I will throw you to the wolves. You're not the only private consultant on my payroll. I have other guys who will kill you in your sleep. Don't mess this up, like you almost did in St. Augie."

"That was a fluke. How was I to know that the old dame saw me? Besides, nobody down there knows me. They can't trace my prints. All they have is a face."

"Maybe you should take a vacation. That was you who burned down Harrigan's house, wasn't it?"

"Yeah, but the cops don't even suspect arson. Nobody knows. But you should know that your former associate is not backing down."

"I know. Nancy offered him three-quarters of a million to settle and he did not even hesitate before declining it. He's going to push this thing one step too far." Van Schank grabbed a towel and started drying off. "Did he learn anything from the widow?"

"They talked about thirty minutes at the café, and she handed him a thick package. I have no idea what was in it. I'd been through the entire house and every inch of his boat. Whatever it was must have been hidden quite well."

Van Schank placed his round spectacles on his face and

scratched his head. "I need to go through Burchette's files and see if there is any damaging material. If Burchette knew who Comstock's partners are, this thing could get ugly."

"What can I do?" Slade's devious mind was whirling.

"Don't take your vacation yet." Van Schank paced to the window and looked down at College Street, now blanketed in snow. "First of all, get us ready to make a fast exit if necessary. Charter a plane at Douglas International Airport and keep it on standby if the trial begins. Make sure you get a wad of cash out of the account." Van Schank had a private account set up for activities that the firm could not directly be a part of.

"Okay, but what about Harrigan?"

"He can't see you again, but turn up the heat one more notch. If that doesn't work, I want you to start working on a plan to take him out of the equation."

"You know Brad Connelly has joined Harrigan, don't you?"

"Yes, but he's weak. With Charlie out of the way, he will fold." He turned quickly. "You can't make it look like a suicide again. It has to be an accident. We don't need any more attention. I can't believe this sorry case has gotten this far; those stupid yokels won't give up."

"Don't worry, Marty, I'll take care of him."

"If I go down, you're a dead man." Van Schank walked out of the natatorium and climbed into the sauna. He would soak for a while and then go find Nancy for an early lunch.

The relationship between Martin Van Schank and Slade went back thirty years to Fort Bragg, North Carolina. Slade was one of Second Lieutenant Van Schank's best products. In his younger, thinner years, Slade had crawled in the mud under North Vietnamese huts and listened to officers making plans. Spying and reconnaissance was a specialty of Slade's. Van Schank had been in Danang three years leading these recon excursions into communist territory when he was approached by a colonel dressed in civilian clothing, asking him to command a black-ops squadron into the Golden Triangle.

Cambodia, Laos, and Thailand were never officially part of the police action, but their unofficial support was greatly needed. Of course, Van Schank took his trusted sidekick, Slade, with him into the green hills of Laos. The Laotian government unofficially offered their support for a fee. There were certain guerrilla factions willing to fight against the NVA, but Van Schank had no money. The deal was struck. Van Schank would take the "China white," or heroin, and funnel it back to the States through a couple of friends who were pilots in the marines. The money would in turn make its way back to the Laotian guerrillas, with Van Schank and his crew taking a small percentage for transportation expenses.

When Van Schank's tour of duty was over, he returned to the States and went to law school at Washington and Lee, but Slade remained in the Far East keeping the operation going. After graduating with honors, Van Schank was hired at the prestigious firm of Stromboldt, Hobbes, and Reimarus. Several years after old man Stromboldt's death, Martin Van Schank was hired as the youngest senior partner in the history of the firm. His ability to generate high-rolling clients had earned him that spot, although no one knew that many of his clients were actually fictional corporations. When Slade had returned to the States, he had started his own security consulting firm in Charlotte. His biggest client was Martin Van Schank.

chapter
THIRTY
FIVE

"He's an idealist." Charles Harrigan, Senior, lifted the gin and tonic to his mouth. "He should have taken the money and run. That's always been his problem; he thinks the world honors Jimmy Stewart heroes who don't compromise."

Brad watched the elder Harrigan take a drink and imagined the taste. "But that's what makes him such a good attorney. He's not a sellout. He really cares about his clients."

"All of the scientists we've brought in still say it's a long shot. If the CDC, EPA, and AMA are not willing to say that silica causes cancer, then most of the medical community is going to side with them. That's the way it is." Charles coughed violently and bent over in his chair, "I'm just glad I don't have to deal with people anymore. Corporations are easy. Life is messy."

"Is that why you left?" Brad watched the old man painfully lift the glass to his mouth.

"That's one of the reasons. That's not all. I really don't care to talk about it. I'm trying to make things right. I figured Charlie couldn't hate me too much if I helped on the biggest case of his life."

"I think just having you here is enough. He needs all the family he can get right now. Personally, I don't see how the guy's even walking. With all that he's been through, he's still forging ahead with this trial. His backbone won't bend, much less break."

Sonny delivered the sausage and eggs to the table. He had stayed late to cook dinner for the strategy session from which Charlie was uncharacteristically absent. The elder Harrigan heard of Sonny's legendary sausage, eggs, biscuits, and gravy from his son and opted for breakfast instead of dinner. Charles and Brad spent the evening reviewing the testimony of the various scientists. Since Dr. Keith Alford was a local boy and Matt's physician, he would be the primary witness. Several experts would buttress his findings and assumptions as to the cause of Matt's death.

Donald Goldberg had been a graduate student at Chapel Hill when he demonstrated a connection between cancer and silica in laboratory rats. Maxine Norvell from Cal-Berkeley, Harold Rutherford from UCLA, and Koshee Patel from Los Alamos would concur with these findings and offer their own studies. Thomas Busby was a political activist from California, pushing Proposition 65, which calls for the regulation of crystalline silica and demands that all forms of silica be listed as a Group 1 carcinogen. He was too radical to testify, but his expertise on the subject made him an invaluable consultant worth the ten thousand the elder Harrigan was shelling out of his own pocket.

According to Busby, the EPA has moved slowly on crystalline silica because of political pressure. Special interest groups, like insurance companies and corporate CEOs, do not want silica named as a carcinogen. The first victorious case against a company demonstrating that silica caused cancer would open a floodgate of litigation on the scale of tobacco and breast implant litigation. Busby told of measures that European countries like England and Norway have taken to monitor silica levels in the workplace. Australia has placed legal limits on the amounts that workers can be exposed to without liability for the employer. They would have a difficult time getting this information to the jury.

Their opponents had one doctor from Duke University whose correlational studies showed no real connection between silica and cancer. The rest of their experts were all from north of the Mason-Dixon line: Johns Hopkins, Massachusetts General, Harvard, Syracuse, and the Mayo Clinic. The two men looked at each other. *Great,* Brad thought, *this Southern jury will have to choose between Yankees and surfers.* The question was, who did they hate worse?

"How can you drink that stuff with eggs?" Brad asked between bites.

"How can you be a lawyer without drinking?" Charles' sarcasm was not well received by someone trying to give up the habit.

Brad looked at the leathery face and white hair. Charles, Senior, was worth millions. He lived in Silicon Valley and had a penthouse in Hong Kong. He flew nothing but first class and wore thousand-dollar suits. Yet he was dying. He was miserably alone and did not even know his own son. Brad decided that giving up alcohol would not be a difficult choice.

"Well, I can't wait around all night for Charlie. I need my beauty rest." Brad collected the dishes and took them to the kitchen. "You can hang out here or upstairs until Charlie gets back."

"Fine." The man answered somewhere between a bark and a growl. "I'll go over the doctors' affidavits one more time and see if there's anything we missed."

The March 1st trial date was closing in quickly. The three men had been working day and night at a fevered pace. Through the diligent work of Brad Connelly, they had a file and brief biography on all two hundred and ten potential jurors. They had several lists. One was in alphabetical order. One list was in order of desirability. There were lists of education, salary, and previous legal history. Brad was physically and mentally exhausted. He, like Charlie, had been working without pay for months. He had two clients who paid him for estate planning, but they were not good repeat customers. Brad's savings had dwindled to nearly nothing, and he was getting more than a little frustrated with Charlie's desire not to take on any new clients to pay the mounting bills.

Brad headed out the door, locking it behind him, thinking about how far in debt Charlie had gotten. Once again, his insurance company was holding out on him, claiming that he fit the profile of an arsonist desperate to make money to pay off his bills. Brad turned the corner into the gravel parking lot and saw Charlie's Blazer parked on the far side of his Porsche. He looked around and saw no other cars in sight and no individuals on the street.

He walked slowly behind the Porsche and found Charlie lying on the ground between the cars. Charlie was unconscious, and blood trickled out of the corner of his mouth. His pulse was weak but constant. Brad turned Charlie's head, and saw that his right eye was dark purple and was swelling at a fast rate. Brad dialed 911 on his cell phone. Within minutes, the ambulance and cops were there.

Brad and Charles drank brown water, which someone had mistakenly called coffee, that they had gotten out of a vending machine in the waiting area of Mercy Hospital's emergency room. After calling Horace Douglas, Brad learned that Charlie had left Kannapolis around eight o'clock. He had met with the Douglases to review their testimonies and to give them a sample of what cross-examination would be like. Charlie pretended to attack them and called them money-grubbing rednecks. He had apologized profusely, telling them that he hated this part of the job, but he had to prepare them for what they might be facing in the next couple of weeks.

However, the Douglases told Charlie they understood that it was part of his job. After Charlie was done, they had prayed for Charlie and the trial. When he left, everything was fine. They knew of nothing else. The police didn't seem to know much either. They had combed the area around Sonny's, but most of the neighbors seemed to have bad hearing and faulty memories.

A third-year resident, named Beth Quinlan, came out of the

trauma room asking for family or friends of Charlie Harrigan. She told Brad and Charles that Charlie had a concussion, several bruises, and two broken ribs. Whoever beat him up did a thorough job. No serious or permanent damage was done, but it would take a couple of days for Charlie to get on his feet again. The only problem was his right eye. Until the swelling went down, they would not know if he would lose any sight in it. They could see him in a few minutes.

Charlie was groggy and dazed. The door opened and the bright light from the hallway hit his left eye, making him wince. An IV poured fluids into his left arm, and oxygen flowed out a tube into his nose. The blood was wiped away, but Charlie looked just as bad. Brad ran to his side and Charles sat down hesitantly in a corner.

"What happened, buddy? Are you okay?" Brad grabbed his hand and gave him a hug.

"Oh, that hurts. Don't squeeze too tight." Charlie gritted his teeth. "Oh man, I don't really know what happened. All I know is that when I pulled into the parking lot I was alone. I went around to the passenger's side to get my briefcase and files. Out of the blue, somebody grabbed me and slammed my face into the side of the Blazer." Charlie moaned and tried to stretch his stiff body.

"Did you see him?"

"No, it was blur. It happened so fast. There were a couple of guys. They smashed my face a few times and then stopped for a second. I remember one of them leaned in real close and whispered, 'Don't you get it yet? Leave it alone. Take the money and walk away.'"

"What'd you say?"

"I said, 'I don't care if you kill me, I've got nothing to lose.' Then they threw a blanket or something over my head and beat the snot out of me. I think one of them took a tire iron to my ribs."

"Wow," Brad looked astonished. "You really think Nancy was behind this?"

"I don't know. Nancy's twisted, but I can't imagine her

hiring thugs. That's our old firm. What do you think?"

"It's not my firm anymore. I'm going to call the judge and tell him what they did."

"Wait a minute. You've got no real proof it was them. Just my word." Charlie groaned. "Let's leave it alone. I'll call ADA Powell in the morning when I feel better and let her know what happened. I told her about Burchette. She's looking into things . . . quietly."

"Well, at least let me go get a continuance from Fitzwaring tomorrow. It will be automatic."

"Are you crazy?" Charlie sat up a little and fell back on the bed immediately. "That's what they want. Delay and intimidate. They want to make us scared and bog down the process. The longer this thing takes, the more it favors them."

"The trial is one week away."

"I'll be ready. These guys are not going to beat me again. I've taken everything that's been thrown at me so far. I'm not backing down. Comstock is going to be sorry he ever met Matt Douglas . . . and me."

Doctor Quinlan stuck her head in the room. "Okay, guys, Charlie needs his rest."

"So she's cute. You got her phone number yet?" Charlie asked Brad.

"Man, I was too worried about you to notice her."

"Go buy her a cup of coffee. I'll be all right." Brad walked out the door, but Charles remained in his seat.

"Son, I don't know what to say. When I saw them put you in that ambulance, all I could think of was the fact that I was going to lose you and I really don't even know you. We've just started getting to know each other and...." Charlie had never seen any weakness or vulnerability in his father. He was not sure how to respond.

"Everything's going to be all right." He tried reassuring his father. "I'll be fine. We have plenty of time to catch up."

"How can you be so forgiving? I'm a rat. I don't deserve a second chance from you. I abandoned you and your mother. I've spent almost thirty years pretending I was happy and that all this stuff gave me joy, but I was miserable. I would imagine what it would be like to have played basketball with you, to have been there when Ashley was born, or to watch you in the courtroom. You know I kept up with everything you did. I still have *The Charlotte Observer* from the day you passed the bar exam."

Charlie was speechless. He stared incredulously at this man he did not even know.

"I'm your biggest fan. You are a better man, a better husband and father, than I ever was. That's why I avoided you all these years. I was ashamed of who I had become. You didn't need me anyway. Look at what a tremendous man you turned out to be." Charles turned away from his son.

Tears rolled down Charlie's face. "I've been waiting all my life to hear that you were proud of me." He sniffed and wiped his eyes. "I do need you, now more than ever. You and Mom are the only family I have. Let's just start over, a clean slate."

His father turned and was visibly frustrated. "How can you forgive me that easily? How can you just start over? People don't change that easily."

"They can. I changed. Actually, God changed me. After Sandy and Ashley were killed, I hated God and everything about Him, but then I discovered the truth about God. I discovered how Jesus suffered and died and forgave the very people who were killing Him. When I asked Him to forgive me, I felt something . . . I can't describe, but for the first time since their deaths, I felt a little glimpse of hope, a reason to wake up in the morning. He took all that hate. I figured God would be angry at me for hating Him, but He took the hate and it's like He wiped it out."

His father was spellbound by Charlie's story.

"God can make you new instantly. We can start over fresh and new. All you have to do is give Him your whole life."

Charles grabbed his son and hugged him with tears rolling down his own face. "I want to start over. Please forgive me."

It was more of a prayer than an apology. Pain ripped

through Charlie's body, but he bit his lip. The last time his father had hugged him, Charlie was six years old. They embraced, and incredibly, the gloomy atmosphere of the trauma room lifted. Years of separation and hurt seemed to be eclipsed by this outpouring of forgiveness and love. Once again, Charlie was a son.

chapter

THIRTY SIX

The phone rang and Betty Douglas immediately picked it up. On the other end was Brad Connelly. "I need to talk to Charlie quick. It's great news!"

"He's sleeping. I hate to wake him."

Betty had been taking care of Charlie as he recovered. It was just three days until the trial, and Charlie still had pain when he walked, but he insisted on going through with it. Betty had brought Charlie breakfast, lunch, and dinner in bed. In all truth, Charlie told her that she was becoming a very proficient paralegal. Charlie would give her instructions and research citations. Betty was very diligent and conscientious in her work. He was ready for trial, but his case still lacked the punch that it needed. At this point, it could go either way.

With three days left, Charlie had started working on his opening arguments. Many attorneys begin with eloquent statements and spend too much time preparing rhetoric that will quickly be forgotten by the jury. Charlie had always gathered all his information and laid out his case, and then formed his opening argument. He wanted to spend the bulk of his time talking about Matt Douglas. The plaintiff's biggest asset in a civil suit is the appeal to the emotions of the jury. When people see human beings suffer, there is a natural tendency to want to place blame somewhere. However, Judge Fitzwaring had effectively taken away his best weapon, at least for the first half of the trial. He would not be able to mention Matt or call his family as witnesses until the second half. If he could not prove that silica caused cancer, their testimony would be irrelevant. If he lost the first part of the case, he could face sanctions and find himself the star of a bar association hearing. This did not concern Charlie; he just could not stand the thought of disappointing his clients.

"I went in and shook him, but he's fast asleep." Betty apologized to Brad who was waiting on the phone.

"Do this for me. Go in and put the phone to his ear."

Betty hesitantly followed orders. Brad yelled into the phone. "Wake up, you sorry ambulance chaser! Get up, boy! We got work to do!"

Charlie bolted upright and momentarily forgot where he was. "Who's this? What's going on?" He grabbed the phone.

"Hey, buddy. Good news." Brad was almost giddy.

He told Charlie about his morning. Brad had gone to the renovation project on Graham Street where Paragon was turning an old warehouse into yuppie condos. He noticed that four Hispanic men were doing all of the sandblasting inside the building. One of the men was blasting rust off the steel beams. A couple of them were not even wearing masks. Brad sat in his car in a crowded parking lot and watched through binoculars. They did the same job all morning until lunch.

At lunch, he observed that Barry Kasick and the older white men got into an expensive pickup and drove off. The Hispanic quartet walked across the street and sat in front of a convenience store eating Twinkies and microwaved enchiladas. They shared a can of beer from a brown paper bag. Brad looked for other crew members, but no one was around. So he approached the men and asked if they could talk. He wanted to talk about their safety, about a lawsuit, about a guy named Matt. Only one man, the oldest in the group, spoke English, and he related the conversation to the others. They were reluctant to say anything.

Brad decided to sweeten the offer. He reached into his pocket and pulled out a roll of twenties. He gave them enough money for each one to buy a six-pack and some cigarettes. He told them he would wait out back while they bought their beer.

Charlie chided Brad, "You never give the money up front. Always after."

"I learned that the hard way," Brad replied. "I waited for fifteen minutes. Finally, I walked back into the store and they were all gone. But the older guy was walking back to the store when he saw me. We talked for about thirty minutes."

The man's name was Diego Strahos. He walked up to Brad and said, "Matt's dead, isn't he?" Then he grabbed Brad and said, "You've got to help. I took over Matt's job when he got too sick to do it. I've got a wife and five children. This is the only thing I can do, but if I die, my family will have nothing."

Charlie was pulling a sweatshirt over his pajamas and trying to listen at the same time, "I've got to talk to him. Right now. Will he testify?"

"He's scared," Brad said. "He's not in this country legally. He's afraid that he'll be deported if he gets involved in anything official."

"I can handle that. I'll make a couple of phone calls—"

Brad interrupted him, "Uh oh, Charlie, I gotta run. I see two guys that look like members of the Village People walking my way. One's got a two by four. See ya."

The Porsche squealed its tires and left skidmarks on the blacktop. Brad turned left onto Fifth Street headed the wrong way on a one-way street. He turned right onto Church Street, where a policeman saw him and flipped on his lights. For Brad, this was nothing. He made two S-shaped turns and stepped on the gas before the cop could ever get close enough to read his license plate number. Brad was on the interstate and disappeared into traffic. The cop gave up.

Charlie and Brad drove along the winding gravel road. They could not believe they were still in Charlotte. They had turned off Rozzelles Ferry Road three miles ago, and this little path was nowhere on Charlie's map. At the end of the path was a cul-de-sac with several mobile homes. Little Hispanic kids ran barefoot kicking a soccer ball. Old ladies were gathering clothes from lines strung between trailers. There were several old pickups and a couple of cars up on blocks. They had just entered a Third World country right there in Mecklenburg County.

They found Diego's trailer with no problem. They knocked on the door. A little girl opened it immediately but was frightened by the white faces. She slammed the door and yelled for her father. A few seconds later, Diego opened the door.

"I'm sorry. The only white people who come here usually cause trouble, either police or crooks, you know. Please sit down." Diego was not inviting them in. He was inviting them to sit on the lawn chairs propped up against the front of the trailer.

Charlie gingerly pulled the rusted metal chair apart and sat down, fearing the ancient lawn furniture might give way. "Mr. Strahos, my name is Charlie Harrigan. I am suing Paragon Group for the death of Matt Douglas. Brad tells me that you might be able to help us."

"I'm afraid of testifying. We can't go back to Mexico. Life is so much better here. There are still rebels in the mountains where we're from and it's very dangerous."

Charlie looked at the squalor surrounding them and could not imagine life getting much worse. "I'm going to work on getting you visas, so you and your family can stay in the country."

"I don't know. It still makes me nervous."

"I've got an idea. Why don't you let me ask you some questions, and you tell me what you know. You may not even have any information I can use."

"Okay, I guess." Diego nodded and opened an ice chest next to him. He offered Brad and Charlie a beer. Charlie declined and thought, *His kids are barefoot in February, but at least the man has beer.*

Charlie asked him about his job and how he got to

Charlotte. Diego was very forthcoming. He told Charlie how twenty of his friends had crossed the border into Texas. Out of fear, they kept moving east to Louisiana. They got jobs harvesting rice. They moved to Arkansas, where they worked in chicken factories. They moved to Florida and picked oranges and grapefruits. After the harvest was over, they were looking for more work. A stranger approached the whole group at a little Mexican bar outside Orlando and told them about a carpet factory in Dalton, Georgia. After the factory closed down, the same round man in a Hawaiian shirt offered them construction jobs in Charlotte. He would give them some money to help them move and pay them four dollars an hour.

Diego had moved every three to six months until he got to Charlotte. He had been at Paragon nearly two years and met Matt on several occasions. He remembered Matt was very funny and bragged about shooting his gun, meaning the sandblaster. When Matt got too sick to work, Diego was ordered to do Matt's job. They would start at seven in the morning, and during the summer, they worked until eight or nine at night. They did nothing but the demolition. When they finished cleaning a site, preparing it for construction, another team would come in and do the actual work. They would move to the next spot and he would continue sandblasting all day long.

Brad and Charlie looked at each other in amazement. The philanthropist of the year was running a sweatshop. He was recruiting illegals and handicapped people, skirting minimum wage laws, and receiving awards for helping people. Somebody in the government was looking the other way. But Charlie still had a case to make. He would have to leave the conspiracy alone for awhile. The Douglas lawsuit was more pressing.

Charlie asked Diego, "Is everyone in this place illegal?"

"Yes, of course. There's eight families here. Most of the men work construction."

Charlie counted quickly. There were eight families, but only five trailers. "Did anyone ever tell you about the dangers of your job?"

"A man named Warner told me to always wear my masks and protective glasses."

"Did they tell you about silicosis?"

"No."

"Did they tell you about pneumoconiosis?"

"What's that?"

"Did they tell you to wash your hands regularly and always wash your clothes good?"

"No."

"Do you cover your ears while you work?"

"No."

Charlie looked at the ground. "Mr. Strahos, if it's possible, I'd like to take you to a doctor tomorrow. Can you get out of work?"

"I don't know."

"I really think you need to be checked out. I'll pay for it, but you could be in some danger. I'll come by and pick you up in the morning, if that's okay."

"Mr. Harrigan, if you can help me stay in the country, I'll testify in court."

Charlie, Brad, and Charles sat around the metal folding table the evening before the trial began. They plotted strategy and argued about the order of the witnesses. They all agreed that the first part of this case would have to be a blitzkrieg. Jurors get bored. Jurors punish extremely verbose lawyers. Jurors want to go home.

The defense strategy was obvious. It was a strategy Charlie had used effectively many times. Delay. Delay. Delay. They would take as much time and call as many witnesses as possible. Their cross-examinations would be excruciatingly long and incredibly complex. They would delve into the smallest minutiae just to bore the jurors. Especially in civil cases involving scientific proof, jurors tend to get lost in the facts and decide a verdict on the most irrelevant observations. This professor was a paid consultant; therefore, he was unbelievable. This scientist had squinty eyes; therefore, he was shifty. This scientist was black; therefore, he got several breaks in medical school and was not as qualified. The jury system was a wondrous invention, but not without its human frailties.

"You could stipulate to what the doctors are going to say," Charles said in between hoarse coughs.

"What do you mean?" Brad looked at him. Brad was not a trial lawyer and had forgotten much of what he learned in civil procedure class at Wake Forest.

"They want to drag out the case. You simply stipulate that all the doctors on our side will say the same thing, and they agree too."

"So it's just our man against theirs? That could be risky," Charlie said.

"Well, not exactly." Another cough and Charles cleared his throat. "Alford is Matt's personal physician. His testimony is different in nature than Goldberg's, Patel's, and the rest. So you would get two to their one."

"Nancy would never agree to that," Charlie said.

"She would if that's what Fitzwaring wanted. Let me work on that. I'll write it up for the pretrial conference." Charlie's father went into the other room and sat down in front of the computer.

"Brad, I want you to go through the juror list one more time. Look for anything we might have missed. Check the medical records, children, and job evaluations. I want people with an innate sense of right and wrong and enough indignation to stick it to Comstock."

"How do I find righteous indignation in a file?"

"Look at church affiliation, college. Check out military service or service occupations. You know, the kind of people who give their lives to others and hate selfish, greedy people."

"I'll give it shot." Brad grabbed the files and went downstairs to make himself some more coffee.

chapter

THIRTY
SEVEN

An early warm spell swept across Charlotte, and spring was not far behind. Charlie skipped breakfast the first day of March. The first day of a big trial always made his stomach nauseated. He had spent the morning reviewing the potential jurors for the last time. He said a little prayer and thought about how Sandy used to wrap her arms around him and tell him that he was the greatest lawyer on the face of the earth and if he happened to lose, she said, that brilliance was not always respected in its time. He longed for her embrace, her touch, her smile. He stopped. Such thinking would derail his train of thought, and he had to be sharp today.

From the second story of the parking deck, he spotted the television cameras on the front lawn of the Mecklenburg County Courthouse. He decided to walk right into the middle of them. He stopped on the front steps of the courthouse. Microphones were shoved in his face. People shouted questions at him. Charlie had been a fascination of the media for so long now that he had stopped reading the newspaper.

"Mr. Harrigan, are you glad to be back in the courtroom?" one perky reporter yelled out.

Charlie straightened his tie and spoke loudly, "I am certainly not happy with the circumstances that brought me here, but I am always delighted to see that the law takes care of the little people who don't have a voice."

"Who attacked you, Charlie?" another shouted.

"I can't say for sure, but it may be the same person who burned down my house." He gave them just enough information for them to speculate about his adversaries. Playing the victim would go a long way in gaining public support.

"Mr. Harrigan, is this lawsuit an attempt to get revenge on your firm for firing you?" The question was an obvious plant and Charlie knew it.

"I have no control over which clients Hobbes, Reimarus, and Van Schank choose to represent. But anyone accused of wrongful death deserves a good defense."

"Charlie, do you miss your wife?"

He glared at the mob. "Don't they have a class on answers to obvious questions in journalism school?" He stormed through the glass doors.

In the lobby, Brad was waiting with Horace and Betty. They walked to the second floor to civil court. In a small witness room, Charlie prepared them for the excruciatingly tedious process of jury selection. He told them that it was important for the jury to see them every day. If the jury got lost in all the science, they needed to be reminded that the trial was about losing a son.

They entered the courtroom and walked down the aisle, through the bar, and sat at the table on the left. Nancy sat directly across the aisle in her red power suit. Her entourage was the four associates, all in dark blue suits and conservative ties. Walter Comstock sat like a rock beside Nancy in a badly fitted gray suit and blue tie. There were no pleasant faces across the aisle, and Charlie realized that it worked to his favor to have this lovely little old couple, whose faces encouraged trust and honesty.

Charlie leaned over to Brad. "Where's my father?"

"He said he would be here. I don't know."

"All rise," the bailiff yelled, and all participants, spectators, and potential jurors stood.

"All right," Judge Carlton Fitzwaring said in his Southern drawl, "let's get this thing started. Horace and Betty Douglas versus Walter Comstock d/b/a Paragon Group. Hmm. Are all the parties present?" He looked for quietly nodding heads in response to his question.

"I don't imagine the two of you have reached any settlement agreement." He looked at Charlie, pleading with his eyes.

"No sir, Your Honor." Charlie stood. "My clients desire a jury to decide the claim. Settlement awards are not the issue."

"Then why did you sue for ten point two million dollars?" Nancy asked. "Mr. Harrigan would not even take part in a settlement conference, Your Honor."

"Stop it, right now." Fitzwaring peered over his bifocals. "I know that you two do not care for each other, but you will address me or the jury, not each other. You will remain calm. You will play nice. Got it?" Both heads were nodding in tandem. "Mr. Harrigan, would you like fifteen minutes to try to settle this thing?"

"That's not what my clients want." Charlie stood firm.

"Well, let's play ball. Clara, will you show the jury pool into the gallery?" The pudgy court clerk sauntered out of a back door feeling very important. The bailiff cleared the courtroom to give the potential jurors room to sit.

After the two hundred and three potential jurors sat down, the judge thanked them for their dutiful response to the judicial process. Seven of the potential jurors had either died or moved out of the county. Judge Fitzwaring lectured them for twenty minutes on their civic duty and castigated all of those lazy people who weasel their way out of a responsibility that our forefathers fought and died for. After that, no one even thought about making any excuses. Fitzwaring then dismissed two pregnant women in their third trimester, saying that he refused to stop every five minutes for bathroom breaks and that he loved babies, but did not want one messing up the marble tile in his courtroom.

He dismissed seven elderly individuals who felt that the strain would be too much, but Stanley Gunderson demanded that he have the right to serve on a jury like everyone else. Anyone who was currently or had recently been involved in a civil lawsuit was allowed to go home, leaving one hundred and ninety three potential jurors. Fitzwaring asked jurors one through twelve to take the stand. Charlie began his questions and used his first of twelve preemptory challenges on an insurance agent. He would definitely be stingy with any cash settlement. Nancy was next and used a challenge on a woman carrying a Rush Limbaugh book without asking her one question.

Brenda Campone was a young, attractive housewife, who posed little threat to either side. Charlie was not crazy about her, but he did not want to burn another challenge so soon. Cecil Miles was a black muffler repairman. He had been injured and on worker's comp for six weeks a couple of years ago. Nancy challenged for cause, stating that he would be overly sympathetic toward the plaintiff, but Fitzwaring denied and invited Cecil to join the jury. Stanley Gunderson was too hard to read. At seventy-six, he was a veteran and retired train conductor. He had driven the Southern line that helped make Charlotte an economic power after the war. He could sympathize with the elderly couple, but he could also appreciate a man who carves out a successful business by his own hands and wants to prevent someone from getting rich off of his hard work. He had a clenched jaw and smiled at neither Charlie nor Nancy.

Daniel O'Leary was a ten on Charlie's scale. A coal miner from West Virginia, he moved to Charlotte after several mining companies closed their doors in the late eighties. However, Nancy's private investigator had discovered that Daniel had lung disease from working in the mines, so he was dismissed. Bonnie Husby was a rotund black lady who managed the graveyard shift at a Waffle House. Charlie liked hard workers, but Nancy knew secrets. She knew that Bonnie smoked and resented people who tried to tell others how to live their lives. Charlie challenged Pah Van Tramm without a second thought.

Asian jurors were notorious for low settlements and voting for the defendant.

Against his better judgment, Charlie accepted Bryce Waterhouse, an investment banker. Charlie had ten challenges left, but the second row of the courtroom had six black women, three midlevel management types, and two Asians. Waterhouse, regrettably, would make it. Fitzwaring seated the next twelve, and Charlie burned three challenges immediately. When asked if there were too many lawsuits, Doug Hibbert said, "As long as the U.S. government screws us every month, I think people should sue as much as possible." The judge did not even wait for a challenge; he invited the truck driver with a suspended license to leave.

Dr. Shelly Chalfandt was an obstetrician on the south side of Charlotte. Very wealthy and very educated, she too was a wild card. Carol Wheeling, the librarian at Central Piedmont Community College, was another questionable choice for Charlie. His challenges were dwindling quickly as the managers were approaching. Kessler Henderson of Kessler's Used Cars was seated next. He was genuinely excited about jury duty. During the breaks, he passed out business cards to all the other jurors. Bernie Hodges was a fairly wealthy black man who mortgaged his house to buy his first dump truck and now had the third largest hauling business in Charlotte.

Nancy torpedoed Charlie's favorites, a man partially blinded in a chemical accident, a widow whose husband was killed in an accident on the job, and a black brick mason. Charlie's last preemptory challenge was between the owner of a dry cleaners and Shascle Deering, a waitress of questionable background. Charlie booted the dry cleaner, assuming that Shascle would simply follow the crowd, which could work in his favor. Charlie had no choice but to watch Kim Pfeiffer, a music teacher who grudgingly relinquished her classes to be there, join the jury. Nancy figured Kim would punish the plaintiff for making her miss school. Nancy's last challenge was another black man. She had no choice but to accept the fiery

Stanley Gunderson.

Charlie gazed over the jury. It was not the best, but it could have been much worse. Five men and seven women. Three blacks. Three small business owners, one of whom, Thomas Landon, was elected as the foreman. A headstrong, retired World War II vet. One doctor and one woman with a seedy reputation. Charlie thought, *Well, this is it. These twelve people will decide the fate of Walter Comstock and the worth of Matt Douglas, a boy whom they never met.*

chapter
THIRTY EIGHT

After two days of voir dire, the jury was impaneled and Judge Fitzwaring gave them instructions. They could take notes and deliberate after the first phase of the case to decide if, in fact, crystalline silica caused cancer. If the jury and judge both agreed, then Comstock's negligence would be the question.

Charlie looked around the room. For the third straight day, there was no sign of his father. Although his father had a history of dropping out of sight at the most important moments in Charlie's life, Charlie thought he had sincerely made a change. He was worried, angry, and frustrated, all at the same time, even though he had no time for such distracting emotions.

Charlie leaned over to Brad. "Have you heard from my father at all?"

"Sorry, Charlie." Brad patted Charlie's shoulder. "He's a grown man. He can take care of himself. Right now, you have more important things to think about. You've got an opening statement in about thirty seconds. During the recess, I'll make some calls for you. You just concentrate on the jury."

As he looked at the odd assortment of individuals, Charlie was not unhappy about the jury, but he had wanted at least one union worker out of the twelve. The foreman was his ace in the hole, a small business owner who had been fired from a large company. Charlie picked up a glass of water and wet his throat. He looked at the jury out of the corner of his eye. Betty patted his knee and whispered that she believed in him. Charlie slowly stood up; he opened his briefcase, and took two steps toward the jury box.

"Good morning, ladies and gentlemen. Thank you for being so patient through the selection process. I know that these days will get long and sometimes boring. I want you to know that I appreciate the sacrifice that you are making to be here. Your job is very important. Matthew Douglas was twenty-three when he died. It is up to you to decide if Walter Comstock is to blame. This case has a lot of scientific proof. A lot of doctors will give their boring opinions about scientific studies, but you can't forget that this case is about Horace and Betty Douglas, who buried their only son. . . . They didn't have to. His death was senseless, useless, and completely preventable."

Charlie turned and walked back to the table. He took another drink of water, so his words could sink in deep. Phase one of this trial would be so scientifically oriented that he had to focus on the personal loss of the Douglases in his opening. He could say practically anything and Nancy Lockman-Kurtz would have to sit there and smile. He placed the glass back on the table and reached into his briefcase. The jurors leaned forward to see what was in Charlie's hand. Judge Fitzwaring frowned, but Charlie ignored him. Slowly, he poured sand into a little pile on the plaintiff's table.

"Sand. Sand, ladies and gentlemen, that's what this trial is about. I know it sounds silly, but something we and our kids build castles out of at the beach can be deadly. All across the world, sand is used in various occupations, like construction. Matthew Douglas spent hours every day inhaling the fine dust created from sandblasting paint and rust. These particles settled in his lungs and caused the cancer that killed him." He turned quickly to the defendant's table. "And Mr. Comstock could have prevented it!"

Charlie walked to his chair and sat down. In fifteen short minutes, he had perturbed the judge, intrigued the jury, and ticked off the entire defense table. Nancy was caught off guard by such a brief opening statement, and when Judge Fitzwaring called on her, she fumbled to find the right papers. Being a professional, Nancy quickly composed herself and walked to Charlie's table. She grabbed a handful of sand.

"Ladies and gentlemen, I am sorry for wasting your time. You do not need to be here today. I have tried to dismiss this case, because it is ridiculous. I am truly sorry about the death of Matthew Douglas. But, ladies and gentlemen, what we have here today is another panic. It's another crisis that the American taxpayers will have to bail the country out of. We have created a culture of victims. If you smoke for fifty years and contract lung cancer, sue the tobacco companies. Get rich. Someone gets shot by a semiautomatic weapon, sue the gun makers. Or sue McDonald's because your coffee is too hot. Losing a loved one is always a terrible thing. My father smoked for forty years and sometimes I still . . . "

She broke off her speech with tears in her eyes. She pulled a convenient tissue out of pocket and dabbed her eyes. Charlie thought for a moment. Nancy's father died in a car wreck. He had attended the funeral with the rest of the attorneys at the firm. Nancy was not above lying about the death of a parent to win the jury's sympathy. She struggled to compose herself and then continued.

She poured some of Charlie's sand on the rail of the jury box. "What is this world coming to? Are we going to have to post danger signs at the beach? 'Warning: Sand may cause cancer!' Will children's sandboxes come with a warning from the Surgeon General? 'Don't let your children eat the sand, they may get cancer!' The death of Matthew Douglas was a terrible loss, but blaming a hard-working businessman, who was trying to help Matthew, will not solve anything. Ladies and gentlemen, you can help turn this society back to sanity. Thank you."

"All right." Judge Fitzwaring banged his gavel half-heartedly, "Let's take a fifteen-minute break and when we get back, Mr. Harrigan will proceed with his first witness." The jury was escorted out and the courtroom bustled.

Nancy walked over to Charlie, smiling. She threw some sand on the table in front of Charlie. "Did you get this out of Ashley's sandbox?" She wiped her hands and walked away. It took every ounce of strength for Charlie to restrain himself from violently attacking her.

Charlie guzzled a cup of coffee, while Horace paced back and forth. Apparently, judges have smaller bladders than the rest of humanity. They need breaks every couple of hours. Charlie hated it. The frequent breaks interrupted his concentration and his train of thought. They walked back into the courtroom. When everyone had settled down again, Judge Fitzwaring told Charlie to call his first witness.

Dr. Keith Alford walked to the witness stand and swore his complete honesty under oath. Charlie stood close to the far end of the jury box, trying to eclipse as much of the defense table as possible. It was imperative the jury focus on the first two witnesses.

"For the record, please state your name and occupation." Charlie studied the faces of the jurors.

"Dr. Keith Alford, chief oncologist, a cancer specialist, at University Hospital."

"That would be the hospital located at the University of North Carolina at Charlotte?"

"Correct."

"Dr. Alford, could you explain the cause of Matthew Douglas' death?"

"Yes, he died from acute lung cancer."

"Objection!" Nancy wasted no time. "Irrelevant to whether or not silicosis causes cancer."

Charlie spun on his heels. "It would not be relevant if your client shot him, but he merely poisoned him."

"Your Honor!" Nancy was standing with her hands on her hips.

"Both of you come here." Nancy and Charlie approached the bench sheepishly. Fitzwaring covered the microphone and whispered. "This is off the record. If you two don't play nice, I'll throw you both in jail for contempt. Don't make fools out of yourselves. Ms. Lockman-Kurtz, you know that Charlie has a right to frame the line of questioning, but I certainly hope it won't take him very long. Now you stay on track and you sit down. Back on the record," he declared loudly. "The jury will disregard that exchange."

Charlie smirked at Nancy. They both knew that jurors were human and rarely disregarded something so volatile. It was Charlie's way of keeping Matthew in the picture. "Dr. Alford, can you please explain what crystalline silica is and how it affects the lungs?"

"Sure." He smiled. "Crystalline silica is essentially what we call sand. It's also found in quartz, granite rock, cristobalite, and tridymite. If someone were to inhale silica dust it would scar and scrape sensitive lung tissue. That's a condition called silicosis. That scarring makes it difficult to breathe, and eventually it can kill a person."

"Doctor, should I be scared the next time I go to the beach?" Charlie noticed a couple of jurors snicker.

"Of course not. What happens is that certain types of occupations use sand. For example, Matthew Douglas operated a sandblaster. Such abrasive blasting causes the sand to break up, forming a very fine dust. The dust is so fine, it can easily be inhaled."

"Why is that?"

"Well, our bodies have little defense mechanisms called cilia or nose hairs. They effectively prevent particles larger than five micrometers from entering the body. However, anything smaller can slip past and be deposited in the lower respiratory system, the trachea, or bronchial tubes."

"How large is silica dust?"

"Some is larger and some is smaller."

"Is silica known to cause certain diseases?"

"Yes, it is accepted that silica causes silicosis, which can lead to tuberculosis or corpulmonale." He went into a very descriptive presentation of the damage that can be done to lungs, while Charlie placed four large pictures of damaged lungs on tripods near the jury box.

"But Matthew Douglas did not contract silicosis, correct?"

"Correct. Silicosis, or scarring of the lung tissue, takes years to develop. Matthew died from lung cancer." Charlie had instructed all his witnesses to use the name Matthew as much as possible to remind the jury.

"What did you find when you examined Matthew?"

"His lungs had an amount of silica dust that was equivalent to someone who had been performing that job six or seven years."

"To your knowledge, how long had Matt been sandblasting?"

"I believe it was less than two years."

"Do you believe the silica was the catalyst for his lung cancer?"

"Yes."

"Did he smoke or do anything else that put him at risk?"

"His grandmother died from breast cancer, but that is the only category where he was a potential at-risk patient."

Charlie quizzed him on specifics of lung cancer and the rate of cancer growth. In some cases, it was possible for cancer to have a quick onset and progression, but that was rare. Dr. Alford suggested that even if a tumor had been present, it was likely that the extreme exposure to silica dust sped up the course of the disease.

On cross-examination, Nancy immediately attacked Dr. Alford's credibility. "You're a surgeon, right, not a researcher?"

"That's correct, but I have—"

"Thank you, doctor. You answered the question. Your explanation for the cause of Mr. Douglas' cancer is just an assumption, right?"

"An assumption based on years of experience."

"Have you ever made any wrong assumptions?"

"As have you, I suppose."

"But my assumptions don't kill people. Do you remember a boy named Steven Bryant?"

"Yes."

"Please tell us about him."

"Objection!" Charlie bolted up. "Outside the scope."

"Credibility, Your Honor."

"Overruled. Dr. Alford," Fitzwaring ordered him to answer the question.

He took a deep breath. "I removed a tumor from his kidney. This was ten years ago. I failed to detect several metastases."

"In fact, you told the parents you got all of the cancer."

"I never say that, because no one can ever be certain, simply because of the nature of cancer."

"He died six months later, correct?"

"The metastasized cancer cells had gotten into his lymph nodes and spread throughout his body."

"Were you sued for malpractice?"

"Yes." Dr. Alford hung his head.

Nancy took her seat and Charlie stood up. "Dr. Alford, were you found liable in that case?"

"No, I was acquitted of all charges."

"Are you currently serving on the board of directors at University Hospital and the North Carolina medical ethics board?"

"Yes, I am."

"Thank you. You may step down."

After lunch, Charlie continued with his expert witnesses. Despite his father Charles' efforts with Judge Fitzwaring, Nancy had not agreed to stipulate. Charlie was still determined to move as swiftly as possible, but Nancy was making it difficult. She had apparently scrounged up every piece of dirt on each expert. Charlie called Dr. Donald Goldberg to the stand. As a graduate student at UNC-Chapel Hill, he had rocked the scientific community in 1984 by suggesting that crystalline silica caused cancer, even without an onset of silicosis. He was currently the head of research at the medical school at UNC-Chapel Hill. The relatively young doctor with chiseled features had already caught the eyes of a couple of female jurors who hung on his every word. They would resent Nancy for attacking such a handsome professional.

Charlie began, "So, doctor, please explain how you demonstrated the connection between cancer and silica."

"Rats are used for scientific experiments, because they are relatively close to humans genetically, sharing eighty-five percent of the same DNA. We injected the rats with high doses of silica mixed in water. Out of thirty-six rats, six developed tumors. My team, since then, has performed two more animal studies showing the same connection."

"How did the medical community receive your findings?"

"The World Health Organization and the International Agency for Cancer Research agreed that silica caused cancer in animals, but said it was only a possible carcinogen to humans."

"Why is that?"

"Objection. Speculation, Your Honor. Dr. Goldberg cannot speak for those people."

"Overruled, I'm sure they gave him some reason." Nancy plopped down into her chair.

"First of all, without getting into specifics, the cancer was a different type than humans contract. Second, humans inhale silica to contract cancer. Since we didn't simulate the exact circumstances, they were hesitant to make a conclusive decision. But truly, I believe the decision is a financial one. Insurance companies and big businesses pay thousands of dollars to prevent lawsuits like this one. It's like the tobacco cases; once the industry loses one case, the floodgates will open and insurance companies will have to pay for all the people who died from inhaling silica dust."

Charlie tried to hold back a smile. Goldberg was not just a researcher and advocate, he was a passionate, persuasive speaker. The blue-collar workers on the jury were on the edge of their seats, drinking in every word. "How did the rest of the world take your news?"

"Well, the United Kingdom banned the use of crystalline silica. Here again, that is a very costly process, but there are many other abrasives that do not cause crystalline silica dust when used, like aluminum oxide, glass or plastic beads, or carbon dioxide pellets. We could recycle carbon dioxide and clean up work environments at the same time—"

"Objection, Your Honor." Nancy was visibly frustrated. "He's sermonizing to the jury."

"Mr. Harrigan, keep your witness on track," Fitzwaring warned.

"Yes, Your Honor. Dr. Goldberg, how widespread is the problem?"

"Since 1968, there have been over 15,000 deaths due to airborne silica. OSHA estimates that this year over one million people are at risk from hazardous silica. Fifty-nine thousand will develop silicosis. One hundred thousand of the million operate sandblasters, like Matthew Douglas."

Judge Fitzwaring called for the afternoon recess and Charlie was beaming. It was a beautiful testimony and his last statement actually made one juror jolt. Thomas Landon owned a small company that repaired houses after fires. He had even operated a sandblaster at one time in his life. Charlie got lucky with him. Nancy had run out of preemptory challenges by the time they reached juror 102, and Fitzwaring denied her challenge for cause that he would be overly prejudicial since he was in the construction business. The judge said that was all the more reason why he would make a good juror. He would see both sides.

After the break, Nancy attacked Goldberg to no avail. He was strong and emphatic.

"The amount of silica dust injected into the rats was one

hundred times what humans are exposed to, wasn't it?"

"Yes, but it had to be, because it would take five years for rats to inhale enough silica to cause tumors. Some rats don't live that long."

"Did the rats develop lung cancer?"

"Not exactly; the tumors were different, of course. But in research, the goal is to see how cells are affected, not to create duplicate diseases. If silica can trigger a mutation in normal rat cells to become cancerous, then the logical conclusion is that it will do the same in humans, regardless of the type of cancer."

Nancy quickly retreated, realizing that she was fighting a losing battle. Goldberg had been questioned by too many panels and research committees around the world to be shaken by one little attorney. Charlie, Brad, and the Douglases had dinner together and reviewed the events of the day. The first day of the trial went to Charlie, no doubt about it. He was cautious and reminded the Douglases that jurors often forget crucial testimony that they hear early in the trial. Tomorrow would be a different story.

chapter
THIRTY
NINE

There was nothing to report, but the media did a good job of repeatedly explaining the obvious. Once again, cameras were outside the courthouse for a civil trial. Maybe it was the amount of money that made the story irresistible. The plaintiffs and defendants were in the normal places waiting for Judge Fitzwaring, who was reclining on his leather couch finishing his morning bagel and the *USA Today*. Five minutes before nine, Charlie's father walked into the courtroom. Casually, he looked around the room and strolled to a chair behind Charlie.

"Where have you been? I've been worried about you," Charlie whispered emphatically.

"I had some business to take care of in Atlanta." Charles began coughing.

Charlie handed him a glass of water. "What kind of business? I need you here. These experts are your guys."

"After that talk we had in the hospital, I went to see your mother."

Charlie tried to remain composed but could not contain his surprise. "Really?" he blurted out.

"Yeah, I got to thinking and realized I needed to apologize to her too. I know I hurt her beyond belief. If I'm really a changed man, I need to do things differently."

"You couldn't wait for the weekend?"

"Don't put things off, Charlie. You never know what will happen. Besides, you still don't get it, do you? I trust you implicitly. I knew you could handle this case. You're a brilliant attorney and you became that way by yourself. Trust your instincts." His father patted him on the shoulder and leaned back.

"All rise," the bailiff commanded.

"Are there any issues we need to attend to?" Judge Fitzwaring looked at Nancy and Charlie, whose faces were blank. "I don't suppose you reached a settlement overnight?"

"No, Your Honor," Charlie responded.

"He won't even entertain the idea of a conference, Your Honor."

"Counsel, come up here." Charlie started to the bench. Nancy marched quickly behind him. "No, Ms. Lockman-Kurtz, just Mr. Harrigan. You may sit down."

"But, but—"

"I said, sit down!" She walked back slowly, burning a hole through the judge's forehead with her eyes. "Charlie, at least talk to her about settling. From what I hear, they might be open to it. I have to be honest. I don't think your chances are very good. Why don't you two go somewhere alone and discuss the weather or something?" To the court, he said, "Let's take a ten-minute recess."

Charlie and Nancy headed to the stairwell at the far end of the courthouse. In between the second and third floor, Charlie leaned against the wall with his arms folded. In the sweetest voice she could muster, Nancy said, "Comstock is willing to settle for one million with everything under seal."

"Two million and an admission of guilt."

"You're crazy. He's never going to admit to anything."

"Don't you get it, Nancy? That's what my clients want. Money is not the issue." Charlie headed back up the stairs, but stopped when Nancy called his name.

"Charlie, last chance." Seeing no visible response, she climbed the stairs past him and shoved him into the wall. "Okay, loser, but I'm getting ready to bury you. You had your shot."

Koshee Patel's father worked hard at a Seven-Eleven in downtown Los Angeles and saved enough money to send his son to Pepperdine. He received his doctorate from Cal-Poly Tech and was currently the head of research and development at Los Alamos Research Facility in New Mexico. Behind Dr. Goldberg, he was the leading doctor researching the effects of silica in the U.S. As Charlie was listening to the witness and watching the jurors' responses, he was also thinking. That whole scene in the courtroom had been organized just for him. Van Schank had probably called Fitzwaring at home and encouraged him to encourage Charlie to settle. Van Schank had been in favor of settling from the start. Charlie took his father's advice and began listening to his instincts.

"Dr. Patel, are you the only one who has demonstrated an increased risk of lung cancer in humans exposed to silica?"

"Why, no. There was a study in Vermont where eighty-four granite-quarry workers died of lung cancer. Quarrying rock creates a substantial amount of silica dust." He was a jovial man, pleasant to listen to with a slight accent. "Out of twenty-six studies on humans, twenty-four have shown that workers exposed to silica have an increased risk of contracting lung cancer."

"What about outside of the U.S.?" Charlie asked.

"Objection. Relevance?" Nancy shrugged.

"I'll allow it." Judge Fitzwaring waved her down.

"In China, for example, tungsten miners are twice as likely to experience lung cancer as the general population. The same is true for tin miners in Australia."

The whole morning, Dr. Patel did an excellent job of showing a causal connection between lung cancer and silica. Charlie and Brad got a couple of hot dogs from a street vendor for lunch and discussed the jury. Brad believed that the jury seemed quite convinced and favorable of Charlie. Apparently, they had developed a very negative image of Nancy. "Brenda Campone and Carol Wheeling actually grimace when Nancy objects," Brad observed. His advice was to cut it short. He told Charlie to finish the experts by lunch tomorrow and rest. Any more witnesses would be overkill.

Nancy had red snapper and white wine at The French Quarter Restaurant with Van Schank. Van Schank had the entire Dallas office scouring the hospitals and facilities that Charlie's experts had come from and discovered some very interesting facts. A couple of associates in the Atlanta office were working with Emory scientists learning everything about silica, from the chemical composition to the rate of death among first-century Roman brick masons. Nancy was well armed for the attack. She rubbed her bare foot up Van Schank's leg as they laughed about the ambush. They kissed, and Nancy headed back to the courthouse in Van Schank's private limousine.

"Dr. Patel, you believe that there is a connection between crystalline silica and lung cancer?" Nancy asked smugly.

"Yes, of course. The evidence seems rather clear."

"What happens if it's true?"

"I'm not quite sure what you mean." Dr. Patel wrinkled his eyebrows.

"For example, if there is a connection, will you receive another federal grant to study the safety levels of silica dust and how much workers can safely inhale to establish new OSHA criteria?"

"I can't say for sure, but usually additional research is needed."

"But if there's no connection, you don't get the money."

"I don't do it for money. People's lives are at stake."

"I appreciate your concern for human life." She was pacing in front of the jury box and spun on her heels. "By the way, do you smoke?"

"Relevance, Your Honor? What is this about?" Charlie stood up.

"You're out of order, Mr. Harrigan. Either object or shut up. But whatever you do, sit down." Fitzwaring's bifocals were beginning to steam up. "Please answer the question, doctor."

"Why yes, I do, but I don't understand—"

"Thank you." Nancy cut him off. "Don't cigarettes cause

lung cancer, too?"

"Yes, they do."

"So even though cigarettes cause cancer, you still use them. Don't a lot of construction workers smoke?"

"I have no way of knowing that." Dr. Patel crossed his arms.

"In that Vermont study you cited, weren't all eight-four of those quarry workers also cigarette smokers?"

"I am not sure, but that may have been in a footnote somewhere."

Dr. Patel was stumbling and grasping for answers. He was on his heels and looked suspicious, as if he were hiding something.

"Don't blue-collar workers have a higher rate of smoking than other professions?"

"I think so, but I have no proof."

"Isn't it true that on surveys and research applications, people tend to minimize the amount they smoke to try to make themselves look good?"

"I don't know."

"Are you familiar with a psychology study at Harvard that shows people have a tendency to underestimate behaviors perceived as negative in self-reports like the ones your research subjects fill out?"

"Objection, Your Honor, counsel is trying to introduce evidence."

"Withdrawn." Nancy smiled at him. "Now, Dr. Patel, are you familiar with studies that show that workers, like coal or tin miners, who are exposed to silica are also exposed to other carcinogens?"

"Yes, I have seen those studies."

"What other carcinogens are miners exposed to?"

"Arsenic dust, radon, maybe some others."

"Arsenic! Radon!" Nancy shouted with outrage and disgust as if she never heard this before. "Aren't those things poisonous?"

"Yes, they are, but it does not eclipse the effect of the silica. As a matter of fact, there is a compounding effect that takes place."

Nancy moved in for the kill. "In your study at Los Alamos, you ignored whether or not someone was a smoker?"

"We did not isolate it as a variable, correct."

"In fact, didn't you violate scientific protocol by dropping one subject, who had cancer, from the control group?"

"After the study began, we learned he did not fill out his personal background accurately and that he was genetically predisposed to cancer. Dropping one person from the control group did not affect the outcome."

"But you did violate protocol? Once the experiment begins, according to scientific method, you can't change the subjects."

"He had not told us the truth."

"The truth is that you should have canceled the experiment."

"But so much work had been done."

"The truth is that you violated the ethical standards of research in your study, isn't it?" Nancy demanded.

"Yes." Dr. Patel studied the floor in shame. "So much money had been spent; to cancel the experiment would have been a waste."

"So it is about the money."

"Objection!" Charlie shouted, but it was too late.

"Withdrawn," Nancy said with a lilt in her voice. She winked at Charlie as she returned to her seat.

Charlie tried to rehabilitate his witness, but too much damage had been done. He cited a Syracuse study that showed the strenuous labor of blue-collar workers often countered the harmful effects of smoking in relation to heart disease. They reviewed an Australian study that had been controlled for cigarettes and still found a higher incidence of lung cancer. But Charlie did not leave his wounded soldier on the front line more than ten minutes.

He had to soften the effects of Nancy's cross-examination. It was four twenty-five and Charlie would not be able to put another witness on the stand. Fitzwaring would dismiss for the day and the jurors would go home picturing Dr. Patel's chin resting on his chest in defeat. He was a brilliant man and a brilliant researcher who cut a seemingly insignificant corner, and it might cost Charlie his entire case.

chapter
FORTY

The jury members took their seats and tried not to look pitifully at Charlie, but it was obvious that he had been obliterated and they had not forgotten about it. Charlie had had trouble sleeping and drew tight little circles on his yellow notepad. He thought about dinner the night before. After the revelation of Dr. Patel, Charlie sat Maxine Norvell and Harold Rutherford in little metal chairs and barked at them. He questioned them, pushed them, and burrowed into their personal lives. After two hours, Dr. Rutherford broke.

He spilled his guts. Surely, Nancy had already discovered this land mine, but at least Charlie had prevented it from exploding in court. Rutherford had been an honors student as an undergraduate. Graduate school had been much more difficult. He had plagiarized a couple of papers and changed grades of other students in the school's computer. In med school, he had cleaned up his act and nothing was wrong with his research. If Nancy got him on the stand, however, she would uncover his past and destroy anything beneficial he could add.

Charlie was down to one witness. As he was drawing concentric circles connecting his original doodle, he muttered a quiet prayer under his breath. Alford was a good witness. Goldberg was extremely impressive. Patel had done a lot right;

maybe the jury could forgive him. Dr. Norvell would have to hit a home run. Maybe the jury would appreciate the brevity of his case.

"Mr. Harrigan, your next witness, please." Judge Fitzwaring rubbed his head.

Maxine Norvell was sworn in and explained that she was a Ph.D. and professor of epidemiology at the University of California at Berkeley. She joined the charge in California to pass Proposition 65, which would officially recognize silica as a carcinogen in California. She had researched crystalline silica since 1974.

"Dr. Norvell, could you explain why Dr. Patel would want to exclude a member of the control group?"

"A control group must fit certain criteria. Apparently, this one person didn't and failed to fill out the personal history forms correctly. I understand the pressure to keep going even when your subject pool is tainted. It's expensive. I have personally forfeited two projects in my career."

"In your professional opinion, were any of his findings altered because he changed the control group?"

"Of course not. The integrity of the experimental group was not bothered. The incidence of cancer demonstrated a correlation."

"Please explain what correlation means."

"A correlation means that two things seem to happen together, but one does not necessarily cause the other. For example, neighborhoods that have churches have a lot of crime. Those two things may not have any relation. There may be other factors. Churches are found in central locations to reach large populations. Maybe churches go where the crime is. Who knows what causes the correlation."

"So cigarette smoking may have also caused lung cancer as much as the silica itself?"

"It is possible, but even in certain coal mining companies that prohibit smoking, there is an increased rate of lung cancer."

Charlie smiled and let this sink in with the jury. "So you are saying that smoking may not even be relevant to our discussion?"

"On the contrary, smoking exacerbates the effects of the silica. It doubles or even triples the harmful effects. The scarring of lung tissue and the growth of mutant cells are exacerbated by smoking." Charlie caught several of the female jurors smiling at one of their own. Nancy would be a fool to attack this witness. Dr. Chalfandt, the female physician on the jury, would probably take it personally.

"Now I had a question about Dr. Goldberg's testimony that you might be able to clear up for me. Why would he inject rats with silica and water one hundred times the amount that humans are exposed to?" Charlie acted outraged by the thought.

"Frankly, I don't think people understand the nature of scientific research. Amounts and procedures are not selected at random. Scientists don't sit around and say let's inject a rat with Mountain Dew and see what happens. We carefully try to simulate circumstances found in nature. A large amount of silica dust mixed with water was used as an attempt to recreate what happens in a work environment."

"How so?"

"Well, fresh silica dust in a rock quarry breathed into the nose is much more potent than any other form of exposure. That fine dust immediately settles in the lungs." A couple of the jurors were actually nodding their heads, indicating that they understood now.

"How easy is this to prevent?"

"That's the worst part about it." Dr. Norvell was becoming very animated. "This disease is one hundred percent preventable. It takes education and awareness. They can use water hoses to wet down surfaces, and vacuums and air filters to suck out the dust rather than blowing it out with air compressors. Using ear, eye, and face masks to keep the dust out of the body is a simple thing. Washing clothes regularly and hands frequently would help prevent exposure. And monitoring the amount of respirable dust is imperative. The dust in the air should be no more than one-tenth of one percent."

"Doesn't OSHA have standards that make it safe to work around silica dust?" Charlie asked innocently.

"Yes, but those limits are twice the level of most other Westernized nations. We are behind Australia, England, Germany, and many others when it comes to protecting the hardest workers in our country. The average life span of someone in quarry and construction is sixty-one."

"How could Matthew Douglas die so young, after only two years of exposure?"

For the first time, Nancy objected with a vengeance. "This is not about Mr. Douglas." Dr. Chalfandt glared at Nancy.

"Hypothetical, Your Honor. This professional is being asked to explain the progression of lung cancer in a given set of circumstances," Charlie defended himself.

Fitzwaring looked at Nancy. He was actually interested in the testimony. "I'll allow it, but make it quick, Mr. Harrigan."

Charlie nodded at Dr. Norvell. "Given an extreme amount of exposure, acute silicosis can develop in a few weeks to four to five years. In a similar manner, with a large enough exposure, lung cancer can progress quickly. The silica dust kills the microphages that fight off infection, and there is nothing to prevent mutated genes from growing and consuming the lung tissue. If there is nothing to fight the cancer, it can kill very quickly. If Matthew's boss had required medical checkups every three months, as OSHA recommends, it could have been caught in time to stop further damage."

"Is there any way to reverse the damage?" Charlie asked.

"No."

It was a brilliant morning. Charlie decided to rest. He had completed the first part of the trial, and if they did not believe Goldberg and Norvell, the jury would not believe anybody. Nancy poked around the edges of Dr. Norvell's testimony, but she was afraid to press too hard. For forty-five minutes, she smirked and conjectured and accomplished nothing, except for wasting the jury's time.

Nancy offered a barrage of experts, scientists, geologists, epidemiologists, and oncologists. All her expert witnesses sang the same tune. There may be a correlation, but there is not enough conclusive evidence to claim with absolute certainty that silica causes cancer. All in all, the witnesses were uninspired and unmotivated eggheads. They were high-dollar professionals who were paid high fees for their services. Nancy had not agreed to stipulate to the testimony of the professionals and took five days to present all of her experts. The jury was brain dead by the end of her case.

Charlie's cross-examination of Dr. Harrison Ballenger of Duke University was particularly striking. Of the various modes of cross-examination, Charlie favored two. He liked the gradual friendly lull into a soft-flowing routine of simple questions and simple answers he already knew. After the witness felt secure in a smooth rhythm, Charlie would hit him with a curve ball. A question so out of the ordinary that the shock elicits an honest response.

But with Dr. Ballenger, Charlie selected his second-favorite technique. The lawyer begins with a hard-hitting indictment that the witness must answer honestly. He jumps from subject to subject without giving the witness time to think about the question or realize the train of logic he is following. The constant bombardment does not end.

Charlie rose slowly. "Dr. Ballenger, how much are you getting paid for your testimony?"

"Money does not influence my scientific opinion." The dignified scholar was offended by the implication.

"That's not what I asked."

"It's not relevant to my findings."

"Your Honor, unresponsive." Charlie raised his hands.

"Dr. Ballenger, just answer the questions that the plaintiff's lawyer asks. Avoid commentary." Judge Fitzwaring motioned to Charlie.

"How much are you paid for this testimony today?"

The good doctor looked at Nancy and back to Charlie. "Ten thousand dollars."

"Did the defense counsel coach you on what to say?"

"Of course not."

"Do you know the witness from Boston University, Dr. Schleigel?"

"Only by reputation."

"Is he a better doctor than you?"

"What? I don't know."

"He's getting twelve thousand. So does that mean his opinion is more valid than yours, or that he said more of what the defense wanted?"

"Your Honor." Nancy stood up.

"Withdrawn," Charlie said without losing his cadence. "Is he a better doctor than you?"

"I don't think so."

"Did you fly down here first-class like he did?"

"No. I drove."

"Doesn't seem fair, does it, doctor?"

"It doesn't matter as long as the truth gets out."

"Whose truth?"

"*The* truth."

"Are you saying Dr. Goldberg is a liar?"

"No. His experiments are not conclusive."

"Is anything about his research true?"

"There seems to be a preponderance of evidence."

"So how much would it take to convince you that silica is as bad as asbestos?"

"I don't know."

"How many deaths?"

"That's not fair."

"Have you ever done manual labor?"

"When I was a teenager."

"Do you have a maid?"

"Yes."

"So you avoid hard work?"

"No."

"If certain diseases are easily preventable, should we do everything we can to spare lives?"

"Yes."

"Can we agree that silica is detrimental?"

"Of course."

"If workers could use other abrasives besides silica, they should do it to protect their lives, right?"

"I suppose."

"We should encourage all blue-collar workers to observe all safety precautions?"

"Of course."

"So we should do everything to help people, except warn them that silica causes cancer?"

"Of course. Wait. No."

"No, we should not warn people that silica causes cancer?"

"Right." He was flustered and confused. "I mean silica doesn't cause cancer."

"But you said there was a preponderance of evidence that it did?"

"Yes, but it doesn't."

"That sounds like a contradiction to me. Are you saying that it might not, so we shouldn't warn people, or that since it might, we should not warn people?"

Dr. Ballenger sighed. "I'm saying that people need to be aware that the possibility might be there."

Charlie had taken a chance of making a negative impression on the jury. But then again, Dr. Ballenger was smug and had swaggered to the witness stand. He left the stand in a much different fashion.

Charlie and Nancy were given ten-minute summations to wrap up this part of the trial. Charlie focused on the fact that insurance companies were paying huge amounts of money to keep this decision from being made, which would lead to numerous lawsuits across the country. Charlie referenced the fact that the International Agency for Research on Cancer had classified silica as a carcinogen, but their own Environmental Protection Agency would not follow suit because of political pressure.

Nancy focused on the fact that this culture has developed a lazy, victim mentality and that people want to get rich off of frivolous litigation. She pointed out that many jobs are dangerous by nature and have inherent risks. Firemen run the risk of damage to their lungs. Stock car racers breathe in exhaust fumes, but no one wants to close the Charlotte Motor Speedway. She argued that correlation does not prove causation and that the jury should carefully consider that.

Judge Fitzwaring instructed the jury. They were to review all the testimony carefully and then decide one simple issue. Did they believe that the testimony proved that crystalline silica causes lung cancer? There would be no admission of guilt by anyone, and discussion of Matthew Douglas was strictly prohibited. Thomas Landon, the foreman, led the twelve into the jury room, and Fitzwaring dismissed the court.

Charlie, Brad, Charles, and the Douglases went to Sonny's and feasted on greasy burgers and crispy fries. They celebrated that Matt had had his day in court and that they had given it their best try, even if they lost. But Charlie could not afford to lose. Charlie had spent every single penny of the insurance money from the house fire to fund this case. Brad had worked only a couple of items to pay his own bills. Charlie was broke and owed Sonny three months' rent on his office apartment. If Charlie lost, he could always follow Dr. Johnston's example and declare bankruptcy.

Charles asked his son to step outside. On Third Street, the lunch-hour renegades rushed through downtown, racing the clock to get back to work by one. Charles put an awkward arm around his formerly estranged son's shoulder.

"I'm proud of you . . . son." Charlie's eyes welled up as his father spoke tenderly to him. "I'm leaving today."

"No. I need you. I've finally gotten to know you. You can't leave." Charlie hugged his father.

"Charlie, I have only a couple of months. I'm going to

spend it with my wife and family. They need me too. I've made amends here. Now I'm going home to set some things right there."

The ugly blue-and-orange taxi that Charles had called for pulled up to the front of Sonny's Teriyaki Grill. They embraced for the last time, and Charles Harrigan, Senior, climbed into the taxi.

"I love you, son." The words that Charlie had longed for all his life melted his heart.

"I love you too, Dad."

The door slammed, but the window rolled down quickly. "I think you won it in there today. Good job, Charlie." The taxi pulled away with Charlie standing on the sidewalk, waving to the father he always wanted.

"Hey, buddy," Brad popped out of the door, "the jury decided in one hour flat. We've got to get to the courthouse."

chapter
FORTY
ONE

The green Blazer ripped through traffic and found a spot in a far corner on the third level of the parking garage. By the time Charlie, Brad, and the Douglases found their place at the table, the courtroom was already packed. Nancy sat stoically, full of confidence and full of herself. Her associates all had yellow legal pads ready to write down the verdict for no apparent reason. Walter Comstock was visibly on edge. His angry eyes and clenched jaw revealed his insecurity. He was worried that Charlie might actually get the chance to put him on trial.

Charlie had been perplexed by the media attention and the large number of spectators in the courtroom. It was such a boring civil case—no gruesome crime scene and no mass murderers. Brad had been asking questions and snooping around. Rumors flew around the courthouse. Lawyers from State Farm, Allstate, Prudential, and Farmer's Insurance had been observing this trial from the start. Speculation from the cute brunette clerk on the second floor was that if the jury decided that silica causes cancer, litigation would spring up all over the country. Individuals would sue mining and construction companies. The companies would sue the makers of abrasive sanding equipment, trying to recoup some of their losses. There might even be cases against the United States government, because OSHA and the EPA had not taken the warnings seriously. Lawyers were lining up with dollar signs in their eyes, wanting to get a piece of the multimillion-dollar settlements.

However, Charlie knew the truth. North Carolina was a great state to be a defendant, but a horrible place to sue somebody. Being a huge tobacco state, no one wanted to open the floodgate of corporate negligence lawsuits. Fitzwaring did everything possible to suck out all the emotion and make the case as difficult as possible, except for outright kicking the case. By the third day of Nancy's case, the jurors' eyes were glazing over, and they were certainly not excited about the prospect of the wrongful death trial following this decision.

As the jury members filed in, Charlie tried to read their faces, but twelve ordinary citizens can be incredibly professional under such intense pressure. They kept their faces down and walked slowly to their seats without showing any emotion. Some lawyers believe that it favors the plaintiff when they do look at them, and some plaintiffs' attorneys think it is the kiss of death. Fitzwaring brought the court to order. After reading the jury's decision, the judge asked the foreman to read the decision out loud to the courtroom.

Thomas Landon stood and cleared his throat. "Your Honor, the jury finds that the use of crystalline silica in abrasive blasting does, indeed, cause lung cancer."

There was a gasp from a couple of insurance lawyers in the gallery. Several reporters ran out the door, and lawyers were dialing numbers on their cell phones to start suing other companies. Nancy stood up yelling, trying to be heard over the commotion.

"Quiet! Quiet!" Fitzwaring banged his gavel. "If you people don't quiet down, I'll throw you all in jail for contempt. Quiet!"

As the courtroom calmed down, Nancy said, "Your Honor, I move for a directed verdict. The plaintiffs did not prove their case."

Horace leaned over to Charlie. "What's she talking about?

They believed us, right?"

Charlie hushed Horace. "Your Honor, with all due respect, this jury was not nullified by emotion. They were moved by scientific opinion."

"Let me take this under advisement. Give me an hour to review the transcripts. If I believe the jury ignored scientific evidence, I will throw the jury's decision out and find for the defendant. If I find for the plaintiff, you need to be ready to present your first witness this afternoon, Mr. Harrigan." Fitzwaring rapped his gavel again as Horace sat in a quandary.

Charlie explained to his clients, "On rare occasions when a judge thinks the jury missed important pieces of evidence or purposefully overlooked the facts, he can reverse the decision. Remember, it happened with that British nanny who shook the baby, but it's very rare."

Brad chimed in, "Well, it'll give us something to appeal."

Charlie knew he couldn't handle an appeal. This case had almost destroyed him already. An appeal would probably be the last nail.

Walter Comstock stormed around the little conference room. He was spouting profanities and shoving chairs out of his way. Two of the associates had gone to fetch some coffee. Nancy and the others were poring over affidavits, just in case she had to cross-examine a witness today. Comstock was being ignored and it irritated him.

"Look, Missy. I'm your client, so get your sorry nose out of that file and listen to me when I talk to you. I'm not paying you good money to lose this case. I knew I should have gotten a man to represent me."

Nancy grabbed Comstock's collar. "Nobody could have done better than I did. It's the jury. You're not the most sympathetic person to look at. Why don't you try looking a little more like a human being and a little less like a drill sergeant?"

The door opened slowly, and the tall figure of Martin Van Schank stood in the doorway in a very imposing manner.

"Children, children, can't we all just get along? Walter, you have never been able to keep your emotions in check. When the heat gets turned up, you have to play it cool. Nancy, why don't you and the others give us a minute?"

As the attorneys left, Van Schank and Comstock sat down at the table. "I guess you've got a plan?"

"Slade is working on something as we speak. Harrigan can't be intimidated and the Douglases are not going to settle. If the directed verdict is a wash, then we will go to work on the jury." Van Schank pulled out a couple of Cuban cigars.

"So what is Slade up to?"

"You realize that one of the jurors owns his own gravel company, right? I got Slade out of those ugly Hawaiian shirts and into a suit. He signed a half-a-million-dollar contract with Bernie Hodges' brother to supply all of Paragon Group's dump trucks. The brother went out that afternoon and got a line of credit to buy five more trucks and hire more drivers. He is going to work on the brother to make sure that Paragon's interests are protected." Van Schank blew out a puff of smoke and laughed.

"I love it." Comstock was giddy. "You got any other irons in the fire?"

"Shascle Deering is in debt and has a kid she's trying to support. There's potential with her. Carol Wheeling's husband is having an affair. We can pressure him to encourage his wife to be sympathetic. Of course, you have the used car salesman. He will be easy." Van Schank took another deep puff. "All you need is four votes for an acquittal. Charlie needs nine to find you guilty."

"Can you assure me those four votes?" Comstock leaned over the table.

Van Schank crossed his legs. "They're in the bag."

"Yeah, you also told me that this case would never see the inside of a courtroom, that the settlement queen would take care of things."

"Don't hold a grudge, Walter. Be flexible."

* * *

Judge Fitzwaring sat down at his bench while the jury remained in the back of the courthouse eating doughnuts and drinking stale coffee. He opened up the file and placed his bifocals on the tip of his nose. The plaintiffs and defendant sat on the edge of their seats, waiting for the judge's pronouncement. Charlie's stomach was doing flips. He could not remember a single case in his career that had had so many ups and downs.

"I understand that the scientific community is still undecided about this issue." Fitzwaring cleared his throat. "I also understand that the law does not have to wait for one hundred percent scientific agreement. For crying out loud, some scientists still don't believe PMS is real, but lawyers use it as a mitigating circumstance in criminal trials. We put tobacco companies on trial with conflicting opinions. It seems to me that humanity will be better served if we call attention to this problem and light a fire under scientists to prove it once and for all."

Realizing Nancy was halfway standing, he motioned to her to remain seated. "Ms. Lockman-Kurtz, if you do not like this decision, then you will have something to appeal in the future. However, I believe that you will find, as I did, that in discretionary matters such as this, the North Carolina Western District Appellate Court usually upholds the brave decision of the lone trial judge. Mr. Harrigan, are you ready to proceed with your case?"

Charlie was holding back a smile, trying to appear professional. "If Your Honor desires, I can begin right now."

The bailiff brought the jury back in, and the judge explained that their decision meant the trial might continue for several days. He also reminded them that if any of them were contacted by either side, they were to immediately let him know. The judge explained that Walter Comstock and Paragon Group were being sued for the wrongful death of Matthew Douglas. He explained the concepts of vicarious liability and passive or imputed negligence. Walter Comstock may never have met Matthew Douglas, but if the way he ran his company and employees placed Matthew Douglas in danger, he was still liable. In business, liability was passed down through the chain of authority. He explained that Paragon Group was a limited partnership and a privately held company, so if the company was guilty, then Mr. Comstock was guilty. Finally, the judge explained all four criteria of the assumption of risks that Charlie must prove.

Charlie rose and called his first witness, Mrs. Betty Douglas. This was his trial now and Charlie would shine. He decided to begin with Betty and end with Horace. The emotion would carry his client a long way. The frail little lady walked proudly to the witness stand with her tissue in her hand. She was ready. For more than a year, Betty had wanted justice; she wanted to tell her son's story and Charlie let her. After a few introductory remarks, Charlie asked about her son.

"Please tell the jury about Matthew."

"Matthew was our only son. He didn't do very well in school, so we had him tested. His IQ was 85. That meant he could learn, but he would always be slow. He graduated from high school when he was twenty. His father, Horace, enjoys woodworking and making tables and things. Well, Matthew loved going out back with his daddy and making things for the house. When we learned about the Project I Can House and that Mr. Grady could find him a job in that area, we were thrilled. You don't know what it's like to have a slow child and the joy you get when he makes some small steps."

She sniffed and wiped her nose. Charlie eased beside her. "Are you okay? Do you need a break?"

"No. I'm fine. Anyway, Mr. Grady taught Matthew how to ride a bus, make sure he got correct change, and wash his own clothes. Then he found him this job with Paragon Group. Matthew could work on the site doing things like picking up trash, and carrying bricks and supplies. Things like that. We would drive by a building he worked on, and he would say,

'That's my building, I helped make it.' "

"How much did he get paid?"

"I think it was four fifty an hour."

"Isn't that below the minimum wage?"

"Well, this job was really like an internship. Mr. Comstock was supposedly helping the community, and technically Matthew was not an employee so much as a charitable contribution on behalf of the company."

"Hmm." Charlie scratched his chin. "Were you aware that Charlie was performing more dangerous tasks, like operating a sandblaster?"

"Objection." Nancy treaded lightly with the mother. "Mr. Harrigan is introducing facts that have not been proved."

"Sustained." The judge motioned to Charlie.

"What did Matthew eventually tell you he was doing?"

"He talked about shooting the gun. We had to really drag it out of him to figure out what he meant. Eventually we understood that he used a sandblaster quite frequently."

"Were you concerned about his safety?"

"Of course. I mentioned it to Mr. Grady and asked him to look into it."

"What did he say?"

"Objection. Hearsay." Nancy did not even look up this time. She was acting bored by the whole testimony.

"Sustained. Move along, Mr. Harrigan."

Betty had no more real facts to offer, but Charlie questioned her twenty more minutes on the loss of a child. She described Matthew's suffering. During those questions, Charlie placed two large pictures of Matthew on tripods right in front of the jury. The first one was a picture of his graduation from high school. The second one was the last picture ever taken of Matthew. His face was thin and gray. Dark circles carved into the sockets under his eyes. He was lying in a bed trying to smile, but the smile was forced and looked painful. Charlie left the pictures there all day. Nancy asked only a few questions on cross.

"Why did you sue for ten point two million dollars?"

Nancy smirked as if she knew something she was not supposed to know.

"I didn't want to sue for money. I really just want an apology from Mr. Comstock. I want him to take responsibility for not protecting my son. But our first attorney said that money is the only thing you can sue for."

"Do you have a lot of money?"

"We're not in debt, but we're not rich."

"So this money could buy you a nice new house or something?"

"Actually, this money will buy a new house for Mr. Grady, so he can help more kids like Matthew."

Nancy knew when to quit and retreated quickly to her seat.

After the testimony of the day, Nancy argued in chambers that the pictures were prejudicial, and if they were not being offered as evidence, they should be taken down. The judge agreed, but gave Charlie the option of replacing the pictures during his summation.

Charlie's next witness was Frank Grady. Grady described his football career at Clemson and the injury to his knee his senior year. He went on to graduate and received a master's degree in social work. He had worked with the handicapped for twenty-five years in Charlotte and his independent living center, the I Can House, was seven years old. He helped teach mildly retarded individuals to live on their own in a hostile world that would take advantage of them. Grady was a tremendous witness. He inspired fear by his sheer size, but he was soft-spoken like a teddy bear. Any man who would devote his life to the underprivileged would never lie.

"Now, Mr. Grady, were you concerned about the type of work Matthew was doing?"

He looked straight at the jury. "Not at first. I'm sorry to say that I didn't notice. We have fourteen people in the house. We had been robbed twice the first few months Matthew had his job. I should have paid more attention. But after a year, I noticed Matthew coughing quite a bit at dinner one night. I had him checked out by a doctor, but he thought it must be allergies. You know those little quick-med places; they don't take the time to get to know the people and find out what is really wrong."

Bonnie Husby was actually nodding her head. She understood and agreed. Charlie liked this. "So what did you do?"

"Nothing." Frank looked at the floor. "Until one day, I noticed Matthew's clothes were piling up. I have to remind my clients to wash their clothes once a week. So I got onto him about wearing the same clothes over and over."

"Are you aware that thoroughly washing clothes is one of OSHA's requirements to prevent the harmful effects of silica?"

"Well, I am now, but I wasn't then. Besides, I called the city manager, Josh Donovan, and he said he would take care of things and make sure Comstock's men would watch out for Matthew. The foreman, Barry Kasick, would keep an eye on him."

"So you didn't worry about Matthew?"

"No."

"Because you trusted Mr. Comstock?"

"Right."

"Is Mr. Comstock a trustworthy person?"

"Objection." Nancy shouted.

"Sustained. Mr. Harrigan." Fitzwaring's tone was very emphatic.

"No further questions, Your Honor." Charlie sat down.

Nancy sauntered to the jury. "Mr. Grady, have you ever received any citations or warnings from the state?"

"No."

"Have you ever treated any of your clients poorly?"

"Of course not."

"Don't you make your clients cry frequently?"

"You have to understand, in some ways, my clients are like children. They have very tender hearts. Sometimes when I correct them, they get upset. It's all done out of love, like a parent."

"Have you ever been sued?" Nancy asked with smile.

"Ah . . . well . . ." Frank looked at Charlie with desperation.

Charlie stood up. "Your Honor, I request a recess."

"No, Mr. Harrigan, sit down."

"Sidebar, Your Honor?" Charlie was persistent.

"Get over here," Fitzwaring grumbled. "What is it?"

"That case was settled and is under seal. Ms. Lockman-Kurtz has no right introducing it into evidence. She's not supposed to know about it."

Nancy shrugged innocently. "I can't help it if all parties involved do not honor the court's decision."

Fitzwaring looked at her. "Do it quickly and get back on track. Now back up, both of you."

"Mr. Grady. Why were you sued?"

He hung his head. "I was sued for physical abuse."

"Thank you, you may step down."

Charlie sprang up, "Redirect, Your Honor?" Without waiting for the response, Charlie started, "Mr. Grady, you would never purposely hurt someone, would you?"

"Of course not. I had a client who was somewhat out of control. He would hit some of the other individuals. He attacked one of the girls upstairs. I grabbed him and threw him off of her. I guess I didn't realize how mad I was, because I was worried about Stephanie. He tumbled down the stairs. He got a concussion and several bruises."

"Were you cited by the state?"

"No. They examined the incident and declared it an accident. The lawsuit never went to trial."

"Have you had any other incidents like that?"

"No," Frank said humbly, but the damage was already done.

chapter
FORTY
TWO

Charlie passed down the corridor of the courthouse, looking at the one-way traffic headed out of downtown on Fourth Street. Brad had still not shown up with their star witness, Diego Strahos. He imagined springing this illegal alien on Nancy. She would hit the roof and object. Charlie would point to their witness list, which included all Paragon employees. Comstock would be forced either to admit that Diego was illegal and therefore not an employee or allow him to testify. Either way, Charlie had a slam dunk for his negligence case.

He had spent the previous day revisiting Dr. Alford, who testified to the vast amount of silica in Matthew's lungs. He would have had to work in an area saturated with the silica dust five days a week, six or seven hours a day, for eighteen months to poison him. Other than a grandmother, who died of breast cancer, Matthew was not prone to any condition or exposed to any other carcinogen that caused cancer.

The bulk of Charlie's case remained with the actual employees of Paragon, Barry Kasick and Dake Warner. He needed Diego to testify to keep the other witnesses honest. The depositions had produced little information that he could use. Charlie would put Mark Ashton on the stand and possibly Joshua Donovan. He would close his case with a stirring account of Matthew's last days from his father. As Charlie was musing over his potential witnesses, his cell phone rang in his pocket.

"This is Charlie."

Brad spoke in staccato, accented phrases. "They're gone. No one. Empty. I don't know."

"Slow down. What's going on?" Charlie noticed a passerby looking at him oddly.

"Diego. His trailer was on a gravel cul-de-sac off Rozzelles Ferry Road, and there were five trailers here, right?"

"Yeah, why?"

"They're gone, Charlie. Nothing is here. No trailers. No kids playing soccer. No coolers full of beer. Everything's disappeared. It's like the apocalypse is happening."

"Are you sure you're at the right place?" Charlie began breathing heavy.

"I've been up and down this road and there's nothing else that resembles this place. This was it and I'm telling you, they have disappeared."

Charlie walked to the stairwell and sat down on the steps. "Let me think. Look carefully, on the ground, in the bushes, see if there's any sign of them."

Brad walked around and his cell phone beeped a warning that the battery was getting low. "There are shells on the ground and some in the grass."

"What are you talking about, seashells?"

"No, bonehead. Bullets. Lots of them." Brad looked around and saw shards of glass. "My guess is that Comstock had some guys come down here and shoot up the place until they all left. We'll never find them."

"No! This can't happen." Charlie banged his head against the cinder brick wall. "They wouldn't allow them to go back to work. Check the emergency rooms and see if any of them happened to show up. Call the cops, and find out if anybody reported the shots or the illegals. Hey, if they were arrested, maybe Diego got caught in the sweep. Call Melinda Powell and get her to help you. Then get here as soon as you can."

"You got it, buddy. I'm not giving up yet." The phone went dead.

Barry Kasick danced around Charlie's questions for an hour. To his knowledge, Matthew did nothing but pick up trash. He never saw him around any abrasive sanding equipment. Barry was given no particular instructions from Walter Comstock about the handicapped employees. Charlie finally decided that Barry would evade any direct answers. Nancy had trained him well.

"So explain your duties and what your team did." Charlie took a stab in the dark.

"Paragon Group has basically four teams. Each team has a different job. My team clears sites, demolishes buildings, and tears down whatever needs to be cleared out of the way to prepare for the next team to come in and frame the new structures that are going up."

"So your team would handle the sandblasting, rust scraping, and digging into rock foundations?"

"Yes, that's part of it."

"Do you follow all of OSHA's recommendations for safety procedures?"

"Of course. If we didn't, the inspector would flag us, and we have had very few citations. Fewer than any other company in the county."

"Inspectors like Mark Ashton, right?"

"I think he may have been one."

"Who are the other inspectors?" Charlie prodded.

"I don't know. I'd have to look it up."

"You knew Mr. Ashton by name. You didn't have to look up his name, right?" Kasick shifted in his seat, and the jury noticed a slight change in his countenance. "In fact, he is the only one of the six city inspectors who visits your site, correct?"

"Again, I would have to look." Barry tried to steal a quick glance at Comstock.

"You're not always there when he visits either, right? I mean, it's one of the other teams he usually inspects?"

"Well . . . it depends on who the foreman is."

"That's not what I asked, Mr. Kasick. Usually, the inspector arrives around the time framing begins, and then when the product is finished. So he would never review you, personally, would he?"

Barry faltered but recovered quickly, "Those things are random. You would have to ask the inspector about that."

"I plan to. Thank you, Mr. Kasick." Charlie headed back to his table as Barry was about to stand. "By the way, Mr. Kasick, what are the OSHA recommendations to prevent silicosis?"

Charlie had never asked him that and avoided it during depositions. He gambled that Nancy had only mentioned the requirements and not asked him to memorize them. Barry shifted and scratched his head. "Well, there's eye, ear, nose, and mouth protection. Training employees. Teach them to wash their hands and clothes well. Use water hoses to clean debris instead of compressed air. Limit the time someone is in an area where abrasive sanding occurs." He paused to take a breath and Charlie jumped in.

"How about monitoring the air?"

"Yes, I was getting to that."

"Is that all?" Charlie gave him ample time to search his brain.

"I think so."

Charlie walked back to his table as if he were going to sit down. The jury scooted forward to see what Charlie was doing. He opened a large black manual. "What about monitoring the effectiveness of your safety program? Is that an OSHA recommendation?" Barry nodded his head. "How about documentation that employees are appropriately trained on certain equipment?" Once again, Barry nodded. "How about food and drinks prohibited in work areas?" Barry nodded as sweat broke out on his forehead. "How about warning them that cigarette smoke may compound the injuries?" Barry nodded and let his chin rest on his chest.

Charlie walked away and turned one more time. He enjoyed this part of his job. "What about Matthew?" Barry looked blankly at him. "Do you think Matthew understood all of these instructions, or do you think he may have needed special clarification and continual supervision?"

"I don't know," Barry quietly said. The answer did not matter, because the jury knew it was true.

Nancy's cross-examination reviewed all of the safety procedures Paragon had in place. They reviewed Paragon's safety manual that was more thorough than OSHA's. She went on for two hours and continued after lunch reviewing meritorious citations Paragon Group received from the city.

Then, out of the blue, she asked, "Do you like basketball?"

"Yes."

"Do you know all of the rules?"

"Sure," he said hesitantly.

"Please explain the rules of basketball."

Barry looked at her, confused. Nancy had obviously not prepared him for this question. "Well . . . you've got the ten-second rule. There's walking. Double dribble. Three-second violation. Personal fouls. Technical fouls." He stopped with a puzzled stare.

"What about the three-point line?" she barked at him. Barry sat stunned and speechless. "What about charging? What about the shot clock? I thought you said you knew the rules of basketball. You must be lying."

"No, it's hard to sit here and list everything, but I know each violation when I see it. I'm not lying."

"Thank you." Nancy sat down.

They took a fifteen-minute recess. Nancy's cross had been effective. But Charlie had not expected much from Kasick. He gained little and he lost little. Kasick was a lapdog for Comstock. He was probably guilty of something, but he was too stupid to be a mastermind behind some scheme. Charlie and Horace were drinking more stale coffee. Betty had brought her knitting because the waiting was making her nervous. She needed something to do.

Suddenly, Charlie heard his name. He spun around and saw nothing. He heard his name again. Brad was peeking out of the rear stairwell.

"Hey, get over here. I got a surprise."

Charlie looked in the stairwell. There was his star witness. Charlie actually hugged him. Diego had a bandage on his forehead and several cuts and scrapes. His clothes were dirty and rumpled.

Charlie was in awe. "How did you find him?"

"I guess that religion stuff is working out for you." Brad was wide-eyed. "I said this little prayer and went to the county jail. They were getting ready to send Diego and his family to the customs holding facility at the airport. They were ready to send them back to Mexico. These thugs in a van came by their trailers last night and started beating the guys with bats and shooting out windows. The people were so scared they took off. A highway patrolman stopped Diego, because his taillights were not working. Then they threw him in jail when they discovered that he was in the country illegally. I stalled them long enough for Melinda to make a call. She met us down there and got him released under my custody. She's working on getting the Strahos family their visas so they can stay here."

"God bless you, Diego." Charlie grabbed his hand. "I'm sorry. This is all my fault. You shouldn't have to go through this."

"It's not your fault, señor. It's Comstock's fault. He brought me and my friends from Georgia to do construction work. We work like slaves. Now you tell me that he was killing me slowly. I'll do whatever I can to help."

Charlie's eyes sparkled. "Brad, wait five minutes after I call Dake Warner and then walk in with Diego and sit on the first row. When he sees him, he won't be able to lie."

"It's a beautiful thing." Brad was smiling. "I can't wait to see Nancy sweat."

Charlie was almost out the door. "Hey, she's a lady. She doesn't sweat."

"I know. Glisten. Glisten like a pig." Brad laughed out loud.

Fitzwaring reconvened the court. Charlie called Dake Warner. Dake Warner was a brusque, burly man. It was beyond Charlie how Nancy missed the appearance of her witnesses. Charlie had little old ladies, and Nancy had rough-looking, long-haired construction workers. By his appearance alone, Dake Warner was an imposing figure, and he worked for a man with an even more ominous appearance. Warner took the stand and looked at Charlie with hatred. After the deposition, Nancy had yelled at Dake, and then Kasick yelled at him. After Kasick told Comstock, Comstock chewed him out. It had been an endless cycle, and it was all Charlie's fault.

"Good afternoon," Charlie said with a broad smile. He got a nod from Dake. "Mr. Warner, would you please tell the jury what your responsibilities are at Paragon Group?"

"Sure, I build buildings." He folded his arms over his massive chest. He expected a laugh and received a couple of chuckles from a reporter.

"Could you be more specific?"

"Yeah, big buildings." He laughed at his brilliant wit.

"Your Honor, request that this witness be treated as a hostile witness?"

Fitzwaring despised people who attempted to be cute in his courtroom. "Go right ahead, Mr. Harrigan."

"Mr. Warner, in your deposition you said that you trained Matthew Douglas to run a sandblaster. Is that correct?"

"I don't remember. I'd have to see it."

"You said that your responsibilities were oversight of safety and training of individuals. Is that correct?"

"I do that along with several other duties."

"Did you train Matthew to operate a sandblaster?"

"I may have, but if I did, I made sure the safety requirements were followed."

Charlie was getting nowhere. He looked at his watch. It had been almost five minutes. "Do you know a man named Diego Strahos?"

"Objection, Your Honor." Nancy darted up.

Charlie spun on his heels. "What could you possibly object to? What grounds?"

"Mr. Harrigan, be quiet. This is my courtroom." Fitzwaring turned to Nancy. "On what grounds, Ms. Lockman-Kurtz?"

She sat down slowly and withdrew her objection.

The judge looked at Warner. "Please answer the question."

"No. I don't know who you're talking about."

"Mr. Warner, does Walter Comstock employ illegal aliens, so you can train them on some of the more dangerous jobs?"

"Objection! Leading!" Nancy shouted.

"That's the nature of a hostile witness. Don't they teach you anything at Duke?"

"Both of you up here now!" The judge slammed his fist in frustration.

Out of the corner of his eye, Charlie saw Dake's face turn pale. Brad had just entered the courtroom with Diego. The defense never expected to see him again after the little hit squad had threatened his entire family.

Fitzwaring warned Charlie and Nancy that one more outburst would send them to jail for contempt. Charlie walked back to his table, looking at his star. He took a drink of water as a drop of sweat rolled down the side of Dake's temple.

"Mr. Warner, do you recognize this man sitting in the front row?"

Dake was looking at Nancy and muttered a garbled, "I'm not sure."

"Mr. Warner, if I were to put this man on the stand, would he know you?"

"Yes," Dake mumbled.

"Keeping in mind that lying under oath is a felony, who is this man sitting in the front row, Mr. Warner?" Charlie stood in the middle of the courtroom pointing at Diego in a deliberately exaggerated pose and waited for the answer.

"That's, ah . . . he, ah, worked at Paragon." Dake avoided looking at the defense table.

"What is his name?" Charlie demanded.

"Diego Strahos."

Charlie saw a couple of jaws drop at the defense table.

"Is he in this country legally?"

"I'm not positive, but I don't think so." Dake was not about to lie about anything else. He had been caught, and now with his shoulders slumped over, he would be very forthright.

"Did you train him to do a job?"

"Yes, when Matthew got too sick to work, Diego became one of the sandblasters."

"Did he do anything else?"

"Not really. Pretty much all day long he was ripping paint off walls and rust off beams."

Charlie paused and looked at his legal pad. "Let me ask you, when you told Mr. Kasick that Matthew was not following all safety regulations, what did he say?" Charlie was looking directly at Walter Comstock.

"He said that if that retard don't know any better, it's his own fault." Another gasp ran through the courtroom.

chapter
FORTY
THREE

Nancy did not question Dake Warner. The jury would never see him again. Charlie called the city inspector, Mark Ashton. Charlie was determined to wrap up his case before lunch. The jury had been through enough, and he wanted them to get the case. Ashton was frazzled as usual and really testified to just one thing. He had conducted the majority of inspections on Paragon Group and had never even met Barry Kasick. One of the other foremen was always on site. In an unwilling exchange, Ashton admitted that Joshua Donovan made the schedule for all surprise and routine inspections.

Charlie questioned Ashton about Brian Beckley, the former Paragon employee who had been hurt on the job, and whom they could not find. Beckley was living in a log cabin in the mountains of Murphy, North Carolina, near the Tennessee border. Unknown to Charlie, he had been paid fifty thousand dollars not to testify. The mysterious circumstances of his injury were never made clear, but a lawsuit had never been filed.

After Ashton, Charlie called Joshua Donovan. The brains behind the downtown revitalization program, Donovan was well respected by the whole community. Charlie had to break him on the stand. If he did not succeed, he ran the risk of alienating his jury by attacking a local legend. Charlie stood reluctantly.

"Good morning, Mr. Donovan."

"Good morning." He was suave and charming. Shascle Deering's eyes danced as she watched him from the jury box.

"Mr. Donovan, why are so many city contracts awarded to Paragon Group?"

"Basically, they have an impeccable safety record, and because they are such a large company, they typically have the lowest bids."

"How does that work? The bidding."

Donovan leaned back in his chair. "Well, we send proposals to all the companies in the area or even out-of-state that are on our lists. They evaluate the job and give the city an estimate of the total costs."

"All of this is confidential?" Charlie asked.

"Correct. No company ever sees any of the bids."

"Would it be possible for one of your employees to leak that information to a friend?"

"Objection."

"Withdrawn, Your Honor." Charlie moved along unfazed. "Why is it that Mark Ashton, the youngest of the inspectors and the only one whom you personally hired, is the inspector who almost always investigates Paragon? Out of fifty inspections, he conducted forty."

"It's coincidence. Whoever is next on the list." Donovan would not be easy.

"Isn't it normal for a company to receive one or two red flags every year?"

"I guess."

"Isn't it odd that Paragon has only received two in the last five years?"

"Not really. That's why Mr. Comstock has received so many meritorious citations."

That was the second time Charlie had heard that phrase. Nancy had trained them very thoroughly. "Would you award government contracts to a company that employed illegal aliens?"

"Of course not."

"So neither you nor Mr. Ashton knew anything about Diego Strahos or any others."

"I can't imagine Mr. Comstock doing such a thing."

"Could you describe this program to help the handicapped that Mr. Comstock was a part of ?"

"Sure, it was the board's idea to give back to the community and provide something like an internship to individuals who could handle minor tasks."

"So they were not employees, but the employer was responsible for them and they were limited in the kinds of activity they could perform?"

"They were only limited by their ability."

After an hour, Joshua Donovan had successfully avoided and side-stepped every question. He portrayed Paragon and Comstock in a positive light and suggested that any problems were created by the dunderheads who worked under him. Charlie was about to wrap up his questioning, when he acted as if he remembered something very important.

"Mr. Donovan, on the wall in your office, you have a picture of yourself in front of an A-6 Intruder in Vietnam."

"That's right. I served three tours proudly." He sat up a little straighter.

"I, along with everyone here, appreciate your sacrifice." Charlie took a couple of steps. "What company?"

"Fifth Marine Air Wing," Donovan said proudly.

"What were your duties?"

"Operating off the *Eisenhower*, A-6's were the first planes in. Basically, we drew the antiaircraft fire so the bombers could come in and knock out military installations."

"Wow." Charlie shook his head. "That's incredible." He paused and said, "Wasn't Walter Comstock in your company? He's in that picture."

Donovan sat frozen. How could he have known that? No one would have ever made that casual connection. "Well, yes, Mr. Comstock and I go way back."

"As a matter of fact, when your plane was shot down, Walter Comstock was responsible for your not being captured by the North Vietnamese, right?"

"He circled the area and covered me at a tremendous risk to himself and his copilot."

"It's interesting how both of you work so closely together now." Charlie decided to take his shot. "Are you the silent partner referred to in Walter Comstock's tiered partnership agreement?"

Nancy shouted, "Objection! Move to strike!"

"Sustained!" Fitzwaring banged his gavel.

Charlie was still screaming questions: "Is that why you're protecting him? Was Oliver Burchette killed because he knew about your secret deal?"

"Bailiff, remove the jury please. Jurors, you will disregard that entire last exchange. It is all Mr. Harrigan's unsubstantiated speculation." After the jurors were escorted out, Fitzwaring cleared the courtroom. "Mr. Harrigan, I am about to declare a mistrial. Regardless, you are going to spend the night in jail. Now what is this wild accusation that you are claiming?"

Charlie approached the bench and handed the judge Burchette's manuscript, one of the twenty copies he had scattered throughout the county in safe-deposit boxes. He even had one hidden under his mattress. "I believe Oliver Burchette was killed because he knew about some shady deals. To protect his interest in the deal, Donovan covered up safety violations at Paragon and fixed bids."

"That's a criminal matter, Mr. Harrigan. You know that."

"Your Honor, they were purposefully negligent concerning my client."

Nancy chimed in, "This whole proceeding is tainted and should be thrown out."

"I'm not about to allow this, but I will look into it. Now after this break, I want you to put on your last witnesses and let's finish this thing. It's becoming a circus and I don't like it."

Fitzwaring stormed down the steps into his chambers for the remainder of the recess.

Charlie had made sure that the jurors did not fall asleep or get bored during this trial. He refused to lose because the jury was tired and wanted to go home. Charlie put Diego Strahos on the stand for twenty minutes. Diego described how he operated the sandblaster for eight hours a day at times and how he wore the same clothes to work every day. No one ever told him that it was not safe. He smoked two packs a day and was now scared that he was going to die like Matthew, and his wife and five children would be alone in a strange country with no support.

Nancy poked around the edges and implied that since he was in this country illegally, he was a criminal. When she said he was taking jobs away from American citizens, Diego looked at the jury and said, "Any of you who wants my job can have it."

Charlie saved Horace for last. Nancy would refuse to cross-examine him, because nothing could be gained. She could ask about the money, but he would give the same speech his wife did. Horace spoke about how it feels to be the parent of a retarded child, how his expectations changed, and how his initial shock gave way to a profound love. They got excited about small victories, and how Matthew's independence and job had given him such a sense of accomplishment.

His voice cracked with anger and sorrow as he replayed aloud Kasick and Warner's brash callousness concerning the safety of his son. Horace pleaded with the jurors to make someone take responsibility. He spoke passionately about the fact that nobody seems to care if blue-collar workers, illegal aliens, or young men with low IQs suffer. Who's going to speak for them? The jurors were moved by Horace, and with that image in their minds, the judge dismissed court for the day.

* * *

The holding cell was crowded. Charlie sat in his suit. He watched the drunks drool all over themselves. The young punks were acting tough, but he could tell that one of the sixteen-year-old boys was scared out of his wits. Charlie leaned against the bars. He was not upset. He had to take his shot and live with the consequences. All he needed was nine jurors to agree with him, and he was not about to hold anything back. Sandy would have acted mad, because she had to, but she would have secretly laughed at him. The great attorney in a cell with common criminals. He slept little that night. In between nightmares and the sobbing that came from the scared little boys, he spent most of the evening telling God that everything was in His hands now. Charlie had done all that he could. About four thirty, he fell asleep.

Nancy began her defense damaged and with little ammunition. She called all the foremen, who testified that no illegal aliens worked at Paragon Group to their knowledge. Any who worked for them must have lied on their job application. Barry Kasick testified that if Diego had lied on his job application, he would certainly lie under oath. He apologized for using the word *retard*. He admitted that under pressure, he often said the wrong thing, but because he lost his temper, he was not a bad person.

Kasick reviewed, in depth, every commendation awarded to the company. Its safety records were reviewed. Workers' comp claims at Paragon Group were at an all-time low. In all, the testimony of the foremen was not compelling. They had little firsthand knowledge of Matthew Douglas.

"According to Mr. Warner, you told him to train Mr. Douglas on the sandblaster." Nancy acted as if she were accusing him to show that she could be tough on her own clients.

"Mr. Warner probably misunderstood. He tends to be reckless and not take orders very well. I have seen him pass the buck many times, because he was lazy or didn't care."

They tried shifting the blame and pointing the finger in all directions. Nancy called the makers of abrasive sanders to testify to their improvements and overall safety. She called federal OSHA employees, who lauded the wonderful work of Walter Comstock. She did just about everything but call the Pope to recommend Comstock for sainthood. In the end, her case seemed unconvincing to Charlie. Then again, she needed only four jurors to bury him. That might be easy to do.

Charlie stood and addressed the jury as he began his closing argument. "Ladies and gentlemen, I want to thank you for your service and duty. I know it has been a long couple of weeks and you have sacrificed tremendously. I also want to apologize for my behavior, but I get passionate about my clients and my work. I get tired of seeing people trampled on and greedy people abusing others just to make a dollar. I get angry when I feel that somebody who can't defend himself is taken advantage of.

"I know you sit there and think that I am some wealthy lawyer, who sued Paragon Group for ten million, two hundred thousand dollars, because I get one-third of the settlement. But that's just not true. I'm not rich and it's not my goal to become rich off of this trial. The reason we sued for so much money is because that is the language that business speaks. Paragon Group is a privately held company, so we don't know how much it is worth. But it must be punished. For it to stop putting its employees in danger, it will have to pay until it hurts. What is a life worth? How do you calculate the value of a child? A parent would do anything and pay any price to get him back."

Charlie walked to his table and stabled himself with his hands. He took a drink of water and held back the tears. "I started this trial telling you that it was about something simple, like sand. Ms. Lockman-Kurtz described how ridiculous it was and that people who sue McDonald's because hot coffee spilled on them are corrupting the system and getting rich. But how many of you really know what happened in the McDonald's case?" Charlie gazed at the jury, and all eyes were transfixed on him. They were eating up every word. "McDonald's company policy is to keep its coffee at the boiling point. The woman who sued was eighty-four years old. She sued because her Styrofoam cup collapsed when she tried to take off the lid. After seven skin graft operations, she was awarded two point six million dollars. That is the net profits off of one day's coffee sales in the U.S. alone. Later, that verdict was reduced to one hundred thousand dollars. Now, let me ask you, if that was your grandmother who received third-degree burns from boiling coffee, how much money would it take to satisfy you?

"Do any of you really think that this lovely couple are greedy rednecks wanting to get rich? I don't think so. Walter Comstock took advantage of their son and killed him. Matthew Douglas inhaled microscopic dust particles hour after hour until lung cancer developed and ravaged his body. We heard how his last days were spent coughing and gasping for breath.

"The defense will surely tell you about Matthew's assumption of risks. Like smoking cigarettes, Matthew knew the dangers of the job. He could appreciate that danger, and chose to disregard it. But Matthew was not like you and me. You heard Mr. Grady. Matthew was a completely trusting soul who had to learn a healthy skepticism of life. He had no idea, no conceivable way of knowing the little particles of dust could kill him. Maybe he was told, but did he understand? Was he told properly? Was he told repeatedly? Did anybody care?"

Charlie turned away. "I care. They care. I hope you do." Charlie walked back to his chair and sat down.

Nancy rose and buttoned her jacket. She was immovable. "I feel for the Douglas family. I have lost parents. We all have lost loved ones, and it's only natural to look to blame somebody. Imputed negligence is based on the relationship between the individuals. But can we really blame Walter Comstock? He cannot look after every single employee. Can we blame Barry Kasick? It's not his fault that Dake Warner was lax in his duties.

CHUCK CHITWOOD

Imputed negligence can go only so far.

"When someone is shot, do we sue the gun company, the bullet company, and the store that sold the gun? No. The shooter is held responsible. Our society has reached a ridiculous point to where a bartender is held liable because he was not paying attention to how much a drunk driver had before he drove his car into another one. Shouldn't we sue the owner of the bar? And the landlord who owns the building that the bar sits on? What about the county that gives the landlord a liquor license? At some point, you must stand up and say enough is enough. We all make choices and we all must take responsibility for our actions."

Nancy walked over to a dry-erase board and started drawing numbers on a board. "Let's assume Mr. Douglas made six dollars an hour and worked eight hours a day, five days a week, fifty weeks a year. If he did that for fifty years, he would earn six hundred thousand dollars. I think that's fair. Mr. Comstock has offered the Douglases more than this to help ease their suffering. He has done everything he could to make up for their loss. Just remember, ladies and gentlemen, the next time somebody sprains an ankle on your property, they might just sue you for millions of dollars."

With that little sermon, the defense rested. Fitzwaring charged the jury and instructed the members to review all the evidence. They would order lunch for the jurors and they could work straight through. Court was adjourned.

chapter
FORTY
FOUR

The hours seemed like days. Charlie paced the diner. Sonny poured coffee into Brad's bottomless cup. Betty did the crossword puzzle in the *USA Today*. Horace stared out the window, holding his picture of Matthew. There had been several attempts at breaking the silence, but the conversations were contrived and forced. By omission, they all agreed to be silent. Reports from the court clerk described how the jury had asked for legal clarifications of imputed negligence. They wanted to review some of the scientific studies from the first part of the trial. They asked for dinner to be sent in, so they did not have to interrupt their deliberations.

Charlie took this as a bad sign. The question was simple in his mind. Either Comstock was responsible for Matthew's death or he wasn't. The jury could be split down the middle, or it could be debating over the extent of Comstock's role in the actual operation of his company. Apparently, the members had some reservations about conviction. All Charlie needed was nine jurors. Finally, he decided to sit down and have a piece of coconut cream pie. He had not eaten anything since he ordered Domino's at midnight.

After seven hours, forty-two minutes, according to Charlie's watch, the phone rang. The verdict was in. Charlie, Brad, their clients, and even Sonny piled into Charlie's Blazer to hear the verdict. Sonny closed down the grill in honor of Charlie, regardless of the outcome. It was six o'clock and outgoing traffic was gridlocked. Charlie blew the horn and tried to force his way through traffic. He turned right on McDowell Street and nothing was moving. It took twenty minutes to travel a quarter of a mile before they finally reached the courthouse.

The defendants were all in place with jaws clenched and angry eyes staring at Charlie. He felt like saying, "This is all your fault. Don't blame me." But he avoided looking directly at them. As the plaintiffs took their seats, Judge Fitzwaring ordered the jury in. Once again, all twelve faces looked stalwartly at the floor, refusing to give away anything.

The judge looked at the foreman, and in great ceremony that Charlie always found ridiculous, Fitzwaring asked, "I understand the jury has reached a verdict."

Thomas Landon stood and boldly declared, "We have, Your Honor." Every day in courtrooms across America, jurists ask each other questions that everybody knows the answer to.

The bailiff handed the slip of paper to Fitzwaring, who opened and read it. He removed his bifocals. "Is this your decision?"

"Yes, Your Honor." The bailiff gave the paper back to the foreman.

"Please read the verdict, Mr. Foreman."

Thomas Landon looked around nervously and took a breath. "We, the jury, find in favor of the plaintiff."

Comstock's head dipped slightly. Nancy looked at the foreman without flinching.

"We award the plaintiff two hundred thousand dollars in actual damages . . ." he took a breath.

Charlie grabbed Betty's hands.

" . . . and in punitive damages, we award the plaintiff . . . twenty-five million dollars."

A gasp of horror sounded from somewhere in the gallery. Comstock's forehead hit the table. Nancy stood immediately, asking for all kinds of motions. Fitzwaring ignored her and repeatedly slammed the gavel trying to force the journalists to sit down and be quiet but to no avail. They were out the door calling the local stations and papers. Tears were steaming down Betty's face as she hugged Charlie. Horace threw his arms around Brad, who was a little unsure of how to react.

"Quiet." The gavel slammed more firmly. "I will have order in my court."

"Your Honor, I want the jury polled," Nancy demanded, doing anything she could to turn back the decision.

The judge asked each juror to state his or her personal decision on guilt. After each juror stood and proclaimed guilty or not guilty, the verdict was ten to two. Nancy began motioning for directed verdicts and all sorts of maneuvers.

Judge Fitzwaring ordered her to sit down. "Ms. Lockman-Kurtz, I understand that this is not the verdict that you wanted, but you can file your objections in appeals court. The jury's verdict stands as read. I want to thank the jury for its diligent service. You are free to go. Court dismissed." The gavel slammed one last time.

Cheers resounded in the gallery and hugs were flowing freely. Martin Van Schank, who was watching the verdict from the back row, slipped out quietly without any notice. Nancy shook Charlie's hand and congratulated him. He knew that she resented every second of it, so he tried to be polite. Comstock gave Charlie a death look and stormed out.

Horace and Betty were hugging each other and laughing through their tears. Brad patted Charlie on the back. "Good job, buddy! You did it!"

"Thanks." Charlie remained in his chair.

He had never quite been sure how to act after winning this type of case. Like Maggie Thomason, Matthew Douglas was still dead. He could not bring either of them back. He sat and thanked his God and hoped that somehow what he had done was enough.

* * *

They celebrated with a private party at Sonny's Teriyaki Grill. Burgers, fries, shakes, and Cokes were all on the house. Everyone involved was exhausted. Charlie would go to bed at nine and sleep for twelve hours. Sonny delivered a chocolate shake to where Charlie was sitting.

"My friend, you are a hero once again."

"I guess."

"You are. You fight and you win. I'm proud of you." Sonny shook his hand.

Horace walked up and said, "I am too. I don't think anybody else would have fought as hard for Matt as you did. I truly thank you. Are we going to get to see you again?"

"Of course, every Sunday, especially if I can come over for dinner. As long as you keep making fried chicken and mashed potatoes, I'll be there."

"You know you are more than welcome." Horace turned to Betty and said, "Well, honey, we better get on the road. You know I don't like driving after it gets dark."

"Okay. Thank you so much, Charlie." She hugged him again and they said good-bye.

"Hey, buddy. I'm going to grab a late dinner with that clerk from the second floor. Do you want to join me?" Brad was hoping Charlie would decline his invitation, but he had to be nice.

"Maybe next time. I'm going to celebrate quietly. See you, buddy." Charlie watched Brad climb into the Porsche and streak through the city.

Sonny looked at him. "You do it better than anybody else."

They sat in silence for a few moments, watching the cars rushing home to their families. Sonny broke the silence. "Each one of those cars contains a person. Each person is on his or her journey. Some are in a good place and some are in their personal purgatory. . . ."

Charlie finished Sonny's thought for him as he continued to stare. "And each one of us further along that journey must help those behind us. That's what you've done with me these past few months."

Sonny smiled and sipped his coffee. "People want to make sense of pain and suffering, but it's just part of the world. We can let the pain destroy us, or we can look for God in the middle of it. On that cross, He didn't wipe out all the pain. He experienced it. He absorbed it. He understands it."

"Somehow in the midst of everything, I have really discovered what you experienced in that POW camp. All the pain isn't gone, and sometimes confusion consumes me, but then there are moments of peace and I feel that God is right here. I can't explain it."

"There are no words for a pain so intense or a God so amazing." Sonny slurped the last drop of coffee from his mug.

"Thanks, Sonny, I don't think I would have made it this far without you."

"I'm just doing my job, same as you." Sonny started cleaning up the dishes and cups. Charlie broke his gaze and pitched in to help.

Charlie woke the next morning to find his picture on the front page of *The Charlotte Observer* once again with the accompanying headline, "Harrigan Does It Again." Printed below the headline was the subheading, "$25 Million." He read the story that recounted the guilty verdict against Walter Comstock and Paragon Group. The story summarized the facts of the wrongful death suit and mentioned Charlie and his two record verdicts in Mecklenburg County. He scanned the rest of the article and smiled.

The phone had not stopped ringing, but Charlie refused to answer it. He opened the paper, and below the fold on the first page he saw a line of pictures. There were Walter Comstock, Martin Van Schank, Nancy Lockman-Kurtz, and Joshua Donovan. Below the pictures was an article describing the indictment of these four individuals for conspiracy, fraud, bid rigging, trafficking in illegal aliens, and it hinted at more indictments related to murder, arson, and assault. Paragon Group had not opened its doors this morning in response to the article. Its boss was sitting in jail, and the company would probably be shut down or bought out. In either case, Paragon Group would cease to exist. Horace and Betty would be very pleased.

The door to Charlie's little office burst open. "Hey, buddy boy, have you seen the front page? We are in business, man."

"What are you talking about?" Charlie looked at Brad.

"Tell me that you're going to take my offer. You know, you and me, our own firm." Brad was bouncing off the walls.

"I don't know if I want to put myself through this anymore."

Brad sat across the table from Charlie. "Check it out. I have gotten calls from Pittsburgh, San Diego, Houston, Colorado Springs, Steubenville—"

"Steubenville? Where's that?"

"I think it's in Ohio or something. Anyway, firms want us to lead a class action suit against companies that deal with silica, maybe even sue the manufacturers. We hit the big time. You can't back down. The world needs people like us."

There was a knock on the door. Their conversation stopped for a moment.

"Come in," Charlie yelled.

Melinda Powell walked in with a handful of newspapers in one hand and a box in the other. "Congratulations, counselors. I didn't know if you had seen the paper, so I thought I would deliver it myself."

"Please sit down," Brad offered her his chair. "Tell us about the indictment."

Melinda cleared her throat and replayed the whole scenario. "I read that manuscript you gave me and started doing some research. Van Schank, Donovan, and Comstock go back to Vietnam. I arrested Nancy, who pleaded for no jail time and told us everything she knew. She filled in many of the missing links that we needed to issue warrants. Apparently, the three of them started bringing heroin back to the States. After they got established in their respective businesses, which were funded by the drug money, Van Schank organized the scam and each one of them got a cut. Comstock's silent partners at Paragon were Van Schank and Donovan. Can you believe it?" She was smiling. "Paragon Group didn't even open today. I think the company is going to be dissolved."

Charlie was stunned. "So they were that corrupt. Was Hobbes or Reimarus involved?"

"I don't think so. It's hard to tell how much they knew, but I'll look into it." She smiled at Charlie. "It was all because of you. Without this lawsuit, I don't know that anybody would have ever uncovered their scam. So Comstock and Donovan are in jail awaiting a bail hearing. The bad news is that Van Schank has disappeared. No one has seen him since the verdict last night."

Charlie looked confused. "Who killed Burchette? Who burned down my house and beat me up?"

Melinda was enjoying telling the story. "Those prints lifted from Burchette's boat that were under wraps at the Pentagon came in a few days ago. Apparently, Van Schank's right-hand man in Nam was this guy named Slade. They were both part of a black-ops mission. No one's willing to tell me what the mission was. Apparently, Slade owned a private security firm here in the city and worked for Van Schank and Donovan, doing the dirty work no one else wanted to do. We think that he and Van Schank fled the country together." She looked dejected.

Brad laughed at the irony. "Great! Another Dr. Johnston."

"Oh, yeah," she brightened up, "Dr. Johnston is in the custody of the police in Cayenne, French Guyana. I'm waiting on extradition. When he gets back to the States, we'll begin his criminal trial."

"Yes, God does answer prayer!" Charlie shouted and gave Brad a high five.

"One more piece of good news," Melinda continued as she held up an envelope, "this is a warrant for your friend, Reverend Billy. He's going to be arrested this afternoon for conspiracy to defraud the public. You can join me if you want to."

"So what's in the box?" Brad was being nosy.

"Well, I just thought I would bring you boys a gift to celebrate your victory." She handed the box to Charlie. "After the verdict, I had some engravers design this for you guys. They finished it this morning."

The box was heavy. Charlie tore into it. "Wow, this is nice."

"What is it, buddy?"

Charlie pulled out the brass placard that read, "Harrigan & Connelly, Attorneys at Law."

"Well, I guess I'll have to do business with you, since Melinda went to all the trouble to make a sign for us." Charlie turned to Melinda. "Thank you very much."

"Thank you. I uncovered a major scam. I could be the next DA because of you."

Brad was acting like a little kid. "Hey, I'll go hang it up outside our door."

"Sure." Melinda watched Brad bolt down the stairs and turned to Charlie. "Charlie, I know that you've been through a lot lately, but I would like to buy you brunch to show my appreciation."

Charlie hesitated and struggled for the right words, "I don't know if I'm ready . . . I mean, you're nice and all, but . . . I'm just not . . . "

"I know. This is nothing serious. Just two friends having a meal, that's all." She tilted her head and smiled sympathetically.

Charlie thought for a moment and grabbed his coat. "Sure, why not?"

They walked down the stairs and out the door. Brad had borrowed a drill from Sonny and was drilling holes into the concrete to announce the office of the newly formed firm of Harrigan & Connelly. Charlie and Melinda walked down the sidewalk headed north on Third Street. They walked in no particular direction with no particular destination.